RUMORS
OF WAR

·CHILDREN OF THE PROMISE·

VOL. I

RUMORS
OF WAR

·DEAN HUGHES·

DESERET BOOK COMPANY · SALT LAKE CITY, UTAH

Library of Congress Cataloging-in-Publication Data

Hughes, Dean, 1943–
   Rumors of war / by Dean Hughes.
     p.   cm. — (Children of the promise ; v. 1)
   ISBN 1-57345-199-1 (HB)
    1. World War, 1939–1945—Fiction. 2. Mormons—History—Fiction.
I. Title. II. Series: Hughes, Dean, 1943–   Children of the promise ;
v. 1.
PS3558.U36R86   1997
813'.54—DC21   96-45548
                                                  CIP

Printed in the United States of America   18961-4624
10   9   8   7   6   5

FOR KATHLEEN

Most of us know the essential facts of World War II. We are aware of the major combatants and the broad outlines of the battles. But unless we lived through those years, how can we comprehend what the war meant to the people? How can we discover the heart of that tested generation? My attempt, through a work of historical fiction, is to recreate that era by portraying the challenges and change forced upon one American family. The family members are Latter-day Saints, so this book and the sequels to follow it become not only American and world history but Mormon history as well.

I have tried to be accurate with details. If my characters go to a movie, you can trust that the film they see was really playing at that theater on that date. If I mention snow on Christmas in Salt Lake City, know that I checked the weather conditions for the day. The war news, heard on the home front, I took directly from the newspapers of the time. I have not changed historical events to fit my plot; in fact, at times I had to adjust my story when I discovered information that rendered my outline implausible or inaccurate. The word *Jap* will probably make you cringe a little, but during World War II it appeared in newspaper headlines almost every day, and racial and nationalistic epithets were part of every soldier's speech. I have probably softened those usages a little, but I didn't want to distort history by taking them out.

I was born in 1943, in the middle of the war, so I have no personal memories of it to rely on. After studying literally hundreds of general and specific works of history, I found that unpublished personal histories were often my most useful sources. I also interviewed many people who were willing to share their memories. I relied heavily, for instance, on the knowledge of Dr. Gene S. Jacobsen. He survived the Bataan "death march" and was held as a prisoner of war in the Philippines and Japan. I read his personal memoir, *Who Refused to Die*, but I also met with him and raised additional questions. I read other accounts from other prisoners in the Philippines, but I chose to base one of my major plots, at least in a general way, on Dr. Jacobsen's experiences. Wally Thomas, however, is not Gene Jacobsen. I invented Wally's responses in the way that a fiction writer always invents—by creating a character and then staying true to his personality.

The entire Thomas family is fictional. There was no stake president named D. Alexander Thomas in Sugar House in the 1930s and 40s. I based President Thomas's character on no particular individual. The experiences of the Thomas family are my creation, but I found the roots of that creation in the accounts of real people. I read, for instance, a number of interviews and personal histories of LDS missionaries in Germany before the war. My account of the evacuation of those missionaries in the late summer of 1939 is based on those actual events, but Elder Mecham and Elder Thomas are fictional.

Sometimes I have chosen to use actual people as characters. Joseph Fielding Smith and J. Reuben Clark are the two most prominent examples. To avoid misrepresentation, I had these characters say things that I took from talks they gave or from accounts in their biographies. The "small talk" is imaginary, as are the scenes in which they appear, but I have worked to portray them accurately.

I don't mean to claim that I have done all that I might have done or that I have not slipped up somewhere. I'm certain I will learn from readers that I've made mistakes. But I spent all afternoon one day trying to find out what building the English department at the University of Utah was housed in during the period of this novel. I could have skipped over that little detail and I doubt anyone would have noticed, but the truth is, puzzles of that kind are fun for me. I loved immersing myself in the time in every way that I could, and I enjoyed tracing down the details I felt I needed.

The Second World War has become the "good war" to many people, but not every young man hurried to a recruiting office on the day after the Pearl Harbor attack. Not everyone accepted rationing with a glad heart. Still, it was a remarkable time. In America, a whole generation sacrificed to accomplish a great purpose. But the war also made deep wounds. Families were not only affected by the loss of life, the sacrifice and stress, but they were also pulled in conflicting directions by the tremendous force of societal change. So this novel, and the volumes that will follow, are an attempt to understand an era that became a significant watershed in world history as well as a "refiner's fire" for the LDS Church and its members. Pioneer Utah was lost forever, and Latter-day Saints were forced into the mainstream of American life. The war, and all that went with it, created a test of strength as mighty as the tests in Jackson County or Nauvoo, or along the trek to the Great Basin. We often tell the stories of the nineteenth-century pioneers, but in the twentieth century there are also epochs of Church history; this series of books will chronicle one of those. My hope is that in looking back, we may turn our hearts—the "hearts of the children"—toward our parents, and that that vision of the past will help us with the trials that may lie in our future.

A number of people have been helpful to me in gathering information and in bringing this first book to clear focus. I appreciate the use of the archives of the History Department of The Church of Jesus Christ of Latter-day Saints, and especially the help of Bill Slaughter. I have also spent hundreds of hours in Brigham Young University's Harold B. Lee library, where I appreciated David Whittaker's assistance. The Provo City Library was another good source, and the staff was always helpful. Most of the members of the editorial staff at Deseret Book read my manuscript and its revisions, and they pulled no punches in the criticism they offered. Especially helpful were Sheri Dew and Jack Lyon. Ronald A. Millett, president of Deseret Book Company, took the time to read every version of the manuscript and to pass along his advice. A number of friends and family members also read the manuscript and gave me constructive feedback: Kathy Luke, Carolyn Rasmus, Pamela Russell, Carol Robbins, Kathryn Manning, Amy Hughes Russell, Tom Hughes, Rob Hughes, Kristen Shawgo Hughes, Shauna Weight, and David Weight.

My wife, Kathleen, has been more a partner than an advisor. She assisted me with my research, she brainstormed with me as I developed the plot, she reviewed my outlines, and she read every word of every draft. She got to know the characters and setting so well that she could always help me think through the issues, the plot, and the tone of the book. I dedicated my first book to her many years ago. This, now, is my seventieth book, and Kathy and I have been married thirty years. It was Kathy who supported my decision to give up a tenured university position to become a full-time writer, and so, in one sense, I owe all my books to her. I also owe her for our thirty good years together. For the second time, therefore, I dedicate a book to her. It's a very small gesture, but I hope symbolic of all I feel for her.

I

Elder Thomas had looked out the window a dozen times in the past two hours. This time he scanned the horizon, a craggy line of spires and boxy buildings in the hazy fall light. But he saw nothing that was alarming. The nearby Jewish ghetto was unusually quiet. Maybe all the warnings were wrong—maybe the trouble was over.

And then he spotted smoke—black and boiling. "It's starting," he said. "They've set something on fire."

Elder Mecham pushed backward from the table, his chair making a scraping noise on the hardwood floor. "Where?" he said. And then, in a moment, he was next to Elder Thomas, his bulk demanding its share of the space.

Elder Thomas pointed at the plume of smoke. It was in the ghetto but rather far off, probably toward the end of the street that people called *Judengasse*—Jewish Street. The elders lived just outside the ghetto in a seedy part of town where apartments were cheap.

"It started burning hard, right from the beginning," Elder Thomas said.

"What is it?"

"I don't know. I can't think what's over that way."

"Let's go look."

"No. We'd better not."

Elder Thomas was the senior companion, the one expected to use wisdom. Out tracting that morning, he had decided—after being warned several times—that he and his companion had better get back to their apartment where they would be safe. Early in the morning, Storm Troopers—the SA—and Gestapo agents had begun ripping apart Jewish homes and businesses and arresting Jews.

Two days before, in Paris, a young Jew named Hershl Grynszpan had shot a German diplomat named Ernst vom Rath, and now the diplomat had died. No one in Germany knew exactly why it had happened—since information was controlled by the Nazis—but the *Völkischer Beobachter,* the party-sponsored newspaper, had been full of indignation, and everyone was predicting trouble for the Jews. The talk, however, was strange. People hadn't told the elders, "I'm furious. I'm going to get those Jews." They had said, "Be careful. It's not safe to be out in the streets."

"What are they doing—burning people's houses?" Elder Mecham asked.

Elder Thomas wasn't sure. In the ghetto all the shops were operated by Jews, including Brother Goldfarb's tailor shop. He was a Mormon but formerly a Jew, and he was no longer allowed to live with his wife and daughter. Hitler had passed a law against Jews being married to Christians. Still, Elder Thomas had never thought that the Nazis would start setting fires. Now he wondered what might be coming—especially for Brother Goldfarb.

"Come on—let's go take a look." Elder Mecham took a couple of steps toward the door.

Elder Thomas hadn't moved yet. But he heard himself saying, "Okay. But we've got to be really careful."

"I'm taking my camera."

"No. Don't do that."

"I'll keep it under my coat. I won't get it out unless I'm sure we're safe."

This was foolish. But Elder Thomas pulled his own camera from a drawer by his bed, and he strapped it over his shoulder. It was November 10 and not terribly cold, but he walked to the wardrobe and got out his wool coat. As he pulled it on, he said, "We're taking a *big* chance. I hope you know that."

The truth was, Elder Thomas hadn't been this excited since the evacuation earlier that same fall of 1938. In September the missionaries had received orders from President M. Douglas Wood to clear out. Germany had lined up troops on the border of Czechoslovakia, and war had seemed imminent. Elder Thomas and Elder Mecham had packed up and caught a train for Holland. And then for three weeks, the missionaries from the West German mission—and from all over Europe—had waited to see whether they would be shipped home. But no one had stopped Hitler; he had gotten his way in Czechoslovakia. The missionaries had returned to their missions, but tension in Europe had remained high, and sometimes Elder Thomas wondered whether he would be able to finish the two and a half years he had been called to serve.

The elders hurried down the three flights of stairs, taking two steps at a time, but as they pushed through the big outside door, Elder Thomas said, "Okay, slow down. Just walk normally."

As they walked, Elder Thomas watched the smoke, gray now, rising in a thick column and then spreading out over the city. Frankfurt was a city of grays and rusty browns—old and worn—but it was beautiful, too, with its ornate cathedrals and its views along the Main River. Elder Thomas had been in Frankfurt only two months, but he had been on his mission over a year. Elder Mecham had come to Frankfurt at the same time as Elder Thomas, in early September, but that had been the beginning of his mission, so his German had not come all that far.

Elder Mecham was taking long strides, and Elder Thomas kept telling him to slow down. Elder Thomas was not short—about five-eleven—but Elder Mecham was a good four inches taller.

The elders walked the several blocks quickly. They didn't go into the ghetto but followed a street along the edge of it. They could still see nothing but smoke, however, until they turned the corner onto the street where the fire was. And then, both of them stopped. "The synagogue!" Elder Thomas said.

That beautiful old building. It had never occurred to Elder Thomas that anyone—even the Nazis—would do such a thing.

The two approached, but they stayed in the background, away from the crowd. The cupola at the front corner of the building had already caved in, and flames were gushing from the roof. The synagogue was a magnificent stone structure with stained glass windows, but the windows were broken now, and inside all was ablaze. Elder Thomas thought of the vaulted ceilings, the dark woodwork, the hand-built stairways—all of that craftsmanship, gone.

A big crowd had gathered, but people were only watching, and they appeared solemn. They stood with their hands behind their backs or their arms folded in front of them. Elder Thomas looked for uniforms—maybe brown-shirted Storm Troopers—but he saw none. Some women were huddled at the back of the crowd in little bunches, but most were men in coats and hats. A few boys were wearing Hitler Youth uniforms, but they watched in awe, clearly more impressed by the furious fire than by political ideas.

"I don't get this," Elder Mecham said. "They're all just watching. Who set the fire?"

"Nazis. Party members, I would guess," Elder Thomas whispered. "These people had nothing to do with it."

"Why didn't anyone try to put it out? It makes me *sick.*"

Elder Thomas felt much the same. And yet, he understood better than Elder Mecham. He had been in Germany long enough to understand the way Nazis operated—and the way the people reacted. Fear was a factor in almost every decision.

"I want a picture," Elder Mecham said. "I want *proof*."

"Maybe we'd just better—"

"Stand in front of me. I'll take my camera out of its case. Then I'll take a quick shot over your shoulder."

"Wait a minute."

Elder Thomas scanned the street, checked behind them. But no one seemed to be paying any attention to them. "Okay," he said. "Just snap one picture, and then let's go. President Wood would die if he knew we were here."

Elder Mecham stepped behind Elder Thomas, but he stayed close, and Elder Thomas could tell he was fumbling to get his camera out. "Hurry. Do it now," Elder Thomas told him.

In another few seconds, he felt the camera, or actually Elder Mecham's big fists, rest on his shoulder, and he held his breath until he heard the shutter release. But then he couldn't resist. "Okay, let me get a shot," he said.

This was not like Elder Thomas. He had been trained by his vigilant stake president father. Elder Thomas's name, David Alexander, the same as his father's, had identified him all his life. At East High, in Salt Lake City, he had been "Alex," but he had also been "President Thomas's boy." His good looks—his dark, wavy hair and earnest brown eyes—gave him the look of a movie star. But there was nothing mysterious or suggestive about the clean lines of his face. He was exactly what he seemed: up front, reliable, even predictable. He didn't break rules.

Elder Mecham stepped forward, and Elder Thomas got his own camera out. He shot around Elder Mecham, not over him, and he took slightly longer to get the picture framed. He had snapped the shot and was pulling the camera back inside his coat when he heard someone say, in German, "What are you doing there?"

Elder Thomas tucked the camera inside his coat, under his

arm, and stepped back to Elder Mecham's side. He tried to appear natural, but his heart was suddenly beating hard. A man was crossing the narrow street and coming toward them. Elder Thomas thought the man must have come out of a house or an alley. He hadn't been anywhere in sight when he had pulled his camera out.

"Making pictures?" the man asked as he walked closer. Elder Thomas took a better look. He saw what he feared: the black uniform with silver trim, the braided hat. Gestapo.

Elder Thomas said nothing for a moment. He was trying to think what to do. "Yes, I took a picture," he finally said breathlessly. "Isn't that acceptable?"

"*Wo kommen Sie her? England?*"

"*Nein. Aus Amerika.*"

And then, in English, "If you think it is not wrong to take pictures, why do you hide your camera?"

Elder Thomas answered in German. "I . . . was not certain."

"What is your name?" the agent said, again in English.

"Alex Thomas. We're missionaries. I'm sorry if I did something wrong."

The agent was silent for a time, as though he were deciding what to do. "Of course you have done nothing wrong. We have no laws against making photographs." His voice had turned sugary, maybe ironic, and Elder Thomas didn't know what to make of it. "I would expect, however, that you would make photographs of our castles and rivers—not of this unfortunate fire."

"Yes. Usually . . . that's the kind of pictures I take."

"It's a terrible thing these people have done, lighting this fine building on fire." The agent was rather hefty but hard, and his eyes, veiled by heavy black eyebrows, were steady. He looked up at Elder Mecham. "Don't you agree, my big friend?"

Elder Mecham nodded, but he said nothing.

"And what is your name, sir?"

"Mecham. Lewis Mecham."

"My, my. Two such fine young men, and here to teach the German people religion."

Elder Thomas said softly, stubbornly in German, "We were uncertain what was happening. We just came to look."

"A Jewish boy killed one of our Germans in Paris. And I'm afraid these people are angry about that. They set this synagogue on fire this morning, and the fire brigade put it out. But the people only came back and started the fire again. It's bad, the things that can happen when people become very, very angry." He hesitated. "Wouldn't you say so, Mr. Thomas?"

He opened his coat and placed his gloved hand on his hip. He was letting the elders see a long nightstick hanging from his belt. His thick lips puckered into a nasty smile, and his eyes held firm, as though daring Elder Thomas to react.

Elder Thomas said nothing.

"So what do you think of these German people, doing this?"

Elder Thomas had had enough of this. "Could we go now? We don't want any trouble."

"Of course you may go, Mr. Thomas. I'm not keeping you here. I thought you wanted to see this terrible fire." He motioned toward the building. "Step closer, if you like."

"We already saw it," Elder Mecham said, in English, his voice showing his irritation.

Elder Thomas knew he couldn't let anything get started. He took hold of Elder Mecham's arm, began to turn him. "We'll go now," he said to the agent.

"*Ach.* Only one matter, first."

The Elders stopped.

"I must have your cameras. You can stop by later and pick them up at the police station down the street, but for now, I must keep them."

This pronouncement had taken on, at last, a commanding tone. Elder Thomas began to pull his camera out, but Elder

Mecham said, "I thought you told us there was no law against taking pictures."

Elder Thomas took hold of his companion's arm again, gripped it tight.

"You are right about that, Mr. Mecham." He smiled, showing his teeth for the first time—brown and blunt. "But your pictures might be helpful. We can study them and perhaps determine who started the fire."

"We got here too late to see who did it," Elder Mecham said, "but I can guess." He pulled his arm forward, trying to loosen Elder Thomas's hold.

The agent's voice was suddenly stern. "I suppose I do not guess so well as you, sir. I must look at all the information I can obtain. Please now, your cameras."

Elder Mecham hesitated, but Elder Thomas gave his own camera over, and then he took Elder Mecham's from him and handed it to the agent.

"You may call at the police station tomorrow. Tell the policemen there that Agent Kellerman told you to pick up your cameras. There will be no problem." He glanced at the cameras. "German made, I see." He smiled again, seeming to enjoy some irony that was lost on Elder Thomas.

Again the elders turned to leave.

"*Ach*, excuse me. One other matter. Do you write letters to your parents in America?"

"*Ja*," Elder Thomas answered.

"When you write this time, tell them not to believe the lies the American press tells about Germany. Tell them we had an unfortunate fire here, and we kept your cameras because we are trying so very hard to find out who started it. Will you tell them that?"

"We'll tell them the truth," Elder Mecham said. "That's what *we* believe in." He was leaning forward a little, using his height and weight to communicate more than his words. Elder Thomas tried again to pull him back.

Kellerman didn't back off. He said, firmly, "Don't make a mistake, Mr. Mecham. I have comrades close by."

"I'm sure you do. You wouldn't dare take someone on by yourself."

Elder Thomas suddenly stepped forward and slid his shoulder in front of Elder Mecham. "Sir, we stopped by to see what was burning. That's all. We're sorry we took pictures, but you have our cameras. We'll be more careful in the future."

"That is right. You will be *much* more careful," Kellerman said. He was looking at Elder Mecham. "I know your names. I'll soon know your address. I wouldn't make another mistake."

"Don't worry. We want no trouble. We're missionaries. That's our only interest in being here."

"You are *foreigners*. That's what you are. And we don't need your kind. We don't need you to teach us religion."

Elder Thomas was angry, but he only said, "We'll go now."

"Heil Hitler," Kellerman said forcefully, and he threw up his hand in a quick Nazi salute.

"*Auf Wiedersehen,*" Elder Thomas said, slowly and emphatically. Then he turned to Elder Mecham. "Let's go," he said in English. The elders turned and began to walk away.

"Wait a moment," Kellerman called. Elder Thomas looked back. "I said 'Heil Hitler' to you. What do you say to me?"

Elder Thomas thought for a moment, but he knew he had no choice. "Heil Hitler," he said, flatly, obediently, but with obvious distaste.

"And you?" Kellerman was looking at Elder Mecham.

Elder Mecham also took his time, and then he said, "I'm not going to say that." He held his ground, staring down at Kellerman.

"Oh, Mr. Mecham, you make a great mistake. You *will* say it. Perhaps not now. But trust me, you will say it. You may even beg me for the chance."

For a moment, Elder Thomas thought of trying to say something to soften the confrontation, to smooth things over.

But there was really nothing to say, and so he merely pulled on his companion's arm and once again said, "Let's go."

The missionaries walked away. But behind them, they heard Kellerman say, "You have not seen me for the last time."

Elder Thomas's anger was already gone, replaced by fear. At the corner he glanced back, and he saw Kellerman still watching. Another Gestapo agent was now at his side.

"I wish I could get that guy out in our back pasture," Elder Mecham muttered. "I'd clean his plow."

"He was *daring* us to try something, Elder. Couldn't you see that?"

"Sure I could. So let him put up or shut up. He can use that big stick of his. I'll still take him on."

"You have no idea what a stupid idea that is, Elder. Gestapo agents can do *anything* they want to do. He could kill you, right here in the street, and not have to explain his reasons to anyone beyond Heinrich Himmler."

"Hey, you didn't say 'Heil Hitler' the first time. You got it all started."

"I know that. I lost my temper. It was stupid of me."

"Everything is stupid around here, if you ask me. What kind of country is this—where you can't even take a picture?"

"Be quiet! Keep your voice down."

"And you have to *whisper* all the time."

Elder Thomas gave up. He kept walking fast and glancing back to see whether anyone was following. He couldn't believe what he had done. President Wood had warned the missionaries dozens of times about things like this. It wouldn't take that much, he had told them, for one elder to get the whole Church in trouble—and get all the missionaries thrown out.

Once the elders got back to their apartment, Elder Thomas said, "We won't go out again tonight. I have branch work to do. And a talk to prepare. You can study."

Elder Thomas was the branch president in Maintal, a little town a few kilometers outside the city. The elders did most of their tracting in Frankfurt, but much of their time was spent looking after the members in the branch. They rode their bikes out along the river to Maintal three or four times a week.

Elder Thomas sat down at his desk and tried to work on his talk, but he couldn't concentrate. He kept wondering what Kellerman might do. And he wondered what more might happen in the city before the day ended. Time and again, he got up and walked to the window. And whenever he returned to his desk, Elder Mecham would soon get up and take a look himself.

After an hour or so, Elder Thomas broke his own edict, and the two walked downstairs and bought wurst at a nearby *Metzgerei*, and milk and cheese and yogurt at a little dairy depot next door. They had no refrigeration in their apartment, so they had to shop almost every day.

As the missionaries ate their cold cuts, they said very little. The horizon was darkening now, the sky faintly orange behind the buildings. If something more were going to happen, it might come after dark. Elder Thomas couldn't help thinking that if a fire started in the ghetto, it could spread through the neighborhood and reach the apartment building the elders lived in. It was a scary thought, and so he didn't bring it up, but it had to be something that Elder Mecham had thought of too.

Elder Mecham had become quiet. He was animated when he was feeling all right, his hands constantly waving in the air or running through his chaotic brown hair, but sometimes he looked terribly lost. He had told Elder Thomas once, "I'm not ever going to learn this language. It just doesn't fit my mouth." And Elder Thomas knew what he was really saying: "I shouldn't have come. I'm not suited for this kind of work."

Elder Mecham was not only tall, he was also twice as dense as Elder Thomas in the chest and arms. He had grown up on a big dry farm near Downey, Idaho, and had always worked hard. He had played football at the "AC"—the Agricultural College in Logan, Utah. Nothing in his life, however, had prepared him to spend his days in a suit, knocking on doors, politely offering pamphlets to skeptical Germans. His overcoat, cut big to fit his shoulders, looked like a two-man tent, and with his hat on, he seemed seven feet tall. When the *Hausfrauen* opened their doors to him, they often stepped back, cowering in his presence.

"Do you think the Jews are catching it today—all over Germany?" Elder Mecham asked.

"I would think so. But that Kellerman guy was lying. All this is coming straight from Hitler."

"I don't see why the Germans put up with that little twerp."

"Most people like what he's doing. Germans almost starved after the World War, and now they're working and eating. A lot of our Church members speak well of him."

"I don't think they're saying what they really think. They're scared of the SS and all these Gestapo agents."

"Maybe some of them are. But you need to learn some fear yourself. If Kellerman shows up again, you'll have to say what he wants to hear."

"I don't worry about that guy. He's all talk. He had his chance to arrest us, and he let us walk away."

"You made him look bad, Mit. He can't let that go. A guy like that has to save face. I'm scared of what he might do."

Elder Mecham shrugged, but Elder Thomas saw he was more worried than he wanted to let on. It crossed Elder Thomas's mind that he ought to call the mission president and ask for transfers for both of them. But that was the last thing he wanted. He loved Frankfurt, and especially Maintal, and he was excited about a family named Stoltz that he and his companion had started to teach. He told himself that he could make things right with Kellerman if he had to.

After eating, the elders tried again to settle down and study, but both were restless. As it turned out, however, they didn't have long to wait. The trouble began suddenly, soon after dark.

It started with shouts, then a crashing noise. Both missionaries bolted for the window.

They could see little, but the noise was terrifying. The yelling was incessant: the shouts of men—forceful and commanding—and then, after a time, shrill screams of women and children and frightened men. And all the while, the breaking of glass, the crashing of heavy objects. The ghetto seemed to be shattering into pieces.

The two elders stood stiff and tense, afraid they might soon see fires. But nothing burned. Only the sounds continued. And then headlights approached and engines roared. At the same time, Elder Thomas heard added voices. "More troops," he said. "Probably Storm Troopers." What followed were increased cries, increased confusion, and neither elder had to say it. They knew that people were being hauled away.

Eventually the missionaries walked away from the window. They sat on their beds. But they didn't study, didn't even talk much. They listened as the sounds continued, on and on: trucks coming and going; the constant shouting; and still, the crashing sounds of things breaking apart.

Neither elder slept much that night. It was the next morning before they ventured out to peer down the narrow *Judengasse*. A few people were trying to clean up the mess, but the refuse was everywhere: feather beds split open and strewn in the street, splintered furniture, smashed clocks, shattered mirrors. And everywhere, broken windows.

A change had come. The Nazis had taken their gloves off, had come out into the open more than ever before.

"Most of the people were not in on this," Elder Thomas said, trying to explain it not just to Elder Mecham but to himself. "Think about the Stoltz family. They would never do this."

"Maybe so. But who's going to stop it?"

Elder Thomas had no idea. He had always felt safe in Germany, even at the time of the evacuation to Holland. But nothing seemed certain now.

"Maybe we should try to find Bruder Goldfarb," Elder Mecham said. "He might need our help."

"No. We'd better stay away. We're in trouble already."

"Come on, Elder Thomas. He's a member of the Church. We've got to do something."

Elder Thomas tried to think what to do. "We can't just walk to his shop," he finally said. "We could be spotted."

"So what do we do?"

"Follow me."

Elder Thomas walked to their apartment house and in the front door, but instead of walking up the stairs he continued on through to the back door and into the courtyard. Then he slipped through a back gate and down an alley. The elders followed lanes and alleys into the ghetto. Each time Elder Thomas reached a street, he checked it out, then hurried across and into another alley. He ended up at Brother Goldfarb's tailor shop, at the back door.

He knocked on the door and then waited. "He might be afraid to answer," Elder Mecham said.

But at that moment Elder Thomas saw a curtain move. "Bruder Goldfarb. It's the missionaries," he whispered.

A few seconds passed, and then the door opened. Brother Goldfarb waved them in and closed the door, but immediately he said, "You must not come here. You must leave now."

"We had to make sure you were all right," Elder Thomas said.

"I'm fine. Don't bother about me. You must not be seen coming here."

"Did the SA come to your shop?" Elder Mecham asked.

"Oh, yes. They came. They broke my windows and turned my machines over. They knocked me around, and they painted *traitor* on my door. But at least they didn't take me off in their trucks."

Brother Goldfarb looked old. He was probably not much more than fifty, but his hair was gray, and he had deep lines around his eyes. He had always seemed stoic, ready to accept his lot in life—given what the Nazis thought of Jews—but now he looked defeated. His voice was flat, his face emotionless.

"Why didn't they take you?" Elder Mecham asked.

"I don't know. They took only men—but mostly young men."

"What will happen to them?"

"I don't know. There were many threats. 'Filthy Jew,' they called me. At first they said they would haul me off and kill me, but then they left. I have no idea what it all means."

"What can we do to help you?" Elder Thomas asked.

"Nothing. You must go. I won't come to church now, but I will worship. I will pray."

"Why won't you come to church?"

Brother Goldfarb looked surprised. "Don't you know? I've been asked not to."

"By whom?"

"President Meis. The Brown Shirts came to the meetings last week. They told him to rip all the hymns from the song-book that speak of Zion or Israel. And they asked him whether any Jews attended his church. He decided it was better to say no."

"But that's not right," Elder Mecham said. "You can go to church if you want to. Come to our branch. In Maintal. You can ride with us on your bicycle."

"No, no. President Meis is right. It will only cause troubles. This time will pass, perhaps, and then I will return."

"Have you talked to your wife?" Elder Thomas asked.

"No. I must not do that. I will stay here. If they will let me sew, I will be all right." Brother Goldfarb nodded, his jaw firm, but tears were gathering in the corners of his eyes.

"We'll check on you again," Elder Thomas promised.

"No. Please don't." He was blinking now. "I'll be fine."

Elder Thomas took hold of Brother Goldfarb and hugged

him. "I'm sorry," he said. Elder Mecham reached around and patted his back.

"I am fine," Brother Goldfarb kept repeating, but when he stepped back, tears were on his cheeks. "*Please*, don't come back. I don't want anything to happen to you because of me."

"We won't abandon you," Elder Thomas said. "But we'll be careful."

Elder Thomas opened the door a crack and looked out. Then he reached back and shook Brother Goldfarb's hand, as did Elder Mecham, and the two slipped out. They followed the back alleys to their building and slipped in the back door. But before they walked upstairs, Elder Thomas went to the front door and opened it an inch or two. Then he shut it again immediately.

"What's wrong?"

"There's a man across the street. Just standing there."

"Gestapo?"

"I don't know. He's not wearing a uniform. He could be an informer. Kellerman could have posted him there."

"Maybe he's just . . . waiting for someone."

"Maybe."

But it didn't seem likely.

2

Wally and Gene were trying to slip out the front door when Wally heard his father's big voice. "Where are you going, boys?"

"Just outside to get a little air," Wally said. He grinned at Gene, but he knew what was coming next.

"Why do you have a football with you?"

"It's Gene's new one. We need to give it a test flight."

"Not today. It's the Sabbath, Christmas or not."

"Before we throw it, we'll have an opening prayer."

Gene laughed, but Dad said, "That's not funny, Wally. Close the door. You're letting all the heat out of the house." Dad was sitting in the living room in "his" chair. He was holding the *Salt Lake Tribune* open in front of him.

Wally stepped inside and shut the door. Most of the snow had melted off the front lawn, but the air was cold this morning, and smoggy. "Hey, Dad," Wally said, as he walked into the living room, "is it all right if I go visit the sick? That's okay on the Sabbath, isn't it?"

"Stick around," Dad said. "We're going to have our meeting just as soon as your mother can get away from the kitchen."

"After that, can I take the car for a little while?"

"No. I want you here. The family is coming for dinner."

This was a pronouncement, stated one word at a time in Dad's deep, authoritative voice, and Wally knew he had no chance of winning any concessions. Still, he pushed ahead. "I just want to run over and see Mel before he dies."

Dad looked curious as he peered through his reading glasses over the top of the newspaper.

"Mel's getting skis for Christmas, Dad. He's sure to break his neck—the way you said I would if I got skis. I just want to see him one last time before he's a goner."

"Maybe he'll only be paralyzed, and you can visit him in the hospital," Dad said. He looked pleased with himself, but he didn't laugh. He hoisted the paper in front of his face again.

Good old Dad. *President* Thomas. He had been stake president for six years, a counselor in the stake presidency before that, and bishop before that. Wally was sixteen, and he couldn't remember a time when his dad hadn't been gone all day on Sunday. Everyone in Sugar House—the south part of Salt Lake City—knew and loved the man. Wally was one of the very few who thought President Thomas could be improved upon.

Wally gave up. He walked through the dining room and into the kitchen. The Thomases lived in a big, white frame house, built before the turn of the century. Dad always said it was a fine home, well constructed, but Wally liked the new one-story brick homes that most of his friends lived in.

Beverly and LaRue, Wally's little sisters, were in the kitchen with Sister Thomas. Beverly, who was seven, was sitting at the kitchen table studying a picture in her coloring book but not yet coloring. LaRue was standing on a stool watching her mother roll lumps of dough into balls. Both girls had on white aprons over their red velvet Christmas dresses.

"Mom, give me your honest opinion," Wally said. "Don't you think Dad is unreasonable, tyrannical . . . bossy . . . and—"

"No, he's not," LaRue said. "He's a sweetie."

"Yeah. If you're nine, and you know how to flash your dimples and get anything you want."

LaRue cocked her head to one side, smiled, and stuck a finger into one of her dimples. Wally tried to stick his finger into the other one—deep—but LaRue twisted away and stepped off her stool. "Leave me alone!" she demanded.

"Mom," Wally said, "I need food before I pass out. The smell of that turkey is killing me."

"Eat a carrot," Mom said. "What did Dad do to you?"

"He won't let me take the car."

"Big surprise. You know he holds a family meeting on Christmas."

"It's not a meeting. He just gives a speech—the same as he does on family night. Gene and I call it 'chloroform night.'"

"Shush." She looked away, but Wally saw, from the side, that her cheek was swelling, and he knew she was smiling.

"Which family is coming?"

"Grandpa and Grandma Thomas. All the Thomases."

"Why doesn't the Snow side of the family come on Christmas? They're not dumb as adobe bricks—like all my Thomas cousins."

"Don't say that, Wally. That's not funny." She turned toward him and tried to look stern, but he could see she was struggling not to smile. Wally took some pleasure in that.

Mom had a smear of some sort of berry—maybe cranberries—across the top of her apron. She was a pretty woman, but squat, and a little overstuffed in her purple Sunday dress. "Wally, you've got the whole week out of school," she said. "You and Mel can run around all you want."

"But you would let me take the car if it were up to you, wouldn't you? Tell the truth."

Mom smiled this time, her big dimples puckering her cheeks like the crowns of apples, but she didn't answer. Bea Thomas was known as widely as President Thomas and loved as much. And even though she said less than her husband, she was quoted more often. She thought for herself, and she had a way of coming out with things that no one expected from a stake president's wife.

Wally tossed a ball of dough into his mouth, and he wandered back to the living room. Then he tried one more time, just to be annoying. "What if I run over to Mel's for *ten* minutes? I'll get back for the meeting, and if I wreck the Nash, I'll jump out before I bleed on the seats."

"Wally, that's enough." President Thomas owned and operated a Hudson/Nash dealership, and every year he got a new car. The Nash "Silver Bullet" that had come out that fall was his current pride and joy. He rarely let it out of his sight.

"All right then," Wally said. "I've reached a decision. I'm staying right here with you."

"Threats won't do you any good either," Dad said, and he chuckled. He was a burly man, a head taller than his wife, even a couple of inches taller than his eldest son, Alex. He had bulldog jowls for cheeks, and he always looked as though he needed to shave—even right after he had done so. The only time he didn't wear a white shirt and tie was when he put on his pajamas.

"This might be a grand time for us to have a father-and-son chat," Wally said. "You could give me some fatherly advice." Wally loved the silence that followed. Dad hated to be interrupted when he was reading the paper, and even more, he hated Wally's facetiousness.

Slowly the paper lowered, and Dad's eyes appeared, his glasses reflecting the yellow light in the room. "Actually, we do need to talk about your grades."

"Now that I think about it, Dad, I'd like to read the paper myself. Do you have the sports section?"

Dad picked up a section of the paper from his lap and handed it over. Then he watched.

Wally laughed as he unfolded the paper. "What?" he finally said as his dad stared at him.

"I just want to see you read something. *Anything.*"

Wally decided he had lost this one, so he ducked behind the paper. Wally's grades hadn't actually been that terrible, but they were below his father's expectations. "You've got as much ability as Alex or Barbara," Dad always told him. "But you're lazy. You're wasting the talents the Lord blessed you with."

Wally didn't want to get into all that again, so he read the sports pages, and Dad went back to the section he had been reading. But it wasn't long before Sister Thomas came to the door and said, "I'm going to let these rolls rise. We could have our meeting now—if it doesn't last too long."

Wally glanced at Dad, who looked a little irritated. And Wally knew why. Dad didn't like to work around other people's schedules. "Go get Barbara and Gene," he told Wally.

Wally got up, hiked halfway up the stairs, and then shouted, "Bobbi, Gene, shake a leg. It's time for Dad's meeting."

Everyone soon gathered in the living room. Mom arrived last, wiping her hands on a dish towel and saying, "Al, I have potatoes boiling. I'll have to check on them before too long." Dad nodded. He asked "Barbara," whom everyone else in the world called Bobbi, to lead them in a Christmas hymn, and he asked Gene to say the opening prayer.

As soon as Gene ended his quick little prayer, President Thomas said, "I know Wally is put out with me that I wouldn't let him leave, but I like Christmas to be a family day. That's how it really ought to be. I hate what I see Christmas becoming."

"If you ask me, it's way too commercialized," Wally said, and he grinned. He knew he had taken the word right out of his father's mouth. Wally glanced at Bobbi, but she gave her head a little shake.

Dad took a breath; he didn't smile. That was a sign he had been pushed about enough. So Wally decided to lay off. "In some ways the depression has been good for people," Dad said. "It's caused us to humble ourselves. But now, as times start to get a little better and folks have a dollar or two in their pockets, they're starting to spend too much money again."

LaRue and Beverly were sitting on the floor, their aprons removed now. They were already beginning to "fidget"—as Dad called it.

"I guess what upsets me most is that members of the Church ought be different. We let the silly radio and the newspapers tell us how to live our lives."

This was dad's favorite topic—the corruption in Zion. Wally could have given the speech himself. But after a few minutes, when Dad had just gotten up a head of steam—condemning the trashy movies showing in town—Mom said, "Al, I've got to check those potatoes really quick, so they won't boil over."

Off she went, and Dad waited. Gene, who was thirteen, was sitting on the floor, leaning against the couch. He was wearing jeans and an old plaid shirt. He looked distant, as usual, but not anxious. Gene was usually one to go along with things and not complain.

Bobbi was sitting on the couch, facing Dad. She had a new navy blue dress on, and her hair was already curled. She was often Dad's main supporter, when she agreed with him, but she had strong opinions of her own, and she never held them back. "Dad," she said now, "the movies aren't really that bad. I saw that Clark Gable, Myrna Loy movie, 'Too Hot to Handle,' and it wasn't vulgar, or anything like that, but the ads made you think—"

"It's the ads I'm talking about," President Thomas said. "I don't have time to go to movies."

Bobbi was about to respond, but just then Mom returned, and Dad quickly jumped back into his speech. "The point is, this is Zion. The mountains you see outside that east window are the very mountains spoken of by Daniel the Prophet. What do we sing? 'For the strength of the hills we bless thee, our

God, our fathers' God.' Do you stop to think what those words mean?"

Dad didn't want an answer. Bobbi must have known that, but she couldn't resist. She had always talked a lot, but now that she was going to the University of Utah—taking literature classes—she had gotten even worse. "I think the mountains symbolize steadfastness," she said. "There's one line in that song . . . I can't think how it goes." She got up and walked toward the piano, apparently to look for a hymn book.

But Dad saw the danger. "It doesn't matter right now," he said. "My point is that we came to this valley to get away from the influences of the world, to escape the evil and the mobs, and to build something. It wasn't that long ago. Do you realize that my Grandfather Thomas was friends with Brigham Young? His father crossed the plains with the second company Brother Brigham brought to this valley. He buried a wife and child out on the plains. And your mother's family—the Snows—were some of the greatest missionaries in the history of the Church."

Bobbi sat down. Dad looked frustrated, as though he had something he wanted to communicate that he couldn't quite get at. Maybe he saw the absence of interest in most of the faces.

"Brigham Young used to talk about 'this people.' Think what that means. We were bound together then—one society. We knew our heritage. But we're becoming like the gentiles. Look at the scandals we've gone through in Salt Lake this year. Gambling dens broken up. Women arrested for running . . . evil houses."

"What women, Daddy?" LaRue asked.

"Just some . . . bad women." Dad looked away from her.

LaRue looked baffled, and Beverly was obviously lost in her own imagination, where she spent most of her life. Mom kept nodding to show her support, but Wally was sure she was thinking mostly about her dinner. And he didn't blame her. Dad was always alarmed about something. Short skirts. Dance halls. Jazz music. The truth was, all the "evil women" in Salt Lake could probably be rounded up and put into one jail cell.

Wally sat back and tried not to let his dad bother him. The sun was at a steep angle this time of year, so the house was aglow with a kind of half-light, made amber by the fire in the fireplace. It all seemed like a scene from a play that Wally had watched before. These three connecting rooms—the living room with the front entrance and parlor to the west and a large dining room to the north—had been exactly the same for as long as Wally could remember. The rose-and-green flowered wallpaper had never changed; Mom cleaned it each year with a pink cleaner—Bennett's dough—and then said, "I think this paper will last us another year." And everything else lasted another year: the hefty gray couch and chair, the upright piano with its claw feet and chipped keys, the knickknack shelf with the little porcelain cats, the mirror with the beveled edges, the picture of a wolf howling in the snow. Even the Christmas tree returned each year to the same spot, always a Douglas fir, eight feet tall.

That was all right. It could all stay like that forever. But Wally wanted to see something else.

"I know you think I sound like a broken phonograph record," Dad said. "But I want you to *feel* how important this is. You are 'children of the promise.' I want to pass on to you what I received from my parents—and I'm not at all sure that I'm doing that. You simply *can't* think of yourselves as being like other people, outside the Church."

Everyone's eyes came up. Even the little girls seemed to sense the urgency in President Thomas's voice.

"I'm telling you, Satan is unleashing his forces against the Lord's people. And we have to stand firm. If this family can't set the example for our stake, who can? Everyone watches us— expects something better from us—and we can't let them down."

Dad was looking directly at Wally, and Wally knew why.

It was he who was Dad's greatest worry. Wally just wasn't Alex—no matter how much Dad wanted one mold for all his sons.

The room was silent. Wally had heard the passion in his Dad's voice, and that was impressive. But something about it seemed too fierce, too self-conscious. Wally had gone through life feeling he had to hold up an appearance to the members of the stake—to the world—and he was tired of it. President Thomas was still looking at Wally, as though he wanted a response. Wally looked at the floor, and when he finally looked back, he could see his father's frustration.

President Thomas picked up his Bible. He thumbed through the pages and then stopped. He let the silence prepare everyone. Then he began the account of Christ's birth, in Luke; read it himself, as always. And Wally, in spite of his complicated feelings, did love the sound of his Dad's voice—the way he let the words roll from deep within himself. There was something genuine about that, and suddenly Wally felt guilty that he was always the one on the outside, always the one disrupting the spirit his father tried to create. One voice in Wally's brain always said, "Don't fight him." But a stronger impulse shouted, "Resist! He wants to run your life for you."

When President Thomas finished reading, Bobbi got up from the couch, kissed her father on the cheek, and said, "Thanks, Daddy. You make it sound so beautiful. And don't worry, we'll be faithful. You've taught us well." Dad was obviously touched. He nodded but didn't say anything.

Little Beverly said, "We liked all the presents, too, even if there were too many."

And that was the irony. No matter how much Dad complained about "commercialism," after Mom bought enough for Christmas each year, Dad went out and bought more. Maybe he bought galoshes and warm sweaters—practical things—but he bought plenty.

"I need to check my turkey," Mom said, and she stood up

and left the room. Wally was sure Dad would have preferred a few final words and then a prayer, but he let the meeting end by default. As everyone wandered off, Wally could see his father's dejection, but Dad brought these things on himself by taking everything so seriously. The man could actually be fun at times, but he seemed to hold that side of himself back.

Relatives soon started showing up. "Bricks-for-brains cousins by the dozens" was Wally's description to Gene. Soon all the usual family-get-together talk began. "My goodness," Aunt Marjorie told Wally, "you're too pretty to be a boy. My daughters would give anything to have your complexion—and those long eyelashes."

"Hey, come on," Wally said. "I'm a rugged guy. I shave twice a month now."

Uncle Everett, Dad's brother from Provo, was standing in the front entrance, pulling off his coat. His laugh sounded like an echo from the bottom of a barrel. "If you're so rugged, how come the coach kept you on the bench all season?"

"He was saving me. I was his secret weapon."

Uncle Everett hung up his coat on the hall tree, and then he walked into the living room. He was still chuckling. "Well, if you're really good, you'd better come down and play for the BY. I'm afraid we had ourselves another miserable season."

"Hey, BYU is doing better," Dad said. "At least they tied the U this year."

"Yeah, well, they've still never *beaten* Utah, and I doubt they ever will."

"I think they will during the millennium," Wally said. "They'll be able to recruit angels to play for them."

Uncle Everett liked that. He slapped Wally on the back, and he laughed again. Then he sat down on the couch across from his brother, who had taken up residence in his own chair. Wally sat on the couch with his uncle. He figured he would rather talk to Uncle Everett than get caught in the middle of all his cousins.

The house was filling up, the aunts gathering in the kitchen and cousins swarming everywhere. Everett's boy, Douglas, was already into an argument with one of Aunt Maurene's daughters—something about his tossing her doll on the floor. Uncle Howard hadn't arrived yet, and Wally knew things would only get worse when seven more kids were added to the chaos.

President Thomas's three brothers-in-law had gathered by the fireplace, and they were chatting and laughing. Wally always suspected that they didn't feel all that comfortable around Dad. Uncle Max, Idonna's husband, always smelled of tobacco, although he never smoked around the family, and Uncle Ray, Marjorie's husband, had never been active in the Church. Uncle Vic was a bishop in Taylorsville, but he was a heavy equipment mechanic with grease under his fingernails; he seemed to gravitate to the backsliders more than he did to the president.

Dad and Uncle Everett talked for a while about the roads—about some bad icy patches at the Point of the Mountain—and then Uncle Everett asked, "What does Alex have to say about Germany? Does he think we're heading into another war over there?"

"He doesn't say much about politics," Dad said.

"This business with the Jews is a terrible shame," Everett said. "Now Hitler is saying that Jewish children can't go to public schools, and Jews can't own their own businesses or be doctors or lawyers—or almost anything else."

"I know. I've been reading about that." But Dad didn't sound as disgusted as his brother.

"Did you read the latest? He's claiming that the Jews owe him a billion marks to pay for the damage that was done on 'Crystal Night'—after that Jewish boy killed the German official in Paris. The Nazis killed close to a hundred Jews that night, hauled off thousands of them, burned down their synagogues and tore up their shops, and now Hitler wants to collect for the *damages*—in gold and jewelry."

"Well, it's a mess in some ways," Dad said. "But I talked to Sylvester Q. Cannon, from the Twelve. He was just over there, and he says Hitler has made some good changes. The country has never been so clean and orderly, and everyone is working."

"Not Jews!"

"Well, I know. I'm just saying—"

"Come on, Al. Of course Hitler's got people working. They're all building tanks and airplanes. And don't think he's not going to use them. Look what he did in Czechoslovakia. He said he was only trying to save the German minority in Sudetenland from the terrible mistreatment they were getting. But watch what he's doing. He's gradually taking control of that whole nation. And it won't be long until he's after Poland."

"Do you think we'll end up in a war?" Wally asked his uncle. That was something Wally worried about.

"Just a minute," Everett said. He got up and strode across the room. He grabbed his son by the arm and pulled him away from a knot of noisy kids. A raging argument had continued there. "Douglas, you leave Emmie and Sheralyn alone. I'm not kidding. If I hear you make another fuss, I'll take you outside and tan your hide."

Wally saw no reason to delay the punishment. But after another warning, Everett returned. Without missing a beat, he said, "I don't know what's going to happen, Wally. But Hitler will keep pushing for the 'living space in the east' that he talked about in *Mein Kampf*. And England and France claim they won't let Poland become another Czechoslovakia."

"Maybe someone has to stop the man," Dad said, "but I don't think it ought to be us. And I don't trust Roosevelt. I think he's getting ready to send our boys over there."

Uncle Everett laughed. He was a history professor at BYU and a committed Democrat. "Didn't you hear FDR on the radio last night? He promised never to get us into another war in Europe."

"Yes, well, he says a lot of things."

"Al, you might as well face it. Utahns love Roosevelt—and this is a Democratic state. A vote for *any* Republican is going to go down the drain."

Dad didn't even try to argue the point.

Wally heard the front door open, and another huge voice boomed through the house. "Anybody home?" It was Uncle Howard from Farmington. He was carrying a little son, and his wife, Aunt Fay, followed with a baby in her arms. After that, the rest of the kids filed in, and cousins dashed toward them, filling the entry with their racket. "It smells great in here. Let's eat," Howard shouted above the noise.

Mom announced that dinner was almost ready. She needed Dad to set up extra tables. Dad, of course, recruited Wally to help him. By the time the tables—makeshift contraptions built of planks and sawhorses—were ready another half hour had passed. But Christmas dinner, as usual, was a grand event, with Grandma and Grandpa Thomas and all the couples—along with Bobbi and Wally—gathered in the dining room. Dad had added all the extra leaves to the table and used a card table as an extension. The small children were housed in the kitchen and the teenagers in the living room. Gene was sitting with some of his cousins, mostly girls, who were all nuts about him. He had a way of lighting up when he got that much attention, and he seemed to be having fun.

Wally ate well—turkey, stuffing, potatoes and gravy, candied yams, cut corn, string beans, pickled beets, sweet relish and dill pickles, cranberry sauce, and those wonderful butter rolls he had been smelling all day. He took another dab of everything as the platters came around the second time. He didn't say much; he listened to his uncles and aunts. Dad was gloating about Salt Lake making the silly decision to install parking meters. He was sure people would shop in Sugar House now. "Who's going to pay to park a car?" he asked his brothers.

Aunt Idonna made sure the other women knew about the

after-Christmas sale at Roe's. "Everything's on sale for eighty-eight cents," she told them. "Two men's shirts, or five pair of socks. All kinds of things. Pajamas. Spring hats. Nice house dresses. But I think those might have been a dollar-eighty-eight."

Wally ate a slice of pie at the table, stalled until the kids had cleared out of the kitchen, and then slipped in for the provisions he would need for a long holdout. He cut three slices of pie—apple, pumpkin, and lemon meringue—and set them on a plate. Then he got out a quart bottle of milk. He was about to make a quick dart through the crowd and up the stairs when Douglas came through the door. "You can't have extra pie," Douglas told him. "Mom said. Aunt Bea, too."

"Hey, this isn't for me. It's for a widow across the street. I'm taking it to her. I'm a wonderful guy, huh?"

"Uh-uh. You're lying. You always lie."

"You're right, Dougy. I'm a thief and a liar. Call in the G-men to arrest me." Just then Grandma came in from the dining room.

"Wally's taking extra pie," Douglas said.

Grandma was a tall woman with a square chin like Dad's and hands like a man's. She set one of those big hands on Douglas's shoulder and said, "Wally wouldn't take extra pie for himself. He's saving it for the poor and the needy."

Wally grinned. "See, Douglas. It's the widow."

"Uh-uh. He's going to eat it all."

"I wouldn't lie to you, Dougy," Grandma said. "Old ladies don't lie. Especially grandmas."

Douglas wasn't buying that, especially now that Grandma was laughing, but Wally finally pushed on through the door, slipped through the crowd quietly, and climbed the stairs to his room. He turned on the radio and tried to tune in something besides Christmas music, but he had no luck. The local stations carried too much pretty dance band music to suit Wally. He liked the bands from New Orleans or New York—jazz bands that liked to "play it hot."

Wally changed clothes, and then he ate his after-dinner feast. Not long after that he heard someone coming up the stairs. He feared it was Gene with instructions from Dad for Wally to come back. But it turned out to be Bobbi, making her own escape. She gave a light little knock and then opened his door. "What are you doing up here?" she asked, smiling.

"I had to leave before I killed Douglas. What's it called when you kill your cousin? Do they have a 'cide for that?"

"In this case, I think it's called justifiable homicide." She leaned against the door frame and laughed, making her usual hissy little sound. Bobbi wasn't knock-out beautiful like LaRue, but Wally liked the way she looked—as though she would always be a little girl, with freckles on her nose and a sweet-kid kind of smile. She and Beverly were the only ones in the family who had light hair—light brown, almost blonde. Mom's hair was like that too, in old pictures, but her hair had grayed a good deal now. Everyone else had dark hair, like Dad's.

"Maybe I can just tape little Dougy's mouth shut for a few years. Even his parents ought to appreciate that."

"Leave a hole for a straw. They can feed him malts."

"Or worms."

Bobbi laughed at that, but gradually her smile disappeared. "You know, Wally," she said, "sometimes you push Dad a little too far. You had him on the edge this morning."

Wally had been lying on his bed, but now he sat up. He had put on a ragged pair of corduroys and a threadbare flannel shirt. He knew that later he would have to put his coat and tie on. The whole family, even all the cousins, would be going down to the Burton Ward for sacrament meeting. It was a Christmas cantata, and Melvin J. Ballard was speaking. After that, President Heber J. Grant would be speaking on the radio—which Dad would also expect him to listen to. Wally figured he would have to live through all that, but for now, he wanted to relax—and not listen to another sermon, this time from Bobbi.

Bobbi shut the bedroom door, and then she walked over and sat down next to him. The two sat facing Gene's bed, which was just a few feet from Wally's. "Wally, what's going on?"

"What do you mean?" He stared across the room at his shelves. There were more balls on them—baseballs, tennis balls, a basketball, a football—than there were books. Wally would have given anything to be a great athlete. He went out for every sport. He always missed the cut, however, or he made the team but not the starting lineup. He played M-Men basketball for his ward, and he did a little better there, but he still spent more time on the bench than not.

"What's this thing you're doing lately? You make fun of *everything*."

"Not really."

Bobbi looked down and placed her shoes—her new black pumps with ankle straps—next to each other. "You've changed, Wally. I think back a year or two, and Dad was your pal. The two of you were always talking about going into the car business together."

"I lost interest in that."

"Why?"

"I'm tired of working at the dealership. Dad drives me nuts. He's never satisfied with anything I do. There's no way he'd ever think of me as his *partner*."

Bobbi got up and moved over to Gene's bed, so she was facing Wally. "Wally," she said, "what's happening to you?"

"I don't know what to tell you. I'm kind of antsy to get out of high school . . . and . . . I want to get away from here."

"What do you mean? Like go away to college? Dad won't pay for that."

"I might join the service. The navy or something."

"You've never said anything about that before."

"That's because Dad expects everyone to go to college. I don't dare bring it up with him." Wally got up and walked across the room to his shelf. Bobbi had to twist to look at him. He picked up his football and flipped it into the air. "Mel is thinking he might go with me," he said.

"Mel thinks you've changed, too."

"What do you mean? What did he say?"

"Just what I told you—that you turn everything into a joke. He told me your big thing lately is trying to see how many girls in the senior class you can kiss."

"So what? He's trying to do the same thing. I'm just better at it than he is."

"So you're the master, are you?"

Wally tried to grin. "I don't kiss and tell."

"You tell Mel—plenty."

Wally rolled his eyes. He couldn't believe Mel would tell Bobbi all this stuff. "Hey, if the worst thing I do is kiss a few girls, I doubt I'll be cast into outer darkness."

"Wally, it's not right to kiss girls you don't really care about. It's just playing with their feelings—for your own thrills. It's all part of this attitude I'm seeing in you now."

"Bobbi, come on. You read too much into everything. I'll get serious when I have to."

"I just worry about you. You've always been my buddy, but you've stopped telling me things." She stood up and smoothed out her skirt. She still had on her pretty dress—dark blue and double breasted, with gold buttons. Her eyes were rather gray, but the blue of the dress brought more color out.

"You wear your skirts too short. I think you need to repent and start wearing pioneer dresses. This is Zion, you know."

"Maybe I should," Bobbi said. "Dad said some important things to us this morning."

Wally folded his arms around his football, like a halfback. He had dark eyes and rich, full hair, and he had a softer look than the other males in the family. The girls at East High said he was "dreamy" looking. He was the tallest of the sons too, about even with his dad.

Bobbi walked to the door. Wally wanted to say something to lighten things. "So are you in love with Phil Clark? Or do you just kiss him for the thrills?"

When Bobbi turned back, Wally was stunned by the color in her face. She always blushed, but she was flushed all the way to her hairline now. "None of your business," she said.

"I think you're playing with his feelings."

"What?"

Wally had never seen Bobbi so unnatural—so undone. Somehow he had hit a nerve he hadn't been looking for.

"Wally, I've never, *ever* told Phil that I love him."

"Well . . . Mom and Dad think you're going to marry him."

Bobbi looked straight at the floor. "I don't know what to do, Wally."

Wally had never imagined anything like this. Phil was already a "done deal" as far as the two families were concerned. Mom said Phil was the best catch in the whole valley. He had served a mission to the Northern States and was now in law school. Wally had heard Dad tell Mom, "That boy is a cut above any young man I know. He'll be a bishop before he's thirty." Phil had moon eyes for Bobbi, too, which was a new thing. She had never had a boyfriend before.

"Don't you think you'd better break it off with him now before it gets any worse?"

Bobbi nodded. "Probably."

There was nothing Wally hated more than to see Bobbi unhappy. "Sis, I'm sorry," he said.

She nodded again, still looking down. "I never encourage him. He's just sure we're supposed to get married, and he won't give up. I don't know what to do. But I've got to decide before long." She turned and left.

Wally was stunned. He had always believed that Bobbi never made a mistake. He walked over and sat on his bed. On the radio, a dance band was playing "Silent Night." He thought about Bobbi for a time, and then he ran the conversation back through his mind and considered the things she had said about him—about the ways he had changed.

Gradually, Wally felt a sadness come over him. He thought of the fun times he and Alex and Bobbi had had on Christmas when they were little. The day had always been so dazzling then—with Santa Claus and all the new toys. He wished he hadn't outgrown all that. He looked over at the other bed, where Alex had once slept. His presence had never seemed to leave the room. And it was that, as much as anything, that Wally wanted to get away from. Of course, there was always the other thing: his father never stopped trying to pile the whole Wasatch Range onto his shoulders, and he was worn out from pushing the weight off.

Wally lay back on his bed, and he looked at the ceiling.

And then an image came to his mind, completely by surprise. He remembered himself pumping hard—terrified, exhilarated—riding his Christmas bike for the first time. Dad had just let go, and he was shouting, "That's it. Keep going."

Snow was piled up on both sides of the walk, and steam from Wally's breath was blowing back into his face. And then everything had gone out from under him. There was a moment of dizziness, and then Dad had been there, hoisting him up, holding him, saying, "Are you all right?"

Wally tried to hold that memory for a time, that feeling, all the concern in his dad's voice, even the smell of his dad's wet wool coat as he pulled him close and hugged him. But the little vision passed almost as quickly as it had come, and Wally's sadness deepened.

3

"Germans do Christmas up right," Elder Thomas had told Elder Mecham. "They celebrate Christmas Eve and Christmas Day, the same as us, but they keep right on going the next day. They call it the 'second day of Christmas.'"

Now, sitting in the Stoltzes' living room on the day after Christmas, Elder Thomas was glad to see Elder Mecham having such a good time. He knew that the first Christmas away from home was tough. Elder Mecham seemed relaxed, however. He was putting away a slice of *Kuchen*, with peppermint tea, and he had already eaten a big dinner of *Sauerbraten*, potato salad, and red cabbage. After dinner Frau Stoltz had lit the real candles on the Christmas tree, and the family and the elders had taken turns leading each other in Christmas songs, German and American. Elder Mecham had a good voice for someone with no training, and Elder Thomas had sung in his high school choir. The Stoltzes had begged the two of them to keep singing, and the missionaries had been willing, but they loved to hear the German songs too. The Stoltzes were not great singers, but they spoke excellent "high German," which made the lyrics wonderfully clear.

Herr Stoltz was a teacher at a *Gymnasium*—a high school for advanced students. The position carried with it considerable honor in Germany. Or at least it always had. Elder Thomas was hearing things now about changes in education under Hitler. Nazis were skeptical about learning. They were dictating what could be taught in the schools and universities.

The Stoltzes had two children: a seventeen-year-old daughter named Anna, who was a *Gymnasium* student herself, and a twelve-year-old son named Peter. He was bright, like his parents, and he seemed fascinated to have American friends. Anna clearly enjoyed having the elders around, too, but she was openly skeptical about the message they brought.

Eventually the singing ended and conversation took over. The Stoltzes had lots of questions about the elders' lives at home. They talked about Elder Mecham's farm, and Peter wanted to know all about cowboys in America. Then Herr Stoltz asked about Salt Lake City and Elder Thomas's family.

After a time, Elder Mecham said, "Herr Stoltz, could I ask you something about Germany?"

Elder Mecham confused his sentence structure, but the words were there, and Herr Stoltz understood. "Certainly," he said. He nodded and waited. He was sitting across the coffee table from Elder Mecham in a straight-backed chair from the kitchen.

"Bruder Thomas and I saw the ghetto after the storm troopers were there. I don't understand why that happened. What do the Nazis have against Jews?"

Elder Thomas was taken by surprise. He had warned Elder Mecham not to ask such questions. Herr Stoltz hesitated a moment and then asked, "Have you no difficulty with Jews in America?"

"No. I don't think so," Elder Mecham said.

Herr Stoltz looked at Elder Thomas. "What about Salt Lake City? Are Jews well accepted there?"

"Heinrich," Frau Stoltz said. She reached over and put her hand on his arm. "We shouldn't—"

"It's all right. We're just talking about America." He looked
at Elder Thomas and waited for an answer.

Herr Stoltz looked formal as he waited, sitting up straight,
holding his tea. The Stoltzes normally heated only the kitchen,
but tonight the living room, with its mahogany furniture, was
warm, and it was filled with the good smells from the kitchen
and from the Christmas tree.

"They're accepted. Mostly," Elder Thomas said, but then he
admitted, "Once I heard my father say that some people
wouldn't shop at one of the stores in the city—because it was
owned by Jews. That's the only time I've ever heard anything
like that."

"I see. And what do Mormons believe about Jews?"

"They're children of Israel, like us," Elder Mecham said.

Herr Stoltz took a long look at Elder Mecham. He was a
barrel-chested man with bulky arms. But his facial features were
delicate, and he had probing eyes that were intensely blue.
"Excuse me?" he said. "What makes *you* children of Israel?"

Elder Mecham glanced at Elder Thomas, apparently aware
that he had gotten in over his head. Elder Thomas cleared his
throat, and then he spoke for Elder Mecham. "We believe in
the gathering of Israel, prophesied in the Bible. When gentiles—like us—accept the gospel, we are adopted into the
tribes of Israel."

"So you see yourselves as brothers with the Jews?"

"Yes. You could say that."

Herr Stoltz thought for a time, and then he said, "Don't say
these things to others. And don't ask Germans what they think
of Jews." He leaned forward and looked at Elder Mecham, "You
are putting yourselves in danger when you bring up such
issues."

Elder Mecham nodded.

"Heinrich, it's Christmas. Let's not talk of this," Frau Stoltz
said. She was an attractive woman, a little thick in the waist,
and worn-looking around her eyes, but the contours of her face

were flawless, as though someone had sculpted her. She was warm, too, not so skeptical as her husband and daughter.

"It's best only to say this," Herr Stoltz said. "Hitler has done much for Germany. We have much to thank him for."

"Papa, don't say that," Anna said. "They'll think it's what we believe." She was looking at Elder Thomas, not at her father.

Elder Thomas was surprised. He thought Herr Stoltz *had* told them what he believed. Herr Stoltz said, calmly, "Anna, I doubt I believe in much of anything."

"It's not true," Frau Stoltz said. "He told me only yesterday that he finds something genuine in the two of you. It makes him want to believe what you teach."

Herr Stoltz laughed softly. "Well, now, don't give away my secrets."

"Let's sing some more now. Let's enjoy Christmas."

"Yes. In a moment, Frieda." But then he said, "My friends, I will trust you. I want to tell you what I feel—in reality."

"Don't, Papa," Peter said. He suddenly sat up straight.

"It's all right, Peter. I need to say this." He looked back at Elder Mecham. "I know it's difficult for you to understand what's happening here. But you have to know our history. The Treaty of Versailles, at the end of the World War, reduced our boundaries, and the reparations we had to pay made economic recovery impossible. People struggled even to put bread on their tables. And then along came Hitler, who offered jobs, who told people to take back their pride. He's rebuilding the military—in defiance of the Treaty. He justifies his actions with grand speeches, puts on magnificent parades, which the people love, and tells Germans that they are superior to all others. I suppose that's something everyone likes to hear."

"He also takes away your freedom," Elder Mecham said.

"Yes. Of course. Hitler is an evil man. A liar. Make no mistake about that. There is *nothing* he will not do."

"Heinrich. Please."

"I am a history teacher. But I cannot teach real history.

Truth, you see, is whatever Hitler says it is. Beethoven, Mozart, Bach—these are great composers. But Mendelssohn is not. Why? Because he was Jewish. Hitler says it is so, and it is so. German history must show that Germanic people—Hitler calls them Aryans—are greater than all other people. Jews, Slavs, Africans, Asians, Gypsies—these are lower forms of life. That is how far this *criminal* has perverted everything."

"I don't understand," Elder Mecham said. "What makes those people so bad?"

"Bruder Mecham, there is no explanation. Hitler is a fanatic. He's been raving this madness all his life. Jews are *dirty,* he tells us. They are the source of every problem—part of a conspiracy to destroy us, to control our finances, to pollute the pure blood of the Teutonic people. It's nonsense."

"Then why do people love him so much?"

Herr Stoltz shook his head slowly back and forth, his eyes taking on a sadness they had not shown before. "It's what I told you before. Full employment. National pride. All those things. And the Jews make a good target. They always have. People like to believe they have an enemy, and hatred of Jews goes very far back in this country. *Judengasse* wasn't created by Hitler. It goes back to medieval times, when Jews were forced outside, beyond the city wall and next to the city dump. Even Martin Luther preached intolerance for Jews."

"We see signs on shops," Elder Thomas said. "'Jews not welcomed here.' That sort of thing. People must believe what Hitler tells them."

It was Anna who spoke up. "Some do. Some don't. But those who don't are afraid to speak up. My friend's father is a minister, and he preached in his church that hatred for Jews is wrong. The Gestapo took him away. They told his family that he's in 'protective custody.' He's been gone for over a year."

"What would Hitler do to you, Herr Stoltz," Elder Thomas asked, "if you taught your students the truth?"

Herr Stoltz folded his big arms over his chest. "Some

teachers have disappeared. We know they go to concentration camps—as the SS calls them—but we have no idea what happens to them. So the rest of us do what we have to do. Personally, I don't teach Hitler's lies, but I don't deny them either. I am a pitiful coward."

"What else can you do, Papa?" Peter asked.

Herr Stoltz didn't answer.

"How would anyone know what you taught?" Elder Thomas asked.

"We are a police state," Herr Stoltz said. "The SS, Hitler's 'protection squad,' has hundreds of thousands of men in it. Every police organization is part of it, and sub-groups have developed. There's the 'security service'—the SD—that deals with 'enemies of the state,' and the *Gestapo*, the 'secret state police,' which supposedly deals with internal disorder. But no one knows who does what. We only know not to say the wrong thing to anyone. There are thousands of informants. Block leaders. Spies in every apartment house. Even children in the Hitler Youth are taught to inform on their parents."

"No wonder people are scared," Elder Mecham said.

Herr Stoltz looked from one elder to the other. "Yes. And now I have put my life in your hands. If you were to tell *anyone* what I have said, I could be arrested. My children have not joined Hitler Youth. That already makes me suspect. There are those, I'm certain, just waiting for me to make a mistake. And you could be in equal danger for listening to what I have said."

"We won't say anything," Elder Mecham said.

"You must also know that Hitler is moving Germany steadily toward war with England and France—and in time, with America. You and I, my friends, are destined to be enemies."

Elder Thomas didn't want to believe that. He always thought, somehow, that Germans would see through Hitler. "Elder Mecham and I will never be your enemies," he said, quietly.

"I hope you're right," Herr Stoltz said. He smiled.

"Herr Stoltz, we have a Jewish friend. He's a member of our Church. He tells us not to visit, but we have gone to see him in the ghetto a few times. We're careful. We go there by back streets. But are we putting him in danger?"

"Definitely. You are also putting yourselves in danger."

"Why? All we do is visit him."

"But you're foreigners. And he's a Jew. The Nazis see conspiracies everywhere. You must not go there again."

Elder Thomas nodded, but he wasn't at all sure he was willing to give up the visits.

"It's Christmas," Frau Stoltz said again, and she patted her husband's arm.

"Yes," Herr Stoltz said. "But let me say one last thing." He looked at Elder Mecham. "As you form your judgment of the German people, think about your own land. You wonder about the attitude toward Jews in Germany, but ask yourselves about the way you think of Negroes and Indians in America. Ask yourself whether you see yourselves as superior to these people."

Elder Thomas had thought of this before—had seen the parallel—but he saw the surprise in Elder Mecham's face. "We don't. . . ." But Elder Mecham seemed to think better of what he was going to say, and he stopped.

"I only ask you to think about it," Herr Stoltz said, and the room fell silent. "I'm sorry. Enough of this. Do either of you young men play chess?"

"I do," Elder Mecham said. "I'm not very good, but I play."

"It's all right not to be so good. I told you that Germans like to be superior. We like to win."

"First, let's sing some more," Frau Stoltz said.

And so everyone sang "Stille Nacht" again, and "O, Du Fröhliche," Elder Thomas's favorite German Christmas hymn. But Elder Thomas didn't feel as warm and relaxed as he had when they had sung the songs before.

After the singing, Herr Stoltz got out the chess set, and he and Elder Mecham walked into the kitchen, where they seated themselves across the table from each other. Peter went with them to watch, and Frau Stoltz and Anna picked up the dishes.

Elder Thomas was left alone, so he decided to join everyone in the kitchen. But Anna came back just as Elder Thomas was getting up. "Papa has never said those things to anyone but us," she said. "He trusts you." She sat in the chair where her mother had sat, across from Elder Thomas, and he sat back down. He hoped Frau Stoltz would return soon. Even though the door to the kitchen was open and Elder Thomas could see his companion, he felt a little strange sitting there "alone" with Anna. "I won't break your father's trust," Elder Thomas said.

Anna smiled and said, "You always do the right thing, don't you?"

"I *try* to do what is right."

With Anna, a smile was always close, flitting into her eyes or appearing as a little arch in her lip. He never knew when she was teasing him—or whether she always was. She had a face like a porcelain doll, the curve of her cheek bones perfect, and eyes almost too blue to be real. Elder Thomas knew he shouldn't notice all this, but he told himself she was only a pretty kid, the same age as his little brother.

"I found a book on Mormons in the library. It says the men in your church marry many wives. Is that true?" She smiled, seeming to take pleasure in making Elder Thomas uncomfortable. He leaned forward, resting his elbows on his knees, and he spoke seriously, without looking at her eyes. "In the early days of our church, certain men were called upon to take more than one wife. It's not something we do anymore."

"Oh, too bad for you. You're so good looking, you might have collected many wives for yourself."

"It wasn't like that."

"No? How was it?"

"It was spiritual. It was—"

But she was laughing. Elder Thomas decided not to talk to her about this. "I think I'll watch the chess game," he said.

"I'm sorry. I didn't mean to insult you." But her eyes were still toying with him. "Don't go."

Elder Thomas sat down again, but he looked toward the other room. He could hear Elder Mecham trying to tell Peter something about football. He was having a hard time explaining the difference between *Fussball*—soccer—and the American game.

"So what do you and Bruder Mecham call each other when you aren't here by us?" Anna asked.

"*Bruder. Or Ältester.*"

"*Ältester?* Are you so old?" She laughed.

"It's our priesthood position. In English, it's 'Elder,' and that's easy. But *Ältester* is hard to say all the time. We usually say *Bruder* when we're speaking German. Or we call each other *Mit*—short for *Mitarbeiter.*"

"Don't you ever use your Christian names?"

"No. It's part of . . . respecting each other. We have to remember we're missionaries, and we have a sacred calling."

She was still smiling, although she actually seemed to be trying not to. "So what is your given name?"

"Alexander," he said. "My family calls me Alex."

"Alex," she repeated in a whisper. "All-ex," she said it, and it sounded better than it ever had before. "I like that name."

"My grandfather was David Alexander, and he was called David. My father is D. Alexander Thomas. But people call him 'President' most of the time—or 'Al.' I'm also David Alexander, so I was left with Alex."

"Why is your father called President?"

Elder Thomas explained about stakes and wards, and a little about Church leadership, while Anna continued to smile, that little arch in her lip appearing again. "So, will you be a president someday. Or a bishop?"

"It's possible."

"And all so serious. At least your church lets you get married. It's not like Catholics."

Elder Thomas smiled in spite of himself, but then he finally took the wiser course. "Why don't we see how Bruder Mecham and your father are doing?" he said.

"Yes. All right . . . Alex."

"Don't call me that. I'm not supposed to—"

"Oh, don't worry. I won't." But she was still using her eyes to tease him. And he could tell she knew how pretty she was—and how awkward that made an *Ältester*.

As Elder Thomas approached the door to the kitchen, he heard Herr Stoltz say, "What do you mean? Who has been following you?"

It was another subject Elder Thomas didn't want to talk about. But now Herr Stoltz had turned to look at Elder Thomas, and the question had become his.

"We're not sure," he said. "Sometimes we see a man outside our apartment. Actually, we've seen three different men—at different times. And sometimes we've seen the same men in other parts of the city. It seems more than a coincidence."

"Trust me—it is not a coincidence. You must tell your leaders. You should leave Frankfurt immediately."

"They haven't seen us go into the ghetto."

"You can't know that. These people are not easily fooled. You must leave. It's important you do so."

Elder Thomas didn't know how to respond, so he said, "Maybe I can talk to our mission president and see what he thinks."

Herr Stoltz pushed the chess board aside. His eyes looked clouded, thoughtful. Finally, he said, "I'm sorry, but it would not be wise for you to come here again. I must think of my family. We can't be drawn into this."

"No, Papa," Peter said. He stood up, stepped to his father, and put his arms around his shoulders. "They're our friends."

"I know. I'm very sorry."

Elder Thomas nodded. "I understand," he said. He wanted to offer some argument, but he could think of nothing to say. "Maybe we'd better go," he said to Elder Mecham, who nodded and then got up from the table.

"Oh, Heinrich, is this necessary?" Frau Stoltz asked. She was standing across the kitchen, near the sink. She had clasped her hands together, and Elder Thomas saw tears in her eyes.

"Maybe it's better—for now," Elder Thomas said. "Maybe later, when we're sure we aren't followed, we could call on you again." Elder Thomas glanced at Anna and saw that all the playfulness was gone from her eyes. She looked shocked.

"Yes. Maybe a little later," Frau Stoltz said.

"It's not just for us. It's for you," Herr Stoltz said. He stood up, and Peter stepped aside. "You need to go back to America and get away from all this. It would cause us great pain if something happened to you."

"I know that," Elder Thomas said. He and Elder Mecham got their coats and then shook hands with everybody, and all the Stoltzes apologized and wished the elders well.

As Elder Thomas walked out the door, he glanced back and caught a quick glimpse of Anna. The shock was gone from her face; what he thought he saw now was sadness.

The missionaries hardly spoke on the way home. Elder Thomas was feeling all sorts of emotions. He had held high hopes that the Stoltzes would eventually accept the gospel, and that chance seemed remote now. But with his disappointment was a good deal of fear. An uneasiness had been nagging at him these past several weeks, but after hearing what Herr Stoltz had said, the fear had turned into a darker, larger presence.

As the elders turned the last corner and then coasted to a stop, Elder Thomas looked up and down the street. The building they lived in was drab and narrow, with only two one-room apartments to a floor. Next door, on the ground floor, was a *Gasthaus* with an outdoor eating area under two big sycamore trees. In September, when the elders had first moved in, the noise from below had been bothersome, and that had seemed inconvenient; now the trees represented shadows, a place for someone to stand out of sight from the window above.

But no one was there tonight. The street was empty. A few remnants of a snowstorm—piles of dirty snow—were not high enough to hide anyone. There were alleys, however, and alcoves at the front of buildings. It was a bitterly cold night, and it seemed unreasonable that anyone would be out there just watching. But Elder Thomas kept scanning the street anyway.

The elders left their bikes in the courtyard out back, and then they walked up the stairs to their room. They were silent, aware of the darkness, and once they got to the room, Elder Thomas took a look out the window. He felt more secure in the lighted room, but that only allowed the other emotion to come back. "I hope someone gets a chance to teach the Stoltzes someday," he told Elder Mecham. "Or that we still can."

"I doubt they'll ever accept the Church," Elder Mecham said. He tossed his hat onto the top of the wardrobe and then pulled his coat off. "Frau Stoltz might, and maybe Peter. But Herr Stoltz has no faith in anything. And Anna doesn't take us seriously." Elder Mecham walked over to the stove. "I'm going to build a fire, unless we're going to bed right away."

"Go ahead," Elder Thomas said. The room had felt warm when they first came in, but now that he had his coat off, he could feel how cold it actually was. He sat on the bed and loosened his tie. "What do you think we ought to do?" he asked.

"About what?"

"About the Gestapo—or whoever is following us."

"I don't know. I don't see how they can arrest us. We haven't done anything." Elder Mecham had stuffed a piece of newspaper into the bottom of the stove, and now he added a few sticks of kindling.

"We can't go see Bruder Goldfarb anymore."

"We have to, Elder Thomas. We can't desert him." Elder Mecham placed a couple of lumps of coal on top of the wood, and then he lit the paper at the bottom. He waited then, and watched. Sometimes the coal didn't catch fire and the whole process had to start again.

"Maybe we should talk to President Wood," Elder Thomas said.

"Maybe so. But if we do, he'll transfer us for sure." That's what bothered Elder Thomas, too. Elder Mecham held his hands over the stove, which was apparently putting out some heat by now, although Elder Thomas couldn't feel it. "I notice that you and Anna can't keep your eyes off each other."

"What?"

"You heard me." Elder Mecham laughed.

"Come on, Elder. She's a swell-looking girl—but she's just a kid."

"Yeah, well, she's seventeen, and you're only twenty-two. I doubt she thinks you're quite over the hill yet."

Elder Thomas didn't reply. He wasn't going to talk about this. "Let's get some studying in," he said. He got his German Bible down from a little shelf by his bed, and then he sat at the table in the center of the room.

Elder Mecham got his scriptures, too, placed them on the table, and sat down across from Elder Thomas, but he didn't begin to read. "What was your family doing today?" he asked.

"I don't know. Taking their presents back probably, trading everything for the right sizes."

"Oh. I don't mean today. I mean yesterday. It still seems like Christmas to me."

Elder Thomas wasn't sure this was a good thing to talk about, but he told Elder Mecham, "In the morning, everyone gets up early and goes downstairs to see what Santa brought."

"What do you do after the presents are open?"

"The kids play with their new toys, and Mom scrambles up

some eggs. She's always telling the little girls not to eat too much candy before breakfast."

"Mothers must go to the same training school. They all say the same things."

Elder Thomas laughed, and now he was seeing the whole picture: the little girls on the floor in their flannel nightgowns with their new dolls or playhouses; Wally and Gene figuring out a new board game; Mom fussing around the house, telling Bobbi that her new sweater will go "just perfect" with her tan skirt.

"My big sisters were quite a bit older than me," Elder Mecham said. "They've been gone from home quite a while. So I remember mostly the years with my little brother going wild with a toy truck or horse trailer, and my little sister telling him to quiet down so her doll could sleep. And Mom saying, 'Now, kids, let's not have any fighting today. It's Christmas.'"

Elder Thomas nodded. He felt the nostalgia seeping in from all sides. He also saw it in Elder Mecham's eyes, and he tried to think of a way to cut it off.

"The bad thing at our house," Elder Mecham said, "was that my dad had very little to do with it. The cows had to be milked no matter what day it was."

"My dad always called us together for a family meeting," Elder Thomas said. "He'd talk to us about 'the true meaning of Christmas.' And then he'd read the Christmas story from the Bible. And that was something to hear." Elder Thomas suddenly felt the deepest stab of homesickness he had known for a long time. He looked down at the table.

"My dad never preached," Elder Mecham said. "He said he'd never stop smoking Bull Durham because if he did, he might get called to be the bishop."

Elder Thomas laughed. "Did he go to church?"

"Not a lot. He always said the farm wouldn't wait, but I don't think he liked dressing up and sitting around in meetings.

I'm not exactly big on it myself." Elder Mecham broke into a sudden, huge burst of laughter.

"When I was little, it seemed like my dad *was* the Church in Sugar House. For as long as I can remember, he was always sitting up front."

"Why is it called Sugar House?"

"The early settlers tried to farm sugar beets, and they set up a sugar processing plant out there. It never really worked."

Elder Mecham nodded. "Your dad must be a good man," he said.

"Yeah, he is. But he's not a man who could talk to me about anything very personal. And he has awfully strict views." Once again, Elder Thomas picked up his Bible. He turned some pages, but he didn't really look at them. He was thinking about his father, his family, wondering what was happening at home.

"Elder Thomas?"

"Yes."

"Could we maybe take some time between now and New Year's and do a little sightseeing? I haven't seen a thing."

"You weren't sent here to be a tourist."

"Hey, I know that. But most of the elders take some time to look around a little. I talked to Elder Daniels at our district conference. He and his companion took a train trip down to the Black Forest. Have you ever done that?"

"No."

"What would it hurt for us to do something like that? Elder Daniels said that President Wood knew they were going, and he didn't mind."

"It's still a waste of the Lord's time and our parents' money, if you ask me." Elder Thomas planted his Bible squarely in front of him.

"So your dad's pretty strict, huh? That must be rough."

When Elder Thomas looked up, Elder Mecham was grinning. Elder Thomas smiled a little too, but he was actually surprised. He never thought of himself as being like his father.

"Look, Mit," he said, "it's hard even to think of relaxing right now. I'm worried about those guys who've been watching us. I don't want to make a mistake and get in trouble."

"Are you really *that* scared?"

"I've been worried all along, but Herr Stoltz made it sound pretty dangerous."

"We haven't seen those guys for a few days. Maybe they've lost interest in us."

"Yeah. Maybe. But they can really stay after people. When I first got over here, a couple of elders got hold of a Nazi flag, and they thought it would be funny to wrap themselves up in it and take pictures. They tried to develop the film and got turned in for it. They had to hightail it out of Germany just to stay out of prison. The Gestapo was only one step behind them all the way."

"Yeah, well, I think maybe the Gestapo takes Christmas off—even if you won't."

Elder Thomas laughed. He suddenly felt a little lighter. "Look," he said, "I don't feel good about running off to the Black Forest, but maybe we could take some time tomorrow and see a few things here in Frankfurt."

"Sounds good to me."

"All right. We'll do that. And now let's study."

But Elder Thomas still had a picture of home in his head, and he couldn't concentrate. He saw his father sitting in his big gray chair, reading in that deep voice of his. He wished he could be home for a few hours, long enough to hug the little girls and Mom and Bobbi, throw a ball around with Gene, and maybe have a talk with Wally. He always had the feeling he wasn't as close to Wally as he really ought to be.

Elder Thomas looked up after a time, and he saw that Elder Mecham wasn't even pretending to study. He was staring straight ahead. "Are you a little homesick tonight?" Elder Thomas asked.

"Either that or my insides are turning to clay."

"Is it that bad?"

"Naw. I'm all right."

"Are you sorry you came on your mission?"

"No. I just wish I could catch on to the language. And I wish the Nazis would go away. I don't like watching what I say."

"What if Herr Stoltz is right? What if we end up in a war with Germany?"

"That won't happen. The Germans won't let Hitler take things that far. They're going to stop him one of these days."

Elder Thomas got up and walked to the window. He looked at the corner lamppost and the circle of light around it. But he was much more aware of all the darkness beyond the light. "I hope you're right," he said.

4

It was another gray day—and cold. Elder Thomas always had branch work to do, and members to visit, but he and Elder Mecham tried to tract every morning for two or three hours. On such cold days, they wrapped themselves up in all the clothes they could get on: long johns, sweaters, overcoats, scarves, hats. Inside the apartment buildings, out of the wind, they trudged up steep flights of stairs and got sweaty. But back on the street—and especially on their bikes—the damp cold cut through everything, and the elders wished they could pile even more layers on.

It was almost noon, this late January day of 1939, and the hours had crawled by with no success. The *Hausfrauen* peeked out of their doors rather than swinging them wide. Then they stayed back in the shadows, in their dark housedresses. Their noses were often all that poked out, perhaps their red cheeks. And in this poor section of town, they showed their browned or missing teeth as they barked, *"Nein, nein—Keine Zeit"* and pushed the door shut in the elders' faces. The missionaries held out their tracts, tried at least to get a little information into the homes, but more often than not the women refused even that.

The grumpier people sometimes complained: "We have our religion. Go preach to the heathens." Or, "Why do you bother

us? We wouldn't join a *sect*." Only Catholics and Lutherans—
called *Evangelisch*—were considered members of "real" churches.

Door-to-door work was always difficult, but lately, with all
the talk of war, and with Hitler's tight controls, it had gotten
harder. Most Germans had nothing against Americans, but
they were wary of doing anything that might be viewed as
careless or even different.

When the elders were about to call it a morning and were
finishing one last building, an elderly man opened his door.
"Yes, what do you want?" he said.

"We have a pamphlet for you," Elder Mecham recited. "It
costs nothing. We won't come back to pick it up later. We only
ask you to read it."

"What are you?" the little man demanded to know.

Elder Mecham wasn't sure what he meant. "We're from the
Church of—"

"No, no. Where do you come from?"

"America."

"What do you want from me?"

"Nothing. We want to give you this. So you can learn
about our religion."

"What religion?"

Elder Mecham took a deep breath. "The Church of Jesus
Christ of Latter-day Saints."

"I never heard of that." The man's white hair, limp and yellowish, had not been cut for some time. Folds of skin seemed
to cut his eyes in half. Red eyes. But he did have good teeth—
or maybe false teeth.

"Members of our church . . ." He still couldn't say that
blasted word—*Kirche*. It came out 'keer-kuh,' and Germans
often had no idea what he meant. So he repeated it, tried to get
the "ch" sound right, and made a noise too much like clearing
his throat. "Members of our church are sometimes called
Mormons."

"*Ach. Die Mormonen.* I know all about that. *Vielweiberei!*"

It was the word Germans used for plural marriage, but it was not easily translated. The picture was lusty—calling up images of a harem. Elder Thomas had acquired a disgust for the word—and for the accusation. His own great-grandfather had been a polygamist and a fine man. He saw no point to this. He decided to step in and end the conversation. "Would you like to read this?" he asked, offering the tract.

The man didn't take it, but he didn't shut the door in their faces either. He was still looking at Elder Mecham. "You're a big man," he said. "What do you do in America?"

"*Ich bin* cowboy," Elder Mecham said, and laughed. Germans knew the English word. They knew the movies, too. Elder Mecham had found it more fun to claim he was a cowboy than a farmer.

"Tom Mix?" the little man said, smiling, his big teeth showing better now—and looking clearly false. He pronounced the first name as if it were "tome."

"That's me," Elder Mecham said. He thought of telling the man that he had a quick draw, but he had no idea how to say that.

At least the man was smiling. "You're a very big man," he said again. "A cowboy."

"Here, read this," Elder Mecham tried again. "You should know the truth about us. Not the lies."

The man nodded. "It's good." He took the tract and said, "*Auf Wiedersehen,*" not "Heil Hitler." And he sounded friendly.

Elder Thomas slapped Elder Mecham on the back. "Good job," he said.

"Yeah, now he thinks Mormons are a bunch of cowboys."

"That's okay. That's better than what he thought before."

The elders knocked on a few more doors, got turned away, and then walked out into the cold. The sky, the apartment buildings, the street—everything—seemed to have blended into a seamless drabness, like a slab of concrete. "Let's buy our lunch today—get something hot," Elder Thomas said.

But Elder Mecham was looking down the street. "What's going on down there?" he asked.

"A Nazi parade. The local party is putting it on. You've seen all those handbills posted around town, haven't you?"

"Oh, yeah," Elder Mecham said. "I didn't know it was today. Let's go take a look."

"I think we'd better stay away."

"Come on. There's nothing they can say about us watching one of their parades."

Elder Thomas shrugged and said, "All right. But let's just take a look and then go."

When the elders reached the corner, they could see that the parade had not arrived, but a crowd had gathered. Many of the people were men on their midday breaks. Stores all closed for two hours at lunchtime. Plenty of women also lined the street, bundled up in their dark coats and warm hats. And school children were bunched together, the boys in their long winter *Lederhosen* and the girls with leggings under their uniform skirts. In the distance, Elder Thomas could see a man carrying a Nazi flag, and behind him a military unit marching in goose step.

"Let's cross the street," Elder Thomas said. "We can stand in that park and stay back from the crowd."

"Why? We can see better here."

"Let's just stay out of the way."

So they crossed the street, and once they were behind the people, back on the frozen ground of the park, no one paid attention to them. They kept their backs to the breeze and tucked their hands deep into their coat pockets.

"I hope they bring out their big *Panzers*," Elder Mecham said.

"They'll have some." Elder Thomas had seen plenty of these parades. Hitler loved to keep his armies in front of the people, and local party leaders looked for any excuse to display military weapons and spit-and-polish troops. Red Nazi flags with the black "hooked-cross"—the swastika—were draped from the buildings and hung from lampposts all along the street. In a couple of minutes Elder Thomas saw the people along the parade route begin to raise their arms. The flag was approaching.

"I'm not doing that," Elder Mecham said, but he glanced around to see who might be watching.

Elder Thomas began to raise his arm and then decided he wouldn't do it either. No one was looking back. The people were stretching their arms, standing at attention. Elder Thomas saw the pride Herr Stoltz had talked about—people who wanted to take back their national spirit.

"This is crazy," Elder Mecham whispered. "I can't believe these are the same people we see in the market place. They've got *fire* in their eyes."

Elder Thomas could see the thrilled faces across the street. After the flag passed by, people dropped their arms, but they began to shout and wave as the black-uniformed SS troops tromped by in their perfect lines, their legs rising in exact unison.

After the SS passed, several big trucks followed, filled with Storm Troopers in their brown shirts and Swastika armbands. They sat in rows, looking straight forward, with rifles held upright in front of them. Women in the crowd had begun to wave handkerchiefs, and gradually more appeared along the street, the white cloths fluttering in the cold wind.

"Look how the women are getting into this," Elder Mecham whispered. "I didn't expect that."

"Watch the kids."

Elder Thomas had always been amazed at the way the German children and teenagers, who usually seemed less demonstrative than American kids, would jump up and down in their excitement and creep out into the street just to be near the noise and the power of the trucks and tanks.

A band passed, and the noise became intense, the waving

all the more ardent. Then a company of goose-stepping soldiers in gray uniforms marched through, followed by eight big
tanks. The tanks made a terrific noise on the cobblestone
street. The drivers stood with their shoulders above the open
turrets. They didn't wave, didn't smile, but they looked exul-
tant.

Behind the Panzers came a troop of Hitler Youth in their
winter uniforms: long black pants, black coats with red swastika
armbands, and black caps and gloves. They didn't goose-step,
but they were skillful marchers, and their devotion was clear in
their stern faces, their tunneled eyes.

And then came the *Bund Deutscher Mädel*—"League of
German Girls"—in their long coats and heavy marching shoes.
Elder Thomas had seen the girls during the summer out on
long hikes in their white blouses and blue skirts. Hitler wanted
healthy women who would mother a great generation. The
Third *Reich* was to stand for a thousand years, and it had to
start with pure, robust parents. Elder Thomas had heard it all,
read it. The propaganda was everywhere.

More soldiers in trucks came after that, and then half-
tracks, a squadron of men on motorcycles, artillery pulled by
giant horses, and Nazi party leaders in touring cars. And overhead, a flight of fighters and then of bombers buzzed low over
the parade route. The crowd continued to cheer and wave.

"I just don't believe this," Elder Mecham kept mumbling.

Elder Thomas hadn't wanted Elder Mecham to see too
much of this kind of thing. Elder Thomas loved the Germans
in the branches and the good people he met in their homes—
people who saved their money to attend operas and concerts;
people who loved books and nature, who spent their spare time
in art museums or strolling in the woods. He didn't know how
to explain this seeming madness for weapons and military
pomp.

"So. We meet again."

Elder Thomas spun to his left. But he already knew the

voice. It was Kellerman, the Gestapo agent. He was wearing his uniform and a black leather coat, but he had opened the coat and pulled it back so his nightstick was showing.

"Good day, Herr Kellerman."

"Heil Hitler." He gave a quick Nazi salute.

"Heil Hitler," Elder Thomas said, and he raised his arm.

"How is it that you let our flag pass you by—at the beginning—and didn't show it proper respect?" He had chosen to speak in German today. And he was looking at Elder Mecham. "A man who reports to me saw you and came to tell me. Needless to say, I was not surprised."

"We weren't certain what we should do," Elder Thomas said.

"I don't want to hear this again. You know *exactly* what you should do." Kellerman spread his legs farther apart and placed his hands on his hips as though to look as large as he could.

"We will salute from this day on," Elder Thomas said, and he tried to sound friendly, not defensive.

"Do it now. Show me. Say, 'Heil Hitler.'" Elder Thomas raised his arm, but Kellerman said, "Not you. I want Herr Mecham to do it." Kellerman looked up at Elder Mecham with hatred in his eyes. He had obviously been waiting for this moment.

Elder Mecham didn't raise his arm and he didn't answer.

"Do it," Elder Thomas said, but Elder Mecham shook his head. So Elder Thomas turned to Kellerman. "I'll talk to him. He hasn't been in Germany very long. He doesn't understand all your customs. But he'll change his mind once I explain."

"You are lying, Herr Thomas." He looked at Elder Mecham. "I want to hear you say 'Heil Hitler.' And see you salute."

Elder Mecham shook his head, slowly and resolutely.

Kellerman pulled his nightstick loose from his belt. "Do it now," he said in English.

"No. I don't have to do that."

Suddenly the nightstick flashed, back-handed, directly into Elder Mecham's face, catching him across the bridge of his nose. Elder Mecham spun away and grabbed his face. Another slashing blow caught him across the head, and he fell to his knees.

Elder Thomas dropped to the ground, grabbed his companion's shoulder, and shielded him with his body from more blows. "Please don't," he pleaded. "That's enough."

Elder Thomas heard Elder Mecham whisper, "If I get up, I'll kill him. Hold me down." Elder Thomas tightened his grip.

"What did he say?" Kellerman demanded.

"He's sorry. He said that he is sorry."

"You lie. I heard him say 'kill.'"

"No, no. He wouldn't say that."

"Get up. Both of you."

Elder Thomas stood up, but Elder Mecham was still on all fours. "Get up, I said!" Kellerman shouted. Suddenly he thrust the toe of his boot hard into Elder Mecham's side.

Elder Mecham took the blow with a grunt, but he hardly moved. Elder Thomas knelt next to him again. "Stand up," he was pleading. And then to Kellerman, "He'll get up now."

And slowly Elder Mecham did climb to his feet. Blood was running down the sides of his nose onto his chin. He wiped his hand through it, smearing it across his lip and cheek. But then he stared into Kellerman's eyes, looking more defiant than hurt.

"Apologize to me—and to my flag," Kellerman said, in German. He looked excited, tense, ready to use the stick again.

Elder Mecham said nothing, but Elder Thomas only let a second or two pass before he said, "He doesn't understand you." And then in English, "Elder, you've got to say you're sorry."

Elder Mecham stood his ground, his jaw set.

"Just say you're sorry."

"*Es tut mir leid,*" Elder Mecham finally said, but his tone said, "Just try it again."

Kellerman looked confused. He had clearly not expected this concession, however insincere. "I'm not finished with you," he said. His thick lips tightened into a grim frown, but it all seemed an act. Under the surface was an obvious well of weakness. "You think you can defy the Führer, but you cannot. My leaders tell me you are harmless boys. But I know better. They will listen to me now. You haven't heard the last from me." He turned on his heels and marched away.

Elder Thomas looked toward the parade. More soldiers were passing by. But many of the people in the crowd had turned; they had been watching Kellerman. Elder Thomas thought he saw concern in their eyes, maybe even fear. They turned away when he looked at them.

"I should have broken his jaw," Elder Mecham said.

"Come on, Elder. That's not what we're here for."

"I'm not going to bow down to that guy, the way you did."

Elder Thomas was frustrated, scared for what might happen if Elder Mecham couldn't learn from this. But he was also ashamed of himself. He wished he hadn't groveled before Kellerman.

"He broke my nose," Elder Mecham said.

"Are you sure?"

"It doesn't matter. It's been broken before."

Elder Thomas took his arm and turned him. "Oh, man, the back of your head is cut too. You're bleeding pretty bad." He reached in his back pocket for a handkerchief and handed it to Elder Mecham, who dabbed at his face and then at his head. "We'd better get home as fast as we can. Come on."

Elder Mecham took a couple of steps and then said, "Don't walk too fast. My side hurts."

"I'll bet he broke your ribs."

"Maybe." He was leaning forward, his eyes squinted and his jaw clamped tight. Elder Thomas heard a little grunt with each step he took. "Do you want to lean on me?"

"No. Let's just get home."

"How are you going to ride a bike?"

"I don't know."

"Let's go to the Stoltzes. It's a lot closer. Maybe they have something they can use to bandage your head."

"They don't want us there."

"I know. But I don't know what else to do. Do you want to go to a hospital?"

"No. The Stoltzes. But take it easy."

Elder Mecham walked slowly, but he didn't break step. He kept going all the way down the block and around the corner. Only on the stairs at the Stoltzes' apartment did he show signs of weakening. The grunts turned into gasps. And then, as he stood at the door, waiting, he let himself slump over, one hand on his knee, the other against his side. The blood had stopped running down his face now, but it was caked on his cheeks and chin, and his hair was matted and dark red.

When the door came open, Frau Stoltz looked at Elder Thomas curiously. She was about to say something when she looked over at Elder Mecham and saw the blood. "God in heaven," she gasped—words Elder Thomas had tried to teach her not to say. "What's happened?" At the same time, she grabbed Elder Mecham by the arm and pulled him inside.

"Gestapo," Elder Thomas said. "We didn't salute."

"*Ach, Meine Güte,* how can this be? Everything is crazy." She pulled Elder Mecham on through the living room and into her kitchen. "Take your coat off. Bruder Thomas, help him."

"He's hurt here, too," Elder Thomas said. He touched his own side. "In the ribs. The Gestapo agent kicked him."

Frau Stoltz threw up her arms in disbelief, and then she disappeared, apparently to find what she needed. Elder Thomas did help Elder Mecham get his coat off, and then his suit coat, and now he could see that blood had been flowing down his neck, forming a huge stain on the back of his white shirt.

"Sit down," Frau Stoltz shouted from another room. "Take your tie off."

Elder Mecham seemed unready for that much movement. He did sit down, but he leaned forward and held his forehead with one hand and his side with the other.

Frau Stoltz came back with towels and rags and a little emergency kit. She went to work quickly. She cleaned up the blood, dabbed iodine into the wounds—the sting causing him to flinch—and she wrapped his head tight with a white cloth. She taped a little bandage over the cut on his nose.

"Now, you must see a doctor," she told him. "I don't know what to do for your ribs. You might be injured inside."

"No. I'm all right," he told Elder Thomas, in English, as though German were too much effort at the moment. "I had some broken ribs before—from football. They heal up."

"I think he needs to rest more than anything," Elder Thomas told Frau Stoltz.

Elder Mecham agreed. He wrapped a towel around his head and shoulders so he wouldn't stain anything, and then he walked to the living room and sat down in a big chair. "I'll be all right in a few minutes," he said. "Then we'll walk home."

Not five minutes later, he was breathing steadily, already falling asleep. But that was not a real surprise. Elder Mecham had been fighting to stay awake his whole mission. Every time Elder Thomas started a lesson, usually in a warm kitchen after fighting the cold outside, Elder Mecham's head began to bob.

Frau Stoltz took the chance to ask more questions, and gradually she got most of the story out of Elder Thomas. He had only just finished his account when Anna came in, and she asked everything again. She seemed more alarmed than her mother, however. "They won't let this drop," she said. "Does the agent know your names?"

"Yes."

She grimaced. "That worries me, Bruder Thomas." She gave his name its English pronunciation, and Elder Thomas felt a familiarity that embarrassed him. He watched her eyes as she studied his. "They should stay here, no?" she said to her mother. "Until Papa gets home. He can tell them what to do."

"Yes. It's good," Frau Stoltz said. "I'll prepare something. Bruder Mecham will want food when he wakes up."

"He always wants food," Elder Thomas said, and he tried to laugh. He glanced at Anna, but she didn't smile. Elder Thomas could see she was getting more frightened as she thought about the situation.

The afternoon passed slowly. Elder Mecham woke up before long, and the elders ate. But Elder Mecham was still hurting, and he didn't have much to say, didn't even eat much. He did describe his own anger, however, made his contempt for Kellerman more clear than Elder Thomas had. And Frau Stoltz and Anna only looked more worried after hearing it.

By the time Herr Stoltz got home, Anna was pacing, and then she blurted out the story. Her version had Elder Mecham standing toe-to-toe with the agent, daring him to take another swing.

"It wasn't quite so bad," Elder Thomas kept saying. "We told Kellerman we were sorry."

"He knows better," Herr Stoltz said, and Elder Thomas heard the anger. "I can't believe you would do this. And I can't believe you would come here. I asked you not to come again."

"Heinrich, what are you saying?" Frau Stoltz said. "They turned to us for help."

Herr Stoltz spoke calmly. "Don't you understand what has happened? You have attacked the pride of a Gestapo agent. He's watching you, waiting for a chance to get revenge."

"He got it. It's over now," Elder Mecham said.

"No. He wanted you to fight back. He needs provocation. Nazi leaders want no trouble with America, and he knows that."

"But we won't fight him. It's all over," Elder Thomas said.

"Not at all. I know these people. He won't be happy until he has knocked the pride out of you." Herr Stoltz took a breath

and then said, stoically, "He won't hesitate to come after me—
or my family. He'll use us to get at you if he knows you are
here. And I have no doubt he knows."

"I'm sorry," Elder Mecham said. "We'll go. I can walk."

"We can make it to our apartment," Elder Thomas said.

"No. You should leave the city," Anna said.

Elder Thomas felt a little unnerved by all the concern, but
he had a hard time believing that Kellerman would continue to
pursue them.

"It's your decision," Herr Stoltz said. "But I have told you
what I think. You should go back to your own country."

"I'm sorry," Elder Mecham said again. "We didn't know we
would cause problems for you."

"I know that. I'm also sorry."

Elder Mecham got to his feet, slowly, breathing hard.

Frau Stoltz was saying, "Oh, Heinrich, how can we turn
them out into the street like this?"

Elder Thomas was looking at Anna. "Don't go back to your
apartment," she said. She followed the elders to the landing.
"Good-bye," she said, in English. Then she whispered, in
German, "Please write to me—or somehow let me know that
you are all right."

"I will," Elder Thomas said. And he took a last look at her.
He saw tears welling up in her eyes.

Elder Mecham walked slowly but steadily down the stairs.
Once he reached the front doors to the building, however, he
stopped and took some short, quick breaths.

"Can you make it?" Elder Thomas asked.

"Sure. The stairs are the worst. Where are we going?"

"I don't know, Mit. Herr Stoltz might be right. Maybe we
should head for the mission home."

"I can't wander all over Frankfurt. I just can't."

Elder Thomas nodded. "Okay. We'll leave our bikes and
take the streetcar. We'll go back to the apartment. And then I'll
get in touch with President Wood. Are you ready to go?"

"Sure. But could you give me a blessing? I'm feeling a little weak."

"We'd better go to a hospital."

"No. Just bless me. And then let's get going."

And so the elders stood in the entrance to the old building, and Elder Thomas reached up high to place his hands on his companion's head. He didn't have consecrated oil with him, but he called on God to heal his companion, and to help them home. And then the two set out.

Elder Thomas liked his companion—Elder Roland Sawyer from Los Angeles—but he missed Elder Mecham. On the day Kellerman had beaten up on Elder Mecham, the two elders had gone back to their apartment and found no one from the Gestapo waiting. Elder Thomas, however, had hurried to the post office and called President Wood and told him the story— or at least most of it. He played down Kellerman's warnings.

President Wood transferred Elder Mecham to Stuttgart after he had him stay a couple of weeks in the mission home. But he kept Elder Thomas in Frankfurt, alone at first. "I need you to keep the branch going in Maintal," he told Elder Thomas. "But don't leave your apartment any more than you have to. Don't tract. And don't take any chances."

For three weeks Elder Thomas led a monastic life, alone and always waiting. But he saw no one watching from the street, and he heard nothing from Kellerman. Then Elder Sawyer arrived. He was older than most new missionaries, even older than Elder Thomas, but he was a quiet, studious man who had a good background in German grammar—although he grew tense when he had to speak. He was pleasant, and less a worry than Elder Mecham, but not nearly so colorful.

For a couple of months after Elder Sawyer joined him,

Elder Thomas stayed away from Brother Goldfarb. But his con-
science bothered him. He felt as though he and the Church
were forsaking a man who now had no contact with his family
nor with the branch members who were his brothers and sisters. It was March now, and Elder Thomas had never once seen
Herr Kellerman. President Wood had told him not to take
chances, but the danger seemed to have blown over by now.

So Elder Thomas made a decision. He wouldn't sneak
through back streets. He and Elder Sawyer would ride down the
Judengasse, and they would visit the tailor shop. One of Elder
Thomas's pairs of trousers was wearing out. He needed to see
whether they could be repaired. So this was a business matter,
and Herr Kellerman should have no complaint about that.

All the same, as Elder Thomas wheeled into the ghetto, he
did feel uneasy. He saw the boarded windows and the closed
shops. He saw the hateful epithets painted on walls and doors,
the bits of glass imbedded between the cobblestones. But what
he watched most carefully were the alleys, the nooks and
corners.

As the elders walked into the tailor shop, a bell on the door
jingled, and a few seconds later Brother Goldfarb came out
from behind a little curtain. His eyes were down, and it took
him a moment to realize who was standing before him.

"Oh my goodness," he said. "How nice to see you. But it's
not wise."

Elder Thomas was surprised to see how much Brother
Goldfarb had changed. He had never been a substantial man,
but now his face was gaunt, his skin only a thin layer over the
bones. Elder Thomas even had the impression that Brother
Goldfarb had lost some hair, his yellowish scalp showing
through on top.

"How are you, Bruder Goldfarb?" Elder Thomas asked.

The question was innocent enough, even perfunctory, but
the reaction was a surprise. Brother Goldfarb's eyes filled with
tears. *"Es geht,"* he tried to say, but his voice choked.

"Have you spoken at all with your wife?"

"No. I've heard nothing from her."

"I'll visit her. I'll bring you word."

"No, no. I don't expect that of you."

But it was not the command Elder Thomas had expected. He knew it was something Brother Goldfarb wanted. "I have tailoring work for you to do. When I come back for it, I'll let you know how your wife and daughter are doing. That can't hurt anything."

Brother Goldfarb didn't argue. So Elder Thomas finally introduced his companion, and then he showed him the trousers.

"These will not do," Brother Goldfarb told him. "I will sew you a new suit. It will be my gift." He was standing behind a counter that was almost as high as his chest. He looked up at Elder Thomas and tried to smile. "That would bring me pleasure."

"No. You can't do that. I'll send for extra money from home. I'll pay you as soon as I can."

"I won't hear of it. You have done so much for me, Bruder Thomas. And I have fabric. That's all I have. I can't really say that I have a business any longer."

"Don't the Nazis give you business?"

"Not business. They make me sew for them. They pay me almost nothing. And they don't let others come here. I've done a little repair work for my neighbors, but most of them are without income now." He stopped and took a breath. "But these are not prudent things to talk about."

"What will you do?"

Brother Goldfarb's eyes squinted against the light behind the elders. Elder Thomas could see a kind of filminess over his pupils. "It doesn't matter very much, I suppose. I have some small savings. I get by. Those of us left here look out for each other as best we can."

"This will end in time, Bruder Goldfarb. The people won't put up with it much longer."

"Please. Don't say those things. They can get you into trouble. Let's measure you now, and then you can go."

Brother Goldfarb came out from behind the counter. He glanced outside. The front window was covered with boards, but he could see through the window in the door. From outside, anyone could see that this tailor was serving a customer. But Elder Thomas felt Brother Goldfarb's nervousness, felt his own, and he noticed that Elder Sawyer kept glancing outside as well.

All the same, before the missionaries left, Elder Thomas said, "Could we have a prayer with you before we go?"

"Oh, yes. Please. You say it for me."

And so Elder Thomas bowed his head and prayed. "Bless this dear, good man," he said. "Protect him and keep him safe. And let his wife and daughter, somehow, sometime, return to him."

Brother Goldfarb broke down at these words, and when the prayer had ended, he embraced Elder Thomas and clung to him for a time. "Oh, thank you," he said. "May it be so."

Elder Thomas was satisfied he had done the right thing in coming, but outside he spotted a man walking slowly, gazing about, not in any hurry. Elder Thomas got on his bike, and he tried to act unhurried himself. Then he went out of his way to say *"Guten Tag"* and to lift his hat as he rode by on his bike. He wanted the man to see that he wasn't skulking about. But from down the street he looked back, and he saw that the man had turned and was still watching.

Elder Thomas told his companion, "If he's some kind of informant we may hear about this. But remember, we came here strictly because my suit was worn out."

Elder Sawyer was riding alongside Elder Thomas in the nearly empty street. Usually something in his downcast eyes made him seem reticent, even uninterested. But now he sounded curious. "I don't understand. Why does anyone care whether we come over here? What harm could we do?"

Elder Thomas smiled. It was Elder Mecham all over again. How could someone fresh from America understand the way Hitler had managed to spread fear, to cause a whole people to live with the assumption that *anything* they did might be misread and dealt with brutally? The unreasonableness of such behavior was the point of it. Justice, for the Nazis, existed only on a grand, historical scale. Individual justice was unimportant. It was also dangerous; it gave people reason to assert themselves.

"I don't know how to explain it to you," Elder Thomas said. "But Elder Mecham refused to understand, and you know what happened to him. If someone should stop us, we can't talk back. We just explain why we were here—and hope for the best." But the elders rode their bikes out of the ghetto, and no one said a word to them.

That night they visited Sister Goldfarb. They found she was not doing much better than her husband. She was working at a large cannery, and she had enough to eat. But she was suspect because of her marriage, and Helene, her daughter, was no longer allowed to go to school. "It's just as well," Sister Goldfarb told the elders. "I teach Helene, and she learns fast. She's a good reader. At school, even though she used my maiden name—Grossen—the children knew. They called her 'Jew girl,' or they said, 'Don't touch her. She's dirty.'"

"Is she all right now?"

"No. Of course not. When we were in the *Judengasse*, she had many friends. That was a happy time for her. Now she has no one but me."

"What do you tell her?"

"What can I say? She's only ten." Sister Goldfarb began to cry. "How can she understand this? She wants to play outside, but the children won't leave her alone. I wish I could tell her to be angry, to speak back to them. But that would be dangerous for both of us."

"I don't understand," Elder Sawyer said. He asked Elder Thomas in English, "Do all Germans feel that way about Jews?"

Sister Goldfarb understood the English, but she answered in German. "Some people have always been hateful. But now, Hitler tells such lies. He has most everyone thinking this way."

Elder Thomas didn't know what to say. Everyone sat quietly for a time. Finally he told her, "Sister, our mission president tells us to trust in the Lord. There's no way to fight the Nazis, but we can survive them. God will help us do that."

Sister Goldfarb, a little woman like her husband but Germanic as Hitler's super race—blue eyed and strongly built—looked at Elder Thomas doubtfully. "I don't believe in God anymore," she said. "I try. But I see no evidence that God cares about me and my little daughter."

"He does, Sister. Don't stop believing that."

The three of them were sitting in Sister Goldfarb's kitchen at a wooden table protected with an oilcloth cover. The room smelled of cabbage and something else, maybe boiled potatoes. But dinner was over now, and Helene was in bed. It was a cool night, and a steady rain had begun to fall.

Sister Goldfarb was twisting a dishtowel in her hands, tightening her grip until her knuckles turned white. "God, it would appear, loves Hitler," she said. "All the Nazis. These are the ones he is blessing now."

"Righteous people have to stand up for what is true, Sister Goldfarb. Then, a better time will come. You see it in the Book of Mormon. Bad times come, and good people humble themselves, and then blessings follow."

Elder Thomas saw a little softening, the muscles around her eyes relaxing. But she only said, "I hope you are right. I will let you believe for me. But I can stand up to no one. For that, I would be taken away, and then what happens to Helene?"

"I didn't mean that you have to . . . do anything. I know you can't fight those people."

"If I can't, who can?"

Elder Thomas didn't know what to say. "We can believe, and pray, even if we can't fight right now," he told her. But after, when the elders were on their bicycles heading home, with rain driving in their faces, Elder Thomas asked his companion, "What could I have said to her? What would have helped?"

Elder Sawyer said, "You did the best you could. I wouldn't know what to say."

Elder Thomas thought of Elder Mecham. He had taken his defiant stance and had gotten his head split open. Even worse, he hadn't accomplished anything. But if that was true, if no one ever organized and fought back, what would happen to Germany?

A week later, the elders returned to visit Brother Goldfarb. Elder Thomas was relieved to see he was all right. No one, he said, had questioned him about the elders' previous visit. Elder Thomas tried to sound optimistic. "Your wife is doing fine," he told Brother Goldfarb. "She and Helene have plenty to eat, a good apartment. And Helene is a good learner."

Brother Goldfarb nodded and looked pleased, but he asked, "What did my wife say?"

"She's not very happy, of course," Elder Thomas told him. "How can she be—separated this way? But she's holding up. And she sent her love. Helene prays for you every night." But he didn't mention Sister Goldfarb's doubts about God.

"Thank you," Brother Goldfarb said. "It's good at least to hear this. But Hitler has vowed to get rid of us, and he will. I no longer doubt that. To him, my little daughter is also a Jew. I hate to think what the Nazis will do to her."

"Don't think that way," Elder Thomas said. "The Nazis rule by fear, but I doubt they have the courage to go beyond that." He saw the uncertainty in Brother Goldfarb's eyes. "Don't give up. She'll be all right. I'm sure of it."

"It's good for you to say this. But you don't know it. No one does."

Elder Thomas wanted to deny that, but he knew better.

"Try on the suit," Brother Goldfarb said. "Be certain it fits. And then you must go."

Elder Thomas did as he was told. Then Brother Goldfarb folded the suit and wrapped it in a bundle, and he walked to the door with the elders. "If you see my wife and daughter, tell them I think of them every day, every hour. I think of almost nothing else."

"I'll tell them."

"But tell my wife, if she can take Helene and leave the country, she should do that. Tell her to get out soon, perhaps to Holland. She might be safe there."

"It's difficult to leave now, Brother Goldfarb. Most Jews want to leave, but only so many are accepted in other countries."

"I know. But tell her to try. They should not stay in Frankfurt because of me. It means much more to me that they are safe somewhere."

"I'll tell her."

"I doubt I will see them again, Bruder Thomas." But he didn't cry. He seemed beyond that now.

On the following morning the elders got up early, as always. Each took a "spit bath" at the sink in their room. It was such an unsatisfying way to keep clean—only taking a real bath at a bathhouse once a week—but something that Elder Thomas had learned to accept. He knew, however, that it was Elder Sawyer's greatest displeasure.

Elder Sawyer's family seemed quite well-off. Elder Thomas had seen pictures of their rambling California home, and Elder Sawyer had admitted, rather reluctantly, that there were two bathrooms in the house. He and his three brothers had had one of them to themselves. But he never complained about the conditions in the elders' apartment: having to walk down the hall to a toilet, and cooking on a hot plate. He made the best of things.

After studying for an hour, the elders cooked *Haferflocken*—

oatmeal mush—and they ate it with milk that they had kept outside on their window sill overnight. Then they settled in to study for another hour before tracting time. Elder Thomas was trying to read the Old Testament in German, and he was struggling with that, but he had his mind well-focused on the chore when a rap came on the door.

It was the time of day when the district president, Elder Dunford, sometimes stopped by, so Elder Thomas wasn't surprised at the knock. But when he opened the door, he saw President Meis, from the Frankfurt Branch. "I must talk to you," he said, and he stepped forward.

Elder Thomas shut the door and then invited President Meis to sit down, but President Meis stood where he was. "There's something you must know," he said. "Bruder Goldfarb was questioned last night. And beaten."

"What? Who did it?"

"That's not for me to say. And that's not important."

"It was the Gestapo, wasn't it?"

Suddenly President Meis's voice sharpened. "It was *you*, Elder Thomas. It was you who got him in trouble. You have been going there even though I told you not to."

"Yes. But . . . only to. . . ." Elder Thomas couldn't believe this. An avalanche of guilt was coming down on him. "Why should they beat him?"

"I don't know that. I only know that a Gestapo agent was at my door early this morning. He warned me. If members of our church contact Bruder Goldfarb again, we won't be allowed to hold our meetings. We'll be disbanded. And I could be arrested."

"Was it Kellerman? Is that who came to your door?"

"That's not your concern."

Elder Thomas saw what was happening. "Elder Mecham and I had trouble with an agent named Kellerman," he said. "But his leaders won't let him arrest us—because we're Americans. He must be trying to get at us some other way."

President Meis was a stout man, a builder by trade. He had a square, solid face, but he also had a kindly smile, with a flashing gold tooth, when he was in the mood to smile. Now his lips were pressed tightly together. He pointed a finger at Elder Thomas. "You have no idea the trouble you are causing. You must *never* go there again. Bruder Goldfarb might have been killed."

"Why didn't they take him away, the way they do the others?"

President Meis looked shocked. "These are not questions for you to ask, Bruder Thomas. They are none of your business. Nor mine. If we want the Church to continue here, we must watch our every step."

Elder Thomas glanced at Elder Sawyer, who was still sitting at the table. His face had lost its color, and he was staring up at President Meis, obviously concerned.

"President Meis," Elder Thomas said, "we did nothing wrong. We visited a member of our branch. He made a suit for me. This is all crazy. What's wrong with this Kellerman? How can he—"

"Stop this!" President Meis said in a fierce whisper. "Soften your voice. You have no idea what you're saying. You are a foreigner. You have no right to tell us what we should do."

Elder Thomas couldn't believe this. But he said more quietly, "President Meis, people are being beaten for no reason. Do you defend that? Do you think it's right?"

President Meis took his time answering. And he spoke with care. "Bruder, I haven't said I like everything that is happening. But I must deal with reality. To the Nazis, Bruder Goldfarb is not one of us. He is a Jew. We must not do anything that will bring harm to him. And we must protect the Church. That's simply how things are."

"How badly is he hurt?"

"It's hard to say. Herr Kellerman wanted me to know that *we* had brought injury to him by contacting him, but he didn't offer any details. And I don't dare approach Bruder Goldfarb. I only hope he was not seriously hurt."

"I'm sorry, President Meis. I didn't think they would hurt *him*."

"I understand that. But you must stay away."

"We will. I promise you that."

President Meis looked at Elder Sawyer. "Do you understand what I have said?"

"Yes."

"And you also promise not to visit him again?"

"Yes."

President Meis turned and walked to the door. But he stopped and looked back. "Do your missionary work and speak of nothing else. I will check on Bruder Goldfarb, if I can." And then he left.

As the door shut, Elder Thomas turned and looked at Elder Sawyer. "I didn't think they would take it out on *him*," he said.

"I don't understand anything about this country," Elder Sawyer said.

The elders went about their tracting that morning, ate lunch, and then went back to the doors, even though they met with the usual reception. In the afternoon, as they returned to their apartment, Elder Thomas, rather automatically, followed a familiar routine. He rode past the Stoltzes' apartment on the off chance that he would see one of them. He had made this little side trip several times, but he had never gotten lucky. Today, however, he was overjoyed when he and Elder Sawyer coasted around the corner just in time to glide past Anna, who was apparently on her way home from school. Elder Thomas braked and pulled over. Then he stepped off his bike and turned around. "Anna," he called out.

She walked quickly toward him. She looked radiant with the cool air brightening the color of her cheeks and her blond hair hanging down over the collar of her dark brown coat.

"How are you?" she said.

"Good. This is my new *Mitarbeiter*," Elder Thomas said. "Bruder Sawyer. He's new, from America."

"Very nice to meet you," she said, in English. "Where do you come from?"

"California," he said.

Elder Thomas could see her struggle to think of another English phrase. Finally, she said, "California has oranges," pronouncing the word "or-on-juzz."

Elder Sawyer smiled a little. "*Ja. Sehr Gut,*" he said.

Anna laughed. "That's about all my English," she said, in German, to Elder Thomas. "But how is Elder Mecham?"

"I talked to President Wood this morning. He said Elder Mecham is doing fine. All recovered. He's in Stuttgart."

She lowered her voice. "And the Gestapo have left you alone?"

"Yes." Elder Thomas thought of telling her what had happened to Brother Goldfarb, but he decided not to.

"And your faith is as strong as ever?"

Elder Thomas shrugged. "I don't understand a lot of things that are happening," he said, "if that's what you mean. But I believe in the things we teach."

She smiled, and he could see the irony in her eyes, the pleasure she found in goading him. "You're a good boy," she said, teasing, using the familiar form of the language.

"Anna, there is a God, and I know what a difference he can make in your life. You need that. Your whole family does."

"I don't know what I believe, Bruder Thomas. Sometimes I pray, the way you told us to do. But I don't get any answers—not that I can recognize."

"Something will happen if you keep praying."

She rolled her eyes. "We'll see."

"What would happen if we came by again? Would your father let us in?"

"No, Bruder Thomas. Don't do that. He wouldn't be happy with me for speaking with you on the street." She lowered her voice. "Things are happening. Hitler thinks he can get away with anything. He made all those promises about Czechoslovakia, and now he's occupied the whole country— and no one is doing one thing to stop him. Now he's tightening down on all of us here in Germany. By law, I must join *BDM*, and Peter must join *Hitler Jugend*. My father is very upset. And worried."

Elder Thomas was holding his bike by the handlebars. He tightened his grip. "Does he think war will come soon?"

"This year."

Elder Thomas nodded. "Well, we won't come by, but we'll pray for your family. And for you. If you keep praying, something good is going to happen. You'll get your answer."

She didn't argue. She smiled with a sort of "if life were only that simple" look in her eyes. But what she said was, "It was wonderful to see you again," this time sounding sincere.

As the elders rode away, Elder Sawyer pumped hard to pull up alongside Elder Thomas. "That's about the prettiest girl I've ever seen," he said with surprising enthusiasm.

"Oh, really? I didn't notice," Elder Thomas said.

"Yeah. I'm sure."

"Elder, I judge a girl completely by her spirit. I pay no attention to her earthly tabernacle."

Elder Sawyer laughed. "Well, you were taking a *very* good look at her spirit, it seemed to me."

Elder Thomas didn't say anything for a time, and the truth was, he was embarrassed. "The problem with Anna," he finally said, seriously, "is that she doesn't care much about the Spirit. Nothing we've said seems to reach her."

"I could see that," Elder Sawyer said. "But, wow, what eyes!"

"She uses them to see all the wrong things," Elder Thomas told him.

6

Wally and Mel were at the track behind East High. Mel was sitting on the grass with his leg bent outward in a hurdler's position, and he was reaching for his toes. Wally was lying on his back, letting the sun heat his body. He wanted Mel to think that he was relaxed, just working on his tan a little, but in fact he was very nervous.

"Are you running a relay or just the four-forty?" Mel asked between stretches.

"The coach wanted me to run the mile relay, but I told him I couldn't do two four-forties." A little wave of nausea passed through Wally as he thought of the race. He sat up. "So he put me in the two-twenty leg of the medley relay. I don't mind that."

"I'm doing the highs and lows again, and the coach told me to try the broad jump. I don't know why. I'm no good at it."

"That's okay. You're no good at the hurdles either."

Mel smiled, and he didn't defend himself, even though Wally had struck a little too close to the truth. Mel only said, "Are you going to try to break your brother's record?"

Wally took a deep breath. "I'll give it a try," he said, but that's not what he was thinking. He had made up his mind, absolutely, that he would do it. He had been reasonably close in some of his practice runs, and today the weather was just right—only a light wind, and the warmest day of the spring so far. Four years before, Alex had set the city record, but Wally was almost sure he could beat the time. He had never done as well as Alex at any sport, so this was the one chance he had left to beat him.

Wally looked toward the bleachers. Maybe a hundred people were in their seats and others were coming in—mostly parents of athletes but also a few students. President Thomas had told Wally that he would try to come, but Wally couldn't see him. Wally knew he didn't need that extra pressure of having him there, but he couldn't help recalling Alex and Dad talking about Alex's track meets after the two had come home together.

This was a duel meet against West High. Later, East would run against South, and then all three teams would meet in the city championship. So Wally knew he would have other chances to break the Big Three record, but he wanted to do it now and not let the pressure build all season.

Wally shut his eyes and concentrated on the smell of the cut grass and the wintergreen smell of the analgesic balm he had rubbed on his thighs, but he felt tight, and so he got up. "Come on," he said. "Run a lap with me." Wally usually had to be prodded to do warmup laps, but right now he wanted to get moving.

"Just a sec." Mel grabbed a towel from his bag and wrapped it around his neck. The two stepped onto the track and began a slow trot. More athletes in warmup suits were showing up now.

The loud speaker, high on a pole above the bleachers, buzzed, and then a deep voice intoned, "Testing. One, two, three, testing." And after a moment, "First call for the shot put, broad jump and pole vault. Report to the scorer's table at the center of the field."

The sound was set too loud, and the vibration shook

through Wally's body. He wished he could run right then and get this whole thing over with.

"It's only March," Mel said. "You don't have to get the record today. You've got all season to do it."

"I know. It doesn't matter that much to me anyway."

"Yeah, sure. That's why all the color's gone from your face."

Wally didn't answer. He listened to the crunch of the cinders under his feet. He thought how different this same backstretch would feel when the race was on. He picked up his pace a bit and Mel had to hurry to catch up.

"You let Alex worry you too much," Mel said. "Sometimes you sound like you hate him."

"That couldn't happen, Mel. No one hates Alex. Dogs love him. Grandmas. Little kids."

Two boys in faded blue warmups sprinted past Wally and Mel, really pressing. "What are they trying to prove?" Wally asked.

But Mel didn't answer. "Wally," he said, "Alex is Alex, and you're you. It's not a contest."

"Tell everyone else that."

Mel let it go, and the two continued their trot around the turn and onto the straightaway. Some girls Wally knew were standing near the track in front of the bleachers. "Wally, Mel—good luck," one of them yelled, and then the others waved and called out encouragement. Wally looked at Gwen Larsen, a girl he had dated a couple of times. When he waved to her, she brightened considerably.

"Win a ribbon for Gwenny," Francene Clegg called out. Gwen slapped Francene's shoulder, then turned to hide her face. All the other girls laughed. Most of them were wearing cotton school dresses, but Gwen had on a dark skirt that hit her above the knees, and long, white stockings. This was the new bare-knee look that college girls were wearing—or so Gwen had told Wally. He liked the style just fine, but he paid even more attention to the way Gwen filled out her pretty yellow sweater. He also noticed that Francene was wearing Chuck Adair's letter sweater. Chuck was East High's all-around sports star. Setting a record in front of Gwen and the other girls would be nice, but outshining Chuck for once would even be better.

"Gwen's got it bad for you, Wally," Mel said.

"Not too bad. She won't let me kiss her."

"Hey, you just started going out with her."

If Wally had been in a different mood he might have vowed that he would kiss her on his next date with her, but he let it go. He glanced again at the bleachers, which were filling up.

"I'll tell you the girl I'd like to go out with," Mel said. "Wait a minute." He stopped, bent over and stuck a finger into the side of his shoe. "I've got a rock in here." He stepped off the track, sat down on the grass and pulled his shoe off.

The loud speaker boomed again, and Wally jerked in response. It was the second call for the field events. Wally still had upwards of an hour to wait for the quarter mile. "Which girl?" he asked, even though he wasn't that interested.

"Lorraine Gardner."

Wally had seen her with the other girls, standing back a little, laughing, but not as involved. He thought she was the best looking girl in the senior class. She had long, slender legs and a little waist, and she had a wonderfully bright smile. But she was not easy to read, and she never showed much interest in Wally. In fact, he always suspected she didn't like him.

"Mel, don't try to play in the big leagues until you've put in a couple of seasons in the minors."

"Hey, I know. I wouldn't dare ask her out. I just think about it sometimes." Mel had his shoe on, and now he got up and stepped back on the track. "But I'll tell you what. She's even big leagues for you, chum. You wouldn't get a kiss from her."

All this chatter was not easing Wally's nerves. He needed to move. "Look, I'm going go to take a few starts," he said.

"Okay. I've got to check in for the broad jump."

Wally was glad to get away from Mel. He ran to his gym bag and got his spikes, sat down and put them on, and then he took some starts on the grass. He broke hard each time, and ran all out for twenty yards or so. Then he did some exercises, took some more starts, watched the hundred yard dash, and then jogged around the middle of the track enough to stay warm. When the announcement for the four-forty finally crackled over the sound system, his nerves sent a reaction through him like an electric shock. At least it would soon be over.

He reported at the scorer's table, waited for the end of the two-twenty, and then pulled off his old gray warmup suit. He took another look along the bleachers, but he knew his dad was not there. He walked onto the track and waited for the starter to call out the names and set the lanes. As it turned out, he was in the middle of the track, a good spot, where the cinders were firm. He gouged out a couple of holes with his spikes and then stepped in to test them. Then he dug the back hole a little deeper, a little farther back, and he took a start. The holes seemed fine, but he wished he hadn't gotten ready so fast. Some of the other guys were still just pulling their warmups off.

"Good luck, Thomas," a boy from West told him—a guy named Farrell. He was strongly built, more like a football player than a runner, but he and a spindly guy named Williamson were supposed to be Wally's toughest competition.

"Yeah. You too," Wally said, and the two shook hands.

Wally turned and walked up the track a few yards and then reached and touched his toes a couple of times.

"Wally, what pretty legs you have!"

Wally straightened up and looked at the girls, who were still standing next to the track. Gwen was laughing, but he knew she hadn't said it. It was probably Francene again. He told himself he was going to fly down that straightaway this time—right past all those girls—and they were going to think he was *dazzling*, like an ancient Olympian.

He smiled at them, or at least tried to, but he could hear his heart pounding in his ears, and his stomach seemed full of helium.

"Runners, take your marks."

Wally turned and walked back to his starting holes. "Good luck, Wally," he heard Mel call out.

As the runners began to place their feet in their marks and crouch for the start, quiet fell over the field. Wally leaned forward and held his arms out for balance.

"Get set!"

Wally tensed. He felt the presence of the runners near him, but his focus was down the track, as though he were looking through a tunnel. No one was going to beat him to that first turn.

Crack. The gun fired and Wally burst from his marks. He jumped into the lead so suddenly that the other runners were already out of his vision as he angled toward the inside of the track and headed for the corner. He had never felt so powerful in his life.

He took the first turn cruising, the chopping sound of the cinders the only evidence that he was even touching the ground. "Hold back," he tried to tell himself, but he couldn't contain the energy that was pulling him into the back stretch.

As he came out of the corner, the whistle in his ears disappeared, and he knew that the wind was now with him, and he was still floating, still running without strain.

"Take it easy, Wally. Take it easy," he heard Coach Morse calling from across the track, and he knew the man was right. But he wanted that record. He would give everything he had, and then gut out the finish, no matter what it cost him.

He could hear no one behind him, and he wasn't about to glance back and foul up the stride he had going. But as he neared the end of the backstretch and started into the second turn, he knew for the first time that he had pushed himself too hard, too early. The pain hit him suddenly. It grabbed at his thighs and burned his lungs, but he didn't let up. He pushed himself into the corner and kept striding hard toward the final straightaway.

But he was slowing. His legs had turned heavy, and as he came out of the turn and picked up the sound of the wind again, he felt his stride break. He almost stumbled, but he muscled his way through and tried to thrust his legs, to find his rhythm again.

He had known all along how much it would hurt, but he had told himself he wouldn't give in to the pain. And so he drove his arms and tried to keep lifting his knees. But the strength was draining from him. His stride was shortening, his lungs giving out.

He heard the girls screaming, everyone screaming. "Keep going, Wally. Keep going. Push!"

It was all as though he were swimming under water, with the sound of the people out there somewhere, above the surface. Still, he tried to respond. He pressed harder. He only had about forty yards to go, a few seconds.

But everything was shutting down. And now he heard the footsteps, heard the crowd noise intensify. And then he felt a runner coming alongside him. Williamson. He could sense the height of him, saw his long arms swinging. Wally reached for something more and held his own, and the two battled forward, both losing speed but straining to match each other step for step.

And then Wally let go. With twenty yards to run, his body simply surrendered. He commanded himself not to give up, but his stride faltered and Williamson was gone. Then, almost at a stop, he took a final step across the line as Farrell slipped by him and took second.

Wally dropped to his knees. He knew, abstractly, that the cinders had cut into his knees, but he felt nothing. He fell forward, scraping his forearms into the track, and then dropped his face onto his arms. He didn't care whether he cut himself. He sucked for air and waited for some relief from the sickness. He wanted to vomit, wanted to do it right there on the track and end the agony. But two people had hold of him, grasping him by the arms and around the middle. They were pulling him up. "Don't," Wally managed to grunt.

"Walk it off," Mel was saying. "You'll be all right."

"Leave me alone," Wally tried to say, but nothing came out. He bent forward and breathed for maybe a minute, and then he found the energy to pull himself free. He stumbled a few steps forward, bent over and put his hands on his knees, then took deep breaths as he waited to vomit. But the relief wouldn't come, and he was coming back to life enough to know that he didn't want to do it here anyway. So he began to walk resolutely down the track toward the first turn. "Let me help you, Wally," Mel was saying.

"Just leave me alone. I'll be all right."

He walked to the end of the bleachers, stepped underneath, grabbed a metal strut and bent over again. And finally it all let loose. He felt the convulsion in his stomach, the acid in his nose, but a second later, he already felt better. He spat on the ground, waited to see whether there would be more.

"Wally, are you all right?"

Wally didn't look back. He knew the voice. It was Gwen.

"Can I do anything for you?"

Wally finally turned around. "No."

"You're all cut up. You're bleeding."

"I know." But now Wally took a better look. Blood was running down his shins from his knees, and black cinders were imbedded in his skin. His elbows were burning now, and his forearms were covered with blood.

Wally couldn't stand to look at Gwen. He kept his head down as he said, "I'll go shower. I'll be all right."

He stepped out from under the bleachers, but now he saw

his coach coming. "Wally, let me have a look at you," Coach Morse said. "How bad is it?"

"Not bad. I just got scratched." Wally glanced up to see that a couple of young boys were leaning over the end of the bleachers. For some reason, that embarrassed him more than anything. The illness was gone now, and the blood wasn't that important. What Wally didn't want was to be stared at. He hated that Gwen was looking so concerned and supportive. All he could think was that she had seen him vomit.

"I've got a first-aid kit out here," the coach said. "Walk back to—"

"No. I'll just go shower." He started to walk away, but it was only then that he realized he had made a decision. He stopped and turned back. "Coach, I'm quitting."

"What?"

"I'm quitting track. I don't like it. I can't do it."

"Wally, you went out too fast, but if you keep training hard, you'll hang on for those final yards and beat those guys. You have a good shot at the city championship."

"No. I can't do it. I'm sorry."

And Wally walked away. He didn't go back to the track for his warmups or his gym bag. He just walked into the locker room. He wanted to get away from the school as fast as he could.

Two hours later, Wally was upstairs in his room lying on his bed. When he heard heavy footsteps on the stairs, he knew his dad was coming. "How does he know already?" Wally asked himself.

A moment later, he heard a knock and then heard his dad's voice. "Wally?"

"Yeah?"

The door came open. Dad took a step inside and then pushed the two wings of his double-breasted suit coat aside and stuffed his hands into his pockets. He was still wearing his hat. Wally dropped his head back onto his pillow.

"Your coach called me. He said you were quitting the team."

"That's right."

"I told him you were probably upset by what happened, but I promised him you wouldn't quit."

"You shouldn't have told him that."

Dad stepped closer. He pulled his hat off and held it. Wally looked away, at the ceiling, but he could hear his dad breathing hard, as though he were trying to control his anger. "I told Coach Morse that I don't raise quitters."

"Only one," Wally said.

"For crying out loud, son, what are you talking about? Can't you take a setback? Your coach told me that you're faster than your brother ever was. All you need to do is put in more work."

"Is that what Alex did? Work harder than me?"

"I don't know. But he always gave it all he had—and he didn't back down from *any* challenge."

"Well, I'm not Alex. Never was, never will be. He's made of better stuff—as you have pointed out to me many times before."

President Thomas stepped closer to the bed. "Sit up," he said. "Look at me, and talk to me like a man." Wally did sit up, and for the first time he looked his father straight in the eye. He was furious, and he didn't mind letting his eyes show it.

"Wally, your team won today—in spite of you. The only relay East lost was the one you were supposed to run. But South is stronger, and the coach says he'll need you to have a chance to win the city championship. You can score some points and help your team—whether you take first place or not. Isn't that important to you?"

Wally had thought this through more than his dad realized. He was *not* going back out on the track. "Dad, I told you. I quit the team. I'm not going to change my mind."

"Wally, there's *nothing* I hate more than a quitter," Dad said, almost shouting. But then he calmed himself and said, more quietly, "That's not your heritage, Wally. That's not who you are. I won't *allow* you to quit."

"You aren't going to make this decision, Dad," Wally said, firmly and acidly. "*I* am."

Wally saw the skin along his father's throat turn deep red, and he sensed that he had won. He suddenly felt powerful. He stood up. "Where were you today anyway?" he demanded. "You always went to Alex's track meets."

"That's not true. I went when I could. And I would have been there today if I could have made it. I can't just drop everything and run off every time I want to."

"You told me this morning you would come."

"No. I said I would if I could get away. But something came up. A man in our stake needed to see me. It wasn't the sort of thing I could put off."

"So it was church business."

"Yes, it was, in this case. I do have my church calling too, Wally. That's something you ought to understand by now."

"Oh, I do understand. You always put the Church ahead of our family. We all know that."

Wally wasn't even sure he believed that. But it was the closest weapon he could find, and he was fighting back.

Dad stared at Wally, and he seemed to calm. Maybe he gave up. "You're pitiful, Wally," he finally said. "You don't have the guts to finish a race, but you won't take responsibility for that. You have to blame it on me—and the Church."

"No. I already admitted that I'm a quitter."

"Well, then, you do what you want, Wally. Quit the team. And quit everything else that's hard in life. And see what that will do for you."

He stood for another moment, as though he hoped for a change of heart. But Wally only said, "Fine, Dad. That'll be my plan. I'll be the family quitter."

"What a shame, Wally. When I think what God has given you, and what you're doing with it, my heart just breaks." He turned and walked from the room. He shut the door, pulled it until the lock clicked. Wally heard the sound like a gunshot, felt the pain of it. He dropped back onto the bed, pulled the pillow over his face, and tried not to cry, but the tears came anyway. He pressed the pillow tighter, trying hard not to let go. What he wished at the moment was that he had the power to keep pressing until he smothered himself.

Wally knew the truth. It wasn't just that he had quit today; it was that he didn't have what it took to win. He had tried as hard as he had ever tried in his life, but something inside him was simply too weak. When Williamson had kept pushing, Wally couldn't. Dad didn't understand that Wally hadn't *decided* to quit. Something inside had decided for him.

He turned on his side and looked at the other bed. Alex had been gone from the room for a year and a half, but he was still hovering over Wally, and there was no escaping him.

7

When Bobbi opened the front door, she found herself hoping that her parents wouldn't be there, or at least that her dad might have gone off to a meeting. She was wearing her new spring outfit: a white flare skirt—the new "skating skirt" look that Sonja Henie had made popular—a lavender vest, white gloves, and a little round hat with a jaunty feather in it. She had spent a long time on her hair, too, which was pulled tight against her head on top but ended in curls. She liked the way she looked, but she knew what was coming that night, and she was nervous.

Phil stepped in behind her, his hand clasped against her waist with a new sense of ownership. She saw her dad sitting by the tall Philco console radio, listening to a news broadcast and reading the newspaper at the same time. LaRue and Beverly were on the floor, sitting cross-legged, playing a card game—Old Maid or Animal Rummy—and Mom was sitting under a lamp, on the couch, stitching on another of her endless needlework projects. At least Wally wasn't there.

"Daddy, Phil wanted to—"

But Phil quickly stepped forward and said, "President Thomas, I'd like to have a little chat with you, if I could."

Everyone looked up. The little girls smiled knowingly.

"Woo, woo," LaRue said, and Beverly giggled. Bobbi glanced at her mother, who gave her a little nod and smile.

"Certainly," Dad said as he folded his paper. "Let's step into my office."

So Phil and President Thomas walked through the dining room to the office in back, and Bobbi was left with the females of the family all beaming at her. She sat on the couch at the opposite end from her mother, and she felt terribly self-conscious.

"Oh, Bobbi, this is so wonderful," Mom said. She smiled contentedly, her dimples appearing. She put down her needlework and reached her hand in Bobbi's direction. Bobbi took her hand for a moment, but she didn't say anything.

"Did he kiss you?" LaRue asked.

And Beverly said, "Hubba, hubba," which brought peals of laughter from both girls.

"Be still, girls," Mom said. "Someday, your day will come."

"That's right," Beverly said. "LaRue's going to marry Rex Halladay. He already kissed her—right on the lips."

"Shut up," LaRue said, and she slapped Beverly's back. "I didn't want him to."

Bobbi didn't need any of this right now. And when she heard footsteps on the stairs, she hoped Gene was the one coming down. But she saw Wally, and her breath caught. He came through the parlor and into the living room. "So what's up?" he said. "I thought you and Phil were on a date." He stuck his hands into his pockets and waited, all the while chewing hard on a stick of gum.

"Phil's talking to Daddy," LaRue said. "And *I* know why."

"Hush," Mom said. "I mean it, LaRue. Be quiet."

"I thought you were going somewhere," Mom said to Wally.

"I am. Mel's coming to get me—if his dad ever gets home with the car. Parents sure can be inconsiderate sometimes."

But Wally had spoken absently. Bobbi knew what he was thinking. She looked at him and tried to seem confident.

"So this is it, huh?" Wally said.

"You don't know that," Mom said. "Maybe those men need to talk about the price of grain."

Bobbi glanced at Wally again. He was nodding as though he were trying to accept the whole idea, but questions were in his eyes. Bobbi wished she had never said anything to him.

"I will say this," Mom said. "I don't know any better people than the Clarks—one of the great families in the Church. And Phil is such a sweet young man."

Beverly got up and came over to the couch. "He's dreamy," she said, and she looked up at Bobbi, her face full of envy.

"He's a wonderful young man," Mom said. "He's going to make something of himself, too."

"Yeah, Mom, but have you checked his teeth?" Wally asked. "What if he has cavities? You can't be too careful these days, you know. Behind that handsome smile could be . . . *tooth decay.*"

Beverly thought that a wonderful joke, but LaRue said, "He doesn't have tooth decay. He has pretty teeth."

Mom let out a little sigh, as if to say, "Wally, you're impossible," but she was still smiling. "I think the Clarks have a dentist or two in the family," she said.

Wally stepped closer to Bobbi and put his hand on her shoulder. "Next time he yawns, stick your head in his mouth and check things out. Don't jump into anything you'll later regret."

Bobbi didn't think Wally was all that funny, but she didn't say it. "At least he doesn't have a cavity where his brains ought to be," she said.

Mom chuckled, but Wally looked down at LaRue. "Wait a minute. Does she mean *me?* Was that an insult or am I just imagining things?"

"She meant you, all right," LaRue said. "You've got a hole in your head. And you're not handsome like Phil."

But the office door was opening. Dad and Phil, both looking pleased, stepped out and walked into the living room. Phil was dressed fit to kill in a gray flannel suit and maroon tie. His hair was combed perfectly, with a wave in the front, and he was showing off those good teeth. He had a square-jaw, square-deal sort of look—every maiden's dream. But Bobbi wished he didn't look quite so pleased with himself.

President Thomas stepped ahead of Phil. He reached for the lapels of his coat, found nothing—since he didn't have his coat on—and then let his hands drop. "Where's Gene?" he asked.

"At the ward house, playing basketball," Mom said.

"Well, I'll talk to him later. At least the rest of us are together—for once." The radio was still on, and a dance band was playing an upbeat song—jitterbug music. Dad stepped over and turned it off. "This is a wonderful occasion," he said. "Brother Clark has asked for Barbara's hand in marriage, and I've told him that we are honored to join our family to his." Phil nodded. He was trying to look serious, but he was glowing.

"Some might think it's old fashioned to ask a father's permission, but it's the proper order of things. Phil is a young man with a wonderful heritage and a wonderful future." Then Dad smiled. "And I look forward to his posterity."

"They can name their kids after you, Dad," Wally said. "The boys could all be named Alexander, and the girls, Alexandria."

Lately, Dad had not had a lot of patience with Wally, but he smiled now. "That's not necessary. Some could be David— or Thomas," he said, and he grinned, but then he cleared his throat. "Well, anyway, we welcome you to our family, Phil. We couldn't be happier." And the two men shook hands.

Mom got up and walked to Phil. "I've got to have more than a handshake," she said. She spread her arms wide, and Phil bent over to hug her. "I'm thrilled to death." Then she came back to Bobbi, who stood up and accepted Mom's embrace. "This is just *perfect*. It's a dream come true," she told Bobbi, and Bobbi felt good about that. It seemed right to please her parents so much.

Dad was waiting, too, so Bobbi pulled away from Mom and turned to him. He seemed unsure what to do, so Bobbi stepped to him and put her arms around him. He hugged her and said, "You couldn't have done any better, Sis."

"Did you two have a nice chat?" she asked him.

"We did. I bargained for two yoke of oxen and a new wagon, but all I got was a pair of goats and an ol' yeller dog."

Bobbi stepped back and gave her dad a little slug on the shoulder. "I'm worth a new Hudson, if you ask me," she said.

"That's what he said, but I told him *he* had to pay *me*."

She punched him again. At the same time, Phil bent down toward LaRue. "You know," he said, "if you're going to be my sister-in-law, you ought to be giving me a hug too."

LaRue stepped forward willingly, and Phil picked her up, gave her a big squeeze, and then set her back down. She looked a little flustered by that, but she said, "I thought you had to be old to be a sister-in-law," and everyone laughed.

Beverly had gotten up now, and she was waiting for her own hug. "What am I?" she asked.

"You'll be my *little* sister-in-law," Phil said, and he picked her up, too. She looked wonderfully pleased when she landed, her face red and her eyes glowing with adoration.

And so it was settled. Everyone had been hugged, and Phil had a plan to formalize the proposal. He had a good sense for such things, for looking after details and making everything just right. Bobbi knew she would always be able to depend on him to handle life with style and propriety—something she didn't do nearly so well.

"Well, now, if you'll excuse us," Phil was already saying, smiling, looking good, using that wonderful, gentle voice of his, "we have some unfinished business ourselves."

"Business?" Wally said. "What do you have to do, write up a contract?" Bobbi felt the words shoot through her, but then she let them go. She didn't want anything to bother her tonight.

Phil gave her his arm, led her to the car, opened the door for her, and then hurried around to the driver's side. Once he had positioned himself behind the wheel and started the engine, he turned to her and said, "I just love your family."

"Even Wally?" she asked, trying to lighten the mood.

"Oh, yeah. He's a swell kid. He'll grow out of that silliness."

"I hope not," Bobbi said rather curtly, but she told herself immediately to be careful. She slid across the seat so she was close to Phil.

"I love you, sweetheart," Phil said, and he gave her a kiss on the cheek. Then he shifted the gears, twisted to look over his shoulder, and backed out of the driveway. He had never called her anything like that before. This was part of the new condition, Bobbi supposed, the new relationship. But Bobbi didn't think she could call him "honey" or "dear" or any of those pretty little names.

"I want to take you to my house so we can tell my parents," Phil said, once he was driving. "But let's do that later. I have dinner reservations coming up in about"—he checked his watch—"twenty minutes. This is working out just right."

"Where are we going?"

"I thought we'd go to the Empire Room at the Hotel Utah. The food is good, I'm told, and they have dancing—Ray Bradford and His Orchestra. Is that all right with you?"

"Sure."

"Is something the matter?"

"No. Not at all."

He patted her leg—something he had also not done before.

"I do want to talk to you about one thing," Bobbi said. She had planned to wait until later, but now she knew she wanted to get this worked out before she had the ring on her finger.

"Sure. What is it?"

Bobbi hadn't thought this out in words, so she hardly knew where to start. She took her hat off and set it on her lap. At the same time, a car in front of them slowed, and Phil had to brake and then shift gears. Bobbi used all this to stall, to think, but no words came to her mind until she actually began to speak. "I want to finish college, Phil. It's important to me. And if we get married too soon, I'm afraid I never will. I mean, never will go back. Or never . . ." She stopped, tried to think. "I just want to wait until then."

"Until when?"

"Couldn't we wait until I graduate? I'm not even twenty yet, so that would—"

"Bobbi, what are you talking about? That's *two* years." She had tried to think how he would react, but she was surprised by the strength of his response, the harshness in his voice.

"I know that. But lots of people are engaged that long. My aunt was engaged the whole time my uncle was on his mission."

"Well, sure. He was gone. But I can't . . . I mean, two years would be way too long."

"I don't see why, Phil."

"Bobbi, think about it." But he couldn't seem to find a way to say it. "I was thinking this fall wouldn't be too soon."

"Then what do I do about college?"

"Why is that so important, Bobbi? Dad's willing to see me the rest of the way through law school. After that, I'll make a good living. I can support you just fine. Why do you need a college degree?"

"I don't *need* it, necessarily."

"Then why bother? You won't have to work—I'll see to that."

"It's something I want to do," Bobbi said. "I made up my mind about that a long time ago." She leaned away from him with her hand on the seat, bracing herself.

"Well, listen. Why couldn't we get married, and then you could keep going—at least for a while?"

"I'd probably have a baby, and that would be that."

"What's wrong with that? What's better than being a mother?"

But Bobbi had a notion about herself, had had it since she was a little girl. She had read about Helen Keller and Madame Curie. She admired Eleanor Roosevelt. And that's how she thought of herself—a woman who could do something.

"I do want to be a mother," Bobbi finally said. "I just want to finish college first. Maybe we could get married when I'm a senior, when I only have a few months to go—six months, or something like that."

"That's still a year and a half from now. Bobbi, come on. We're in love. How can we wait that long?"

Bobbi knew what that meant. But she had never felt the urgency that she sensed from him. He never got out of line, but sometimes when they kissed, he held her very close and then pushed himself away in an act of obvious self-control. It was something she wondered about. Why didn't she feel the same ache? She actually longed to feel that way, had imagined sometimes that she would someday have that kind of need for someone.

"Bobbi, I can wait. But not two years. Not even a year and a half."

"So what are you saying? You're the one who decides?"

Phil turned onto State Street and drove north, with both hands on the wheel. Bobbi knew he was angry. She saw the little muscle by his ear form a lump as he clenched his jaw. She almost wished he would explode, really fight with her. "Bobbi," he finally said, "I don't know how to say this. I don't want to sound like a tough guy. But I do think, before we get married, we both need to know who wears the pants in the family."

"I have a nice new pair of slacks. You told me they look good on me."

"Bobbi, this isn't funny. You know what I'm talking about."

"Yes. I know exactly. You want to make my decisions for me." She was being nasty now, and she knew it, but he might as well know what he was up against.

"I didn't say that, and you know it. But I am going to be the patriarch in our family. I am expected to lead."

"Oh, *yes* sir. Just command me and I will obey." She slid a little farther away.

Phil took a long breath, held it longer than seemed possible, and then gradually let it seep out. "Bobbi, you've never talked to me like this before."

"And *you?* You've never talked to *me* this way. This is the first I've heard about you being my boss."

"I didn't say that."

"'Patriarch' doesn't mean you *rule*—that's what a boss does."

"Who leads *your* family?"

"My dad—more than he should. Mom ought to stand up to him more often than she does."

Phil turned now, took a good look into Bobbi's eyes, but she didn't blink. "I can't believe I'm hearing this. You haven't been raised this way."

Bobbi felt the guilt—more than she wanted to. "Phil, come on. I'm not trying to steal your *pants* from you. You can patriarch me all you want, but you can't make decisions by yourself and tell me to like it or lump it."

"Do you really think I would do that?"

No. She didn't. But it took her the better part of a minute to talk herself into saying, "I'm sorry, Phil. I know you aren't that way. But our first decision is to set a date for our wedding, and I don't want to get married right away. I can't just say, 'Whatever you think' when I feel that way."

Phil was nodding, thinking. "Listen, honey, I think we need to talk this through—maybe get our parents' opinions, and—"

"No."

"What?"

"You know what my dad would say. So would yours."

"And maybe for good reason."

"I don't care. All you patriarchs are not going to get together and overrule me."

"Bobbi! What a thing to say."

And she knew it. She was being irreverent, and even though she rather liked the feel of it, in the long run she couldn't do this. "I'm sorry," she said. "Phil, I really am. But if a girl has a right to determine anything, she ought to be able to choose her own wedding date."

"Why can't we decide together?" Phil was driving more slowly all the time, seeming not to concentrate on the car, and the traffic was streaming past them.

"We can, I guess. But I'm not going to be pushed into going ahead with it this fall."

"Fine. I can live with that. But I can't live with two years. Can't we find some middle ground?"

"I don't know."

Phil braked, gently, for a red light. "Well, okay," he said. "This will be our first challenge. We'll learn about talking things out and finding answers. We'll ask the Lord, for one thing. We really should have done that already."

And yet, even that bothered Bobbi. She had the feeling that once all the patriarchs got lined up with Mom and Phil's mom—and they started claiming that God was voting on their side—she would get steamrollered.

But what was she thinking? The Lord should strike her down this instant. Why couldn't she just be happy she had found such a good man? And thankful. There were beautiful girls at the U who were crazy with jealousy that Bobbi—freckle-faced little Bobbi—had managed to harvest the pick of the crop. She slid back and took Phil's arm. "I don't mean to be difficult," she said. "Maybe I have to get used to the idea. It's all a big adjustment for me."

And with that, she saw Phil's chest rise, his chin come up.

He was the pants-wearer, after all. Bobbi couldn't help being annoyed by his satisfaction, but she told herself that she loved him, and that she would make this work.

"It is a big adjustment," he said kindly. "But we'll know when it's right. And I promise you, Bobbi, I'll treat you like an angel. I always will. That's what you are to me, and I could never treat you any other way."

So what was all that business about wearing the pants? Bobbi wondered. But she said nothing more. She leaned her head against his shoulder. "I know you'll treat me right," she said. "I just hope I'll treat you the way I should."

"Hey, you're feisty, all right. But it's one of the things I like about you."

"Phil, I feel like I'm walking into a dark tunnel, and I don't know who I'll be when—and *if*—I get to the other end. I've always thought for myself, and I don't want to give that up. Can you understand that?"

"Of course, honey. A man feels those things too. I like my independence as much as the next guy. But I want to be one flesh with someone I love. And I want to create a posterity. It's a beautiful thing, Bobbi—the greatest thing there is in life."

Bobbi believed all that, always had. But why did he make it sound so . . . *functional?*

He patted her leg again and then left his hand on her thigh. "You're just a little frightened of having a man in your bed. There's a lot to get used to."

Bobbi sat up straighter, moved her head away from his shoulder.

"Oh, hey, I'm sorry. I don't mean to sound like that. I'll always be tender with you. I promise that, too."

Bobbi didn't doubt that either. But she didn't want to think about it. She didn't want to think at all.

At the Hotel Utah she ate her dinner, made light conversation, and danced. Phil was a wonderful dancer, smooth, and when he held her close, she nestled against him. The band was lovely and the room magnificent. The beautiful gold leafing, the dark woodwork, the crystal chandeliers, the medieval murals high up on the walls—it was all perfect, and she tried to take it in so she would never forget it.

Then, when Phil walked her across the street to Temple Square and led her to a lonely bench, she saw all of his planning, and she couldn't help smiling. He knelt on one knee and asked her, "Bobbi, will you marry me, here, in this temple, for time and all eternity?"

"Yes, I will," she said softly, almost delicately. Then she leaned over and gave him a little kiss.

He got out the ring then—the one they had chosen together. "I had the jeweler put a few more diamonds in the arrangement—more than we originally talked about," he said. "I just felt you deserved something as beautiful as you are."

And the ring *was* pretty—with a large diamond in the middle and lots of smaller stones. It was going to knock her friends' eyes out. Bobbi felt a surge of excitement. Phil kissed her again, then held her for a long time. "You've made me the happiest man in the world," he whispered.

The two walked back across the street. Bobbi was shivering by now, the evening having become cool. Phil took off his suit coat and dropped it over her shoulders, wrapping his arm around her. Then they got into Phil's car and drove to his parents' house. Bobbi hugged her new in-laws-to-be, including Phil's teenaged brothers, laughed at their teasing, felt touched by Phil's mother's tears, and leaned her head on Phil's shoulder once again on the way home. She was relieved to know that her inner struggles were over. Her fears had been natural enough—cold feet—but now she felt secure. She had done the right thing, and when she did that, things always worked out fine.

But after he had kissed her at the door, held her for a long time again, and professed his love one more time, she wondered why she hadn't found the voice to say the same to him. And when she walked upstairs, she was sorry to see that Wally was home and that his door was open—as though he were waiting for her.

She tried to walk softly and go straight to her room, but Wally heard her and came out, wearing his old green pajamas. "Sis, are you okay?" he asked.

"Of course."

"Did he give you the ring?"

She stretched her hand out. She had thought of waking her parents and showing them—she knew they expected it. But she had decided they could see it in the morning.

"Wow, that's a lot of stones. That much weight is going to stretch your arm."

"It's pretty, isn't it?"

"Yeah. I guess. Are you sure you're okay?"

"Wally, that one night I talked to you, I was just in a bad mood—and sort of upset with him. But we've worked everything out. I'm really happy now."

"You don't seem all that happy, if you want to know the truth."

"I'm just thinking about everything. It's a happy event, but it's also sacred. I'm just feeling really thankful and pleased."

"Well, okay. That's good. But it seems like it ought to be exciting, too."

"Oh, it is. I'm excited. Really. But it's one thing to think about getting married when you're a little girl. It's something else to know you're grown up, and you have to take on the responsibilities that come with marriage."

Wally gave her a curious look, as though the words didn't sound right to him. The light was shining behind him from his room. It silhouetted his messy hair, and it caught his eyes enough to show his confusion, but he didn't raise any questions. "Well, anyway," he said, "I hope you're going to be really happy and everything."

"What about you? Are you going to be happy?"

"Sure. I'm always happy."

"Is Dad still upset with you for quitting track?"

"Sure he is. But he's never said another word about it. And personally, I think it's the smartest thing I ever did. I'm just trying to live the Word of Wisdom—not do things that hurt my body. And trust me, running hurts."

"Wally, I used to think you were the most transparent kid who ever lived. But you've gotten complicated. I can't figure you out anymore."

"Nothing to figure out," Wally said. "I'm fine."

But he didn't seem fine to Bobbi. "Why are you being so nice to me? I'm getting married, not dying."

"I'm all choked up." Now he was grinning. "Once you're gone, I get to ship Gene down the hall. That's a wonderful moment in a guy's life—when he gets his own room."

"Yeah, I've had mine for a long time. Now I have to let some *guy* move in. I hope he picks up his dirty socks."

"That's your job. Men have *important* things to do."

Bobbi turned and walked away. "That's how you men think, too," she said.

"Not Phil. He bows and scrapes for you."

"Good night, Wally," Bobbi said. And she stepped into her room. Then, without turning the lights on, she walked to the window. The moon was casting a glow through the apple tree. Bobbi could see the dark limbs, like arms. She thought of all the times she had climbed that tree when she was a girl—those summer days when the apples were still not ripe. Dad had always told her not to eat the apples yet, that they would make her sick. But she had eaten them anyway, green, and she had loved them. Now, she remembered herself perched in those limbs, a salt shaker in one hand, an apple in the other, and suddenly she wished more than anything that she could have that time—that Bobbi—back.

When the knocking began, Elder Thomas thought he had overslept. But the room was dark, and he realized it was still early. The next thought, of course, was that it was Kellerman. But why? They hadn't done anything. They hadn't gone anywhere near the ghetto.

Elder Thomas grabbed his robe, which he had left hanging over a chair the night before. The knock was back, more persistent this time, but not hard. Elder Thomas felt somewhat calmed. He didn't hear Kellerman in it. But he stepped to the door, still unsure, and opened it a little. He was surprised to see Peter Stoltz standing there, wide-eyed, his hair ruffled as though he had just gotten out of bed.

"Anna is very sick," he insisted. "Can you come? Mama wants you."

"Yes. Yes. Come in for a moment."

"No. I'll start back on my bicycle. Come as quickly as you can."

Elder Sawyer was already getting out of bed. Both elders dressed quickly, saying little to each other. But in the courtyard, when they were getting their bikes, Elder Sawyer asked, "Do they understand about administering? Is that what they want?"

"Yes. I think so. We told them about it."

The elders pumped hard. They left their bicycles in front of the Stoltzes' building, and they hurried up the stairs. When they reached the landing, Peter was standing in the doorway. "Come in," he said. He walked on through the living room to a hall and then stopped by a door and motioned the elders in.

Inside, the room was lighted dimly by a single lamp in the corner. Frau Stoltz had been sitting by the bed. She stood up, still holding a basin and a wash cloth. She set them down on a little stand by the bed, and then she wiped her hands on her apron. She reached out to Elder Thomas. "Thank you," she said.

"What's wrong?"

"Influenza." Elder Thomas heard the despair in Frau Stoltz's voice.

"How bad is she?"

"Not good—not at all. The doctor comes every day. But now he says we can only wait and see. Her fever is very high."

Elder Thomas stepped closer to the bed, and he was astounded by what he saw. Anna's eyes were sunken, her face skeletal and white. Frau Stoltz had been wiping Anna's face with a damp cloth, and her hair was matted. She seemed to have no substance, as though she were as thin as the sheet over her. She was dying, Elder Thomas realized, and he felt a sudden panic.

"She was talking to us until last night. But now she is sinking." Frau Stoltz began to cry. "Will you bless her? Can you bring her back?"

Elder Thomas had administered to only one other person in his life—a woman who had been only mildly ill by comparison. No one had ever asked him to bring someone back from the edge of death. "We do have the power," he said, frightened to make a promise and at the same time disappointed with himself that he didn't feel more certain.

"Please do it, Bruder Thomas. Please. She's my life."

Elder Thomas nodded. He reached into his pocket and

grasped the little bottle of oil. "Where is Herr Stoltz?" he asked.

"He doesn't believe in this. He allowed me, finally, to send for you, but he wants nothing to do with it. He's very angry right now, Bruder Thomas. He can't bear this. I don't know what he'll do."

Elder Thomas could feel the weight. He wished he had his father with him, or an apostle—someone with deeper faith, greater power. "Will Herr Stoltz at least come in? He should be here for the blessing. He could say a prayer, or—"

"No, no. He refuses. He told me it's superstition, and he won't be part of it."

Elder Thomas nodded, and he considered for a moment. "Frau Stoltz, I need . . . to be ready. I want to pray. Could I go into the living room for a moment?"

"Of course. Go ahead. But don't take too long."

Elder Thomas looked at his companion. "Come with me," he said, and the two walked to the living room. Elder Thomas wanted to include poor Frau Stoltz, who needed the prayer too, and Peter, who looked so desperate. But there were things he needed to say to the Lord—things he didn't want them to hear.

So the elders knelt together, and Elder Thomas prayed. "Father in Heaven," he said, "I'm scared. I'm not big enough for this." And then he explained that the Stoltzes were honest and good, that they were worthy of such a blessing. "Please, Father, don't let my weakness stand in their way. Trust in Frau Stoltz's faith more than in mine or Elder Sawyer's. She called us here because she believes in our power. But our power is thy power, Lord, and we are nothing without it."

Elder Thomas's voice came close to pinching off. "I've never been asked to do anything so important as this, Lord. I trust in thee to put the right words in my mouth—that I may speak thy words, not mine."

When Elder Thomas got up from his knees, he was feeling

better, but he was still scared. He looked at Elder Sawyer. "It'll be all right," Elder Sawyer said, but Elder Thomas seemed to see there a reflection of himself—someone young and nervous, not an Alma or a Parley Pratt.

Elder Thomas wiped the tears from his cheeks. He took a breath. He wanted to walk back into that bedroom with some confidence, but his thoughts were running fast. What if he blessed her to live but she died? What would Herr Stoltz say? What if he put his hands on her head and didn't know what to say?

"You anoint her, okay?" Elder Thomas told his companion. "Just do it in English."

When the two returned to Anna's bedroom, Elder Thomas nodded to Frau Stoltz to assure her, but he could feel his hands shake as he handed the vial of oil to Elder Sawyer.

"What's Anna's full name?" he asked Frau Stoltz.

"Anna Eleanore Stoltz." Frau Stoltz was grasping her hands together, her fingers tightly laced. "What should I do?"

"You and Peter just stand here close. Listen to the blessing. Pray with us. Add your faith to ours."

Peter nodded and stepped close. His eyes were wide, almost frantic.

Elder Thomas touched his companion's shoulder, and Elder Sawyer stepped forward. He leaned over and let a little drop of oil fall onto Anna's forehead, at the hairline, and then he turned and handed the bottle and the lid to Elder Thomas. It all seemed rather awkward, but Elder Sawyer did say the prayer all right. And then Elder Thomas stepped closer to join him.

Anna's bed was low, and the elders had to bend down and reach rather far to place their hands on her head. Elder Thomas felt the heat in her head, heard her take a longer breath, as if in response to the touch. Then he felt something else. As he shut his eyes, he felt his chest swell and fill with calm. All the shaking stopped—and he knew.

The words were easy. He sealed the anointing and then he

said, "Anna, you have important reasons to stay upon this earth. We command you in the name of the Lord to be restored to your full health and well-being. Return to us and be healed."

Later, he would try to remember what he had said, but what he would remember more than anything was the feeling that had come over him: the overwhelming love he felt for the Lord, for Anna and her family, and the light that seemed to fill him up.

When he ended the prayer, he turned to Frau Stoltz, who was crying audibly. She grasped Elder Thomas around the shoulders and pressed her head against his chest. "Will it be so?" she said. "Can it really happen this way?"

And instantly Elder Thomas felt the first doubt. A moment before, he hadn't questioned at all—he had known. But Frau Stoltz seemed unsure, and when he looked at Anna she seemed unchanged. Her breathing was imperceptible. She seemed gone already, the same as when the elders had entered the room.

It was Elder Sawyer who said, "She is fine. I know it."

That was the best Elder Sawyer could do with his German, but Elder Thomas felt another surge of confidence. He patted Frau Stoltz on the shoulder and said, "Trust in the Lord." But he couldn't bring himself to use the strong words he had used in the blessing, and he wondered why.

As the elders left the room and turned down the hall, they could see into the kitchen where Herr Stoltz was sitting at the table. When he heard the elders coming, he looked up. "This was my wife's desire," he said. "I want you to leave now and not come back." He seemed hostile, his voice brittle with anger.

And it was that voice that Elder Thomas remembered as he and Elder Sawyer bicycled back to their apartment. He had seen nothing but light for that minute or so during the blessing, but now he felt the darkness in Herr Stoltz's angry eyes, and the desperation in Frau Stoltz's.

It was a hard morning, but Elder Sawyer kept reassuring

Elder Thomas. The Spirit had told him the words were right—
Anna was going to recover. Elder Thomas envied Elder
Sawyer's faith. He tried to be as strong. But he was already trying to think how he could console the Stoltzes, explain what
had happened if the blessing wasn't granted. And that only led
to the worst thought of all: a world without Anna.

When would he know how all this had come out? If she
died, would the Stoltzes let him know? Elder Thomas was not
patient about such things, and all morning he was tempted to
bike back and at least ask whether anything had changed. But
instead, the elders put in their usual study time, and then they
went out to knock on doors. Elder Thomas had the feeling that
he had better work hard, keep doing his duty. He wanted—
needed—a blessing today, and he had to be worthy.

He was preoccupied during the tracting hours. He stayed
within himself and kept asking questions. What will I say to
Frau Stoltz? To Peter? What will happen to Herr Stoltz? He
tried to picture Anna's recovery, the joy that would bring, but
he had to force himself to think of it. His worries had taken
over. At some point during the morning, he even allowed himself to ask whether he believed in blessings, whether he even
had a real testimony of the gospel.

A cool gray mist was hanging over the city that March
morning. Elder Thomas felt it, the grayness pushing its way
into his spirit. By eleven-thirty, instead of twelve, he was saying, "Elder, why don't we head home and get some lunch?"

"Should we stop by the Stoltz's?" Elder Sawyer asked.

"You heard Herr Stoltz. He doesn't want us to do that."

"How are we going to know?"

Elder Thomas shook his head. "Maybe Frau Stoltz will send
Peter again—if there's good news. If things don't go well, I'm
not sure we'll hear from them."

"Don't say that, Mit. She's getting better."

"I know. I just . . ." Elder Thomas didn't know what to say.

But he didn't think making a lot of claims was going to help. He had to be ready for whatever happened.

As the missionaries coasted to a stop at their apartment, Elder Thomas saw a man standing near the front door. His first thought was that the Gestapo had returned. But then he recognized that barrel chest, those thick arms and legs. It was Herr Stoltz.

At the same time, Elder Thomas saw the stiffness, the grave look on Herr Stoltz's face. Elder Thomas hated to think what he was about to hear. The idea crossed his mind that Herr Stoltz was there to curse them, to tell them that their blessing had only given his wife false hope before the end.

Elder Thomas stepped off his bike and hoisted it over the curb. Then he set it down and walked straight to Herr Stoltz. It was only when he got close that he saw the calm in the man's face. "How is she?" Elder Thomas finally dared to ask.

"I came to tell you," Herr Stoltz said. "After you left—only a short time after—the fever left her. She is getting better. She is sitting up now. She had a little to eat."

All the agony suddenly released in Elder Thomas, and a sob broke from his chest. "Thank God," he said, forgetting to speak German. Elder Sawyer came up behind him and put his arm around his companion's shoulder. "She's all right," Elder Thomas told him, feeling something much more powerful than he had expected.

Herr Stoltz didn't speak for a long time, but when Elder Thomas had gotten out his handkerchief and had managed to clear his own eyes enough to see again, he saw that tears were in Herr Stoltz's eyes, too.

"I don't know what this means," Herr Stoltz said. "I cannot say for sure that your blessing made any difference. It might have happened anyway." But these were only his words. His voice was completely changed. He sounded humbled.

"Herr Stoltz, I am never very sure about such things myself," Elder Thomas said. "But I want you to know this:

When I put my hands on her head, the Lord filled me with truth. I felt it. I knew she was all right."

"It's that simple for you?"

Elder Thomas wanted to say yes, but he told the truth. "No. After I left your house, I doubted myself. I thought maybe I had only felt what I wanted to feel. I've been worried all morning."

"So which is it?"

"The blessing was a miracle, Herr Stoltz. I'm sure it was. Believe that, and don't let my weakness cause you to doubt."

Herr Stoltz ran his hand across his cheek and quickly flicked away the tears that had dropped onto his face. "Bruder Thomas, you are a remarkable young man," he said. "You trust. You believe. But you don't lie to me. You didn't have to tell me that you doubted yourself."

"I wish I hadn't. I hope I can get to the point where I don't do that."

"Perhaps. But your honesty means much to me. It gives me reason to trust you. It makes me think you really did feel something from God."

"I did, Herr Stoltz."

"I would like to believe in miracles, Bruder Thomas. I can't say that I do. But I am thankful to you. And I'm thankful to God . . . or fate . . . or whatever brought my dear Anna back. And I'm sorry for the way I treated you at my house."

"You were afraid," Elder Thomas said.

"Yes. I was." But he had said all he could say. The tears were streaming down both his cheeks. Elder Thomas wanted to wrap his arms around the man, but Herr Stoltz was still a little too formal for that. And so Elder Thomas wiped his own eyes again and allowed the silence.

Finally, Herr Stoltz said, "Anna wants you to come back. She wants to thank you."

"Of course. Should we wait until—"

"Come now, if you can. It would mean very much to her."

"Yes. We can come."

"I'll take the streetcar back. You go ahead on your bicycles. You will get there before I do."

"We'll go with you on the streetcar, if you like."

"No. I need the time. I need to think. I haven't felt this good inside for a long time. I want to enjoy that."

Elder Thomas understood. He turned to his companion. "Do you want to have lunch first, or should we go now?"

But Elder Sawyer must have known there was only one answer to that question. His eyes were wet, too, but he was smiling. "Let's just go," he said.

"I'm sure my wife will feed you," Herr Stoltz said. "She'll want to feed you every day from now on."

Elder Thomas thought he knew what that meant, but he decided not to ask. All that would take care of itself.

Herr Stoltz seemed to see the question in his eyes, however, and he answered. "I regret what I told you before. You may come to us. I care not what the Gestapo has to say about that."

"Good. We want to keep teaching you. And we would like you to come to church."

"Yes. I thought about that on the way over here. I want to attend your church—at least once."

Elder Thomas smiled. He had more than one visit in mind. "Good," he said again. "We'll work all that out. We'll see you at your house." He shook Herr Stoltz's hand, and he felt the man pressing back, offering as much affection as he knew how to give.

The elders began to walk away when Herr Stoltz said, "Just a moment. Could you do something for me?"

"Of course."

"Could you say a prayer? I want to be grateful, and yet I'm not sure how I'll feel about all this in the future. It would be more truthful if you said it for me."

And so the three walked into the courtyard, behind the

house, where they could be alone, and Elder Thomas prayed. He thanked the Lord for the blessing, and he asked a blessing on Herr Stoltz, too, called him 'Bruder' for the first time. "Let him feel thy Spirit," Elder Thomas said. "Let him know the truth of what happened today—and the truth of the restored gospel."

Herr Stoltz didn't say "Amen," but he shook Elder Thomas's hand again, grasping it even tighter than before.

The elders didn't ride hard on the way to the Stoltz's. They were feeling more thankful than excited, and so they enjoyed the time to talk. They compared their feelings, the sure word they had received, and Elder Thomas chastised himself a little for the concerns he had expressed afterward. "I know we have the same priesthood as the apostles do," Elder Thomas said. "But it's hard to picture the Lord paying attention to guys like us."

"Hey, if I had given the blessing, I would have felt the same way," Elder Sawyer said. "But I heard you, and it was like this whole new voice, like some authority coming from you that I couldn't have imagined before. I *knew* that you knew."

It was all very difficult for Elder Thomas to imagine about himself, and he knew that he would probably doubt again. Still, he would never be exactly the same person. His faith had moved up a notch, and there wasn't any going back from that.

When the elders knocked on the Stoltz's door, Frau Stoltz was the one who answered. She grabbed Elder Thomas immediately, and she clung to him and cried. Elder Thomas thought she was going to soak his shirt before she was finished, but he was crying again himself. He had never thought himself capable of this much emotion.

Peter was still there, too, and like his father, he didn't intend to embrace the elders. But Elder Thomas took him in his arms anyway, and Peter didn't seem to mind. "Thank you," he kept whispering. "Thank you, Bruder Thomas."

Elder Thomas patted him on the back and told him, "Don't thank me. I didn't do it." But Peter kept repeating the words.

And then Frau Stoltz motioned for the elders to follow her, and they walked to Anna's bedroom again. She was sitting up, with two big pillows behind her. She still looked white and delicate. Elder Thomas stepped close and reached out to shake her hand. She took his hand, but she kept it, held it. And Elder Thomas saw something new. Her eyes were alive, but they were quieter than before. "Thank you," she said.

"It's all right. We only—"

"I heard your voice. I was very far down. But I heard you call me back."

"Really? I didn't think you even knew we were here."

"I didn't know. I was leaving. I felt comfortable. I wanted to go, and I was moving toward something good. And then I heard your voice. I knew I had to come back."

"That's . . ." But Elder Thomas had no idea what to say. "That's good," he finally offered, feeling stupid for not saying something more meaningful.

"I feel different," Anna said. "I'm not the same person."

"It's all right," her mother said. "It's not a bad change."

"I know," was all Anna said. She was looking up at Elder Thomas, and he saw something there that embarrassed him. She was still holding his hand, and finally he thought to pull it away.

9

Bobbi hesitated outside Professor Stinson's office and almost walked away. But she told herself she was being silly, and she tapped on his door. "Yes? Come in," she heard him call, and she couldn't help smiling. There was something brash in calling out that way, in not bothering to come to the door.

She opened the door about half way and looked in. "I just wanted to ask a quick question, Professor Stinson."

He was seated at his desk, but he let his chair swivel around, and he was already smiling, as though pleased to have someone—or maybe Bobbi—stop by. "Come in. Sit down."

"Oh, I'm not staying that long," Bobbi said. She stepped into the room, but she kept her hand on the doorknob. She had been in the office once before, but again she was amazed by the chaos. Books and papers were stacked everywhere—or perhaps *dropped* was more accurate. A dusty basketball was lying in the same corner where it had been before, and a picture of Henry David Thoreau was propped on his desk, leaning against a wall, still not hung. Next to it was a hotplate with a coffeepot perched on top, and the air was full of the smell of coffee. "I'm working on my paper, and I couldn't remember what you said about foot-note style," Bobbi said. "Is Turabian all right?"

Professor Stinson laughed and tossed his hands in the air.

"I don't care. Just stick something down there. I never check the footnotes anyway."

"Oh. Some professors are very—"

"I know. I always got my footnotes wrong in grad school. And some of my profs made a big thing of it. But as long as I wrote something brilliant, they forgave me." He laughed again with a little boy's kind of elation, his voice putting like a motor. "And I've got to admit, I was *always* brilliant."

"You went to Columbia, didn't you?"

"For grad school, yes. Amherst, undergrad. And my dad's a professor at Yale. You're looking at a thoroughbred—good genes, good training. The only thing I lack is demeanor."

"And footnotes," Bobbi said.

That set off another surge of laughter, which delighted Bobbi, but she was hardly prepared when Professor Stinson stood up, thrust his hands into his pockets, and said, "Bobbi, you are absolutely wonderful. Do you know that?"

Bobbi felt her face turn hot. She couldn't think of a thing to say.

"I mean it. You're twice as bright as anyone in *any* of my classes, and you're always right with me. Don't you see me directing my lectures to you? Sometimes I forget anyone else is there."

Bobbi had certainly noticed, and it sometimes made her uncomfortable, but she kept the eye contact because she loved the amazing range of emotions in his subtle green eyes, and she liked to watch for his smile, lurking and then bursting out with joy in response to a comment—more often than not his own. He was the youngest professor Bobbi had taken a class from, and even though he wasn't exactly handsome, she found him—when she admitted the truth to herself—disturbingly attractive. She also knew, just on the edge of her consciousness, that the question about footnotes was more an excuse than a reason for stopping by.

"What are you going to do, Bobbi? And don't tell me you

want to teach high school. You need to teach at a college. It's the only life for someone who likes to think." He motioned at a chair in the corner. "Sit down."

Bobbi did sit, even though she had told herself she wouldn't stay long. "I'm not sure what I'll do," she said.

Professor Stinson sat in his desk chair again. He had already taken off his tweed coat and tossed it onto a radiator near his desk, and he had undone his tie and loosened the clasps on his suspenders so they looped loosely on his chest. Bobbi could see some muscles under his white shirt; apparently he hadn't spent all his life reading and thinking.

"I saw you showing off your new diamond ring the other day," he said. "It's big as a baseball."

"I wasn't showing it off. Some girls wanted to see it."

"Well, in any case, I suppose you're getting married before long. But I hope you don't drop your studies when you do."

"All that's a little unclear right now," Bobbi said, "but I'm not getting married right away."

"I would think not. You're awfully young." He exaggerated the words and let his eyebrows rise, as though shocked.

"Not really. My grandmother had two children by the time she was my age."

"That is such a Mormon response," he said, but with a tone of affection more than criticism.

Bobbi used it, however, as a chance to ask something she had wondered about. "What's it like to come from the East and live here—with all us Mormons?"

"Well, I'll tell you." He let his head roll back, ran his fingers through his hair, and then looked at the ceiling as he thought. "My first year—three years ago—I was baffled. If I'd taken a job on some South Pacific island, I couldn't have been more confused by the culture. But I like it here now. There are things I don't like, but on balance, it's a good place."

"What don't you like?"

He answered without hesitation. "There's no curiosity in

Mormons. They've got all the truth they want. And they're suspicious of any fellow who's been transported across state lines from one of Satan's universities."

Bobbi laughed. She thought of her dad's admonitions about the godless doctrines she would have to discern and reject—especially from non-Mormon professors. "I've suspected all along that you're a devil in disguise," she said.

The words were out of her mouth before she realized how flirtatious they sounded. And she saw his response. He glowed with pleasure. It was time for her to leave. She stood up.

"Wait. Wait. Where are you going?"

"Oh, I just—"

"Finish your question. You only asked me what I don't like."

"All right." She sat down again. "What do you like?"

"The goodness." He nodded firmly. "I'm serious. Mormons are good people. My parents are Episcopalians. They go to church with nice people, well-educated and impeccably groomed, and they carry on a reserved sort of comradeship with them. But Mormons roll up their sleeves and turn religion into irrigation ditches and a side of beef for a needy family."

"My mother's response to any problem is to take in a meal. It doesn't matter whether a family has had a death or a birth or the son has been thrown in jail—she shows up with food."

"With apple pie. Right?"

"She's actually a lemon meringue specialist."

Professor Stinson grinned. "Wallace Stegner was still here the first year I came. He used to tell a great story about J. Golden Kimball. Did you ever meet him?"

"He spoke at our stake conference once—and ate dinner at our house."

"Really? Did he get some of that lemon meringue pie?"

"He certainly did."

"Did he swear?"

"No. We were all disappointed about that."

"I wish I had met him. Wallace made him sound like someone

I'd love. The story goes that old J. Golden blessed a young man and prophesied that if he would go on a mission the Lord would provide him, when he returned, with four good mules. Well, the boy served his mission, came home, and found no mules. He wasn't one to complain, but he mentioned the discrepancy to Brother Kimball. So J. Golden gave the young man four fine mules of his own—and that didn't exactly please his wife. But Golden told her—and Wallace always imitated him with a high, squeaky voice—'Just never mind about that. If the Lord won't keep his damn fool promises, then I will.'" Professor Stinson grinned. "Now that, to me, is Mormonism."

Bobbi enjoyed the story, but she didn't like the simplistic summary. "That's only part of who we are," she said.

"Tell me what you mean. I'm really interested to know."

"Well . . . I know we're practical. We've had to survive a lot of things. But there's a profound theology behind everything we do."

"Actually, I've read a good deal about that."

"Then you know that learning is important to us—even if we are suspicious of irreverent fellows like yourself." She smiled at him. "When your goal is to become like God, you know that you have to understand *everything*."

"But tell the whole truth," Professor Stinson said. "You don't want to be *like* God. You want to *be* gods."

"People misunderstand that. They think we're trying—"

"Hey, I love it. It's the most audacious belief in all of Christendom. It's downright impertinent."

"No. That's not true. It's a very humbling idea—if you think about it the right way. We're not trying to put ourselves before God. We're trying to reach our full capability."

He nodded, and he seemed to take the idea seriously. Bobbi loved the thoughtful respect that came into his eyes. Professor Stinson's feathery hair was beyond control, and his hands were constantly in motion, as if they had a will of their own. But amid all that wildness, Bobbi saw so much in his eyes—warmth, irony, fun, and genuine interest in almost every-thing, including her. When it came to impertinence, the man could point no fingers, but just when Bobbi would conclude that he was insufferably arrogant, she would discover again the fairness and kindness in those gentle eyes.

"That's fascinating to think about," he said. "I wonder what kind of god I would make?" He laughed, but then he added, "I do like this eternal progress thing Mormons believe in. It makes heaven sound like an interesting place. I've always thought of heaven as entirely too *restful* to suit my tastes. But if I had a whole eternity to keep discovering things—with a mind that could handle it—that would be appealing."

"Then why are you making fun of it?"

"I'm not."

"You sound facetious. Don't you believe in a life after death?"

Professor Stinson leaned forward in his chair and put his elbows on his knees. "I don't know, Bobbi. It seems unlikely to me. But I'm open to the possibility."

"Do you ever go to church?" Bobbi thought she was being bold, but he didn't seem to mind the personal questions.

"I haven't for a long time. But preachers always want to give me answers. And I like questions much more than I like answers." His sneaky smile appeared. "That's the real devil in me, Bobbi."

Bobbi was suddenly self-conscious about the way he was looking at her. "Well, I'm glad you warned me," she said, and she decided to leave. Soon.

"You have a taste for questions yourself. Where did you get that?"

"I don't know." But it crossed her mind that she did know. Something about her father's certitude had always elicited from her a subtle sort of skepticism. She didn't rebel or deny; she simply wondered, *How can you be so sure?*

"Well, I think you're remarkable. I don't know where you

came from. It's hard to believe you're home grown. And your father is a stake president, isn't he?"

"How did you know that?"

Suddenly he was the one blushing. "Oh. Well . . . I talked to one of the other professors about you. He lives out in Sugar House—knows all about your family."

Bobbi felt certain she should leave now. There was nothing exactly wrong with his talking about her, but his embarrassment seemed to imply something that she didn't know how to deal with.

"Tell me about your fiancé," Professor Stinson said. "Is he worthy of you?"

"I think most people would ask the question the other way around," Bobbi said. "He's very . . ." But Bobbi couldn't think what to say.

"Very what? Handsome? Rich? Righteous?"

He was all those things, and yet Bobbi heard the irony in her professor's voice. "He's good. He's . . . very kind to me."

Professor Stinson rolled his chair back a little and extended his legs, and then he crossed his arms over his chest. Bobbi could see that the fabric over his elbows had worn thin. "He's in law school, isn't he?"

"Yes." But once again, she didn't know how he would know that. She looked past him, through a smudged and dusty window. Outside, students were moving in a steady stream around and across the University Circle. Eleven o'clock classes had just ended, and lots of people were heading toward the union. Bobbi realized she was supposed to meet Phil across the street at the University Inn for lunch in just a few minutes. She suddenly felt guilty.

"He must be someone very special. You wouldn't fall for just anyone. Does he love ideas as much as you do?"

That seemed almost purposeful, as though he knew very well what sort of man Phil was. "We find a lot to talk about,"

Bobbi said, but the words sounded feeble. She stood up. "Well, anyway, thanks for your time, Dr. Stinson, and—"

"Don't call me that."

"What?"

"It seems so silly. And formal. Just call me David."

"No. I . . . couldn't." She stepped to the door. "Anyway, thank you."

He got up. "Let me say just one more thing. And you take it however you want."

"Is it about footnotes?"

He laughed in a burst. "No. Not footnotes. I guess it's about your getting married, but it's more about you getting your Ph.D. and becoming an English professor."

"I doubt I would ever do that."

"I know. But I want you to think about it." He tucked his hands into his pockets. Then he waited until she looked at him. "I tell most of these students that Thoreau sat by Walden Pond for a year, and they say, 'What in the world for?' But you're not like that. I watch your eyes, and I can't believe someone so alive is sitting in front of me, just drinking all this stuff in. It would be a tragedy for you to hide yourself away in a house—with a dozen children to raise and no time to think and read."

But this angered Bobbi—maybe partly because it also pleased her so much. "I don't think there's anything finer in life than being a mother," she said.

"Actually, I agree. But what I'm saying is that there are other things, too. I don't know about you, but I want to see everything there is to see on this planet, feel every emotion, think every thought. I want to chew up life and swallow it—and then lick all the good juices off my lips." He smiled at his own image. "I don't think being a mother should mean that you have to cut yourself off from life."

"I would never do that."

"Maybe not, but . . . well, I've said enough. I saw you with your boyfriend one day, and I got some sort of impression. But that's none of my business."

"What impression?"

"No, really. I've said enough. The truth is, I was probably just jealous."

And now Bobbi felt the heat start in her face and spread. She had to get out of there. "Thanks for your time," she said again, quickly and awkwardly, and she slipped out the door, down the hallway, and out of the Liberal Arts Building. She told herself that he was the devil, indeed, and that he had been entirely improper to say such things. She also vowed not to watch him in class the way she had, not to engage his eyes so often.

That night Bobbi went to MIA. All too often lately she had missed her Gleaners' class. But even with her paper due the next morning, she decided to go. Sister Holmes had talked to her at church. "Too many of you older girls aren't coming," she had said, "and the younger ones need your example. More than anyone, as the president's daughter, you need to show that you don't think you're too good for Gleaners just because you're out of high school."

Bobbi never liked that kind of pressure, but she did respond—although she purposely chose to arrive late enough to miss opening exercises. Normally, there were a couple of short talks, and often one of the Beehive girls played a piano solo or sang. She decided she could live without all that.

In class Sister Holmes talked about prayer, something Bobbi cared very deeply about, but the woman used every cliché. She explained that God always answered prayers; sometimes he answered yes, and sometimes no. Bobbi had wondered all her life about that. How could she identify an answer if "nothing" was as much a response as "something" was? She considered asking about that, even offering some of her own thoughts, but she was certain Sister Holmes wouldn't appreciate that sort of discussion.

So Bobbi hardly opened her mouth, and her mind

wandered. She tried not to think about Professor Stinson and what he had said about Mormons and curiosity, but all Sister Holmes' simple answers—with no challenges from the class—kept bringing the thought back. Toward the end, however, Bobbi's friend Lorene Paulson told a little story. She had needed special help in a speech class. She had always been terrified to get up in front of groups, but she had prayed just before standing up, and a calm had come over her. She had given the best talk of her life.

And Bobbi believed that—believed in Lorene's faith, and in God's willingness to help. And then, as always, Bobbi felt guilty. She had sat through this whole lesson questioning and doubting, offering nothing in the way of support or testimony. She knew she ought to do that now, but she couldn't muster the spirit. And that made her feel even worse.

When class ended, Bobbi tried to slip away. She really did need to get home so she could type up the final version of her paper. But as Bobbi stepped toward the door, Sister Holmes said, "Bobbi, just a second." All the other girls filed out, and each said good-bye to Bobbi as though they recognized they owed her some special respect—because of her age, and probably because of her family.

"How are you doing?" Sister Holmes asked. She was folding up a lace tablecloth. The room was nothing more than a cubicle in the basement of the ward house, but Sister Holmes had hung a picture of Christ on the wall and decorated the table with an arrangement of tulips, red and yellow. At one point in her lesson, she had suddenly pulled out one of the tulips, cast it onto the floor, and stamped on it. Sister Holmes was a delicate woman who dressed in gabardine suits and always wore a hat and gloves. Her sudden movement, the severity of it, had shocked the girls. Doris Christiansen, one of the younger girls, had gasped out loud and then giggled at her own response.

"When you forget your prayers," Sister Holmes had said

dramatically, "that is what you do to God. You take his gift—
the sweet, wonderful opportunity to communicate with him—
and you *crush* it. If a young man brought you a flower, would
you step on it? I don't think so. You would cherish it. But your
Father in Heaven offers you, daily, something far more pre-
cious, and all too often young women throw his gift away.
Don't ever do it again. Say your prayers *every* single day."

Bobbi did pray every day—and often with more than a
sense of duty. But something in the little demonstration seemed
unnecessarily hard on the girls who forgot at times.

"I'm fine," Bobbi was saying now. "Just busy. I've got a paper
due tomorrow."

"I suppose this time of year, you start looking forward to
summer."

"I do. But I like college. After I work a few weeks in the
summer, I'm usually ready to go back to school." Bobbi
laughed. She wanted to be congenial, but she also wanted to
leave.

"Where do you work?"

"At a candy shop. All I do is box chocolates all day. It's kind
of boring."

Sister Holmes nodded, rather stiffly. "Is your wedding this
summer?"

Bobbi picked up something in Sister Holmes' voice, a hint
of nervousness. It wasn't much of a stretch to think that
President Thomas—or even Sister Thomas—had asked Sister
Holmes to explain the advantages of a short engagement.

"We haven't set a date," Bobbi said, and she tried to leave it
at that. "But Phil still has two years of law school to go, and I
have two years of college."

"There are great temptations during an engagement, Bobbi.
Aren't you worried about that?" Sister Holmes set the tablecloth next to the vase of tulips. She stood with her hands at her
sides and her neck very straight.

"Sister Holmes, don't worry about that. Phil is very respectful.

We've never done anything . . . you know . . . even slightly wrong."

"Sometimes, when they least expect it, young people think it's all right to do a little necking, since they're engaged and all, and then . . . mistakes can happen."

"I know. We're careful about that." Bobbi wanted to tell her that her real worry was that she couldn't work up any excitement about sharing her bed with this man—that the thought of it made her more nervous than aroused.

"Still, familiarity advances easily—and almost without notice. I think a wise course is to marry reasonably soon, once a couple has settled on marriage." She patted her hair, but it needed no fixing; it was piled in stiff black rolls on the top of her head.

"Well, thank you, Sister Holmes. That's something we need to think about."

"Bobbi, I don't mean to pry. I just know how difficult it is to avoid temptation."

And suddenly Bobbi couldn't resist. "Did you and Brother Holmes find that a tempting time, Sister Holmes?"

"Oh, no. I didn't mean that. We never . . . not at all." The woman's face had turned white, not red.

"But you were *terribly* in love, weren't you?" Bobbi thought of Brother Holmes, who tied his ties much too short and always looked a little dismayed, as though he had wandered into reality accidentally.

"Oh, yes. We were very much in love."

"How did you know—when you first fell in love?" Bobbi was a little more serious about this question.

"Well . . ." Sister Holmes relaxed a little. She touched the table with her fingertips. "When I met Brother Holmes, I felt very safe with him. Gerald wasn't the best looking boy I'd dated, and he's not dashing and romantic, but I knew I could rely on him. He would take me to the temple, and he would be responsible to me and our children."

"Did you feel excited about him?"

"Well, yes. I did." She thought for a moment. "But not the way a young girl gets all moony-eyed about a movie star. I knew Gerald wouldn't be impulsive or cross or cruel, and I knew he would hold down a good job. That may not sound romantic, but I have girlfriends who married cute boys who turned out to be just that—boys. One of my friends is divorced now, and it just breaks my heart when I see her."

Bobbi nodded. She was sorry she had goaded Sister Holmes. She really was a good woman.

"Bobbi, the novels young people read—and the movies— can give a girl the wrong idea. Marriage is not all hearts and flowers. It's mostly learning to work together as a team."

Bobbi nodded again. But the description sounded too much like two workhorses pulling a heavy wagon. "Well," she said, "I need to get home." She reached down and pulled one of the red tulips from the vase. "May I have this?" she said.

"Of course."

Bobbi was almost to the door when Sister Holmes said, "Bobbi, it is hearts and flowers, too. I sometimes wish Gerald were one to give me flowers, or to be a little more romantic. I'm just saying that it isn't *all* about that."

"I know. I understand."

Bobbi left. But out on the street, with the sun down and the fertile smells of spring in the air, she felt an uncomfortable absence of life within her. For a moment, she allowed herself to think of Professor Stinson. She ran his words through her head: "Bobbi, you are absolutely wonderful." But she couldn't dwell on that. She sniffed the tulip in her hand, and then she breathed in the night air. Curiosity was fine—and so were powerful feelings—but Professor Stinson made too much of all that. There were more important things. Still, she sniffed the flower again, and she thought of Brother Holmes. And suddenly she shuddered.

I 0

Elder Thomas, dressed in white, was standing near the swimming pool. The little congregation was sitting on wooden
chairs, and there on the front row was Elder Sawyer, next to
Peter, both of them in white shirts and pants, and then Anna
and her mother, in white dresses.

Brother Stoltz was next to his wife, but he was wearing a
dark suit. He looked thoughtful. Elder Thomas hoped that
Brother Stoltz felt a little left out. Maybe that would work as
an incentive for him to take the same step soon.

The smell of the old bathhouse, pungent with soap and the
minty oils from the sauna, was not exactly what Elder Thomas
would have preferred, but the place was clean, and after the
business day had ended, it was the best facility in town for a
baptism. Brother Meis was there with his wife and two young
children and a few of the other members from the Frankfurt
Branch: Sister Dittmar and Sister Holzmeier, widows and
friends; young brother Fetterman, the only returned missionary in the branch; Brother and Sister Müller, who had moved
to Frankfurt from eastern Germany, where the largest Church
branches were; and Brother Richter, an older man who was
counselor in the branch presidency along with Brother Müller.
Elder Thomas had the only hymn book in the room, so he had

chosen an opening hymn that everyone knew: "I Need Thee Every Hour."

In the confines of the bathhouse, the music swelled, even without accompaniment, like a grand choir. *"Ich brauch Dich, O Ich brauch Dich, Jesus, ja Ich brauch Dich."* Elder Thomas swung his arm mechanically. He had some music training, but he was never quite confident that he knew what he was doing when he led the singing. He continued to watch Brother Stoltz, who wasn't singing with the others but was looking at the concrete floor.

Brother Meis gave what was supposed to be a short talk on the ordinance of baptism—but which turned out to be a long dissertation. As usual, he had something to say about the millennial reign that would be ushered in soon. Elder Thomas was sitting in a chair near the edge of the pool, in front of the others, and he tried not to squirm, but this was the sort of thing that bothered Brother Stoltz. He could almost believe in the Church until someone got off on subjects that seemed a little too mystical for his practical mind.

The sermon ended, eventually, and then Elder Thomas added a few words about the gift of the Holy Ghost. He told the Stoltzes, "I know that you have felt the power of the Holy Ghost. Anna, on the day you were healed of your illness, the Spirit told you that the power of the Priesthood was real. All of you saw the miracle and felt the Lord's power."

Sister Stoltz nodded her confirmation, and so did Peter. Anna's eyes had been down, but now they came up, and she smiled, ever so slightly. Her eyes were suddenly the brightest color in the drab room. The thought occurred to Elder Thomas that he had never in his life seen anything so beautiful as this scene—these people he loved, dressed in white.

"Brother Stoltz," Elder Thomas said, "I know that you too have felt the Spirit. You are right to wait for your baptism until you feel completely prepared, but I have seen tears in your eyes. I have seen how moved you have been by the change that has taken place in your family—and the change in your-self."

Brother Stoltz leaned back in his chair, and he looked at Elder Thomas. He gave no sign that he agreed, but his look was warm and friendly, as it had been since the day that Anna had been healed. Since that day, Elder Thomas and Elder Sawyer had been in the Stoltz home almost every day. They had designed discussions to answer Brother Stoltz's many questions. Anna had questions herself, but her attitude had changed. She no longer challenged the missionaries; she was trying to understand.

Brother Stoltz responded well to certain concepts. The plan of salvation made sense to him. The justice of the plan, the way it avoided the harshness of the hell that was taught by most Christian religions, rang true to him. What was much harder for him to believe was that God himself had visited Joseph Smith.

The elders had hoped to baptize the entire family, and they had been concentrating on getting Brother Stoltz ready. Then Elder Thomas had received word that he was being transferred. "The truth is," President Wood had told him, "the signs point toward war. Any day now, we may all be evacuating. I need you to do your best in Heidelberg to get those Saints ready to take over for themselves."

Missionaries usually waited for a family to apply for baptism, but when Elder Thomas got his transfer he decided to ask the Stoltzes whether they were ready. Above all, he was afraid he and the other missionaries would receive word that they had to leave, and the Stoltzes would be left unbaptized.

Sister Stoltz was quick to say that she was ready, and so were Peter and Anna. But Brother Stoltz sat quietly for a painfully long time, and then he said, "I want the others to do this. But I can't. Not yet." And that's how things stood now. Brother Stoltz did seem touched by what was happening, but he was going to make his decision his own way, and on his own schedule.

Elder Thomas had had his chance to perform baptisms before, and so he thought it only right that Elder Sawyer have this opportunity. He had suggested that, and the family had politely accepted. But later, Sister Stoltz had found a chance to tell Elder Thomas that "the children" were disappointed. They would like to have Elder Thomas perform the baptism, if possible. "Could Elder Sawyer baptize me, perhaps, and you do the others?"

Elder Thomas had found himself in an awkward position. Peter liked Elder Sawyer, and it was hard to believe that he cared. Or in other words, maybe Sister Stoltz had been embarrassed to say that it was Anna who had made the request. But Elder Sawyer understood.

Elder Thomas finished his little talk, and he asked Brother Meis and Brother Müller to come forward to serve as witnesses. Then he invited Elder Sawyer to lead Sister Stoltz into the waters of baptism. Elder Sawyer walked to the stairs, on the left side of the pool. He looked unsure of himself, his face almost as colorless as his shirt. But he took Sister Stoltz's hand and helped her down the stairs. When he stood a little too close to the center of the pool, Elder Thomas reminded him quietly to step nearer to the end.

Sister Stoltz grasped Elder Sawyer's wrist, just as the two of them had practiced in her living room. Elder Sawyer raised his arm to the square and pronounced her full name—the sound echoing around the room—and then he said the brief prayer. His hand came down, and Sister Stoltz pinched her nose between her fingers as Elder Sawyer lowered her, backward, into the water.

She was under the water only a second, barely submerged, before Elder Sawyer pulled her back up. She came up gently and ran her hands over her face. Then she looked up at Elder Thomas, and that glimpse, that look of satisfaction, meant as much to him as anything he had experienced on his mission. It was that same joy he was feeling as Anna took his hand, and he walked with her down the stairs into the warm water.

He moved Anna into place, pushing gently on her shoulders. Then he raised his arm and pronounced the words. *Anna Eleanore Stoltz. Beauftragt von Jesus Christus, taufe ich dich im Namen des Vaters, und des Sonnes, und des Heiligen Geistes. Amen."*

He placed his hand on her back and then lowered her into the water. She was buoyant, seeming to possess no weight at all. He let the water drift over her, made certain she was all the way under, and then lifted her up. As her face broke the surface, she was already blinking, and her hair had pulled back away from her face. She didn't let go of his arm, even after she was standing. She turned and looked into his face, little rivulets of water still running over her skin, tiny drops clinging to her eyelashes. *"Danke,"* she said.

Everything seemed so pure. Elder Thomas could feel the vibrations of the Spirit, affirming his faith, telling him he was in the right place at the right time, that life had led him to this moment. At the same time, as the two looked into each other's eyes, Elder Thomas felt an admission pass between them. He looked away quickly, pulled his hand back, and stepped away, concerned that others in the room might see what was in his eyes. He walked with Anna, held her hand as she climbed the stairs, but looked away when the water draped her dress tightly over her pretty figure.

And then Peter was there, smiling as though he were about to start some adventure. He climbed quickly down the stairs, continued to smile as Elder Thomas said the prayer, and then bent his knees and leaned backward against Elder Thomas's hand. As he came out of the water, he smiled cheerfully, wiped the water away from his eyes, and then slapped Elder Thomas on the shoulder. "Now I'm a Mormon!" he said.

But, of course, there was more to it. Once all of them had changed their clothes and returned to the pool area, the elders and the branch presidency circled the three new converts, one at a time, and confirmed them members of the Church.

When the meeting was over—after a closing hymn and prayer—Elder Thomas walked to Brother Stoltz. "I hope you feel good about this," he said.

Brother Stoltz shook Elder Thomas's hand. "Oh, yes," he said. "This was very nice. Very moving."

"And soon it will be time for you."

Brother Stoltz looked into Elder Thomas's eyes. "Perhaps. I have no way of judging this. Tonight I wanted very much to believe. But I don't trust emotion. I don't want to make a decision and then later doubt my rashness."

Elder Thomas didn't know the word Brother Stoltz had used. But he understood the idea. "You won't ever do anything in a hurried way," Elder Thomas told him. "I understand that. But keep studying, and keep praying. I want to get word, before long, that you have joined your family in the Church."

"I *will* keep studying, and I certainly will attend church. I like the people in the branch, and I like the feeling there."

Elder Thomas felt something new. Brother Stoltz was making deeper commitments than he had made before. But now others wanted to shake Brother Stoltz's hand, and so Elder Thomas stepped away and spoke to Sister Stoltz. Anna was there too, but she said nothing. Elder Thomas was feeling some embarrassment around her, and he thought she was too.

"Bruder Thomas," Sister Stoltz was saying, "could you and Bruder Sawyer come over. I have *Kuchen* for you. And something small for you to take with you when you leave."

And so the good-byes were delayed a little. After everyone had a turn at welcoming the new members and congratulating them, the elders left with the Stoltzes and rode the streetcar back to their apartment. It was dark outside now, a cold April night, and the evening was getting away. In all the busyness, Elder Thomas still hadn't packed. He was leaving on an early train in the morning. But it didn't matter. He didn't plan to get much sleep that night. He preferred, in this city he had loved so much, not to sleep many of his final hours away.

On the streetcar, Anna and her mother sat in front of the elders, and Peter and his father took the seats behind them. Peter was still excited, and he kept leaning forward to talk to the elders. "You must stay, Bruder Thomas," he said over the noise of the streetcar. "You must tell your mission president this cannot be. Let's call him up. I'll tell him myself."

Peter was only joking, of course, but his father was quick to tell him to be quiet. And Elder Thomas knew why. It was not wise to talk about missions, or to call each other "brother" in public. Religions were suspect these days. Hitler considered any viable organization a rival to his power.

Elder Thomas continued to watch Anna. Her hair, which was tied in a dark-blue ribbon, was still wet and shiny and hanging straight. When she turned a little, he could catch glimpses of her cheeks and the soft skin along her neck and jaw. She was carved so delicately. He wanted to talk to her personally, before he had to leave. But he couldn't do that, absolutely *wouldn't* do that.

By the time the little group reached the apartment building and climbed the stairs, the sun was setting. But inside, the Stoltzes didn't turn the lights on. The living room glowed with the soft light from the windows. Anna, unusually quiet, sat in her usual place, the same as she had during the lessons, at the end of the coffee table, near Elder Thomas. She was sitting straighter tonight, however, and the tinted light made her skin glow. Elder Thomas kept glancing at her, and all too often he caught her glancing at him.

They ate cake and drank herb tea, and they chatted, but now everyone seemed to sense that the joy of their togetherness was ending, that the leave-taking couldn't be put off much longer. Elder Thomas had been through this before in his first city, but he had never felt this loved. This was his family in Germany, the people he cared most about, and he knew that the chances were strong that he would never see them again. Even if the missionaries stayed, the most he could hope for was to see them briefly at a district conference.

"I was wondering," Elder Thomas said, "whether you have a picture of your family that I could take with me."

"Well, now," Sister Stoltz said, "you have guessed my little secret. I told you I had something for you. It's only an amateur photograph, nothing very nice, but I had it framed, and I think it's a nice likeness." She handed him a little package.

"Thank you," Elder Thomas said, and he pulled the wrapping loose. He looked at the picture, and it was a good likeness—especially of Anna. But the problem was, the faces were beginning to swim as Elder Thomas's eyes filled with tears. He looked around and thanked everyone.

A long silence followed. Elder Thomas got out a handkerchief and wiped his eyes. And when he looked up again, he could see that everyone else was also fighting tears, even Brother Stoltz. And poor Peter had begun to sob. "Can't you stay?" he said. "Why do they make you go?"

"Elder Sawyer will be here."

"I know. But why can't you *both* stay?"

But no one answered the question. Elder Thomas glanced at Anna and saw the tears on her cheeks.

Sister Stoltz finally said, "Excuse us, Bruder Thomas. We don't mean to make things more difficult for you. But you are like a son to us now. We were in such a dark time before you came. But you—you and Bruder Mecham and Bruder Sawyer—brought the Lord into our home. And it's what we needed."

"The Lord will still be with you," Elder Thomas said.

"But we want *you*," Peter said, the sobs coming again.

Elder Thomas could hardly stand this anymore. He wished he could think of something lighter, happier, to say.

"Bruder Thomas," Brother Stoltz finally said, "tell me honestly. Won't you be leaving Germany soon?"

"I don't know. We keep hoping this trouble will pass

away—the way it did before—and we won't have to leave. I was called to serve two-and-a-half years, and that's what I want to do."

"Things are different this time," Brother Stoltz said. "Hitler says he wants Danzig returned to the *Reich*. But that's not the real issue. He can swallow all of Poland, and he won't be satisfied. Europe will be drawn into this—all the world, perhaps. Hitler will keep pushing until it happens."

Elder Thomas had been hearing this kind of talk from others lately, but he didn't want to believe it.

"If war begins," Brother Stoltz said, "you could be in danger. Kellerman has not bothered you lately, but during a war, foreigners will be rounded up, I'm certain, and Kellerman will try to find you. Did you register today that you are leaving Frankfurt?"

"Yes."

"By now, he must know. Certainly, he is having you traced. He will make contacts in Heidelberg, I can assure you."

"I've thought of that, Brother Stoltz," Elder Thomas said. "But I don't know what to do. All of the missionaries could be in danger. Our mission president has us on alert. If we get a telegram, we are to leave immediately."

"Where has he told you to go?"

"The Netherlands."

"Yes. That is probably the best, the quickest way out. But you may not have time. Your president should get you out long before the war actually begins. If it were up to me, I would send you home right now."

Elder Sawyer said, "The Lord will look after us—don't worry about that."

Brother Stoltz took a long look at him. "I don't know about that," he said. "Jews are being taken away—more all the time now. And all of them are praying. I don't know what God is up to, if you want to know the truth. But he might have stopped

Hitler long ago, if he had had a mind to, and he hasn't. Look what happened to Bruder Goldfarb."

"It could have been worse," Elder Thomas said weakly.

"Yes. And in a better world, such a thing would never happen."

Brother Goldfarb, according to President Meis, had been roughed up but not severely injured. Elder Thomas had not dared to visit him again, and he wondered whether his spirit hadn't been broken, maybe his health besides.

"Be careful," Sister Stoltz said. "Say, 'Heil Hitler' whether you like to or not. Don't take any chances at all."

"There's something else you should know," Bruder Stoltz said. "I hesitate to bring this up, but if something happens, you would perhaps always wonder, and so it might be better to say something now." Elder Thomas felt a kind of stiffness come over all the Stoltzes. "As you know, Anna was forced to join *Bund Deutscher Mädel.*" Brother Stoltz hesitated. "Now, certain SS men would appear to be . . . pursuing her."

"Pursuing her? What do you mean?"

Herr Stoltz's jaw tightened. "These degraded animals—Himmler's men—are being told to have all the babies they can. With their wives, or with unmarried girls. They search out Germanic-looking girls—blond, healthy young women—and they tell them it is their duty, their glory, to create babies for the *Reich.*"

Elder Thomas was too stunned to respond. Anna was looking down at her hands, which she had gripped together in her lap.

"Anna has protected herself so far. And I *won't* let this happen to her. I'll die first. But that means, one day, we may suddenly be gone—and I don't know where we might go."

"Would you try to get out of the country?"

"There's little chance of that," Brother Stoltz said. "But we would . . . well, let me be completely honest with you. We will not give in to them. And running may not be possible. I fear we could be taken away."

Elder Thomas suddenly felt sick.

"My husband is making the picture too dark," Sister Stoltz was quick to say. "These SS men don't want anyone to know what they are doing. They usually don't push the girls too hard when they resist. At least that's what we have heard. Anna will be able to avoid them. I know it. God will look out for her, just as he did before. You made promises to her, in your blessing, and I believe in those promises."

The silence returned. But after a short time, Sister Stoltz said, "We can't leave each other like this. Let's sing together, and then let's kneel and pray together. Everything is going to be all right. I feel certain of it."

And so they sang hymns together. And then to everyone's surprise, Brother Stoltz said the prayer himself. He asked for a blessing upon Elder Thomas, on Anna, and on all of them. He asked that somehow they could all survive Hitler's evil, that the Church could survive. "Lord, I struggle to believe anything at all," he said. "But please, let those who are good triumph over the evil men who want to rule our world."

When the prayer ended, everyone stood. And they all knew that something very significant had happened. Brother Stoltz had never said the family prayer before, and he had often expressed his doubts about prayer. This was his honest effort to show faith, but it was also his gift to Elder Thomas— to show him that he was trying, that he was making progress.

Elder Thomas knew that, and he walked to Brother Stoltz. He embraced the man, and Brother Stoltz accepted the affection, even wrapped his arms around Elder Thomas. Then Sister Stoltz grabbed Elder Thomas and hugged him for quite some time, patting his back and saying, "Oh, my goodness. This is so heavy for us."

Peter hugged Elder Thomas, too, and cried, and then Anna was next. But Elder Thomas knew he had to be careful. He held his hand out to her, and she clung to it for a couple of extra seconds and then whispered, "*Auf Wiedersehen.*" Tears were streaming down her face.

Elder Thomas nodded and tried to seem as business-like as he could. "Yes." He tried to say good-bye, but his throat had tightened, and he didn't dare speak. He walked to the door. People were saying things, offering good wishes, saying good-bye, but Elder Thomas couldn't get a word out. He took a last look around, nodded to everyone, and caught one last glimpse of Anna. She was leaning against her father, who had taken her under his arm. And in that instant he knew: he was going to get back to her somehow, sometime.

He hurried down the stairs, ahead of his companion, and then on the way home, he rode his bike ahead. He fought back the tears by saying to himself, over and over, "I'll see her again. Somehow, I'll see her again."

Bobbi was sitting across from Phil, a white linen tablecloth between them. "You have to have dessert," Phil was saying. "The rice pudding is the specialty here."

Bobbi knew that. She had eaten at Lamb's Cafe before. She even loved the rice pudding. But she didn't want any tonight. "I just couldn't," she told him.

"I won't take no for an answer." He looked at the waitress, who was waiting with her notepad in one hand and a pencil in the other. "We'll both have the rice pudding," he said.

The waitress scratched the order on her pad, tucked the pencil behind her ear, and walked away. "I don't *want* any pudding," Bobbi said, allowing more of an edge to her voice than she had intended.

"I know. But taste it. And if you don't want it all, I'll finish it. I can never get enough of the stuff."

Bobbi was relieved that he hadn't picked up on the irritation in her voice, and at the same time, she was rather annoyed that he *hadn't* noticed. Still, she let it go.

"Honey, we need to make a decision about our wedding date," Phil said. "You keep saying we'll talk about it, but we don't. Both our mothers want us to tie down a date so they can start to plan."

"I don't see why that's so important. They'll have plenty of time."

"It would just be good to have things settled."

Lamb's was packed, and something about discussing their wedding date in the middle of this crowd seemed ridiculous. Bobbi was sure the couple at the next table was listening to their conversation. Phil always spoke louder than he needed to.

"Here's a suggestion—just something to think about," he said. "What about a Christmas wedding? Maybe get married right after fall-term finals and then have the Christmas break to go somewhere. We could go to a ski lodge—with a fireplace in the room and a furry bear rug on the floor." He smiled and winked.

"I don't ski."

"Hey, who cares about skiing?" Phil laughed, but he stopped rather quickly when Bobbi didn't. "Look, it's just a thought. What do you have in mind? We could sail to the Hawaiian Islands if you would like that better."

"Let's not talk about it here."

"Fine. But just tell me when you *will* talk about it. We've been engaged for a month now, and everyone I talk to wants to know our marriage date. It gets embarrassing."

Now it was Phil's voice that had the edge. Bobbi knew she was making things difficult. "I don't know, Phil. I've been so busy with term papers, I haven't had time to think."

"What's wrong with talking about it tonight? Let's just figure something out."

"I already told you I don't want to get married that soon. Christmas is much sooner than we talked about." The man and wife at the next table glanced at Bobbi. She was embarrassed. Even Phil ducked his head.

The waitress, in her mustard-colored dress and white apron, arrived with the rice pudding. She made a little curtsy out of placing each bowl in front of them. "Thank you," Phil told her, smiling confidently. "I love this stuff."

"Everyone does," the waitress said, obviously pleased with Phil's warm smile. It struck Bobbi all over again how girls must envy her to be engaged to such a classy-looking man. He had on a double-breasted blue blazer with a regimental striped tie. He called it his "sports outfit," since he usually wore suits.

Phil scooped a large spoonful of pudding into his mouth. "Ummm, that's good," he said. The waitress continued to bask in his attention until she realized she had no reason to stay. When she walked away, Phil told Bobbi, "Now give that rice a try."

"I've eaten it before, Phil."

"Hey, not with me. Has some other guy been bringing you down here?" He gave Bobbi a blast of that big smile, as though he knew how well it worked.

Bobbi didn't answer, but she remembered coming here with her dad, sitting at the long counter, looking at herself in the mirrors, feeling grown up to be on a luncheon date with Daddy. She took a mouthful of the pudding and was reminded how much she did like it, especially how much she had liked it then. Still, she pushed the bowl across the table to Phil.

"That's all you're going to eat?"

"I told you, I'm full."

"You eat like a bird." He ate another spoonful and then added, "I guess I'd better not complain. I want you to stay as slim as you are now. I don't want one of those girls who gets married and then puts on fifty pounds the first year."

"I'll try not to be an embarrassment to you."

And this time the irritation was unmistakable. Bobbi saw the little shock of surprise in Phil's eyes. "Hey, honey, I didn't mean anything like that."

"I know," Bobbi said, and once again she wondered what was wrong with her. Why did she say things like that?

After Phil finished both puddings and paid the bill—and left a nice tip for the waitress—he and Bobbi walked up Main

Street to the car. Phil opened the door for her, held it while she got in, and then strode around to his side.

"Phil, I'm sorry I was grumpy with you," she said as he got in the car.

"Oh, no. Not at all. I have no business shoving food at you. It's your own choice whether you want dessert or not."

"You just wanted two bowls yourself," she said, trying to sound friendlier.

"Hey, you got me—dead to rights. I'm a bona fide rice pudding maniac."

She slid closer and tucked her arm through his. "Well, I know how to please you. Now, if only I knew how to cook. The only thing I'm trained to do is correct your grammar."

He laughed, and then he twisted and checked the traffic. Bobbi was glad they were back to small talk. But then Phil said, "You know, Bobbi, you really might want to think about changing your major. Reading Chaucer and Milton may not help you much when it comes to raising a family."

Bobbi was instantly angry. "Oh, you're right about that. There's no value at all in reading books. It fills a housewife's head with a lot of useless ideas."

Phil took the shot with a reflex hunch of the shoulders, and for a time he drove in silence. "I'm sorry, Bobbi," he finally said. "I'm a practical guy. That's just how I think. It's actually good that you're studying the great books. That's something you can give the kids that I can't."

Phil was amazing. Every time Bobbi got close to giving up on him, he did something like that. He was a dear person, so quick to recognize his own mistakes. If only Bobbi could stop reacting and just love him. "It's okay. I need to be more practical. I will be, I'm sure, when I have to worry about lumpy gravy and crying babies."

"You're going to be a wonderful wife, Bobbi. You're going to keep me on my toes."

"I *hope* I'll be a good wife."

"I'm going to keep you on your toes, too—because I'm going to be kissing you all the time."

Bobbi didn't respond for a time. And then she said, "Phil, do you mind if we go home early? I don't feel that well tonight. Maybe that's why I'm being so cranky with you."

"Sure, honey. I was planning to stay up late studying tonight. It's probably better if I get an early start. But one of these first nights we have to talk about our wedding date."

"I know."

Phil took Bobbi home, and she did stand on her toes to kiss him at her front door. Then Phil stepped in long enough to greet Sister Thomas, who was sitting in the living room, reading. As he closed the door, she said to Bobbi, "You're home awfully early for a Friday night."

"I know. I don't feel too well."

"Are you coming down with something?"

"I don't think so. I'm just . . . tired, I guess."

"Well, go to bed early then."

"I will." Bobbi walked to the stairs.

"Bobbi, come here for just a minute first, will you?"

Bobbi stepped into the living room. Her mother had been listening to a record on the phonograph, but it had come to an end, and she hadn't gotten up to change it. Bobbi heard the static and the little click as the needle kept repeating its circle in the same groove. She walked over to start the record over, but Sister Thomas said, "Just turn that off."

Bobbi did, and then she sat down on the couch next to her mom. Sister Thomas placed a marker in her book, and she set the book on an end table that was covered by a pretty lace doily. She dropped her hands to her lap and looked straight ahead, not at Bobbi. "Are you happy?" she asked.

"Sure."

"Are you in love?"

Bobbi almost decided to give the "right" answer, but she

had wanted to talk to her mother about this, and now was probably as good a time as any. "Where's Dad?" she asked.

"Gone to bed, of course. Answer my question."

"I don't know whether I love him or not."

"Are you serious?"

"Mom, I used to think love hit you so hard that you heard bells—and that was that. But that's never happened to me, so I don't know what to think."

Mom looked at Bobbi, and Bobbi wondered what she was thinking. Sister Thomas was forty-seven, four years younger than her husband. Bobbi had heard the story of how Dad, a college senior and returned missionary, had fallen head-over-heels for "Little Bea," a twenty-year-old sophomore, and how Mom had quit college so they could get married after Dad's graduation. But it was hard to picture. Mom was still pretty, with her deep dimples and her lively smile, but she and Dad didn't really fawn over each other; Bobbi wondered whether they ever had.

"Bobbi, why did you tell Phil you would marry him if you aren't sure you're in love?"

"I don't know that I *don't* love him. He's good to me. He's handsome. He has a good future. And all the girls at the U wish they could bump me off and steal him."

"Those sound like impressive qualifications—not love."

"I know. But what can I say? I don't hear any bells."

"How do you feel when he kisses you?"

This was getting into an area that made Bobbi uncomfortable. When Bobbi had been about twelve, she and her mom had had a talk about "personal matters" and "hygiene," and a hint or two had come across about babies, but it had all been so vague that if Bobbi hadn't picked up information from other sources, she wouldn't have even known what they had talked about.

"It's okay when he kisses me. It's fine."

"Bobbi, people will tell you that . . . that part . . . is not important. But it is. It's very important. If he kisses you, and holds you in his arms, and you don't feel . . . something . . . then this whole thing might not be right." She was blushing by now, but she added, "I'm afraid when we talk to girls at church, we make marriage sound like it's all family prayer and gospel study, but there's more to it than that."

Bobbi laughed. "I think the girls know on their own that they aren't hearing the whole story."

Mom laughed too. "Bobbi, the point is, I wouldn't marry him if you don't feel . . . you know . . . some excitement."

"Daddy will blow a hole in the roof if I call off the engagement."

"Maybe. But if he does, we'll patch it up. I can't think of anything worse than marrying a man you don't love."

"I know. That's what I keep thinking." She leaned back and folded her arms.

"Is there someone else?"

Bobbi instantly sat up straight again. "No. Not really."

"Not really? What's that supposed to mean?"

"There's someone I wish Phil were a little more like. But he's not someone I'm interested in."

"Why not?"

"He's not LDS for one thing. He's not someone I could even think about marrying."

"Oh, Bobbi."

And they both knew what she meant. "Don't worry. I won't let anything develop between us."

"But he's setting off some bells, isn't he?"

Bobbi took a breath. "Yes."

"Now I wish I hadn't asked. This is worse than I thought." She looked at Bobbi and rolled her eyes. But she was smiling—at least a little.

"No, it isn't. I won't let anything happen."

"Maybe you already have."

"No. Absolutely not."

"Bobbi, after I met your dad, I wanted to be with him every second. Other boys didn't interest me at all. I suspect that's how it ought to be. I just don't think this is a good sign that you're thinking about someone else."

"I'm not—not really." Bobbi tried to imagine President Thomas causing bells to ring so loudly that Mom had forgotten everyone else. Bobbi did know he had been a handsome man—she had seen the wedding pictures. He had looked a lot like Alex, with the same boldness, and maybe a little more glint in his eye. But she couldn't imagine him as romantic—or passionate.

"So what are you going to do?" Mom asked.

"I don't know."

"Oh, Sis, this is so hard for me. Phil could make bells *clang* for me. I just don't see the problem."

"Maybe *you* ought to marry him."

"Maybe so. Or LaRue could. We're both nuts over him."

Bobbi got up. She looked down at her mom and smiled. "Dad had better get some of the old fire back, or he'll lose you."

"Don't worry about your father. He's got *plenty* of fire."

"Really?"

But Mom was blushing again, and Bobbi knew that she was too. It was time to head upstairs.

On the following morning, Saturday, Sister Thomas got up almost as early as she did on weekdays. President Thomas was already downstairs in his office, doing some sort of Church business, but he would want his breakfast soon. He always went to the dealership on Saturdays, the same as any other workday, but he usually allowed himself a little later arrival time.

Once Sister Thomas had the bacon and eggs on, she gave a little knock on her husband's office door. "I'll be right there," he answered. And in another couple of minutes, he pushed his way through the swinging door and into the kitchen. "Who's up?" he wanted to know.

"No one," Mom answered. "No one in this whole town. You're the only man I know who wants his breakfast at six-thirty on Saturday."

"Half the day is gone," he said, but he was grinning. He sat down at the kitchen table, which was set only for him. "Aren't you eating?"

"I will a little later—when the kids are up."

"Everyone ought to be up by now—so you don't have to cook all morning."

"Yes, and pigs would fly if they were good little pigs." She set a plate in front of him. It was his usual breakfast: two eggs, fried, over easy; two strips of bacon; two slices of toast.

"Thanks, honey. Has the paper come?"

"I don't know. I haven't checked." The truth was, she had chosen not to look. She wanted to talk to him and not have to watch him read his paper while he ate. She sat down at the table across from him. "Have you talked to Bobbi about her wedding?" she asked. Sister Thomas was wearing an old cotton bathrobe with rips in the elbows, and she had her hair pinned up. That was something President Thomas didn't like, but this early on Saturday morning, he was going to have to live with it.

"No. I've asked her a couple of times when it's going to happen, but she won't give me an answer."

"Do you think she's really in love with Phil?"

"What?"

"I asked her last night why she didn't show more excitement about getting married, and frankly, I didn't like her answers. I don't think she knows what she wants."

President Thomas looked utterly baffled. "I don't see that at all," he said. "Bobbi isn't a giddy little girl. But any young woman in her right mind would be thrilled to marry Phil."

"Maybe so, Al. But *our* girl is struggling."

President Thomas stopped with his fork halfway to his mouth. "Bea, I just can't believe that. Struggling about what?"

"She's not really sure she loves him."

"That's nonsense. What's not to love about the boy?" He decisively shoved a big chunk of fried egg into his mouth.

Sister Thomas knew she was on thin ice with her husband. She didn't want him to go crashing up the stairs to wake Bobbi. "Love isn't quite that simple, Al. You know that."

"I'll tell you something, Bea." The president set his fork down. "This is the kind of silliness we let young people get away with these days. My Grandfather Thomas walked across a pasture to the next farm and told my grandmother he wanted to marry her. She hardly knew him, but he was an honest man from a good family. She accepted, and that was that. That's how people did it in those days. And they had good marriages, too."

"You're right, Al. I'm glad *I* didn't marry for love. I just took the first offer that came along."

President Thomas began to smile. "You were *nuts* over me. Admit it," he said.

"And shouldn't Bobbi be nuts over the man she marries?"

"Yes. Definitely. She should be nuts over Phil Clark."

Sister Thomas knew that her husband was being ironic, but she also knew what he expected. "Well . . . maybe she was just feeling blue last night. I don't know. But we need to back her up, whatever she decides."

"No. I think that's exactly the wrong thing to do. She's found a good man, and she needs to go forward and not look back."

"So why didn't you marry LaVerl Stevens?" Sister Thomas asked. "You went with her a whole year, and you told me yourself that your family thought you ought to marry her."

She had him, but it took him a good long while before he could bring himself to say, "That was different. She had a squeaky little voice that drove me crazy." He began to chuckle as he spread apricot jam on his toast.

Sister Thomas wasn't going to be derailed at this point. "Al, young people these days are different from our grandparents. They think for themselves whether we like it or not. And Bobbi is about as independent as any girl I know."

"You say that as if you admire her for it. Maybe she would be better off if she listened a little more and didn't get her back up the way she does."

"Yes, and if you had listened better, you'd be raising a bunch of squeaky-voiced little kids with LaVerl Stevens."

"And maybe I'd be better off. She never talked back to me."

"I think you're right. You got more than you bargained for, didn't you?"

They sat and smiled at each other for quite some time, but then President Thomas said, "I love you, Bea. And I love that daughter of yours, who's just like you." His smile faded. "Sometimes, though, I feel like this whole family is heading off in all directions and I can't do one thing to keep us on track. Everyone in my stake seems to think I'm a pretty wise fellow. Why can't I get my own kids to think so?"

"That's probably the same thing your father said when you broke it off with LaVerl."

President Thomas waited until he had finished chewing and had swallowed. "He did say that. He told me outright. And a year later, he told me I had done the right thing to wait—that you were head and shoulders better than LaVerl."

"Well?"

"It proves I'm smarter than my dad," President Thomas said. "It doesn't prove that *my* kids are smarter than I am." He grinned.

"You're hopeless," Sister Thomas said. She reached out and gave his hand a little slap.

But President Thomas looked down at the table, and when he looked back up, his wife saw his concern. "I know I overrate my own wisdom," he said. "And I know the kids have to think for themselves. But I see them walking right off cliffs sometimes, and the minute I say, 'Take a look where you're heading,' they act like I want to hogtie them to the back porch."

"Oh, come on. Alex has never come close to a cliff in his life. And Bobbi is wise beyond her years."

"I notice you didn't mention Wally."

"He's just young."

President Thomas thought about that for a time. "You're right about Alex. He'll listen. But the boy would rather think than *do*. I don't know how to get him to be more practical."

"Life will take care of that."

"Maybe. In time. But he might have to learn some hard lessons. And Bobbi will, too. But it's Wally, right now, who worries me sick. He's told me already that he doesn't want to go on a mission. And I'm afraid if he did go, he'd *quit* the first time it got a little hard."

"We just need to be patient with him. He'll be all right."

"I hope so. But I don't see any sign of it yet. And I worry about the other kids, too. Gene is a good boy—easier to deal with than most of our kids—but the only thing he really cares about is sports. And LaRue's ten years old and already has a mouth on her."

"I worry more about Bev. She lives too much in LaRue's shadow. She doesn't know how to speak up for herself."

President Thomas shook his head. "I had no idea raising kids would be like this," he said. "I thought all I had to do was teach them the truth and they would follow."

"It gets worse. My mother says she worries more about her grandkids than she did about her own children."

President Thomas pushed his plate away even though there was another slice of toast on it. "I'll tell you the worst part, Bea. This business of being a parent in Zion is going to get harder. Things are changing way too fast around here."

Sister Thomas sometimes grew weary of her husband's lectures on the problems in Zion, but she felt his honest concern now. She reached across the table and took hold of his hand. "I still think our kids will be okay," she said.

"I sure hope so," President Thomas said. He sat for a long time, smiling a little, seemingly lost in thought, but when he finally got up from the table, he took his wife's hand and pulled her up from her chair. Then he took her in his arms. "I love you," he said. "I'm glad I didn't marry LaVerl." And he kissed her longer and more ardently than Bobbi ever would have expected.

Sister Thomas liked that, but when her husband was gone, she sat down at the table, ate his slice of toast, and tried to think what she could say to Bobbi. But everything had been said. And the truth was, she felt much like her husband: she wished she could just tell Bobbi what to do. The choice seemed so obvious. If only her kids' problems were still skinned knees and bad colds. But wishes weren't fishes, she told herself, and she got up and cleared the table.

1 2

It was one of those perfect April evenings in Utah when spring is trying—one last time—to muscle winter aside. Wally was on his first date with Lorraine Gardner, and he was driving his dad's Nash. That, in and of itself, made this a special occasion. The car, retail, sold for over eight hundred dollars—and it *felt* expensive, too. The ride was cushioned, and the upholstery was more plush than any furniture in the Thomas home.

Wally had taken Lorraine to the lavish new Centre Theater, downtown, and they had seen "The Story of Vernon and Irene Castle," with Fred Astaire and Ginger Rogers. Wally liked the dancing, but he thought the story was pretty corny. Still, Lorraine had loved it, and Wally was in a better mood than he had been in for some time.

The past few weeks had been hard for Wally. East had lost its track meet to South, and Wally knew he might have made the difference. The guys on the team were furious about it, too. Wally had heard most of the complaints secondhand, but a few of the boys had confronted him and told him what they thought. Wally hadn't defended himself. In fact, he had passed it all off with apparent nonchalance. No one knew what he really thought, not even Mel.

Tonight Wally was feeling an almost desperate need to

have fun. Not only was he an outcast at school, but a stiff compromise had set in at home. Dad had always expected a great
deal of his kids, but he was usually good-humored about it.
Now, he joked with Gene and the girls, but around Wally he
had become reserved and distant. But that was exactly what
Wally didn't want to think about. He was going to prove he
could still work his charm with the girls—even the untouch-
able Lorraine Gardner—and then he would announce to Mel
what he had accomplished. Poor Mel would be in agony.

So Wally drove far south of Salt Lake to Thirty-Ninth and
State, and he and Lorraine drank malts at the "Do Drop Inn."
Then he took her for a ride into the foothills. He followed a
dirt road that curved its way onto a prominent crest where the
lights in the northern part of the valley were clear in the distance, and then he turned off and stopped the car.

"Wally, come on," Lorraine said. "I don't do this."

"Do what? Look at the lights?"

"You know what I'm talking about. I don't park."

"What do you do, *drive* forever?"

Lorraine laughed. "I don't park with *boys*."

"Okay, here's the deal. I'll keep my distance. And you keep
hugging that door, the way you've been doing all night."

"Or, better yet, we could go home." But she didn't seem
adamant, and Wally considered that a good sign. He wanted
to get some idea what her eyes were saying, but the moon was
angling through the back window, and he couldn't see her face.
What he could see was her pretty hair, loosely curled and
almost down to her shoulders. In the moonlight, it looked the
color of varnished oak, light and rich and shiny.

"So what are you worried about? Don't you trust me?"

"No. I don't. I know what a Romeo you are."

"*Me?* Hey, that's not true at all."

"No? Then tell me, Wally, what are you *really* like?"

The question seemed more sarcastic than genuine. Wally

could see he had his work cut out for him. "Lorraine, can we be serious for a minute?" he asked.

"No. I don't think so. You're never serious."

"I know that's how I seem." Wally leaned forward, took hold of the steering wheel, and put his chin on his hands. "But I do think about serious things."

Lorraine laughed. "Like what?"

Wally waited, and then, sounding solemn, said, "I'll tell you what I've been thinking lately. We're going to graduate in a couple of months—and then what? It's very possible that the boys in our class will end up fighting—maybe dying—in Europe."

"My dad says we'll never get involved over there."

Wally allowed some time again, and then he said, "I hope he's right. But I think war is coming, and when it does, I don't see how America can stay out of it."

"And you're really worried about that?"

"Well . . . it makes a guy stop to think about his life and what he wants to do with it." He leaned back and shut his eyes.

"So what *do* you want out of life, Wally?"

Wally thought he heard the sarcasm again, but he pushed ahead anyway. "I used to think about making money, but that's not so important to me now. What I picture is a nice house, great kids, and above all, a *perfect* wife. That's what counts."

"So what's perfect? Rita Hayworth?"

"I want her to be pretty, if that's what you mean. But I want someone who's not just pretty on the outside. I know it sounds trite, Lorraine, but I want someone just like my mother."

Lorraine didn't react for a time. "Your mother is a wonderful woman, Wally," she finally said, and her voice had become as solemn as Wally's. Or maybe too solemn. Was she making fun of him?

"I think a lot about being married," Wally said. "I see myself sitting by a fire on a winter night, reading a good book, and then I imagine myself looking over at my wife and suddenly going absolutely weak all over—just because I love her so much."

"That's *so* nice, Wally. I'm glad you can talk to me this way."

Wally heard the words he wanted to hear, but the tone was wrong. He folded his arms and looked down. "I know you have no reason to believe any of this, Lorraine. I don't reveal my true self very often. No one really knows me."

"Oh, I think the girls at East High do."

Wally could see little more than the silhouette of Lorraine's face and hair, but he could see a spark of reflection from her eyes, like fire. "What?"

"Gwen Larsen and I are very good friends, Wally. We talk about everything. Think about that."

Wally realized he was in trouble. "Look, Lorraine, there's something I need to tell you."

"That you can talk to me better than any girl you know?"

"I didn't say that."

"And I wouldn't if I were you."

Wally tried to think what to do.

"Wally, you drove Gwen up here—probably to this same spot—and you told her all the same baloney. Then you kissed her—her first kiss—and she floated on air for a week. But that was three weeks ago, and since then, you haven't even called her."

"That's not exactly . . ." Wally had started a sentence with the hope of discovering an end to it along the way, but nothing came to him.

"I can't believe you, Wally. You really *hurt* her."

"I didn't mean to. I'll ask her out again sometime."

"No you won't. It's just a game you play. You take a girl out until she starts to like you, but once you kiss her, you've won, and you look for another challenge."

Wally was surprised. Maybe that *was* the game he played, but girls had their own games. "Oh, come on," he said. "Don't make such a big thing of it. Gwen *wanted* me to kiss her."

Lorraine's head snapped around. "You're such a *drip*, Wally. Take me home—right now."

"Hey, talk about playing games. You were just waiting for me to say something that I also happened to say to Gwen—so you could jump all over me."

"That's exactly right. And I *got* you, didn't I?"

Wally couldn't think what to say for a moment, but he realized he was smiling. "Well . . . yeah."

Lorraine laughed and then leaned back against the door. "You're a sad case, Wally. I really don't like you at all." But her voice had lost its venom.

Wally was surprisingly relieved. It was good to have the game finished, even if he had lost. "Lorraine, I didn't mean to hurt Gwen. I didn't think about it that way."

"Don't you care about people? Something like that—a first kiss—means a lot to a girl. Didn't you stop to think how she would feel if you never asked her out again?"

Wally thought for a few seconds, and then he told the truth. "Not really."

"Wally, that is so pathetic."

"Maybe so," Wally said, and he found himself wondering about himself. "Honestly, I think there's something wrong with me. Everyone seems to know how I ought to feel about things, but most of the time, I don't feel anything at all."

It was a strange moment. Wally had never said anything like that before, but the words, as though they had come from someone else, struck him as right, and they seemed to reformulate his entire view of himself. There was something missing in him, he realized, and he didn't know what it was.

"A lot of boys are like that," Lorraine said, softly. "Maybe girls, too. I don't know."

"So what do I do about it?"

"Grow up, I guess."

A frightening sadness had come over Wally, but he wanted to keep talking. "Let's go out and sit on the grass," he said.

"Wally, why?"

"I don't know. It's nice out tonight. And I like to talk with you."

"I wouldn't use that line if I were you."

"No. I didn't mean it that way." Wally opened his door and stepped out, and to his surprise, before he could walk around the car, Lorraine got out too. So he stopped in front of the car and sat on the grass. Lorraine didn't come near him, however. She chose a big boulder several feet away, and she sat on that.

Wally could see her better now with moonlight falling across her face. Her skin was radiant in the delicate light, and she was wearing a simple dress—flowered and knee-length. He could see her slenderness, the subtle curves of her body. What he couldn't guess was what she was thinking. He knew that most girls found him good looking, and he had always cared about that. He wore argyle sweaters and expensive slacks to school, and he took time with his hair. But Lorraine had never paid much attention to him, and now, after the things he had done and said, this would certainly be his only date with her.

"What are you going to do after you graduate?" he asked her.

"I'm going to work this summer and then go to the U in the fall. What about you?"

"I don't know. I want to get away from Salt Lake."

"Really? Where do you want to go?"

"I've thought about joining the service."

"I thought you were afraid of going off to war."

She was teasing him now, and Wally was embarrassed. He let the question go by and merely said, "I want to see some other places." He lay back on the grass and looked at the sky. Away from the smoke of the city, the Milky Way was thick as a smudge of chalk across a blackboard. "What do you want to do with your life, Lorraine?"

"I don't know. Get married, have kids, wash on Mondays,

iron on Tuesdays—all the regular things. But I want to do something else before I commit my whole life to that."

"Like what?"

"I don't really want to go to college. I'd like to get a job and earn some money of my own. And then I'd just . . . I don't know . . . maybe take some trips."

Wally laughed. "So why don't you do it?"

"My parents say college is the best place to meet a good husband. And I guess that's right."

"If you ask me, the U is an extension of East High. All the same crowd will be up there. I want a change in my life."

"What does your dad say about that?"

"I'm not going to let my dad make my decisions for me anymore." Wally felt some dampness on his back, even through his sweater. He sat up. "My dad will never be satisfied with anything I do, Lorraine. So why try to please him?"

"Wally, come on. I know your father. He came to visit my mother when she was sick last year, and he give her a blessing. He was so tender with her, and he told my dad, 'Don't worry. She's going to get better.' You should have heard his voice. I didn't doubt for a minute after that. There's just no way you're going to convince me that he goes home at night and turns into some sort of bad guy."

Wally didn't say anything. He knew the tender side of his father, knew the confidence the man had in the promptings he received. And Wally understood entirely why people in the stake loved him so much. But he also knew what it was like to live within the compass of his authority.

"You love your father, don't you?" Lorraine asked. It was a simple question, seemingly offered as a reminder more than a query, but Wally was surprised by the confusion it set off. "I guess I do," was all he could think to say, but he knew the real answer was too complicated for him to explain.

"Look, Wally, I do need to go home now." She stood up.

Wally hesitated. He knew she was disappointed with his

answer, but he couldn't think what to say. He finally got up too. "Will you go out with me again?" he asked. He stepped a little closer to her.

"No, Wally. I told you. I don't like you."

"That's all right. I don't like me either." He tried to laugh, but they both knew he was telling the truth, and it was an oddly personal, even poignant moment.

"Don't say that," she said, and she reached out and touched his arm. "Wally, you'll be okay. You're just trying to figure yourself out. Most guys our age are doing that."

"But I'm not finding any answers."

"Are you really that unhappy?"

"I don't know. I'm not sure what I am. I just feel . . . lost."

"Oh, Wally." She reached her hand behind his head, rested it on the back of his neck, and then touched her cheek to his cheek for a moment. "You'll be okay," she said.

Wally felt a kind of weakness come over him. "*Will* you go out with me?" he asked.

"Wally, I didn't mean it that way. I just feel bad for you."

"I know. But will you?"

"No. I'll be your friend. That's all."

"How about next Friday? Would you be my friend that night?"

She was silent for a long time. And then she said, "Okay. But not on a date. We could talk some more, if you want."

The two got back into the car, and Wally drove her home. He said very little along the way. He was still lost inside himself and sort of numb from that one little touch.

At the door she was careful to keep her distance. She only said "Thanks" and went inside. Wally walked to the car and got in, but he didn't want to go home. Suddenly he wanted to talk to Mel. He looked at his watch. Eleven-ten. He didn't have to get the car home until midnight. And so he backed out of the driveway, drove half a block to Thirteenth East, and turned north. Mel lived a couple of blocks up the street, close to East High.

When Wally pulled up in front of Mel's, he could see that most of the lights were out, and he didn't want to get anybody out of bed, so he walked around to the back, where he found that Mel's bedroom light was on. He tapped on the window.

In a few seconds, Mel appeared, and the window slid open. "Oh, no," Mel said. "You wouldn't be here if you didn't have something to brag about."

Wally grabbed the window sill, pulled himself up, and then swung a leg inside. He was trying to think of something funny to say. He didn't want Mel to know what had happened.

"Be quiet," Mel said. "Tim's asleep."

Wally heard the big band music on the radio. He thought of teasing Mel about being home on a Saturday night, but the words wouldn't come. "Gene Krupa's band comes on at eleven-thirty," he said, just to say something, but his voice sounded flat.

"There's no way you kissed Lorraine Gardner," Mel was saying at the same time. "Don't even try to make me believe that."

Mel was an ungainly kid with a skinny neck. He had a tendency to get pimples, especially near his ears, and his reddish skin made them shine like beacons. He was rather broken out now, in fact, and in his pajamas, he looked terribly young for his age.

Wally turned Mel's desk chair around and sat down. "I want to talk to you about something," he said.

"Hey, what happened? Did you kiss her?"

"No."

"Did you try?" Mel sat down on his bed, facing Wally.

"No. She saw right through me. I didn't get anywhere."

"What? The champ gets KO'd? Joe Louis, down for the count?"

Wally laughed a little, but stiffly. "Yup. I guess so."

"What's wrong?"

"Nothing."

Tim stirred in his bed and then sat up. He looked around, bleary-eyed. "It's okay," Mel said. "Go back to sleep." Mel laughed and then turned back to Wally.

But Wally didn't want any more probing. "Mel," he said, "right after graduation, let's do what we talked about. Let's join the navy."

"I don't know if I want to, Wally. My dad and I talked about it, and he—"

"Don't give me that, Mel. We both know what our fathers will say. But who cares? We'll never have another chance to do something like this. We can see the world—sail the seven seas." He spread his arms wide and managed to smile. "Just think how much fun we could have."

Mel leaned forward and put his elbows on his knees. "I don't know if I'd like that kind of life," he said.

Wally stood up, furious but not wanting to show it. "Okay. Fine. Never mind." He walked back to the window. "I'll send you postcards so you can see what you're missing."

"Hey, come on, Wally. I'll give it some thought. But it's not something you just jump into."

"Mel, that's exactly what it is. For once in my life I want to take a leap and see where I land. I'm tired of everything around here."

"What happened tonight?"

"I told you—nothing." But then he added, impulsively, "She felt sorry for me, Mel. That's what she told me."

"Why?"

"Because I'm a mess. You know that. I'm a complete mess, and she felt bad for me."

"Come on, Wally. You're not a mess. You're fine."

"That's not what the guys on the track team are saying."

Mel looked down at his bedspread, ran his fingers across the bumpy brown chenille. "They're just mad right now. They'll forget about it."

"No they won't. They'll be up at the university this fall, still hating me. And my dad will still be wondering how he managed to raise a quitter."

Mel didn't look up, didn't say anything.

"I just want to go where no one knows me—and start over."

"Wally, you can't decide anything tonight. You're upset. Lorraine must have gotten to you."

"Maybe so. But let's think about this—seriously."

"Okay. We'll talk about it."

Wally sat down on the window sill and was about to swing his legs outside.

"Don't feel bad about getting shot down by Lorraine," Mel said. "You're not the first, and you won't be the last."

"I know that. I'm fine."

"Hey, I'm the sad case around here. I've only kissed one girl all year, and that was Alice. It took me about twenty tries before she let me give her a little kiss on the porch."

"That's your mistake, Mel. Never kiss them on the porch. Kiss them on the lips." Mel laughed a little too hard, but Wally welcomed the new mood. That was what worked for him; he was always better off to be funny, not to think so much. "I've tried the veranda a couple of times," he said, "but all in all, the lips are still the best."

"Wally, do you like her or something? Is that what's bothering you?"

"Lorraine?"

Mel nodded.

"She's all right." Wally swung his legs outside, and he dropped to the ground. "I'll see you," he said.

"You're okay, aren't you, Wally?"

"Sure."

Wally walked to the car and got in, even turned the ignition on. But he didn't push the starter button. He sat and stared straight ahead. He tried to put a name on what he was feeling, but nothing occurred to him. He longed to catch a highway and head somewhere—California, maybe. Or all the way to the East Coast. Instead, he started the car and drove slowly home. And he told himself along the way that he was going to join the navy, no matter what Mel decided.

"Elder Smith, do you have just a minute?"

Apostle Joseph Fielding Smith looked up from the papers on his desk. "President Thomas. Of course. Come in."

The apostle and the president had known each other for more than twenty years, and they had met on stake matters many times. In recent years they had also seen each other at East High events. Some of their children, about the same age, were good friends. All the same, they addressed each other with their titles, and President Thomas stood with his hat in his hand until Elder Smith stood up, shook his hand, and then invited him to sit down.

"I'm sorry to bother you," President Thomas said. "Your secretary said you wouldn't mind."

"That's right. She thinks I have nothing to do around here." Elder Smith sounded terse, but he smiled, and President Thomas knew he was teasing.

"I was wondering what you think might happen with our missionaries in Germany."

"Reuben Clark is the one you ought to ask. He knows people in the State Department, so he keeps up on things. Anything I know, I hear from him."

President Thomas nodded. "I guess that's right, but I read

in the paper that you're on your way to Europe in a few days, and I thought you might have looked into things a little."

Elder Smith was about ten years older than President Thomas. He was a slight man with white hair, receding a little, and wire-rimmed glasses. He had a way of looking closely at a person, as though he could see inside. President Thomas knew that Elder Smith's crustiness was all on the surface, that he was actually a kindly man; all the same, the president was a little nervous around him. "That's one reason I'm going to Europe," Elder Smith said. "President Grant wants me to review the whole situation. Right now, I don't know what to expect."

And that seemed the end of it. President Thomas rolled his hat around in his fingers. "Well, thanks. I'm worried, to tell you the truth. I know we want to keep the missionaries there if we can, but it looks dangerous to me, the way things are going."

"It is dangerous, President. But we have to preach the gospel—and we can't do that by pulling all our missionaries home every time there's some trouble."

"I know."

"But it's another matter to have your own son there, isn't it?" Elder Smith smiled again. "I know about that. Switzerland is safe for now, I suppose, but I still worry about my son Lewis. With Hitler after Poland and Mussolini grabbing up Albania, I wonder what's to stop one of them from going after Switzerland?"

"Someone is going to stand up to them somewhere."

"Yes, and when that happens, our missionaries could get caught in the middle. We understand that. But the Brethren pray about this every day. We'll do the right thing, and we won't wait until it's too late. You just have to trust us on that."

"Oh, I do. I was just wondering what you had heard."

"What's wrong, Al? You seem a little down in the mouth."

President Thomas set his hat on the chair next to him. "I do have some other things on my mind. I guess I feel that a stake president's family ought to set the right example. And my family has me worried."

Elder Smith got up and walked around to the other side of his desk. Several chairs were arranged in a half circle, and Elder Smith sat down in one that faced President Thomas. "What's the trouble?" he said. "I know Alex is doing well, and I heard that Bobbi is marrying the Clark boy. He's a fine young man."

President Thomas decided he wouldn't bring up his concerns about Bobbi. "It's Wally I'm worried about," he said.

"Is he the one who played ball with my son Reynolds?"

"Yes. He's a year younger. He graduates in June."

"He's a nice boy. Reyn always liked him. What's he been doing? Breaking the Word of Wisdom? Missing church?"

"Oh, no. It hasn't gone that far. But I don't think the Church means much to him."

Elder Smith chuckled. He had taken his coat off and was wearing a gray vest. He crossed his arms over his chest and gave the knot of his tie a little pull. "He's not serious and devoted the way you and I were at that age. Right?"

"I was pretty serious, Elder Smith."

"We all were. And the older we get, the better we were."

President Thomas laughed. "Maybe so," he said. "But you haven't had much to worry about with your kids."

"I worry about all of them, and that's one reason I married again. I felt like my younger kids needed to have a mother in the home."

Less than a year before, Elder Smith had married Jessie Evans, an attractive, rather flamboyant woman, much younger than he was. She was a trained opera singer, known throughout the valley for her music, but she seemed the last person a quiet, scholarly man like Elder Smith would marry. President Thomas had seen the two together many times since then, however, and they seemed very happy.

"Wally works for you down at the dealership, doesn't he?"

"Yes. In the summers."

"Has he ever worked for anyone else?"

"No. But he's lazy. The only way I can get him to work at all is to hire him myself."

"I'd let him get out from under your thumb. Give him some room. These sons of stake presidents and bishops get tired of trying to live up to their fathers' expectations. They need to take on some responsibility of their own."

"I doubt he'll look for a job if I don't hire him again."

"Find him a job. Get someone to make him an offer."

"I guess I could do that."

"And show that boy some love and patience. Growing up isn't easy these days."

"All right. I know that's true."

"Well, fine. And don't worry so much. Are you all right? Your church work isn't getting you down, is it?" Elder Smith had slid toward the front of his seat, and President Thomas knew it was time to go.

"No. I'm fine."

"Are you making a living?"

President Thomas smiled. "We manage to eat."

"You drive a new car every year, I notice."

"I know where I can get a good deal. Come down and I'll make you one, too." The two laughed, and President Thomas felt some of the load lift from his shoulders. The two stood up.

"Just between you and me, President, I don't think Alex will be in Germany much longer. Many of the people of Europe have hardened their hearts to the gospel. We try to teach them, but very few listen. Now they're going to reap the consequences of their pride. I see some terrible times ahead for them."

"It looks that way to me, too."

"We've got plenty of problems in this country, too, and I fear we're going to be drawn into the troubles in Europe. President Roosevelt keeps asking everyone to pray for peace. What he ought to tell people is to *repent* and then pray. That's the only course that's going to save us now. It's all in the Book of Mormon. The Lord will only prosper us and protect us when we're righteous."

President Thomas had not thought of it that way before, but it all rang true to him. "So what can we do?"

"The only thing I know is to call the members to repentance. Too many of our leaders want to soft-pedal everything." Elder Smith smiled. "I know what the members think of me: I'm the crankiest old buzzard in the Church. But I read the scriptures, and they tell me to cry repentance *unceasingly.*"

"That's what I find in the scriptures too."

"I'm glad to know that. I was starting to think I was using a different set from everyone else."

President Thomas laughed.

"President, our missionaries have been preaching the gospel abroad for a hundred years. And we've come a long way: three quarters of a million members, more than a hundred stakes, thirty-five missions. But we've got a long way to go. I see too many of our members slacking off. I walk down the streets here in Salt Lake, and it seems like half the people are smoking cigarettes. Our sacrament meeting attendance is terrible. I don't understand what's happening, but maybe the Lord has to get our attention—so he can carry out his purposes."

President Thomas nodded solemnly, but Elder Smith seemed to sense that he had gone on a bit of a tirade. He laughed. "Anyway," he said, "how's Bea doing? I haven't even asked you about her."

"Fine. The only problem with her is that she thinks she's right all the time. And it turns out most of the time that she is."

Elder Smith laughed and slapped his friend on the back. "Well, I'll tell you this. When Ethel died, I thought my heart would break. But Jessie has brought me back to life. And my kids love her. So I'm not grouchy *all* the time."

"I heard you and Jessie sing a duet. I had no idea you could sing like that."

"It's not a duet. It's a 'do-it.' She makes me *do it* whether I want to or not."

They laughed and shook hands.

Early in June Wally graduated from high school and took a summer job on Mat Nakashima's farm. Brother Nakashima had called and asked whether he wanted to work for him, and for Wally the chance to get away from the dealership had been welcome. So far, the work had actually been rather fun, too. Wally got to act like a boss at times, and he worked mostly alone—without anyone watching over him. He was outside, too, not cooped up in a hot showroom or a stuffy garage.

Wally did the plowing to keep the weeds down between the rows of trees, and he hauled bins of cherries to waiting trucks. After work each day he helped figure the earnings of the pickers—mostly local boys and some itinerant laborers. He paid them in cash from a metal box, and he joked with them when they complained about being tired.

When the last picker was paid one afternoon, Mat asked Wally to move the empty bins back to the orchard, ready for the next day's work. As Wally climbed onto the tractor, Brother Nakashima said, "Wally, you're doing a good job for me. I appreciate it."

"Thanks. I never drove a tractor before in my life, but I'm getting the hang of it. I like this work. Maybe I'll run an orchard of my own someday."

"And not sell cars?"

"That's one thing I *don't* want to do."

Mat was young, in his thirties, but he was more formal than any man Wally had worked around. He sounded more like a professor than a farmer. "Well, I was a little bit the same," he said, "but I didn't stray too far from my father's business. He raised vegetables, so when I was growing up, I always had my back bent and my nose in the dirt. Maybe that's why I decided on an orchard. I can look up, not down." He laughed.

"It's a good business, I would think."

"Some years it is." Mat gripped the shoulder straps of his overalls and smiled. He was strongly built, with powerful shoulders and a stout neck. "We get a late frost as often as not, and then we do more worrying than picking. Sometimes I wish I had chosen something else."

At the dealership, the employees had treated Wally like the "owner's boy." No one had ever carried on a man-to-man conversation with him. Mat had seemed rather quiet at first, but he was opening up a little more each day, and Wally liked that.

"All in all, I've done all right," Mat said. "I have to save from year to year, but Sharon and I don't spend much, so I don't need to get rich. We plant a garden, we keep some chickens and a milk cow, and we raise a couple of calves each year. So we don't worry about going hungry."

The Nakashimas lived beyond Twenty-Seventh South, where there were lots of orchards and farms. They had a nice little house, three sons, and a baby daughter. Wally ate lunch with the family every day, so he was getting to be friends with the boys. Sharon was much more outgoing than Mat, and she seemed to like Wally. She had teased him about being "every schoolgirl's dream" until Wally finally admitted that the one girl he really liked only wanted to be friends with him. No one else—not even Mel—knew how much he cared about Lorraine.

"Personally," Wally told Mat, "I think I'd like to be rich. You know—live in a fancy house and drive nice cars." He pulled off his old hat and wiped his forehead with his sleeve.

"Then maybe you *should* stay with your father's business."

"No. My dad and I don't get along well enough. I want to do something on my own."

Wally had hinted about this before, but Mat had never commented. Now, however, he said, "Things aren't always easy between fathers and sons. I had my difficulties, too."

"What kind of difficulties?"

"Mainly, my father stayed with the old ways from Japan, and that bothered me. For one thing, he never would call me Mat." He smiled. "He called me Matoshi, my real name, even in front of my friends. I hated that. But I learned from him—and then he died quite young. I wish I had him around now."

"Did you two argue?"

"Not a lot. Japanese sons aren't supposed to do that. But I was always caught in the middle. I was the only Japanese boy in my high school, and I wanted to be like everyone else. I didn't want my friends to meet my family—since my parents spoke so little English and were . . . you know . . . so different. There for a while, I wasn't very respectful to my father."

"But it sounds like you worked things out."

Mat thought for a time, the way he often did, before he responded. "Mostly, I just grew up," he said. "But I made one choice that was hard on my folks. When I joined the Church, I went against my father's will. He couldn't understand that."

"What religion was he?"

"Buddhist. He didn't mind so much that I added something to my faith. It was rejecting all the old ways that bothered him."

"Didn't you live in our neighborhood back then?"

"That's right. My father's farm wasn't too far from you. It's all filled with houses now. When I first joined the Church, your dad was my bishop. He got me through some hard times."

"My dad did?"

"I'll say." Mat stepped closer to the tractor and looked up at Wally. "Some of the members didn't want a Japanese boy in the ward. I think they were afraid I might want to date their daughters. But I'll never forget; your dad stood up in sacrament meeting one night. He never mentioned me by name, but he told the ward what it meant to be a Christian. Everybody in that chapel knew what he meant, too. And they responded." Mat looked away and blinked, took a few seconds, and then added, "There's no man on this earth I love more than your father."

Wally was amazed.

"You probably don't know this, but your father performed my marriage. Sharon is from Brigham City. I met her through a cousin of mine who used to live up there. Your dad always told me I'd be wise to find a Japanese girl if I could, and when I met Sharon, who's Nisei like me—born in America—I went crazy over her. She joined the Church, but she had to go against her parents, the same as I had done, and her family pretty much disowned her. During those first couple of years we were married, your dad spent hours and hours with us—and especially with Sharon—just getting us through all that. Sharon never says your dad's name without reverence. You must have noticed that."

"Mat, all that's hard for me to imagine. The sermon you said he gave in sacrament meeting—that I can picture. But whenever he talks with me, he just ends up telling me what to do. I know he spends a lot of time with members of the stake, but I can't visualize him being patient with people—and listening."

Mat smiled. "I don't know, Wally. You and I don't seem to be talking about the same man."

"I think you're right," Wally said. He pulled his work gloves from his back pocket and put them on. He got ready to start the tractor, but he could see that Mat was still watching him, that he had something more to say.

"Someday you'll be a father yourself, and you'll see everything from the other side. Your father is trying hard to do what's best for you. Sometimes he has to lay down the law."

"I know that. But he could talk things out with me. I'm not a little kid anymore."

Mat nodded. "No, you're not," he said, and he let the matter go. But Wally could tell that Mat was holding back. As Wally drove the tractor away, he tried to think what Mat might have said. Maybe, "But you're not as grown up as you think you are, either." And somehow those words cut deep, even deeper than if Mat had actually said them.

The following Sunday was stake conference. Sitting all morning on the hard benches of the Granite Stake Tabernacle was bad enough for Wally, but returning in the afternoon, when the building was blazing hot, seemed enough to kill him off. So he wasn't in a good mood when his father got up to give the closing sermon. President Thomas told some good stories in the beginning and was rather funny, but then he began to hammer away at the "iniquity" in the Salt Lake Valley. "Apostle Joseph Fielding Smith recently told me never to stop crying repentance to this people," he told the congregation, "and I never will."

He had begun to speak with almost an hour left in the meeting. Wally held out a little hope that he might stop a few minutes early. But with four o'clock coming up, he was still going strong.

"I believe," he said in conclusion, "and I am not alone in this belief, that Church members may soon face the greatest test we have ever known. The pioneers faced hardships. And the depression has been a challenge. But this next great trial will tear our families apart and thrust our children into danger and temptation. This valley will deal firsthand with the depravity of a wicked world. It is time, my brothers and sisters, to gather our families about us and to seek repentance for our sins, that we might be prepared for a very dark time."

Wally was surprised by all this. He knew his father believed that war was coming soon in Europe, but what was this about a test for the members in Salt Lake? Dad, as usual, was taking himself too seriously. Wally tried to picture his dad comforting Sharon Nakashima. He was amazed that the man hadn't said, "Don't feel so sorry for yourself. Look how many pioneers had to leave their families behind when they joined the Church."

After, as the stake members filed out, many of them stopped the Thomases. "My goodness, Bea," people would say, "that husband of yours outdid himself today. That's one of the finest sermons I've ever heard."

One man even told Bobbi, "Your father ought to be an apostle, if you ask me. He can preach with the best of 'em."

Beverly had fallen asleep on her mother's lap, and now she was sleep-walking her way up the aisle. LaRue looked little better, the curl gone from her hair and her eyes glazed. Gene seemed lost inside himself. But Mom and Bobbi were willing to talk to everyone, and Bobbi kept saying, "It was a wonderful conference—one of the best we've had." Wally wondered whether she could possibly mean it. Had all these people actually *liked* his father's talk—or did they just think they had to say so?

Wally had almost made it to the door when his bishop, Morgan Evans, took hold of his arm. "I want to speak with you for a minute," he said. He pulled Wally into one of the pews. "I've been worried about you lately, Wally. How are you doing?"

"Fine."

"You haven't been coming to MIA or playing baseball with the Junior M-Men. Is there a reason for that?"

"Did my dad ask you to talk to me?"

"No, no. I just wondered." Bishop Evans wiped the sweat from his bald head with a ragged blue handkerchief. Wally didn't doubt his concern, but he was not someone Wally felt close to. The bishop managed a feed store in Sugar House, and he farmed on the side. There was nothing false about him, but he had little sense of how to get to know the boys in the ward.

"I don't know, Bishop. I've just lost interest. I'm not much of a ball player, to tell the truth."

"You've always played for us in years past."

"I know."

"Why don't you come out this week?"

"I'll think about it."

"Wally, did you think about the things your father said today? Did any of it go to your heart?"

Wally was holding his suit coat over his arm. He shifted it and threw it over his shoulder. "Not enough, I guess," he said.

Bishop Evans seemed to accept the honesty. "Well, son, don't drift away. You need to stay involved with the Church."

"All right," Wally said. "I'll try to come to MIA more often." But he promised nothing more than that, and Bishop Evans seemed to know better than to push any harder.

Wally finally escaped the hot building, and he was overjoyed to get home. He pulled off his church clothes and put on a short-sleeved shirt and a pair of jeans. He was tying his shoes when Gene walked in. "Boy, that building was hot," Gene said. He was unbuttoning his white shirt.

Wally looked up. "Just once you would think Dad could let the meeting out early. I don't know why he thinks he has to preach for a solid hour."

Gene didn't comment, but Wally saw the look in his eyes. It always bothered him when Wally criticized Dad.

"And then the bishop gets all over me because I've missed Mutual a couple of times."

"Why aren't you playing baseball?" Gene asked. He sat down on his bed and pulled off a shoe, not bothering to unlace it.

"Because I don't want to. The last I knew, playing baseball wasn't one of the requirements for the celestial kingdom."

Gene pulled his other shoe off, stood and slipped his church pants down, then sat again and pulled them off. But he didn't say anything.

"Whether I go to Mutual is my business."

Gene walked to the closet. He got out a hanger and draped his trousers over it without bothering to get the crease straight. "What about the Word of Wisdom?" he asked. "Is that your own business too?"

"What?"

"You know what I'm talking about."

"No, I don't."

Gene hung up his pants and then walked back to his bed. He stood there in his underwear, facing Wally. "You came in drunk Friday night," he said.

"I was *not* drunk."

"You'd been drinking. And smoking, too. I could smell it."

Wally got up from his bed. "Yeah. That is my own business." But Wally felt ashamed. After a few seconds, he said, "Look, Gene, I'm not going to start drinking all the time. It was something I just wanted to try."

"Wally, you're going to ruin our family."

"For crying out loud, Gene, what are you talking about? I took a couple of drinks. One time."

"I don't mean that. You hate Dad. You do everything he tells you not to do."

"No, I don't. If I did that, I'd leave this place."

"Why?"

Wally felt bad when he saw the hurt in Gene's face. He softened his voice when he said, "Gene, I just need to get away. It's nothing against the family."

"Stay until Alex gets back. I want us to be together again." Gene stepped to his chest of drawers and pulled out a pair of cords.

"We'll never be together again, Gene. Not for long."

Gene was stepping into his pants, but he glanced toward Wally, and Wally saw how upset he was.

"We're all growing up, Gene," Wally said. "We'll go our separate ways. Bobbi's getting married. Alex will too. That's just how life is."

Gene sat on his bed, his back to Wally. "I hated it when Alex left," he said. "I don't want anyone else to go." He was straining hard not to let his voice show his emotion.

Wally didn't know what to do. "Hey, get your baseball glove," he finally thought to say. "Let's go out and play some catch."

"We can't. It's Sunday."

"Dad isn't home yet."

"That doesn't matter. We're not supposed to do it." He looked around. "Don't you understand that, Wally?"

Gene finished dressing and left the room. And Wally was left to wonder about himself. Why were so many things clear to his family that simply weren't at all clear to him?

14

Wally and Lorraine were lying on their backs watching the fireworks. "It's so strange," Lorraine said. "Every time there's a flash, it feels like the light is coming right at us."

Wally laughed. "I know. I love that feeling."

"It scares me, but I like it too. It's like the sparks are going to keep right on coming and crash on top of us."

Wally laughed. "Yeah. You love to take chances as long as you know there's no real danger."

"Hey, that's not true. My friends tell me I shouldn't be spending so much time with you. They think *you* are dangerous."

Wally heard the thump as another rocket took off. He could trace the path by the sparks, could hear the hissing sound. Then the burst came, and again he saw the illusion—the expanding blast, the light reaching toward them, as though it were much closer than it really was.

In the quiet that followed, Wally asked, "What's so dangerous about me? I haven't even tried to kiss you."

And it was true. He had never kissed her, and yet they had been together often all summer. He had, however, held her in his arms—on the dance floor. Wally was a good dancer, and Lorraine had begun to accept invitations that clearly were dates. Mostly, they went to Friday night ward dances, but sometimes Wally splurged and they went to the Rainbow Rendezvous downtown, or to the Avalon Ballroom south of Sugar House.

Today, the Twenty-Fourth of July, they had gone to the "Covered Wagon Days" parade in the morning and then shared a picnic lunch in Liberty Park. They had each gone off to family parties that afternoon and hadn't planned to be together again, but Wally had called and said, "Let's drive out to Lagoon and see the fireworks." He had expected Lorraine to turn him down, but she had agreed. By the time they had gotten to The Lagoon, an amusement park near Farmington, the dance floor was already so crowded they could hardly elbow their way in. But they had danced for a time and then wandered over to the fun house.

Lorraine knew she had to hold her skirt down as she walked in, but a blast of air had still lifted her dress enough to show her pretty legs, and Wally hadn't minded that at all. The two had then laughed to see themselves in the distorted mirrors, and they had crashed on the floor together as they tried to walk through the big rolling barrel. Lorraine wouldn't get on the saucer, which spun until it threw people off in all directions, but she did grab a burlap bag and hike to the top of the immense slippery slides. She tried to race Wally, but he reached the bottom ahead of her.

After, the two had waited in line until they finally got a ride on the roller coaster, and then they had walked to the swimming pool—the biggest in the state—and watched the swimmers for a time. By then, the fireworks were starting.

"My friends all know you," Lorraine was saying now. "They say you're waiting for your chance to *attack* me."

"That's true. And guess what—tonight's the night."

"At least you warned me."

Another little thud sounded, and a rocket shot through the darkness. Wally watched for it but couldn't pick it up. When it burst, it was something new, a larger explosion. And then several more followed in rapid succession.

"Big finish," Lorraine said.

And it was. Five explosions followed quickly, one after the other, and then one more, higher, bigger than the rest, in brilliant red. It lit up the whole sky.

Wally and Lorraine were lying on the grass not far from the pool. Wally had claimed it was best to watch fireworks lying down. Lorraine had accepted that, but she had also kept her distance. "That's the end," she said now. "I need to get home."

"The night is young, my dear. What's the hurry?"

"I'd better not be late. My parents weren't very pleased about my taking off again tonight."

"Okay. But first we need to do something dangerous."

"No."

"It's the safe kind of danger that you like."

"All the same . . . no."

"I knew you'd like the idea," Wally said. "Tonight we're Bonnie and Clyde. We're going to pull off a heist."

Lorraine didn't agree, but she laughed, and Wally took that as a good sign. The two got up and walked to the parking lot. The band had begun to play again, and Wally hummed along with a new Hoagy Carmichael tune called "I Get Along Without You Very Well." It was a beautiful song, and Wally, on impulse, turned to Lorraine. "Let's dance," he said. She laughed, but she let him take her in his arms, and they danced the rest of the song, out among the cars. When the music stopped, he let go of her and bowed, and then they continued on to the car, but he wished they could stay late and dance every dance. He was always happiest when he was holding her.

Wally had his own car now. Dad had seen no need for another car in the family, but he had relented and made Wally a good deal on a trade-in. It was a '32 Ford coupe. Wally was making two dollars a day, and he had managed to save thirty dollars for a down payment. Since then he had paid another twenty, but he still owed a hundred. He had promised to work part-time when college started, and to keep paying off his debt at five dollars a month. That would be hard, but Wally loved his little coupe, and it had given him more freedom than he had ever known before.

When Wally got into the car, he was surprised to see that Lorraine was sitting closer than usual. All day, he had had the feeling that she was growing more comfortable with him. And also, all day, he had wanted to kiss her. He knew better than to force that, but he believed it would happen before long.

He didn't tell Lorraine where they were going. He was sure she would back out if she had time to think about it. But the girl was entirely too strict, and Wally wanted her to try something a little more risky. He drove back to Salt Lake on Highway 89 and then turned east on Twenty-First South. This was taking them home, but when he continued east through Sugar House and parked the car near the Country Club golf course, Lorraine finally demanded to know what was going on.

"You'll find out. Just follow me."

Lorraine hesitated, but then she did get out of the car. Wally took her hand and walked across a big field of dry cheat grass, south of the golf course, to a place where a long, steep drop-off led down to one of the fairways. As he started down the hill, Lorraine asked, "Are we allowed to go down here?"

"Yes. Can't you tell? I'm allowing it. Just be careful with your skirt. I'll carry you across the creek."

"Creek?"

Wally was pulling her along now, and he didn't explain. But when they came to the creek, he bent and took off his shoes, and then he rolled up his pants.

"Wally, what's this all about?" she wanted to know.

"It'll only take a minute. It's just something fun." He turned and took hold of her, picked her up, and then walked carefully into the shallow water. He loved the smell of her when he got that close. When he set her down on the other side, he was tempted to hold on to her and try to kiss her—and just find out, finally, what she would do. But he didn't. "Okay," he whispered, "follow me, but stop when I tell you to."

"Why are you whispering? Are we trespassing?"

"Well . . . a little, but—"

"How can you trespass 'a little'?"

Wally laughed. "Let's say it's only a minor trespass. We're not hurting anything. But don't talk too loud." He took her hand. The pond he was looking for was not far away, but he couldn't see very well. He tried to judge the firmness of the earth under the grass as he inched his way down a little slope. When he felt softer footing, he said, "Okay, stop here."

"You're going wading?"

"Yes."

"Maybe I'll go in too. I can hold my skirt up."

"Really?" They both laughed. But then Wally thought better of it. "No, you'd better not. It's a muddy mess. Just stand on the bank, and I'll throw our *take* to you."

"Take? What are you going to do—catch fish?"

Wally laughed so hard he had to reach for Lorraine to get his balance. "Not fish," he whispered. "Golf balls. These ponds collect a lot of them."

"Is it okay to take them?"

"Yeah. It's more than okay. It's great. We wouldn't want the fish to eat them and get sick."

"Are there really fish in there?"

Wally was trying to roll up his trousers a little higher, but he was laughing harder than ever. "Lorraine, I'd like to be a salesman and call at your house. You'll believe anything."

"It's stealing, isn't it?"

"No. It's free enterprise. If I'm enterprising enough, the golf balls are free." Wally had his pants ready now. "Okay, here I go. Maybe I'd better just stuff my pockets. You might not see the balls coming at you if I throw them."

Wally fully expected Lorraine to tell him not to do it—that

it was wrong. But she surprised him again when she began to giggle. "This is crazy. How can you find them?"

"With my toes."

For some reason that struck Lorraine as very funny. Her laugh was usually soft and sort of husky, but she was cackling now. "My dad would die," she said.

Wally stepped into the water and worked his way out a little from the bank. "The golfers get the ones close to the bank. I'll have to get out a little more," Wally said.

"Do you even golf?" Lorraine asked, and the question got her laughing again.

"Not yet. But I'm getting ready to start. I've got a whole bucket of balls at home. Mel and I have done this lots of times."

"Are you finding any?"

"Not yet." But then Wally felt the familiar hardness under his foot. "There's one," he said, and he reached down for it.

Lorraine was giggling again.

"Hey, they're thick right in here," Wally said. He reached into the water, got one, swished it in the water to get rid of the mud, and then stuffed it into his pocket.

He had five or six in his pocket when Lorraine said, "Hey, I think I want to come in. It's no fun just standing here."

"You'd better not. You'll hate me if you ruin your dress."

"I'll stay close to the edge and just cool my feet."

"Okay. Go slowly though. It's slippery." He could see her outline, just enough to know that she was bending over, taking off her shoes. He could hardly believe she would do something like that. "This crime stuff is fun, isn't it?" he whispered.

"You're the criminal. I'm only going . . . Wally! A light!"

Wally saw it too. A flashlight was coming toward them. Wally began to slosh his way toward the bank, but he slipped in the mud and went down. He caught himself with one hand and came up scrambling. "Run to the tree," he said. "I'll catch up."

"I can't see."

Wally heard the panic in her voice. As he came out of the water, he grabbed her arm and took off running, pulling her along. There was a big spruce tree near the creek, maybe fifty feet away. He ran toward it, not really seeing it, but before long he was catching hold of its prickly needles. "Ouch," Lorraine was saying at the same moment.

"Get behind," Wally whispered, and he pulled her to the back side of the tree, away from the flashlight, which he glanced to see was coming nearer. But the light was shining on the pond, not toward the tree, and Wally thought they were safe. "Just stay still," he whispered. "I don't think he saw us."

She had hold of him, grasping one arm, and he could feel by her grip that she really was scared. The light flashed past the tree a couple of times, but no one came near. And then they heard a voice: "Stay out of this pond. I'll call the cops on you next time."

Then, silence.

The voice had been young. The guy was probably a teenager who was hired to water at night. His boss had told him to scare off kids who got into the ponds, but it was obviously not a huge thing to him. He had heard the voices, the laughter, and walked over, but he was giving up already. Wally waited a good two minutes, without speaking, and then stepped out far enough to take a look. "He's gone," he said, and he began to laugh.

"Oh, Wally. What if the police had come?" But her voice was light. She had apparently liked the excitement. "Let's get out of here," she said, and now she was laughing again.

"Okay. Let me get you across the stream. Then I've got to find my shoes."

Lorraine began to cackle again. "I forgot about my shoes for a second," she said. "I almost left them."

"Shush. It was that laugh of yours that tipped the guy off in the first place."

She laughed all the harder. "You got all wet, didn't you?"

"And muddy."

"See. Crime doesn't pay."

"Sure it does. It pays in golf balls."

"No. I learned my lesson. Give me those balls. I'm throwing them back in the pond. And then I'm going to confess to my bishop and repent."

"You repent. I'm moving on to bigger crimes. Tennis balls."

"No, Wally. Don't do it. It could lead to bowling balls."

"Basketballs."

"Globes."

Wally could think of nothing bigger. He was laughing too hard anyway. He slipped his arm around Lorraine. She leaned against him and continued to giggle.

"Come on," he said, and he picked her up. He made his way back across the creek, but this time, when he put her down in front of him, he didn't let go. He stood close to her with his arm still around her waist. She didn't step away, and so he took his chance. He bent a little, felt his nose touch hers, and then turned his head and kissed her. For three or four seconds, she let it happen, didn't exactly kiss him back, but didn't stop him either. And then she stepped away.

"No, Wally. I don't want to do that."

"Why?"

"We're just friends." She turned and began to walk up the hill. Wally didn't follow. He said, softly, "I love you, Lorraine."

She spun around. "Wally, what a stupid thing to say. Don't ever say it again." She turned again and hurried away.

Wally had said the words suddenly but not impulsively. He had thought to tell her every time he had been with her lately. He worked his way along the creek until he found his shoes, and then he sat down and put them on. When he finally caught up, Lorraine was leaning against the car, facing him. "I do love you," he said. Lorraine opened the door and got in. But Wally caught the door before she could close it. "Isn't it obvious?"

"I know that you feel something for me," she said. "But it's not love, Wally."

"I want to marry you."

She pulled at the door, and he let her close it. Then he walked to the other side and got in. "Wally," she said, "please don't do this."

"Lorraine, listen. I've decided to go to the U this fall. I've changed my mind about the navy. I want to keep dating you—and then I want us to get married."

"Wally, I'm not going to talk to you about this. I don't think we'd better see each other anymore." She rolled her window down. The car was warm inside. "Please, take me home now."

Wally wondered why he had said anything. He had known how she would react. But he was tired of feeling this way about her and acting as though he didn't. "Lorraine," he said, "why do you say that? What's wrong with my being in love with you?"

"I've told you from the first—we can only be friends. Let's go." She folded her arms and sat straight and rigid.

"No. Let's talk. I think you have some feelings for me, too. Why can't that develop into something?"

"I'm sorry, but you're not the kind of person I want to marry."

"There's nothing wrong with me. I'm going to be successful. I'll be a good husband. What else do you want?"

"Wally, you don't know what you want out of life. You just float along with the current."

"I just told you—I'm going to college. I'm signing up this week."

"Oh, is that so? And what are you going to major in?"

"Business. I've thought all about it. I'm going to have my own business—of some kind. And I'll do all the things you want me to do. I'll make something of myself."

"And what about the Church?"

"What about it?"

She turned and leaned closer to him. "Wally, you don't care about the Church."

"You don't know that. I go to church every Sunday."

"Wally, you don't get it. I happen to *believe* in the Church. I want a husband who feels the same way."

Wally tried to think what he could say to her. He didn't want to claim anything that wasn't true. "Lorraine," he said, "I know I've been mixed up. But I know what I want now. I want *you*. I'll work hard—the way I've done this summer. I'll do good things with my life. I'll be a good father. And I'll be true to the Church. Don't worry about that."

"You can't want those things because of me. You have to want them because they really matter to you."

Wally didn't know what else to say. He only knew that he woke up in the morning thinking about Lorraine. And this summer, working in the orchard all day, he thought about her virtually all the time. He hurried home each night and called her, hoping she would want to see him. He longed for moments when she showed even the slightest sign that she cared about him.

"Wally, I do like you. I have more fun with you than anyone. But that's just the point. Fun is what you're good at. And dancing. In all the time we've spent together, this is the first time you've said anything about your goals—or about the Church—and I had to bring those things up."

"Then why haven't you told me to get lost before now?"

Her voice had lost all its irritation when she said, "I like you more than I should. I wish I didn't."

"Will you keep going out with me?"

"Why, Wally?"

"Because we like each other. Let's just leave it at that, if that's all you feel for now."

"Oh, Wally. It just won't work."

"Just keep seeing me. That's all I ask. I won't push you to think about the future."

She didn't say yes, but she also didn't say no, and so Wally left it at that, and he drove her home. And as he drove to his own home after, he thought about praying, about promising to reform himself if he could just have her. But he hadn't prayed for a long time now, and he thought God would consider him a phony if he tried.

Wally parked his car out front, and then he walked to the house. His parents were sitting on the porch.

"I'm glad to see you home at a reasonable hour," Dad said. "Your sister got in a little while ago, too. It's a miracle to have everyone home before we're in bed."

"What are you doing up so late?" Wally asked, just trying to say something before he walked on by.

Mom said, "It's *stifling* in the house tonight. This porch is the only place we could get a breath of air." Then she got a better look at him as he stepped under the porch light. "Wally, what did you do? You're all covered with mud—or something."

Wally didn't want to tell the truth, but he didn't have the energy—or the heart—to think up a story. "I slipped in a pond. Up at the golf course."

"What in the world?" Dad said.

"We go in there after golf balls." Wally stepped to the screen door and hoped he could get away. "It'll wash out."

"Wally," Dad said, "I don't think that's an honest thing to do. Those balls don't belong to you."

Wally took a breath. He didn't want to hear a lecture. "Okay," he said, but he couldn't resist saying, "It's not that big of a thing, Dad."

President Thomas stood up. "What isn't, Wally? Honesty?"

Wally had no idea how to respond to that. He merely stood and looked at his dad.

But Dad backed off. "Look, Wally, I don't mean to sound like an old fogy. It's not grand larceny. But I just don't think it's right."

Wally was surprised. He could tell that his dad had caught himself and was actually trying to sound less strict than usual.

But Wally couldn't resist saying, "Alex used to do it. That's where he and his friends always got their golf balls."

"Well, that doesn't make it right."

"I know." Wally thought of saying, "I just wanted you to know that Alex isn't perfect either." But it wasn't worth it. Wally knew he wasn't going to gain anything by bringing up that comparison.

When Wally reached his room, he was depressed by the heat—and by everything that had happened. He walked to the open window, where he could see the moon rising over the mountains. Behind him, he could hear Gene breathing, deeply and steadily. He thought of being married to Lorraine, of lying in bed with her at night, hearing her breathe. But it wasn't going to happen.

"I get along without you very well. Of course I do," he sang, and he thought again of holding her in his arms, out in the parking lot, and then of those few seconds when she had allowed him to kiss her. "Except perhaps in spring. But I should never think of spring. For that would surely break my heart in two."

15

Elder Thomas and his companion, Elder Taylor, decided they should go about their work normally and assume for the present that they would be able to complete their missions. But it wasn't easy. It was late August now, the twenty-fifth, and Hitler's troops were lined up on the border of Poland. All the people of Heidelberg seemed to be holding their breath, waiting to see whether Hitler would dare march into one more country.

The Nazis had been setting up this confrontation for months. The newspapers were full of accusations against the Poles, and Hitler was making his usual claim that the German minority in Poland was being mistreated. He was also demanding that Danzig, part of Germany before it had been taken away by the Treaty of Versailles, be returned. In addition, he wanted a corridor through Danzig and on to East Prussia, so he could build an *autobahn* and a railroad passage.

Most Germans seemed to agree with the Führer—if they said anything at all. But some of the members of the Church admitted their fears to the elders. In Czechoslovakia, Hitler had signed a treaty and then ignored it. But he wasn't likely to get away with that again. France and England and the other democracies seemed ready to stand firm with Poland this time.

And now, this week, Russia had signed a "non-aggression" pact with Germany. The lines were being drawn for a great European battle.

So tension—even dread—was in the air. Germany had been building its armaments at breakneck speed, in defiance of the treaty. Still, it hardly seemed possible that the military was strong enough to take on the great powers of the world. And no one wanted to think of another war like the last, when Germany had been devastated.

On that Friday morning, Elder Thomas and his lanky young companion, Wayne Taylor from Kanab, Utah, rode their bikes to Heidelberg's *Alt Stadt*—the "old city." But as they knocked on doors, they found people preoccupied and nervous. Some even asked, "Don't you know what's happening? You should leave the country while it's still possible."

Elder Thomas kept reassuring his companion that things had looked very bad the year before but that all the trouble had evaporated, and the missionaries had stayed. All the same, he knew that this was different, and not as likely to be resolved.

After lunch, the elders went back to their work, but tracting had only gotten more difficult. "Don't bother us now," people told them. "The Führer is on the radio." The elders were about to give up and go back to their apartment when an elderly man told them, "Come. Listen. You should hear this."

And so the elders walked into the apartment. Elder Thomas had once heard Hitler speak in person—in Frankfurt. The strange little man had raged, his black hair flopping over his eye as his head bobbed and his arm chopped. The Führer had shouted his allegations, his vows, and the people had cheered after every sentence. Just as the crest of the noise would pass, he would fire out the next blistering sentence, the words only half the import, the passion—the rhythm—having the greater impact. "*Sieg! Heil! Sieg! Heil!*" The crowd had chanted wildly at the end. "Hail victory!"

Elder Thomas heard the same pattern now, the voice a little

muffled on the radio but still conveying that intensity, still strident with passion. Hitler was denouncing foreign powers who had robbed his country of its natural rights, and he described the atrocities committed upon German residents in Poland. However much Germans loved peace, however much they hated war, the Poles need not think that Germans would abandon their brothers and sisters.

"This is right," the elderly man said. "We want no war. We'll start no war. But we'll do what is required. The Poles are attacking us across the border. It's they who want a war." His eyes focused on Elder Thomas, dared him to disagree.

But Elder Thomas only said, "Maybe we should come by another time," and he and Elder Taylor left.

Outside the door, on the landing, Elder Thomas stopped and looked at his companion. "We'd better wait until this broadcast is over," he said. "No one will talk to us right now."

And so they got on their bikes and pedaled back to their apartment. And when they arrived, they found what Elder Thomas had been fearing for days: a telegram. Their landlady had apparently accepted it and then pushed it under their door.

Elder Thomas felt the breath go out of him. He didn't have to open it; he knew what it would say. But he sat down on his bed, picked up a letter opener from his little night stand, and sliced the top of the envelope. "Leave for Holland immediately," the telegram said. "Turn over all Church records to local leaders. Contact the mission office before you leave."

The next few hours were maddening. The elders had to find branch members and turn over records, but more important, they had to give them encouragement to carry on. Heidelberg had a fairly strong branch, but the members depended on the missionaries, who had been like an extension cord, their power coming from the source, in Salt Lake City. It was frightening to pull that plug and know that for a time—possibly a long time—the members would have to manage on their own.

As it turned out, getting train tickets was more of a problem than Elder Thomas had expected. Trains were being taken
over by troops as the army mobilized for the massive buildup
on the Polish front. The train schedule was tentative, and
according to railroad officials, unpredictable from this point on.
Elder Thomas tried to purchase tickets to Holland, by any
route available, but the man at the busy ticket booth could
offer nothing definite, and he became impatient. Finally, he
said, "I can sell you tickets for Frankfurt, leaving early in the
morning. From there, you will have to see what you can do."

Elder Thomas had known that he might pass through
Frankfurt, the next big city to the North, and that would bring
him tantalizingly close to the Stoltzes, but he saw no way he
could take time to visit them.

That evening the elders took much of what they owned to
members: bicycles, books, household items. And they packed
their trunks late that night. After, they lay on their coverless
mattresses and tried to sleep in the oppressive, humid heat.
Neither slept much at all, and they were up before sunrise.
They walked to the *Bahnhof*, hired a taxicab, and drove back to
their apartment for their trunks. They had little concern for
the expense at this point since they knew they were only
allowed to take ten deutsche marks with them when they left
the country.

The train, even though it was departing at 5:35 A.M., was
extremely crowded. For a time the elders thought they would
have to leave everything behind. They paid a porter something
extra, however, and got the trunks on, but then had to stand up
in a crowded, already hot passenger car.

The train ride should have lasted a couple of hours, but it
took four, with a long delay in Mannheim, where more soldiers
got on. The elders wondered whether they might be forced
off, but they pushed themselves into a corner and tried to
remain inconspicuous.

Elder Thomas listened to the soldiers talk about the war.

They spoke of their certain victory—if the Poles refused to negotiate. But Elder Thomas watched one young man, maybe nineteen, who was standing opposite him. The chugging of the locomotive, the rattling of the tracks, along with all the talk, made the noise intense in the car. And somewhere in all that confusion, the young man seemed lost in thought, staring ahead, perhaps feeling homesick already and wondering what it would be like to fire a weapon at someone—or be fired upon. It was a memory that would stick in Elder Thomas's head long after. And when he heard people talk of the well-trained, fierce German fighters, he would picture that boy with the thin face, staring at nothing, like a homesick kid going off to summer camp for the first time.

At the Frankfurt train station, the elders were able to get their trunks off the train, but it was clear to them now that this wasn't going to work. They needed to leave much of what they were taking and pack what they could in suitcases that they could carry more easily. Suddenly Elder Thomas realized that he had an excuse. "The Stoltzes are not too far from here. They can help us," Elder Thomas said. "I want to talk to them anyway. I want to see whether Brother Stoltz isn't ready to be baptized."

The elders carried their trunks outside, but they found a taxi hard to procure. Finally, they spotted one arriving and ran to the driver before he had opened the door to let his fare out. They offered him money, lots of it, and then they ran back for their trunks. They piled the baggage in the back of the car and then offered the driver another bonus if he would get them out of the confusion and to the Stoltz's place quickly.

The driver took them almost too seriously, driving rather recklessly, but he made it. And then, once at the Stoltz's apartment, Elder Taylor stayed downstairs with the trunks while Elder Thomas ran up to the apartment.

Elder Thomas was hoping that everyone would be home on a Saturday morning. But Sister Stoltz was the one who appeared at the door. She took a moment to accept the shock and then grabbed Elder Thomas and hugged him. "Oh, my," she said when she finally calmed down, "the others are not here. They will want to see you."

"What time do they come home?"

"Early on Saturdays. Anna comes home from work at noon. Heinrich and Peter get home from school a little later. But you *must* stay until they come. Absolutely."

Elder Thomas looked at his watch. It was after eleven. He didn't know how long it would take him to buy suitcases, repack, and purchase train tickets. What he did know was that he was going to see the others before he left. He had to talk to Brother Stoltz. It was his last missionary effort, and he couldn't leave until he had carried it out.

And so the elders carried their trunks upstairs, and they walked to a leather-goods store, where they bought good suitcases. Then they walked to the post office, where they called President Wood.

"We're in Frankfurt. We couldn't get tickets to Holland," he told the president. "Can anyone help us?"

"Not really. Are you at the train station now?"

"No. But we're close."

"Go there. Buy tickets for Amsterdam, but you'll need tickets on to London by ship. We just got a call from the border. If you can't prove you're continuing on through, the Dutch border guards won't let you in. Do you have enough money to do that?"

"I think so. We can't take any with us, can we?"

"Only a little. You might give some to members if you want, but I would keep a reserve. You'll need to eat, and the way the trains are jammed, it could take a day or two to get out."

"President, do you know the Stoltz family, here in Frankfurt?"

"Yes, of course."

"Before we go, I want to talk to Brother Stoltz and see whether he's willing to be baptized."

"You'd better not take time for that. If you can get out, just go."

"But the family needs to be united. And he could be such a big help in the branch once we're gone."

"I know, Elder. But my concern right now is to get all of you out of Germany before this war starts and the borders close."

"Are all the missionaries gone from Frankfurt?"

"No. We're trying to close out the office. We have a million things to do, and Sister Wood is trying to finish up some lesson materials the members can use. But we're hoping to leave by tomorrow—or maybe the next day."

Elder Thomas wondered. If the president's missionary work could keep him another day, maybe his own work could too. Still, he knew what he had to do—he had to obey his mission president.

And so the elders walked to the train station, and they stood in a long line. But the harried clerk was not a lot of help. There were no tickets available on any train leaving Frankfurt that afternoon or evening. Finally, he said he could sell them tickets all the way to Amsterdam on a train leaving the next morning, but he couldn't guarantee that the schedule would hold overnight. Elder Thomas was too elated to worry about that. He had his answer. Now he had to stay.

And so the elders hurried back to the Stoltz's, and they repacked their bags, leaving behind all sorts of things for Sister Stoltz to keep or to pass on to other Church members.

Elder Thomas was on his knees in the living room, packing, when the door opened and Anna stepped in. She looked tired but beautiful. She didn't say anything, but Elder Thomas saw her swallow, as though she were trying to find her voice.

"*Guten Tag*," Elder Thomas said lightly, trying to sound casual about being there. He stood up.

"What. . . ." But she didn't finish.

"We're leaving Germany," Elder Thomas said.

"I know. We heard. But I didn't expect you here."

"We're leaving our trunks behind." It wasn't much of an explanation, but he didn't want to go through the whole story.

"How long will you be here?"

"We leave in the morning." Elder Thomas finally thought of his companion. "This is Bruder Taylor," he said.

Elder Taylor shook her hand. "It pleases me," he said softly.

Sister Stoltz had come into the room now. "Isn't this wonderful?" she said, and she walked to Anna and put her arm around her waist. And then she added, "I'm preparing something to eat. Anna, you keep them company until it's ready."

Anna nodded, and then she sat down on the couch. Elder Thomas knelt by his suitcase again, but he kept looking at her. "Where are you going?" she asked.

"To the Netherlands. And then . . . I don't know."

"Bruder Meis told us the last time you went to the Netherlands, you came back—after three weeks."

"Yes. But it won't happen that way again. President Wood said we won't be back."

She nodded, and he saw the sadness in her eyes. "It will be nice for you, to see your family."

"We may not go home. We may finish our missions somewhere else. No one knows for sure." Elder Thomas looked down at the things in his trunk, but he couldn't think what to do with anything. All his concentration was gone. "How's the branch doing?" he asked.

"Good. Everyone is kind to us. I teach the small children in Primary. Mother teaches the older ones."

"That's good, Anna. What about your father? Does he go with you?"

"Yes. Every week."

Elder Thomas finally heard some animation in her voice.

He looked up again. "That's what I was hoping. Do you think he'll ever join the Church?"

"I think he wants to. He's never quite certain. You should talk to him while you're here."

"I plan to."

Elder Thomas looked down again. She had begun to smile, to accept the joy of the moment, however brief. But the discussion stayed on the surface, and the problem was, there wasn't much to say. They talked about the people in the Frankfurt branch, and they glanced back and forth at each other, both so self-conscious that it was actually easier not to look.

"Does anyone know anything about Bruder Goldfarb?" Elder Thomas asked.

"No one can contact him directly, but President Meis gets reports from someone. All we hear is that he is still there in his shop, alone."

"I wish I could go there today. If it were only dangerous to me, and not for him, I would."

"Don't do it. Maybe there's something we can do—at some time. If there is a way, my father will do it." And Elder Thomas had to accept that. He had no other alternative.

By the time the elders had finished packing and Sister Stoltz had brought in some coldcuts for them to eat, Peter showed up. He had hardly calmed down before Brother Stoltz came in. They all talked about the evacuation of the missionaries, about the possible war, about the change that would come to all their lives.

"Bruder Thomas," Brother Stoltz said, "a long time ago I told you we might end up enemies. And you said we never would."

"We never will, Bruder Stoltz."

"Yes, I believe that's so. You and I cannot be enemies. But America may follow the other countries into the war. And you missionaries returning home could become soldiers. Whether you like it or not, you could come back to this soil to shoot at us."

"I couldn't do that." Elder Thomas was sitting at the kitchen table. He looked up at Bruder Stoltz, who was standing by the kitchen door, but he couldn't look at him long. He knew he was making a promise he might not be able to keep. And yet some things were so deeply contradictory that they seemed impossible.

"Our missionaries will never shoot at us," Sister Stoltz said. "Not even Hitler can make that happen."

"There is no end to the evil men can do," Brother Stoltz said. "We have seen enough already to know that." He looked at Elder Thomas. "This Kellerman—the Gestapo officer—came to us one day. He said you had been followed here many times, and he wanted to know what our connection to you was."

"What did you tell him?"

"We told him that we attended the same church. But he didn't care about that. He was only here to frighten us. It's what these men do. When they have nothing better to do, they go about making life a terror for anyone they can."

"Will he bother you anymore now?"

"Who knows? If he asks me what I think of the Nazis, I ought to tell him. Someone needs to stand up to them."

"And die," Anna said. "Please don't talk that way." She walked over and took hold of her father's arm.

"Oh, I won't. Don't worry. I'll be like every other German. I'll sit by and let this happen. Our nation will be destroyed, and I'll do nothing at all about it."

The room fell silent.

"What about the SS men?" Elder Thomas was finally brave enough to ask. "Have any of them bothered Anna?" He looked at Brother Stoltz, unable to pose such a repugnant question to Anna herself.

"We have been fortunate in that matter," Brother Stoltz said. "So far."

"She is strong," Sister Stoltz said. "These men don't like strong girls. They like the ones they can convince easily—ones who *like* the power of such brutal men." And then she added, "Bruder Thomas, the Lord *is* looking out for her—just as you said he would. Anna will be all right."

"At least it's what we hope," Brother Stoltz said, not offering his usual cynicism.

"Bruder Stoltz, you need to be baptized. You may not be able to stop Hitler. But you can bring your family together. You can bring the priesthood into your home." He stood up, so he could look directly at Brother Stoltz.

Brother Stoltz was still wearing his suit from work—the only suit Elder Thomas had ever seen him in. He hadn't even taken off his tie. He looked down and rubbed his hands together, and he didn't say no.

"Anna tells me you go to the branch meetings," Elder Thomas said. "And you like them."

"Yes, that's true. I like the hope it offers."

"Do you pray?"

"Yes. I do that."

Elder Thomas was not surprised but pleased, and he liked Brother Stoltz's tone of voice. "What do you feel when you pray?"

"I like to pray. I enjoy the thought that there actually is a God and that he cares about us—even in all this disorder and ugliness. But I don't know. Perhaps I feel good when I pray only because I want to hide from the possibility that there is no one to help us."

"At some time, you have to listen to the Spirit. Accept it. Not discount it every time you feel it."

Again Brother Stoltz looked toward the floor, and he rubbed his hands together. "I made a little test for the Lord," he said. "It's not the right thing to do, I suppose, but I did it."

"What test?"

"Last night, I talked to Bruder Meis. He told me that the

missionaries were leaving. I knew how much my family wanted to see you, and so I asked the Lord to send you here."

"Heinrich, you didn't tell me that," Sister Stoltz said.

"I know."

"Why was that a test?" Elder Thomas asked.

"I told the Lord, 'Send him here if you care about us.'"

"We didn't plan to come this way, Bruder Stoltz. But it was the only city we could get tickets for. And we couldn't get a train for the Netherlands until tomorrow. So maybe God made it happen."

"It's possible."

"Oh, Heinrich. You ask and you receive. And even then you doubt." She too walked to him, took hold of his other arm.

"But how does one know? What if the elders hadn't come? Would it mean there is no God? It's all so difficult to know."

"Bruder Stoltz, we are here. I wanted to come. I think you should be baptized. Now. Tonight, before we go."

Brother Stoltz's head came up, and those intense blue eyes, like his daughter's, filled with tears. "That's what I told the Lord. I said, 'Send Bruder Thomas. I'll take that as a reason to commit myself. I'll be baptized.'"

"Then you will, Heinrich?"

Brother Stoltz looked at Anna, and then at Peter, across the room, and then he turned and took his wife in his arms. "*Ja. Ich bin bereit.*"

I am ready.

Elder Thomas could hardly believe he was hearing this.

"But let's do it quickly. If I think very long, I'll change my mind. I feel something very strong right now, but I'll question it soon. I know I will."

Elder Thomas stood. "I'll go find Bruder Meis. And I'll check at the bathhouse. I don't see any reason we can't do it tonight."

"It's good," Bruder Stoltz said.

Peter ran to his father and grabbed him, and Anna reached

around and hugged him from one side while Sister Stoltz still had him from the other. The four stood together, holding each other, while the missionaries watched. Elder Thomas had never known such joy in his life—nor such sorrow. If only he didn't have to leave.

Elder Thomas and Elder Taylor were able to find President Meis, and he knew the man who ran the bathhouse. These were chaotic times for everyone, but the owner was more than happy to rent his establishment for the evening. President Meis, however, suggested something that added a new layer of difficulty. His second counselor, Brother Richter, was an older man whose health had been bad all summer. Brother Stoltz had already been a big help to the branch, but he could do more if he were called to the branch presidency. The only problem was that a missionary had served as district president, and he had already left.

And yet, everything fell together. President Meis was able to take a streetcar to the mission office, and President Wood authorized the reorganization of the branch. He sent one of his counselors, another missionary, to take care of it. And Brother Stoltz accepted the call, before his baptism.

A little group gathered together at the bathhouse that evening. Outside, trucks full of troops were roaring through the city, and all the talk was of war. Inside, Elder Taylor, who was about to perform his first baptism, sat next to Brother Stoltz, dressed in white. The handful of members sang with power, and Elder Thomas talked about peace.

"We search for peace, and we find very little," he said. "Men are aiming guns at each other right now, preparing to make war. Soon, perhaps, the only place we'll find peace is within ourselves and in Jesus Christ. We must trust that in the end, all will be well—as our favorite hymn tells us.

"I want you to know that you will *always* be my brothers and sisters. Nothing will change my heart. Or Brother Taylor's. The day will come when we will be united again. I hope that war won't come, but if it does, trust that members of the Church all over the world will pray for you, will love you, will be waiting for the day when this darkness clears."

Elder Thomas invited Elder Taylor and Brother Stoltz to come forward. Once in the water, standing next to Elder Taylor, who towered over him, Brother Stoltz looked up at Elder Thomas. He seemed more resolute than joyous, but he did look calm.

After the baptism, the Saints sang hymns as they waited for Brother Stoltz and Elder Taylor to change clothes. And then, when they returned, Brother Stoltz sat down on a chair next to the pool, and the brethren gathered around him. Elder Thomas confirmed him a member of the Church. He blessed him that he might become a man of great faith, that his doubts might disappear. As he said the words, he felt Brother Stoltz begin to shake. And when the prayer was over, Brother Stoltz stood up with tears on his cheeks and something new in his eyes. He wrapped his thick arms around Elder Thomas.

President Meis then ordained Brother Stoltz an elder, and Elder Buhl, from the mission office, asked the members to release Brother Richter and to sustain Brother Stoltz as second counselor in the branch presidency. The members were not surprised, and of course, every hand went up. Once more the men gathered around, and this time Elder Buhl set Brother Stoltz apart.

The closing hymn was "God Be with You Till We Meet Again," but Elder Thomas wished he had never chosen it. He could hardly get through the song, and everyone else was struggling too.

Brother Meis closed the meeting with a tearful prayer. He asked the Lord to protect and bless the missionaries as they departed, and he prayed that other missionaries would soon return. "But now, while they are gone, please strengthen those of us who remain, that we might carry on the work," he asked. And Elder Thomas tried to picture it. Would there be battles here eventually—soldiers, artillery, even bombs?

When the prayer ended, there was only silence, but finally Sister Stoltz turned and embraced her husband. Anna and Peter followed, and the members lined up to shake Brother Stoltz's hand. Elder Thomas was watching them when he felt a touch on his arm, and he looked to see Anna next to him. "I must say something to you," she whispered.

The two were not far from the others, but the rumble of the echoing voices was loud in the tiled room. "Thank you," she said. "Thank you for what you have done for my family."

He turned toward her, but he stepped back just a little. "Believe me, Anna, this has been my pleasure." He knew he sounded overly proper, but he also knew it was the only way he should talk to her.

"I'm afraid I won't see you again," she whispered.

Elder Thomas's breath caught. He couldn't let her get too personal. "We can always remember each other," he said, and instantly he hated the words. She was looking up at him, those huge eyes swimming in tears. "Anna, you're young," Elder Thomas said, but he didn't dare add to that.

"I'm not a child. I know what I feel."

Elder Thomas had to end this. "Anna, I'll pray for you," he said, trying to sound like a missionary. "I'll always remember you and your family. I hope you'll all be kept safe."

"Will you write to me?"

"Yes. Yes, I will." And he knew that once he was released,

he could be more open with her. "But if war comes, letters might not get through."

"I know. But let's try. Do you want to write to me?"

"Yes. Certainly." But that was all he said. He stayed under control.

It was on the train the next morning that he missed her so deeply that he wished he had said everything, mission rules or not. He wished that he had begged her to wait for him, and that he had promised to return to Germany as soon as he could. There were so many things he didn't know about her, so many hours he wanted to spend with her. And now she was just . . . gone.

"Are you okay?"

Elder Thomas was staring out the window at the countryside—watching Germany disappear from his life. He and Elder Taylor had found seats at first, but as the car got crowded, they got up and gave their places to a woman and her daughter. Now they were standing at the back, leaning against the wall behind the last seat. Elder Thomas was next to the window; looking out gave him something to do besides stare at the crowds of people.

"I'm okay," he said. "It's a hard time for all of us."

"I feel like I've been cheated out of my mission," Elder Taylor said. "Until last night, it didn't seem so bad. But being with that branch and performing the baptism, now I feel like I'm supposed to be here."

Elder Thomas saw a couple of soldiers glance at them, surprised to hear English. Elder Thomas wasn't sure it was a good idea to bring attention to themselves. "I feel that way too," he said quietly. "I would have been going home in February anyway, but I still wish I could stay until then."

Elder Thomas watched the pastures and garden plots outside. He saw women in long skirts, their heads wrapped in scarves, and men in high boots and wool trousers. It was

Sunday morning, but they were working—maybe because of the impending war.

The train was slowing now. Elder Thomas could see they were coming into the outskirts of a city, and he knew it had to be Bonn. He watched as they passed through an industrial area and then slowed to a stop in the big train station. The elders were staying on board here, so they held their places in the back. The only problem was, very few people got off, and more were trying to get on—many of them soldiers.

But no one ordered them off, to their relief, and even though the train remained in the station much longer than seemed necessary, when Elder Thomas heard the big steam locomotive begin to chug and grind, and felt the car move again, he knew they were edging closer to Holland.

Elder Thomas listened to bits and pieces of the conversation around them. He heard a soldier say, "Poland would be crazy to get anything started. They will be destroyed if they do—utterly destroyed."

So the talk went—confident, boisterous at times, and yet exaggerated. The men sounded a little too much as though they were trying to convince themselves.

Another hour went by, and the train pulled into Cologne, *Köln* in German. Here, the elders had to change trains. They grabbed their suitcases from an overhead shelf, and they tried to work their way through the crowded car. More people were trying to get on the train, and they weren't waiting for passengers to get off. For a time it seemed as though the elders wouldn't make it, but a policeman barked, "Let these people through."

The crowd in the aisle gave way enough to let them slide past, and they managed to make their way out onto the platform. But the crunch of people there was almost as bad. "We have to get inside," Elder Thomas shouted above the noise. "We have to find out what track our next train is on."

And so Elder Thomas worked his way through the crowd,

holding his suitcase up to his chest. Elder Taylor followed. Inside, they found a board with all the trains listed. "Track number four," Elder Thomas told his companion. He looked around for the right gate. "That way," he said, and he began to push through the crowd again.

"The schedule means nothing," a man said to him, in English.

Elder Thomas turned toward a young man with thick glasses and a cigarette in his mouth. "Excuse me?" he said in German.

"The train may be there. It may not. Tickets mean nothing. Even if your train is there, you may not be able to get on."

Elder Thomas nodded. "*Danke Schön,*" he said, but he pushed ahead anyway. They had to try.

The station was suffocating, hot and humid, and the smell of the people was almost intolerable, but Elder Thomas was sure he didn't smell good himself at this point. He wanted to strip off his suit coat, but it would be one more thing to carry.

"How much time before the train is supposed to leave?" Elder Taylor asked.

"Forty minutes—if the schedule means anything," Elder Thomas shouted over his shoulder. "Did you understand that man?"

"Some."

"Let's hope the right train is here."

"What about food?"

"We'd better not worry about that for the moment. If the train is here, let's get on. If it hasn't come in yet, we'd better hold our places on the platform and get on as soon as we can."

"If we have to wait on the platform, one of us could find something—at least some mineral water. I'm really thirsty."

"Yeah. We'll see."

But the two had come to the gate now, and Elder Thomas reached into his pocket to get out his ticket. A railroad official, however, was already shaking his head. "We have tickets for Holland," Elder Taylor told him. "Through Nijmegen."

The man, wearing a flat cap and cotton jacket, continued to shake his head. "That train is canceled," he said. "It's going to Poland."

"We're Americans. We're leaving the country. How can we get to the Netherlands?"

"You can't. The border is closed."

"Excuse me?"

A large man was eager to get by, and he was pushing Elder Thomas aside, slowly but persistently. As he slipped on past, he complained under his breath.

"The border is closed. No one can go through."

"What can we do?"

The official cocked his head to the side and shrugged his shoulders. "Move back, please," he said, and his look of indifference was almost more than Elder Thomas could stand. How could the man not make some effort to help, or at least to advise them? Elder Thomas stepped away and set down his bag. He looked at Elder Taylor. "We've got a problem. The border is closed. Holland must not be letting refugees in."

"Why not?"

"I don't know. Last year we got through without any problem. But there weren't so many people trying to get out."

"What can we do?"

Elder Thomas was trying to think. "If we can get to the border, maybe we could convince the guards that we're American missionaries and should be allowed to pass through on our way home. But we have to get there. Let's try to get to a ticket booth and find out whether *any* trains are going to the border."

"Can we use these same tickets?"

"I don't know."

Elder Thomas knew the next question. Where would they get money to buy tickets? The elders had given most of their money to President Meis—for any members who needed help. The elders had enough money for food, but only for a couple of days. They hadn't thought that anything like this would happen. They were expecting to be out of Germany before the day was over.

"Let's not panic," Elder Thomas said. "We need to ask questions—try to figure something out."

Elder Thomas pushed his way toward a ticket booth, and then he got in a long line. But when he finally got to the booth, the man inside the cage was no more helpful than the man at the gate had been. "Maybe some trains will go that direction. I can't say. But you won't get across," he said. "You should try to get to Belgium, perhaps, or maybe Denmark."

"Could we trade in our tickets for others?"

"No, no. I'm sorry. That's not possible."

"But the train is canceled. We should get our money back."

"We can't do that. I'm sorry. You must step aside. Many people are waiting."

"We have no money. We have no way to get out of Germany."

"I'm very sorry. I can't help you. Please step aside."

So Elder Thomas stepped away from the booth, and he tried to think. "Maybe we can call President Wood," Elder Taylor said.

"Maybe. But the phones are jammed. I doubt we could get through to him."

All the same, they tried. They waited in another line until they got to a telephone booth, and they placed their call. But the operator told Elder Thomas, "The call will not go through."

"But couldn't you—?"

The line went dead. Elder Thomas stepped out of the sweltering booth, and for a moment the air of the train station felt almost cool. He took a long breath and then said, "We need to eat something, and we need to think." And so they walked outside and found a little *Gasthaus* that was open on Sundays. They ordered bratwurst and sauerkraut—with a large mug of apple juice. And they felt a little strength come back. But they could think of no way out of their mess. "We'll have to keep calling the mission office," Elder Thomas told his companion. "Maybe later in the day the phoning will slow down."

"At night, maybe. How soon is President Wood leaving?"

"He wasn't sure. Soon."

It was not a comfortable thought. What if the president closed the mission office before he realized his missionaries were stranded? "We need to stay in the train station and keep our eyes open for missionaries. Others might be stuck here too—or will be before the day is over."

And so the elders walked back to the station. But in the mass of people, they could spot no one they recognized as missionaries. Every hour or so they tried to call the mission office, but each time they got the same result: the operator replying that the call would not go through.

The elders spent some of their time outside, where they only had heat to deal with, not the sauna-like closeness, and not the ubiquitous body odor. When night came, the crowd diminished, but the calls still would not go through. The elders finally found a place in a corner, stretched out as much as possible, and lay their heads on their rolled-up suitcoats.

Toward morning, Elder Thomas finally drifted off into a shallow state of sleep. But he hadn't been asleep long when something slammed against the bottom of his foot. He sat up suddenly, startled and wide awake. What he saw above him was a policeman—not SS but local. "Get up!" the man demanded.

Both elders scrambled to their feet.

"You can't sleep here," the policeman said. He was a grim-looking man with lumps over his eyes, like a boxer.

"I'm sorry. Our train was canceled," Elder Thomas said.

"What are you? Americans?"

"Yes. Missionaries."

"Show me your papers." Both elders dug out their passports and minister's credentials. The man gave them a cursory glance. "Let me see your train tickets," he demanded.

The elders complied once again, and this time the policeman took more time. He was heavy, and he stood with his mouth open, breathing audibly. Finally, he said, "These are worthless. You cannot go to the Netherlands."

"We know that," Elder Thomas said. "But we're trying to leave some other way—maybe through Denmark."

"Why didn't you go last night?"

"We used the last of our money to buy the tickets that were canceled. And now we can't get our money back."

Elder Thomas hoped to a win a little sympathy; instead, the policeman seemed to take the words as an insult. "That is not our fault," he said, leaning forward. "Germany didn't close the border. The Netherlands did."

"Yes. I understand that."

"You can't stay here. You're vagrants. This station is already too crowded. We don't need foreigners—tramps—sleeping on our floors."

Elder Thomas knew better than to argue. "That's fine," he said. "We'll leave."

The policeman stepped closer. He breathed into Elder Thomas's face. "At this moment you are only vagrants. Any day now—any hour—you will become enemies, foreigners in a country at war. All borders will be closed. If anyone stops you then, you will be jailed, immediately."

"We want to leave. Can you help us contact our leaders in Frankfurt? All the telephone lines are busy."

"That's not my problem. You must leave this station. Don't let me see you again."

So the elders picked up their baggage and walked outside, and they kept going until they reached a little park. They found a bench there and sat down, and they talked things over, but every possibility seemed closed to them.

"Elder Taylor, have you been praying all night?" Elder Thomas asked.

"Sure."

"Me too. But let's have a prayer together, okay?"

And so they knelt together by the bench. Elder Thomas called on the Lord to deliver them from the trap they were in. "Please help us find a way out," Elder Thomas said. "We place ourselves in thy hands. Show us what to do."

The sun was just beginning to rise, causing a little line of clouds to glow, pink and gold. Elder Thomas sat back on the bench and tried to get an answer, to hear the voice of the Lord telling him what to do.

"What about members here in *Köln?*" Elder Taylor asked. "Maybe they would help us."

"I've thought about that. We could find the church, maybe, but I doubt anyone would be there on a Monday morning."

The two fell silent for a time, but then Elder Thomas found himself saying something that came as a surprise even to him. "We need to get back into that train station."

"Why?"

"If President Wood knows about the border closing, I would think he'd try to send help in this direction."

"How would they find us in all that confusion?"

"I don't know. But they won't find us out here."

"What about that cop?"

"We'll watch for him, but before long the place will be as crowded as it was yesterday. I doubt he'll spot us."

"Do you think that's what the Lord is telling us to do?"

Elder Thomas shut his eyes and tried to find a voice within himself. But then he said, "I don't know, Mit. But it's the only thing that feels right to me. What about you?"

"I don't know. But if that's what you're feeling, let's do it."

And so they walked back. They stepped into the station but stayed near the open doors, and they scanned the crowd. For the moment, Elder Thomas was primarily looking out for the policeman. "Let's keep our bags close to this exit," Elder Thomas said, "and then let's take turns working our way through the crowd. If any missionaries are in the building, maybe we can spot them."

"Okay. Do you want to go first, or should—"

"Wait. Listen."

Elder Thomas was not sure. He listened intently. Someone was whistling on the other side of the station. It was hard to tell, but he thought he recognized the tune.

"Do What Is Right!" Elder Taylor said, and suddenly both elders were grabbing for their suitcases.

"Over there, on that baggage cart," Elder Thomas said, and at the same moment, he thought he recognized the missionary. But it was too good to be true. "Come on." A big guy in a dark suit had crawled up on top of the baggage cart and was whistling for all he was worth.

Halfway there, Elder Thomas finally knew for sure. "It's Elder Mecham, my old companion," he said.

"I hope he's got some money."

Elder Thomas was thinking the same thing. As the elders neared the baggage cart, Elder Thomas began to wave, and he saw Elder Mecham grin. "Hey, Elder Thomas," he said, looking delighted, "I'm glad you recognized my song. I can't carry a tune in a bushel basket."

"It sounded like a chorus of angels, if you ask me."

Elder Mecham waved his elbows, pretending they were wings. "That's me, the Angel Lewis." And then he pointed. "Look! Another pair of elders. And two sisters with them."

As it turned out, these four had been in the station only a short time, having gotten in during the early morning hours. But an older couple also appeared, and they had been stuck in the station even longer than Elder Thomas and Elder Taylor. Elder Thomas knew Elder Norbert and Elder Peterson quite well. Sister Edwards and Sister Price, along with the couple, Elder and Sister Pfortner, he had met at district conferences.

Elder Mecham had gotten down from the baggage cart by the time the missionaries collected in a little group. Everyone was shaking hands but still looking rather serious until Elder Mecham said, "I've got tickets. And plenty of money."

"Did President Wood send you?" Sister Price asked.

"Yeah. I got into Frankfurt last night and stopped at the mission office. The president had gotten word about the border being closed, so he had me buy tickets for Amsterdam—and for Copenhagen—and he gave me five hundred marks. Then he sent me out looking for missionaries. I'm glad to find eight in one place, but I still have twenty-three to locate."

"What did he say for us to do?" Elder Norbert asked.

"He thought you could still get through the border if you had tickets on to London. Joseph Fielding Smith was with President Wood in Hanover when all this started. Elder Smith and his wife got out that way, and they're in Amsterdam. But I'm not sure that will work now. You might want to try it, since it's close, and then, if that doesn't work, head for Copenhagen. I'll give you enough money to buy more tickets if you have to."

Elder Mecham reached inside his suitcoat and pulled out his billfold. He was pulling out bills when a loud voice sounded. "*Was machen Sie da?*"

The whole group turned at the same time. A policeman—not the one Elder Thomas and Elder Taylor had dealt with but another local officer—had come around the baggage cart. He stepped up close to Elder Mecham.

"Nothing," Elder Mecham said. "I was just trying to find my friends."

"You shouldn't be getting up there like that."

"I'm sorry. I won't do it again." He laughed.

"Have you papers?"

"Yes, of course."

The policeman was a slim man with a strong jaw and short, well-trimmed hair. He studied the papers thoroughly but briskly, and then he handed them back to Elder Mecham. "Are you leaving Germany?" he asked.

"Yes."

"I see you have money. You cannot take that with you. Give it to me."

"It's for my friends. We're all missionaries. We have to buy tickets to Denmark."

"I told you, give me that money." The policeman stepped closer and held out his hand. His eyes were still as stones.

Elder Mecham, who was much bigger than the policeman, held his ground, the billfold still in his hand and tucked against his chest. "I can't give it to you," he said. "I promised to get all our missionaries out of Germany, and we need this money to buy train tickets."

"You have a great deal of money there—much more than enough."

"No. I'm looking for thirty-one missionaries. I promised to help them all."

"I will decide that. Give me the money." He stepped closer and extended his hand again.

"No."

"Come with me, then," the policeman said.

"Where?"

"To the police station."

"No. I can't do that. I need to stay here."

The policeman had stepped away, expecting Elder Mecham to follow him. Now he stepped back. "Have you gone mad? I am arresting you. You must come with me."

"I can't. I won't go."

The two stood absolutely still, staring into each other's eyes. Elder Thomas felt as though his heart had stopped.

"I told you to come with me. Instantly."

Elder Mecham seemed to think things over this time. Several seconds went by before he said firmly but quietly, "No. I'm staying right here."

17

The policeman glanced around at the other missionaries, and then he focused on Elder Mecham again, who was a full head taller than the policeman. He seemed to be considering his options. He certainly knew he couldn't overpower Elder Mecham, but he could possibly call for help. He gradually turned and began to scan the crowd, obviously looking for other officers.

But surprisingly, it was Elder Mecham who pointed off toward a station exit. "I won't leave the station, but I am willing to talk to those military policemen over there."

Elder Thomas couldn't think what Elder Mecham was doing. But the policeman jumped at the chance to get the big elder over to other authorities. "Yes," he said. "We will go to them."

Elder Mecham set out, the policeman following, and the other missionaries trailing along in single file. Elder Mecham made his way to the officers and then said, "I'm an American missionary. I'm trying to leave Germany." Then he explained about the money he was carrying.

Elder Thomas was amazed by Elder Mecham's improved German, but even more by the authority in his voice. He and the others stayed back and let Elder Mecham handle the situation himself.

"This man wants to take my money," Elder Mecham said. "And that's not right. I'll give up any money I have left when I reach the border, but he has no right to take it from me now."

The two German military policeman listened, but their faces, their steady eyes, revealed no reaction. The taller of the two, a man who looked to be a match for Elder Mecham, said, "We will decide what is right. That's not for you to say."

"I told him he was under arrest," the local policeman said. "But he refused to go with me."

"You resisted arrest?" the big officer asked.

"I made a promise. I have to help my friends. And this man wanted to steal my money from me. I couldn't let him do that."

"What do you mean, 'steal'?" the local policeman demanded. He took hold of Elder Mecham's arm. "You will be very sorry you said this. Come with me to the station now."

But no one moved. Elder Mecham looked at the big officer and said, "This is wrong. You know it is. We have a right to leave your country. I have a right to help my friends."

"Enough talk," the local officer said. "Help me take him."

The two military officers glanced at each other, as though to measure the other's response. And then the bigger man asked, "What were you going to do with this man's money?"

The policeman let go of Elder Mecham's arm and faced the officer squarely. "You have no right to question my honesty," he said, his voice full of indignation.

But the officer said, "I do question it. I trust this man's honor more than yours. Leave now. I'll handle this matter."

"You have no authority over me."

"I'm taking authority. What are you going to do about it?"

"I can return with more officers from our station."

"Yes. But you won't."

The policeman stood his ground for a time, and then he said, "You have not heard the last from me," and he walked away. But he sounded defeated.

"Just a moment," the military policeman said to Elder

Mecham. He walked to a desk near the exit. He picked up a pen, dipped it in a bottle of ink, and wrote something on a sheet of paper. Then he brought the note to Elder Mecham. "This may help you, if someone else stops you, but I can't guarantee it. You must leave the country as soon as possible."

"I have to look for other missionaries," Elder Mecham said.

"I understand that. But I wouldn't take long." And then he reached out his hand. "Good luck," he said, in English.

Elder Mecham thanked him, and then he walked to the other missionaries. "That was amazing," Elder Peterson said.

"Not really," Elder Mecham said. "Germans believe in honor."

"Maybe so," Elder Thomas said, "but how did you know to talk to these army guys? I thought you were getting yourself into a bigger mess."

"I don't know why I did that. I said it before I'd thought about it—and as soon as I did, I thought I'd made a mistake."

"The Lord *is* looking out for us," old Brother Pfortner said. He was an American, but a native German. He spoke English with a heavy accent. "God told that officer what was right."

Elder Thomas felt a chill go through him, and he felt sure that Elder Pfortner was right. He finally thought to close his eyes for a few seconds and say a prayer of thanks.

"Look, I need to keep going," Elder Mecham said. "I can't tell you exactly what to do. You'll have to take whatever trains you can catch. I hope the conductors will honor these tickets." He looked at the Pfortners. "The Dutch might be stricter about letting the young missionaries through—but maybe you can make it the way Elder Smith and his wife did."

"Yes, yes," Sister Pfortner said. "We must try this. We can't make it the other way."

Elder Thomas hated to think what might happen to them if they didn't get across the border, but he thought the Lord would help, somehow.

Everyone talked things over after that. Elder Thomas

agreed to go with Elder Mecham to find the stranded missionaries. Elder Taylor decided to leave with the others for the border, and then to head north to Denmark if that didn't work. And so everyone went together, for the moment, to see whether they could catch the train to Bentheim, on the Dutch border. The man at the gate said the train was going to be late. Everyone else decided to wait, but Elder Mecham and Elder Thomas found a train heading to Oberhausen, a closer town, and they got on. The train was slow in getting started, but when it pulled out of the station, the elders knew they were moving toward the area where some of the missionaries might be—which was better than waiting in *Köln* for a train that might not come for another hour.

Along the way, the elders talked about their experiences since they had last seen each other. Elder Mecham was excited to hear all about the Stoltz family, and Elder Thomas was overjoyed to know how much Elder Mecham had grown as a missionary.

Elder Thomas was also impressed with the way Elder Mecham led the way when they got off the train in Oberhausen. He strode to the ticket booth, and he worked out the next plan. There was a "milk run" train that stopped in every town along the border. It was just the right thing, except that it was very crowded. Elder Mecham bought tickets anyway, and then the elders boarded and found standing room. The train was under way before Elder Mecham said, "I hope you don't mind how I'm doing this, but President Wood told me to follow my impressions and somehow find those missionaries. I said, 'Don't worry. I'll find them.' So I feel like I've got to be the one to carry this through."

"That's good, Mit. I like being the junior companion."

"You were the best senior I could have had, Elder Thomas. You showed me how to do this work. I don't have any patience with elders who waste their time."

"Did you ever take that trip to the Black Forest?"

"Heck, no." Elder Mecham laughed. "Some of these missionaries are running around all over. But after the Lord saved my skin in Frankfurt, I made up my mind I was going to give him his money's worth." He smiled and dropped a big hand on Elder Thomas's shoulder. "I guess if the Lord can make a half-baked missionary out of me, he can do just about anything."

"I hope he doesn't bake you till you're done," Elder Thomas said. "You're about right—a little doughy in the middle."

Elder Mecham picked up his hand and gave Elder Thomas a pretty good whack on the shoulder. And he laughed, in that big voice of his, causing everyone in the car to look his way.

The plan was to get off in the first border town; then they could work their way north. But as the train was pulling into one of the towns still a few kilometers distant from the border, Elder Mecham suddenly stooped and looked out the window.

"Let's see," he said. "I'm thinking maybe we'd better get off here and take a look."

"I doubt anyone would—"

"Come on. I think we'd better."

"Should we leave our baggage on board?"

"Uh . . . no. The train won't be stopped long." He reached up and grabbed his own bag, nothing more than a satchel, and then pulled down Elder Thomas's bigger suitcase. He pushed his way past a few people and stepped off the train, carrying both bags.

Elder Thomas caught up quickly and took his suitcase from Elder Mecham, who walked into the little one-room station and looked around. A few people were sitting on the benches inside, but certainly none were missionaries. A man just inside the door asked, "What can I do for you?"

"Have you seen any Americans?"

"Not that I know of."

"Let's get back on the train before it pulls out," Elder Thomas said. "We don't want to get stuck here."

"Just a minute." Elder Mecham walked on through the

station, stepped outside, and scanned the area. "When we were on the train," he said, "I got this really strong feeling that we ought to stop here. And now I don't know why."

"Maybe it was just—you know—a mistake."

Elder Mecham didn't answer. He was still looking at the street that led away from the train station.

"We'd better get back on the train, Elder."

Elder Mecham stood for a moment. "Maybe so," he said quietly. But then he took a step forward. "No. We need to take a look around here."

"Look around?" Elder Thomas couldn't believe this. There was nothing to look around at. The town was a tiny village. If missionaries had ended up here for some reason, surely they wouldn't have left the train station.

Elder Mecham picked up both bags again, and he marched away, taking those long steps that Elder Thomas remembered all too well. The day was getting hot now in the early afternoon, and Elder Thomas saw no reason to walk so fast. They could check out this whole town in ten minutes—at an easy pace.

"Where are you going?" Elder Thomas finally asked.

"I'm not sure. I just feel like I need to keep looking."

Elder Thomas was losing patience. He believed in the Spirit, but this was sounding downright silly. Maybe Elder Mecham had become a little too zealous in all his newfound faith.

The elders passed some shops—a *Bäckerei* that smelled wonderful, for one thing—and then came to a *Gasthaus*. "Let's take a peek in here," Elder Mecham said.

This was the one place in the village that was worth checking, so the two stepped into the little restaurant, which was filled with long tables, most of them empty. Elder Thomas took a quick glance and was about to turn, when he came to a stop. Two men were sitting at a nearby table—wearing suits.

Elder Mecham burst into laughter. "Hey, Elders," he said.

The missionaries looked up, one twisting in his seat. Both were wide-eyed. But in another second they were scrambling out of their seats and heading toward Elder Mecham. "How did you know we were here?" one of them was asking.

"I didn't know. You're just lucky the Lord knew. You did your best to hide from him."

Everyone shook hands. Elder Thomas was somewhat acquainted with one of them, Elder Thompson. The other said his name was Elder Maw.

"How did you end up here?" Elder Mecham asked.

Elder Thompson was a tidy young man, normally, but he hadn't shaved for a couple of days and his tie was hanging loose. "We got to Bentheim, and they wouldn't let us through. So we got on a train—without tickets—just hoping no one would notice. But a conductor kicked us off here. We just spent our last few pfennigs to buy some apple juice. We didn't know what we were going to do after that."

"I never would have gotten off that train," Elder Thomas said. "It was all Elder Mecham. It's a miracle we found you."

"I'll tell you what," Elder Mecham said. "God told me—just as clear as a bell ringing—to get off here. I've never had such a sure feeling in my life. Then ol' doubting Thomas got me worried, and I almost gave up. But God wouldn't let me do it."

"Are you serious? You got off the train to look for us?"

"I just felt something. I just . . . knew."

A long silence followed, and Elder Thomas saw the awe in both elders' eyes. "We've been praying—a lot," Elder Thompson finally said. His eyes had filled with tears.

Elder Mecham took his billfold out. "I'm going to give you money for tickets," he said. "But I don't know how to tell you to get to Denmark. You'll have to follow your own inspiration."

And so the elders walked back to the train station, and Elders Thompson and Maw got tickets on a train to Hanover. Elder Mecham and Elder Thomas waited until the next train came through, and then they departed for the border. They found four more missionaries in one little border town, this time in the train station. And then, when they reached Bentheim, they walked off the train and immediately spotted a whole group of elders.

"Elder Thomas," one of them called, an elder named Sanders who had come over on the boat to Germany with Elder Thomas.

Elder Mecham walked ahead. "I have money," he said. "President Wood sent me to find you."

"We're okay," Elder Sanders said. "We have tickets."

"Where did you get the money?"

All the elders laughed. They were a tired-looking group, all with unshaven faces and wrinkled suits. "It's a long story," Elder Sanders said. "We got across the border, to Oldenzaal, but the Dutch border guards stopped us and told us we couldn't enter the country. So we called the mission office in Amsterdam, and the mission president told us he would send someone with money for tickets to Denmark. But we got sent back across the border before anyone could reach us."

Elder Sanders put his arm on another missionary's shoulder. Elder Thomas didn't recognize him. "This is Elder Kest," Elder Sanders said. "He came from Amsterdam. He's leaving in a few minutes to head back. His story is the one you need to hear."

"How did you get into Germany?" Elder Mecham asked.

Elder Kest smiled. "I got to Oldenzaal," he said, "and the guards told me the missionaries had been sent back to Germany. I didn't know what to do. I tried everything I could to get a visa, but I couldn't get one, so I got on the train anyway. And for some reason, the border guards didn't check my passport. They just let me go."

"That's impossible," Elder Thomas said.

"I know. But it happened."

"But not on the German side," one of the elders said.

"I got arrested on this side," Elder Kest said. But he was still smiling. "The German border guards took me into a little room and asked me all kinds of questions. And they searched me. They took some tracts I had and read them. And then they started confiscating everything I had in my pockets."

"Did they take your money?" Elder Mecham asked.

"Yes. But I had bought tickets and brought them with me. I knew those guards were going to take them, so I took them out of my pocket and just set them on the table. But they just let them sit there—right in plain sight."

"Why?" Elder Thomas asked.

"I don't know for sure. I know this sounds crazy, but I don't think they saw them. I set them down, and no one even blinked. It was like they couldn't see them." Elder Kest motioned with both hands past his eyes, as if to indicate a veil.

"So did you get them back?"

"Yes. They told me to go back into Holland on the next train—leaving in forty minutes—and they would give me back my things. But the tickets were still on the table. As I got up to leave, I reached out and picked them up, and I swear, no one seemed to see me do it. It's like they were blind to it. I walked out with the tickets, and they let me go. Then it was another miracle that I found the elders. I asked around, and someone had seen them and told me where to look."

Elder Thomas thought of Elder Pfortner's words again. "The Lord is looking out for us."

"So you have a way to get back to Amsterdam?" Elder Mecham asked.

"Yes. The train should be here any minute now."

Elder Mecham nodded. "Let me give you some more money. And before you go, if it's all right, I'd like to have a prayer with all of you."

They walked outside and found an alley where they could step off the street. Elder Mecham thanked the Lord for his guidance, and he asked a blessing on Elder Kest and all the German missionaries that they would be able to leave the country safely. By the time he had finished, Elder Mecham was fighting to control himself, and after, all the missionaries had tears in their eyes. They shook hands all around and wished each other the best. Confidence seemed high, but Elder Thomas knew everyone would feel a lot better once they were actually out of Germany.

Elder Mecham and Elder Thomas talked things over again. They considered all the possible routes that missionaries might have taken to the border, and where the two of them might look for the ones they still had not located. They decided they would have to head south again, retrace their steps, and check some of the towns farther from the border.

For another day and night, Elder Mecham and Elder Thomas tried everything they could think of, but they found no one else.

By the time they had made the trip south and then all the way back to Bentheim, it seemed highly unlikely that they could have missed anyone. But they walked outside, knelt, and prayed. When they were finished, Elder Mecham said, "I feel like the others must have managed to get out somewhere—without our help. What do you think, Mit?"

"Well, I don't see any reason to go south again. But more than anything, I trust what you're feeling. God is working through you, Elder Mecham."

It would have been more like Elder Mecham to deny that, but he said, "I know. And I feel like it's time for us to see whether we can get out. President Wood told me not to stay so long that I couldn't get out myself."

As it turned out, the next twenty-four hours were the worst of all. The elders had slept very little the night before, catching winks on trains when they could get a seat, and lying on a train station floor for a few hours. But now they found that the trains heading toward Hamburg or anywhere north were being taken over by troops. At every station they were warned not to board, that they might get to the next train station but then be booted off and end up stranded. But they got on trains that were heading somewhat in the direction they needed to go, and they kept working their way closer to Denmark. Three different times they seemed trapped, with no way to continue north or to return to their last city. But each time, they managed to find another train.

When they reached Schleswig, they knew they couldn't be more than thirty or forty kilometers away from Denmark, but it was early in the morning, and the elders hadn't had any real sleep for three days. And worse, what they had been seeing outside made them feel that the war would probably begin that day. They had seen convoys of tanks and artillery moving on the roads and highways, blocking traffic, filling villages with their noise. And armaments were appearing everywhere. Anti-aircraft guns were set up in church steeples and on top of buildings. Every bridge they crossed was guarded by machine-gun emplacements.

In Schleswig, an official came through the car announcing that the train would travel no farther north. Everyone must get off. So the elders climbed off the train, again very worried. But they saw people jumping off the platform and running across the tracks to the train across from them.

Someone shouted, "It's going to the border. It's leaving now." The elders bolted after the others. They jumped off the platform, ran across the tracks, and then climbed up the other side. They were about to head for the nearest car when a man yelled. "You two! Stop!"

Elder Thomas took a couple of steps toward the train, but a policeman was running toward them.

"Stop! You can't do that."

Just then Elder Thomas saw the departing train jerk and begin to roll forward. "We must catch that train," Elder Thomas told the policeman. He took another step in that direction.

"No. You have broken the law. Where are you from?"

"America." Elder Thomas looked at the train, which was rolling a little faster now. He couldn't think what to do.

"Look how many are crossing," Elder Mecham shouted at the man, above the noise. Several more people were down on the tracks, and some were just climbing up on the platform.

The policeman shouted, "No! You must not do that." He turned back to the elders. "Stay here. You are under arrest." Then he ran along the platform, yelling for everyone to stop.

"Come on!" Elder Mecham yelled to Elder Thomas, and he reached down and grabbed both suitcases. He took off after the train, running hard. Elder Thomas was almost sure they were making a mistake, but he took off after Elder Mecham.

"Stop! You men, stop!" the policeman was shouting. But Elder Mecham kept running, and Elder Thomas was not about to stop and go back alone.

The only trouble was, the train was picking up speed. Elder Thomas could see what he had to do. He sprinted past Elder Mecham, gained some quick ground on the caboose, and then leaped onto the steps. "Forget the bags," he yelled to Elder Mecham. He reached his hand out for him.

But Elder Mecham had drawn even now, and he tossed Elder Thomas's suitcase to him. Elder Thomas shoved it behind him and then caught Elder Mecham's little bag. In the effort, however, Elder Mecham had lost some ground on the train.

He put on a burst of speed—all he had—and leaped. He got a foot on the bottom step, and Elder Thomas grabbed him by the arm, but the big guy was dangling, unable to reach the handrail with his other hand. Elder Thomas was clinging with everything he had, but he could feel Elder Mecham slipping from his hold.

And then another hand reached over Elder Thomas's shoulder and caught Elder Mecham by his suitcoat. A big tug shifted Elder Mecham's weight forward, and he was able to swing himself around and catch hold of the handrail. He was on!

Elder Thomas took one last look and saw the policeman waving a fist, his mouth wide open, yelling some last curse at them. But they were on the train, heading toward the border.

And it was the conductor himself who had pulled Elder Mecham on board.

"I should have let you fall," he muttered. "You should not do that." But his gruffness seemed to take some effort.

The elders stepped inside the caboose and shut the door. "We have to get to the border," Elder Thomas said.

"Yes, of course. I understand that."

"We have money—but no ticket."

"Everything is crazy," the conductor said. "People are getting on any train they can. No one has proper tickets." He turned and walked away.

The elders were still trying to catch their breath. "I was about to slip off," Elder Mecham said, but he was laughing. "If I had landed back on the platform, that cop would have had me."

"I doubt that. You would have fallen on the tracks and broken your head wide open."

"Ah, no. My head is too hard for that." He grinned, and then he said, "Let's go see if there's a seat somewhere in this train. I'm a little tired."

The train, as it turned out, was not crowded. Troops were heading south from this part of Germany, and most people who were fleeing the country had apparently already made their way out. The two missionaries sat down, and Elder Thomas took some more deep breaths. They were going to make it, he told himself.

"I hope everyone else got out," Elder Mecham said, and that, of course, was the last worry.

The train stopped at a couple of little towns after that, and it stayed longer than seemed necessary, but finally, about mid-morning, it chugged to a stop at the border. And once again, everyone was told to get off the train.

The elders lined up at a little guard station and waited for their turn to be processed. Elder Thomas couldn't believe the relief he felt. As they were waiting, however, a guard walked along the line, looking at everyone. When he reached the elders, he stopped. "Americans?" he asked.

"Yes."

"Come with me."

Elder Thomas couldn't think why they would be singled out. Most of the people in the line were foreigners. But the elders were marched into the station and into an office. There, they faced an older, balding man who looked up at them through thick glasses. "You two were arrested in Schleswig— and you ran from the police. Did you think you could get away with that?"

Elder Thomas's breath seemed to lodge in his windpipe. It seemed impossible that they could come this close only to be stopped now. He tried to think what to tell the man, but he didn't think excuses were going to impress him.

"You broke the law. For that you must be punished."

"We just want to leave Germany before the war breaks out," Elder Mecham said.

"Yes. And why are you so desperate? Are you spies?"

"We're missionaries."

"I'll let others decide what you are. I only enforce the law." He stood up and called for the guard.

"We have this," Elder Mecham said. He pulled out the letter that the military policeman had written for him in *Köln*. The man read it carefully and then said, "This means nothing. This officer simply accepted the story you told him." He looked at the guard. "Call the police. Have them come for these men."

"Wait a minute," Elder Mecham said. "We're not liars. We *are* missionaries. We crossed some railroad tracks—with a lot of other people—but that's the only thing we did wrong."

"That's why you were arrested? For crossing railroad tracks?"

"Yes."

"And nothing else?"

"Nothing else."

The man stared at Elder Mecham for several seconds, seemed to test the idea, and then he said, "Go. Cross the border. You're only making my day more difficult."

He handed back the papers, and the elders left. They waited in line again, gave up most of their remaining cash, allowed the guards to check their passports, and then, suddenly, it was all over. They walked across the border and into Denmark.

On the Danish side, they were stopped and checked again, but by then they could see, standing not far away, President Wood with two other missionaries. The three of them were beaming.

As soon as the elders passed on through, they hurried to President Wood, who grabbed one of them in each arm. "You're the last," he said. "Everyone is out now."

"All thirty-one? We couldn't find some of them."

"They all got out. Some got through the border before it closed."

"What about the Pfortners?"

"They're safe in Amsterdam. The guards let them go through."

Elder Thomas and Elder Mecham turned and threw their arms around each other. "The Lord did it, Mit," Elder Mecham said. Elder Thomas began to say a silent prayer.

President Meis said the opening prayer himself, and then he said, "These are strange circumstances for our first meeting as a branch presidency, but I think we need to carry on as always."

Brother Stoltz nodded, but he was feeling nervous about this. He knew nothing of Church leadership, and he felt the absence of the missionaries. Brother Meis leaned back in his chair. "I believe we will defeat the Poles quickly and decisively. And that could be the end of this. If everything settles down, the Church might be willing to send missionaries back before long."

Brother Stoltz hardly knew how to react. He understood the hope to have the missionaries back, but President Meis sounded unconcerned, maybe even satisfied, about the attack on Poland. "Brother Meis," he said, "England and France have declared war against us. I see no way that this can end quickly."

"The Führer can negotiate with them. He's done so before. Why should those countries want to fight over Poland? They know we deserve to have Danzig back."

"Hitler won't stop with Danzig. He'll take the whole nation, just as he did in Austria and Czechoslovakia."

"It's what those people wanted. They chose to be part of the *Reich*. They voted."

"Voted? They voted the way we do. Yes or no to Hitler—with men checking the ballots to collect the names of those who vote against him."

But President Meis didn't answer. "Bruder Stoltz," he said, "those countries are better off now—being one with us."

"You believe that?"

"Yes. It's what I understand. And I'm pleased we're fighting to get back what belongs to us."

"Read *Mein Kampf*, President Meis. Hitler is doing what he said he would do." Brother Stoltz's voice had become intense. "He's grabbing up every country he can get his hands on. Then he constructs outrageous lies to justify anything he does."

President Meis looked stunned. He glanced at the door and then whispered, "You must not say such things. Who knows who might hear you?"

Brother Stoltz lowered his voice, but he struck the desk with his fist, and he said, "If you care about the gospel, you should pray that someone stops Hitler. *Kills* him, if possible."

"Brother Stoltz, this is treason. You could be put to death. Bruder Müller and I could die for listening to you."

The three were sitting in a room President Meis used as an office for the branch, in rented space above a store, but the office was really just a closet. President Meis sat behind a small desk, and the counselors sat opposite him, very close, on wooden folding chairs.

"I'm sorry, President Meis," Brother Stoltz said. "But this is how I feel. If you cannot work with me, tell me now."

President Meis forced a finger inside his collar and tugged. He was not heavy, but he was strong, his collar squeezing his thick neck and his bulky shoulders stretching his suitcoat and pulling under the arms. "Perhaps I believe too much of what I'm told," he said softly. "And you are a *Gymnasium* teacher, more knowledgeable than I am. But I support my Fatherland. I will always do that."

"We can differ on this," Brother Müller said. "What matters

is that we all believe in Christ—and the restoration." Brother
Müller was a white-haired man, about sixty. He was lean, and
he usually seemed rather stiff. But his voice was tender now.
"That's fine," Brother Stoltz said. "I'll say nothing more
about politics. But in time you will agree with me. We cannot
love Christ and Hitler any more than we can love God and
Satan."

"Many members disagree with you," President Meis said.
"They think the Führer is doing what must be done." He placed
his hands on the desk before him, and he leaned forward. "But
Bruder Stoltz, the gospel is more important than any of this."

"That too is a treasonous statement, President Meis.
Nothing is more important to Hitler than the *Reich.*"

President Meis looked down at the desk—his hands—and
then he said, "We must make the best of our circumstances, and
we must keep the Church alive in Germany until missionary
work can begin again. If you say the wrong thing and get us
killed, how can that do any good?"

"Then you're telling me that Hitler is a murderer—but I
should support him."

Clearly, President Meis had no good response to that. It
took him some time to say, "We must do what is expected of
us."

"I do," Brother Stoltz said. "I care too much about my family to take chances." He hesitated, and then he added, "I won't
bring this up again. And I do believe we must find a way to survive. But don't ask me to praise Hitler."

"Fine. I don't expect that. Let's worry about the people of
our branch and what we can do to look after them."

"That's fine with me."

And so the three pushed their chairs back and knelt in the
crowded little room again. "Please, Lord," President Meis said,
"help us to work together and to bring peace to our members,
no matter what else happens."

When he finished the prayer, he stood up, and he shook

Brother Stoltz's and Brother Müller's hands again, and they started over. They discussed the problems that lay ahead. The members had a much larger load of work to handle themselves now that the missionaries were gone, and the Maintal members were left without leadership. Plans had to be made for someone to visit them and preside over their meetings.

When the meeting ended, everyone felt better. German troops were blitzing through Poland, and people all over the world were waiting to see how the European democracies would react. But the branch presidency would keep the Church going in Frankfurt, no matter what happened, and Brother Stoltz, in spite of his differences with President Meis, felt some closeness to him.

Elder Joseph Fielding Smith had managed to find a flight, and he and his wife, Jessie, had arrived from Amsterdam in Copenhagen. Elder Smith had overseen the arrival of the missionaries, and now he was working to make arrangements for them to sail back to America.

It was a strange time for the missionaries. After all the excitement and anxiety of the evacuation, suddenly they were living like vacationers. Each morning they met with Elder Smith at the branch house, and he led them in discussions, but after the class they were free to wander through Copenhagen, take pictures, and visit tourist sites. It would have been very pleasant if the missionaries hadn't been hearing the news.

German forces were destroying Poland in spite of some limited help by the French. Warsaw was under siege, the artillery fire constant and the people in terror. It was only a matter of days until Poland would fall. And now Russia had marched in from the North, ready to grab up its share of the spoils. That was apparently the deal Hitler had made with Stalin. The great question was what would come next. Would Hitler attack France? Or would the French army move across the Maginot Line and try to stop Hitler, maybe with the help of the Royal Air Force? All of Europe was blacked out at night, and everywhere civilians were expecting bombs to begin falling.

But the bombs were still not dropping, and the missionaries were thrilled to have time each day with Elder Smith. Elder Thomas had known him for as long as he could remember, but he still knew what an opportunity he now had. And Elder Smith obviously liked teaching, even surprising, the missionaries. One morning he told them, "Here's something you probably never thought of. The land masses of the world were all together at one time. You can look at a map and see the continents like pieces of a jigsaw puzzle spread apart. Priesthood power, one day, during the millennium, will bring those continents back together. That's part of the restoration of all things." He nodded and looked around, obviously pleased with his own concept.

After class one day, Elder Thomas lingered after the other missionaries had left. "Elder Smith," he said, "I'm wondering whether this war breaking out now could be part of the winding up scene in the last days."

"Well, now, let's not speculate," Elder Smith said. He pointed at his black leather scriptures, then pounded his forefinger on the cover. "Too many people want to think up the truth when all we really need to know is right in the scriptures."

"Oh, I didn't mean—"

"That's fine. That's just fine. Nothing wrong with the question. But let's look in the scriptures and see what they say. Where do we need to look, Elder Thomas? What do we know about the last days?"

Elder Thomas hadn't realized what he was getting himself into, but he could see that Elder Smith was delighted to play the schoolmaster. "Matthew, I guess," Elder Thomas said.

"Yes, certainly. There are signs mentioned there." Elder Smith walked over and sat down in a chair, and he motioned for Elder Thomas to sit next to him. He set his Book of

Mormon on another chair and then opened his Bible. He thumbed through the pages, which were marked and written on, the corners of the pages tattered. He found Matthew 24 quickly, but he didn't look at it. It was all in his head. "Have you seen nations rising up against other nations, Elder Thomas?"

"Yes." Elder Thomas was still trying to locate Matthew 24.

"All right. That's one of the signs. But it's been going on forever, hasn't it? Have you heard of any false Christs?"

"Well . . ."

"Of course you have. Have you heard of wars and rumors of wars?"

"Yes."

"Famines? Pestilence? Earthquakes?"

"Yes."

"Nothing new in any of that, is there? All those things have happened. But what does Christ say about that?"

Elder Smith turned and looked directly at Elder Thomas, who finally looked up from his Bible. "He says that's not the end."

"Exactly right. 'For all these things must come to pass, but the end is not yet.' They are the 'beginning of sorrows.' So things are bad, with Hitler raising up one nation against another, but it's going to get worse. What do you know about Jerusalem? What do we learn from Zechariah?"

"There's supposed to be a great battle in Jerusalem."

"Yes. Now that's hard to envision right now. But it will happen. And then the stone cut out of the mountain without hands . . . you know that scripture, don't you?"

"Daniel."

"Yes. That's right. It will roll forth, and what?" He leaned a little closer, and he raised his finger, almost touching Elder Thomas's chin.

"Consume the whole world."

"Well, that's about right. It becomes a mountain, and it fills the whole earth. And what is this stone?"

"The gospel going forth to all the world."

"That's right. And that still has to happen."

Elder Thomas thought about that. "So the end might be a long way off yet."

"Now wait." Elder Smith held his finger in the air, and he gave his head a little shake. "Don't be too quick to say that. Things can happen quickly. And no one knows the time. Isn't that what we're told? The bridegroom cometh, but no one knows the day nor the hour. Where's that?"

Elder Smith was still leaning toward Elder Thomas, making him self-conscious. "Uh . . . Matthew . . ."

"Matthew 25. That's right. Now here's what I have to say to you, Elder Thomas. Look up here now. Look me in the eye."

Elder Thomas had been turning to Matthew 25, but now he did as he was told. "Everyone wants to know the hour. And there is the answer right there in the scriptures. When will it be?"

"No one knows."

"That's right. You and I don't know. The prophet doesn't even know. So stick to your knitting. Don't worry about it. You go home and serve the Lord. President Wood told me you were one of his best missionaries, which is exactly what I would expect. You need to get home and marry a woman in the temple of God, raise up a fine family, and serve the Lord in whatever capacity he calls you. And trust me, he's going to call you. Do you understand what I'm saying to you?"

"Yes." Elder Thomas felt strangely out of breath.

"You probably need to go to college. But don't get caught up in it to the point that you start to think you know everything. You read the scriptures, and you learn from that. And you follow in your father's footsteps. When the Lord comes— which may very well be in your time—you be ready. That's the whole point of the parable, isn't it? Keep your lamp ready. Be prepared. Does that settle that matter for you, Elder?"

Elder Thomas was nodding.

"Good. You run along now. Jessie wants me to go look at some museum. She'll walk my legs off and tell me all about everything, and I'll say 'uh-huh, uh-huh,' and she'll think she's educated me a little. She needs that."

Elder Thomas smiled when he realized that Elder Smith was joking—although he hadn't cracked a smile. Some mornings, at the meetings, Sister Smith had sung to the group. Once she had even talked Elder Smith into joining her. And one day he had surprised everyone by saying, "When the Prophet sealed Sister Smith and me, he commanded me to kiss the bride. And I always do exactly what the prophet tells me. I keep that commandment as often as I can. Some day, you young men should do the same."

But now Elder Smith was saying, "Let me tell you one more thing. I haven't told the others yet, but I will before long. It looks like we're sending you home. You don't have six months left on your mission, do you?"

"No. Only about—"

"Well, then, you'll be going home. It isn't worth sending you off to Nebraska or Kentucky or somewhere and just let you get settled in a little before we ship you home. Those with more than six months to go will finish their missions somewhere in the States—or maybe Canada."

Elder Thomas hardly knew how to react. Suddenly his mission was over and he hadn't had a chance to complete the full term. Something about it felt incomplete.

"Wish me luck," Elder Smith said as he stood up. "If I don't get just the right sound in my 'uh-huhs,' Jessie will chastise me something terrible. She's not a woman who will settle for a half-hearted 'uh-huh.'" Finally, he laughed.

Elder Thomas laughed too and said, "I do wish you luck, Elder Smith. And thanks for talking with me."

"Let me tell you one more thing. You have the ability—and the heritage—to become a great man. You could easily end up sitting on the highest councils of the Church. Don't strive for it, but do your duty—serve with all your heart—and the Lord will use you. I feel that in you, Elder."

He nodded, seemingly to seal the words, and then he walked away. During the rest of Elder Thomas's stay in Copenhagen, he thought of those words constantly, wondered what his destiny would be back in Utah. And he wondered about the other part of his future. What would happen in Germany?

After about three weeks, the missionaries were divided into two groups and shipped out. Elders Thomas and Mecham made certain they ended up on the same ship. They sailed on the *Mormachawk*, a freight ship that had been set up with cots down in the hold to handle passengers. Another part of the hold was inhabited by cattle, with all their pungent smells. The passage, especially in the beginning, was rough, and most of the missionaries spent many hours leaning over the rail. The steward finally brought a big metal tub down to the hold so the elders wouldn't have to run quite so far to vomit. But the smell only added to the problems, and Elder Thomas tried to spend all the time he could out in the fresh air. Some nights he slept on deck rather than going down into the hold, where he always became sick immediately.

The only baths the missionaries could take were cold, salt-water showers, and the food was terrible. After a few days, however, the weather improved, and the rest of the trip—another week or so—went much better. The missionaries gathered in groups each day, and they continued the gospel study that Elder Smith had started. Elder Thomas was one of the more knowledgeable of the missionaries, and he found himself called on to answer questions. He liked to play the Elder Smith role a little, to push the others to state what they knew from scripture, and quote chapter and verse. He wasn't nearly so good at it as Elder Smith, but he was better than most, and that made him appear quite the authority.

Toward the end of the voyage, Elder Thomas and Elder Mecham sat up late one night talking and looking at the stars. It was a cool night in early October, and they shivered a little, but the sky was enormous, and the stars were clear. It was too good to pass up after all the cloudy days they had seen at sea. So the two of them lay flat on their backs on the deck and looked at the sky.

They talked about their futures, and Elder Mecham said he was going to take college more seriously this time around. He wanted to settle into a major and find something he could build a career on. "I'm thinking about forestry," he told Elder Thomas. "They have a forestry school at the AC. And I like the idea of working outside."

"I think that's a good choice," Elder Thomas said. "I can see you doing something like that."

"So what are you going to do? Do you still want to study history?"

"I think so. I can't think of anything else I'd rather do. I have an uncle who's a history professor, and I've always loved to talk to him."

"You'd be a good professor, too. It's hard to think of you doing anything else."

"Of course . . . maybe we'll all be soldiers." Neither spoke for a time after that. Elder Thomas looked at the stars and imagined them falling from the heavens. So many calamities were coming, but he had never thought, until lately, that those "wars and rumors of wars" would involve him.

"I pray every night that I won't ever have to fight Germans," Elder Mecham finally said.

"Me too."

The two lay there, the universe stretched out overhead. Elder Thomas was always awed by the idea that God could see and understand so much. In the presence of such vastness, it seemed rather selfish to bother him now with personal concerns, but Elder Thomas began to pray—not about the war or the German Saints this time—but about a small matter: a young woman he wanted kept safe.

He closed his eyes to shut out the stars for a moment, and he tried to see her face. But the image wouldn't come. What he saw instead was a parade: tanks resounding on cobblestone streets, goose-stepping soldiers, trucks, artillery, blood-red Nazi flags. When he opened his eyes, it was hard for him not to think of the universe as something cold and immovable. And so he shut his eyes again and tried to picture God, his Father— someone who cared—and he prayed for a miracle. He asked that Anna might be protected, that he might see her again, that he might have the chance to ask her to marry him.

And there, out under the stars, suddenly a tremendous warmth and calm filled him, the same power he had felt at the moment he had placed his hands on Anna's head to bless her. He was sure he had his answer. She was the one he was supposed to marry, the one he *would* marry.

19

The door was open part way, so Bobbi stuck her head in and said, "David?"

Professor Stinson rotated in his chair and then stood up. He looked elated. "Bobbi. I was hoping you would come by." Fall-term finals were over, and David was reading tests. He had on a sports shirt and a white V-neck tennis sweater. He actually looked stylish—just a little out of season.

"I turned in my last paper, so I'm finished. But I wanted to bring you this." Bobbi was holding a gift wrapped in red and green Christmas paper.

"Bobbi, you don't have to bribe me. I already gave you an A." He smiled and reached for the package.

"Oh. I'll keep it then." She pulled it back, but he stepped closer and took it away from her.

Bobbi had completed her second class with Professor Stinson, whom she now called David at times, but only when no one else was around. The two had talked many times during the term. The conversations usually started with Bobbi's questions about the Puritans or Emily Dickinson—or whatever she was studying at the time—but they had a way of continuing down the hallway and into David's office. And then, more often than not, the talk turned to other matters, and at some point Bobbi had begun to express her frustration with Phil. She and Phil had agreed on a wedding date, but she had managed to put it off to June 16, at the end of her junior year. That had seemed a long way off in the fall, but now, with Christmas near, it was beginning to seem close.

David tore off the wrapping paper and looked at the gift—a book. "Oh, my," he said, and then he opened the cover and looked through the first few pages. "Bobbi, I don't believe this. It must have cost you a fortune."

"Not really. Mr. Weller made me a good deal."

"But it's a first edition."

"I know." Bobbi had not intended to buy him a Christmas present, but she had been downtown in Zion's bookstore, and she had looked through the used books. When she had come across this handsome edition of Henry James' *The Ambassadors,* she couldn't resist buying it for him.

"This is wonderful. The binding is beautiful."

"I'm glad you like it. I thought you would."

"You *knew* I would." He looked at her for a moment, smiling a little, but those green eyes of his looked serious, intense. "Bobbi, I don't think, in all my life, anyone has known me so well. I've told you things I've never told anyone."

It was time to go. This sort of thing was happening too often lately. Bobbi was never so happy as when she could spend time with him—and never so miserable. "I've told you things I *shouldn't* have told anyone. I hope you keep my secrets."

He nodded, smiling more now. She loved the way he studied her face, as though he were trying to discover any hint of what she was thinking. "I didn't get you anything. I thought about it, but I didn't know whether I should."

"David, I didn't expect us to *exchange* gifts. I just saw this, and I wanted you to have it."

He looked at the book again, turned it over in his hands. "I think the proper response is to give you a kiss."

"Oh, I think not." But she didn't step back. She was confused about her relationship with David and well aware that she was playing with fire, but she loved these moments when his attraction to her was so obvious.

"There's another reason I should kiss you."

"Oh, really?"

"Yes. A sprig of mistletoe is hanging over your head, and you know what custom requires in that case." She began to look up, but he placed the palm of his hand on the top of her head. "Don't look. That implies that you don't believe me."

"Oh, I would never suggest that." She smiled, knowing she was flirting, wanting the kiss at the same time she was telling herself she wasn't going to allow it. She loved the excitement when he stepped closer. In fact, she almost let it happen, but when he bent a little, she finally stepped back. "I need to go," she said, her voice barely a whisper.

"I'm sorry. I didn't mean to—"

"That's okay. I just need to go."

"Could I maybe see you—during the holidays."

"No. Of course not." But the idea was wonderful to her, and she watched a subtle dimple form in his cheek when he sensed that he had a chance.

"We *need* to talk," he said, and now he was trying to say things with his eyes, and she was suddenly nervous.

"There's nothing to talk about. You know that."

"Bobbi, you can't marry Phil. You know you can't."

Bobbi looked out the window, where the afternoon sun was angling across the snow. It was bright out there, and Bobbi had felt good all day. She didn't want to think. She had only intended to surprise David with the gift and then go home, relieved that her last paper was in. "I know I've made Phil sound awful sometimes. But he's not so bad as you think."

"He couldn't be as bad as I think. Because I think you'll *hate* him if you marry him."

Bobbi wanted to deny that, but she sometimes wondered

whether that would be true. She looked back at David, whose eyes were still trained on hers. "I've got to go," she said again.

"What about college? What would he say if you told him you wanted to stay on for graduate school?"

"I don't know. He would think it wasn't necessary, but if I told him it was important to me, he might try to work something out—at least at some point in my life."

"This is crazy, Bobbi. He has no right to decide things like that for you."

"You're the only person I know who feels that way."

"You Mormons," he said, and Bobbi could see his frustration. His shoulders lowered as the air seeped from his chest. "I'm sorry. I don't mean to intrude. It's your life—obviously."

Bobbi pulled the door open. "Well—I won't have a class with you next quarter, but I'm sure I'll see you."

"I don't want to go the whole holiday without seeing you."

"David! You shouldn't say things like that."

He walked closer but stopped and pushed his hands into his pockets. "You're right. I'm being unprofessional. Let me put it another way." He cleared his throat and then said, formally, "As your professor, I feel an obligation to discuss your career options with you. Would you like to meet with me sometime?"

"Yes, of course. We should talk about that at some point."

"How about tonight?"

She smiled.

"I'm serious." He took hold of her wrists. "Meet me tonight. I won't do or say anything I shouldn't. But we could celebrate the end of the term together. It's a lonely time for me right now. I need something like that."

"I can't meet you. What if someone should see us?"

"Meet me downtown."

"Are you serious? Everyone in Sugar House knows me, and half of them will be Christmas shopping tonight."

"Okay. Meet me here on campus. We'll find somewhere to

go. Give me *one* evening of your life—before Phil gets you forever."

Bobbi expected to say no. But the word didn't come, and when he said, "Okay?" she found that she was nodding. And when he said, "Seven?" she nodded again. "Out in front of this building. I'll think of someplace to go."

And once again she nodded, but she said nothing at all. She left quickly. Halfway down the hall, she almost turned back to tell him she couldn't do it, and then on the bus, she remembered that she had told her parents she would go to a family party with them. Phil had promised Sister Thomas he would come along to meet some of the Snow family.

Bobbi would have to stand David up. It was the only thing she could do at this point. But half an hour later, she was telling her mother that a professor of hers had gotten himself into a bind. An emergency had come up, and he had asked her to mark a set of papers for grammar—before he read them for content. "It's actually a compliment to me," she said. "Most professors would never ask an undergraduate to do something like that. I know he'll write me a good letter of recommendation someday."

"But Bobbi, my mother is expecting you. She wants her sisters to meet Phil."

"Maybe Phil could go with you, and then I could run over a little later. If Dad will let me take his car, and you two drive with Phil, I could meet you there. The party doesn't start until eight. I should be there by nine or so."

Mom accepted that, and Bobbi felt terrible to think herself capable of such effective lies. But Dad was a tougher sale. He wanted to know who the professor was. "I don't like the idea. Taxpayers provide his salary. Why can't he do his own work?"

"He normally would," Bobbi told him. "It's an emergency. Something in his family."

"Or bad planning."

But Dad let it go. And now Bobbi only had to talk to Phil,

who turned out to be the easiest. He was impressed that professors in the department thought so highly of Bobbi. But when he asked which professor it was, Bobbi lost her nerve. "Dr. Wilson," she said, and she heard her voice rise to a higher pitch. But Phil didn't notice, and after Bobbi put the receiver back on the telephone, she felt guiltier than ever.

In spite of her doubts, however, at 6:45 she was starting her dad's new Hudson, and she could hardly contain the tumult inside her. She knew she had to end all this, but she too wanted this one evening before she took the wiser course.

When Bobbi showed up in front of the "LA"—the Liberal Arts building—David was already there. But the problem they had been putting off was real now. They really couldn't be seen together anywhere on campus, and they couldn't go to a restaurant. "Listen," David said, "don't take this the wrong way. If I promise to be a gentleman, will you walk down to my apartment?"

"I don't feel good about that, David."

He laughed, the steam gusting from his mouth. "I'll sit on the opposite side of the room. I won't *try* anything."

"And you won't start claiming that your ceiling is covered with mistletoe?"

"There's not a sprig in sight. I promise."

But he was flirting with his eyes, and so was she. This was all so dangerous and thrilling she could hardly stand it. "Let's drive down. Someone might see us walking."

And so they walked off campus and then drove the Hudson down First South. When David opened the door to his apartment, Bobbi was surprised. The room was a little cluttered, mainly with books, but it was surprisingly clean. He took her coat and hat, offered her a seat on a little sofa, and then sat across the room, as he had promised. He was still wearing the tennis sweater, and Bobbi was a little embarrassed she had dressed up so much—in a pretty green dress with black, high-heel pumps. At least she had left her gloves in the car.

David's chair was tattered but comfortable, with a floor lamp next to it. Bobbi could tell he spent a lot of time there. "What do you do every night?" she asked. "Do you read all the time?"

"No. I play some squash, or basketball, with another professor. Or I go swimming sometimes. I even go out for a drink once in a while." He smiled. "But I do spend lots of hours sitting right here."

"My goodness. The life of a professor *does* sound stimulating. You're doing a marvelous job of recruiting me."

"At least I make a *handsome* salary."

Bobbi laughed, but then David told her how much he actually did love his life. He spent his days reading, lecturing, talking to other professors. "That isn't work to me," he said. "I come home, fix something to eat, and get lost in my books. And being alone is good in some ways. Sooner or later I want a family, but for now, these are my years to learn and contemplate."

Bobbi wondered. She couldn't imagine a life that wasn't full of activity and people. "Why didn't you go home for Christmas?"

"I couldn't afford it."

"What's Christmas like in Connecticut?"

David leaned forward and smiled. "It's terrific and just awful," he said. "My parents are lovely people—I really mean that—but they're painfully formal. Both my brothers are lawyers, and my brother-in-law is an investment banker. We eat a lot of good food, and we're all very witty and charming. But I don't know, there's just too much posturing and name-dropping for me. I take off with my nephews and nieces. We go ice skating or sledding, or I get a snowball fight going."

"It doesn't sound much like the world I've grown up in."

"What's your Christmas like?"

"Lots of family around. This year it's going to be nice with Alex home."

"What's it like to have him around? Is he still *zealous?*"

Bobbi had to think about that. "He's not preachy, if that's what you mean, but he's gained some depth. I feel a kind of quiet confidence in him now."

"He's got all his pockets full of truth. That weighs a fellow down."

"What he has is *faith.*"

David had been looking down, but his head came up quickly. "I'm sorry," he said. "I'm not making fun of him. It's just that the returned missionaries I've taught all seem to think they . . . well, never mind."

Neither spoke for a time after that until Bobbi finally said, "David, you don't feel comfortable at home anymore, but you're not really comfortable here either, are you?"

"Well . . . no. But I get by all right." He stood up. "Let's see, can I get you something? I have Pepsi Cola, or—"

"No. That's all right."

He grinned. "Have you ever tasted alcohol?"

"Yes. In cough syrup."

"I guess you wouldn't want . . . no, never mind."

"That's right. Never mind." Bobbi was beginning to feel awkward, but maybe that was good. It would be something to remember when she became unsatisfied with her life.

He sat down again, leaned forward with his elbows on his knees. "Salt Lake isn't so Mormon as everyone thinks. I could find a congenial group of friends here—especially at the university—and do just fine. But I think I'd rather move on before too many more years."

"Why?"

"If I stayed, I'd have to burrow out a little cave and live in the middle of Mormonism. And I don't want that. I would either want to be part of it or away from it."

"Could you ever join the Church?"

He laughed. "'The Church.' We both know which church *the* Church is."

Bobbi was embarrassed, partly because of her provincialism,

which he was teasing her about, and partly because her question was so transparent—and they both knew it.

"I don't like the pressure Mormons put on each other. You can't just be religious; you have to *show* it. Still, you really *are* religious. And that's the thing I envy: that certainty. I wish sometimes I could share in that."

Was that something to build on? Bobbi allowed herself a little fantasy. One day she would bump into David on campus, and he would say, "Guess what? I've been looking more deeply into your church, and I've decided to join." Then, suddenly, everything would be different.

David seemed to know what she was thinking. "I doubt I could ever feel the way you do about *the* Church"—he smiled—"but maybe I could . . . find a way to . . ."

"Fake it?"

"No. I wouldn't do that."

Bobbi felt the fantasy vanish, and suddenly she wished she weren't there. She thought of making an excuse and leaving, but she decided to keep things neutral, to make cordial conversation, and then to leave gracefully, with all this behind her. So she asked David about his time at Columbia, about his childhood, and David asked about life in a stake president's home. It was all very polite, but the magic Bobbi had both feared and desired simply wasn't there.

After an hour, which actually passed rather slowly, Bobbi decided she'd better make her escape back to her own life. "I need to leave," she said. She had told him earlier about the family party. Now she stood up.

"I'm sorry," David said softly. "This didn't turn out the way I had hoped."

"What were you hoping?"

"I don't know." He stood up, and he ran his fingers through his hair. "I think we're both kind of nervous."

"Yes. I think so."

He walked over to her. "But I still have a problem."

"What problem?" She knew better than to ask, knew she should leave—but she wanted to hear the words.

"I'm in love with you, Bobbi. You know that. I think about you all day, every day." She took a long look into his eyes, gave him a tiny little nod, and then walked to the chair where David had placed her coat. "Do you feel something for me, Bobbi?"

She looked back at him. "Yes. You know I do. But—"

"I know." He followed, and he helped her on with her coat. Then she walked to the door. "Bobbi, I shouldn't have said those things about Phil. Maybe you two will be all right."

She nodded. "I have to decide about that—soon."

And that was the end. Bobbi reached for the door.

But he was walking toward her. Bobbi knew she should put her hand out and stop him, but she wanted this. He took her in his arms and kissed her, and then he held her close. "There must be a way. Somehow," he said, his mouth by her ear.

But already Bobbi's wiser self was pushing itself back into control. "I just don't think so," she said, and she pulled away.

"We need to talk more. Maybe if we left Utah. We could find a church that we could—"

"No. You know I wouldn't do that."

"All right . . . but. . . ."

"I shouldn't have come. I need to—"

But then he had her in his arms, and they were kissing again. He slowly ran his fingers over her hair. She felt the tingling run along her neck, then spread all through her. But once again she pulled away. She was surprised when the first tears dropped onto her cheeks; she hadn't known she was crying.

"Bobbi, I think I *could* be a Mormon—in my own way. There's so much about the Church that appeals to me."

"Don't, David. You know that wouldn't work."

"Why not? Let's think about it. I'd be willing to study the Church more, or . . . I don't know. Bobbi, I don't want to lose you."

Bobbi was crying harder now. She wanted this, but she

didn't trust it. And she knew she had to leave before she made promises she wouldn't be able to keep. "I've got to go," she said again.

"Will you talk to me more about this?"

"I don't know. Probably not." She opened the door and stepped out, and she hurried down the stairs and out to the car. She had to get to the family party, but she couldn't go while she was in this state. And so she drove for a time, stalled longer than she should have before she finally pulled up in front of her Grandma and Grandpa Snow's home. And then she went inside and told her lies again: the students' papers had taken a little longer than she had expected. No one seemed to doubt her, but then, never before had she given them any reason to do so.

Bobbi slept much later than usual the next morning—partly because she had struggled for such a long time to go to sleep. When she finally did wake, she looked toward her window and saw that snow was falling. She was glad for that. At the university the skies had been clear lately, but her home was deep enough into the valley to have been locked in the dark blanket of soot that sometimes covered the valley for weeks. This storm would clear some of that.

During her wakeful night, she had told herself over and over that she had to make things work with Phil. If she didn't like him at times, it was because of her own attitude more than anything that was wrong with him. Things would never work with David, and it was time to stop playing with ideas that were not just useless but also dangerous. The ache she was feeling would go away if she got the right thoughts in her head.

But she kept thinking of the kisses, of the way she had felt when he had held her. And those feelings were far too powerful to push aside. She heard his words over and over: "Bobbi, I don't want to lose you." And try as she might to force the thought away, she kept wondering whether she and David couldn't find some answer that would work for both of them.

She was still lying in bed when she heard a squeal and then

an angry voice from the bedroom next door. She didn't worry too much about it until she heard Beverly begin to cry, but then she got up, walked to the girls' room, and opened the door. "What's the trouble?" she said.

Beverly was sitting on her bed, but now she jumped off, ran to Bobbi, and threw her arms around her. "LaRue says Santa won't come to me."

Bobbi held on to Beverly but looked across the room to LaRue, who was standing by her bed, still in her flannel nightgown. She defiantly cocked her head to one side and said, "She never does what Mama tells her to do."

"I just forget sometimes," Beverly moaned, pressing her face against Bobbi's middle. And Bobbi had to smile. Beverly lived in her own world, always imagining, always playing games with her dolls. The real world of chores and duties sometimes slipped her mind. Mom scolded Beverly for that now and then, and LaRue found her mother's words handy as weapons when the girls got upset with each other. Bobbi was sure LaRue no longer believed in Santa Claus, although she had never announced that to her family, but her knowledge gave her power over her sister, who was clinging to belief.

"If you're bad, Santa doesn't come, does he, Bobbi?" LaRue demanded. "Jesus doesn't love bad people either."

"Jesus loves everyone, LaRue. You should never say that."

"Well, if you're bad, he won't let you go to heaven."

"LaRue, your sister isn't bad. She forgets sometimes. You're the one being bad right now."

Beverly let go and twisted around. "Yeah!" she said.

LaRue stuck her tongue out.

"Now you're both being bad," Bobbi said. And she began to walk away. But the words struck Beverly hard, and she began to cry again. Bobbi turned back and knelt in front of her. "Oh, honey," she said, "don't worry. You're not bad." She looked up. "Can't you two be nice to each other?"

"Does Jesus love us?" Beverly asked, swallowing now, trying not to cry.

"Yes. No matter what you do, he loves you. But it's still important to be good."

Bobbi left after that, and she walked back to her room, to the window, and she watched the snow falling through the limbs of the apple tree. She didn't want to be bad either, she told herself. But why did the choices have to be so complicated?

2 0

Christmas day started out like all the others, except that Alex was back and, as always, had a way of becoming the center of things. He played with the little girls, and they fussed over him, sat on his lap, and laughed with him. When Alex asked who was going to win the Rose Bowl, Gene, who read every word in both newspapers' sports sections, gave Alex the whole rundown on why he figured Southern Cal would beat Tennessee.

Wally couldn't help feeling a little jealous, but he was waiting for his special little pleasure in watching Mom and Dad open their presents from Beverly and LaRue. Mom had asked Wally to go Christmas shopping with the girls, and Wally had liked that. He had taken them downtown on the trolley, which they loved to ride. The city had been great—so busy that it was hard to walk along Main Street. Music was playing; people were waving and greeting each other. The street lamps were wrapped in red and white like candy canes, and high-arching evergreen bows were draped across the streets.

Wally loved it, and he had fun with the girls. They spent most of their time in W. T. Grant's, the "five and dime store." The girls looked at potholders and fancy combs, screwdrivers and shoe-polish brushes—everything. They walked up and down the aisles, picked up half the items in the store, it seemed, and all the while chattered about the many choices. Wally teased them constantly, showing them that the shoe brush looked like Hitler's mustache and using an eggbeater to muss their hair.

Finally the girls settled on the right gifts. For Mom, they chose a little music box that Wally had to "go halves" on. It cost $1.29, and the girls, together, had only a dollar to shop with. Wally also helped out on a 49-cent tie. It was an ugly thing, maroon with a flock of ducks flying south across it. Wally loved it mainly because he knew Dad *would* wear it. He would feel he had to, because of the girls, but also because it had been paid for and ought to be put to use.

After shopping, Wally and the girls had gone to Walgreen's and ordered strawberry sodas. Beverly and LaRue loved to watch the "soda jerks" toss the dips of ice cream in the air and catch them in the big glasses and then, with a flair, run soda over the ice cream and create lots of pink foam. He knew, too, that they both liked to look at themselves in the mirrors behind the counter and admire their pretty new winter coats and hats.

But even after all that, it was Alex they wanted to be close to, now, on Christmas day. That was partly because Alex was gone a lot in the evenings—because he had gone to work for Dad—but Alex also knew that the girls got tired of Wally's teasing.

Mom loved her music box and thanked the girls—as well as Wally. And Dad hated the tie but pretended he didn't, which was perfect. "Thank you for helping them, Wally," Dad said with an ironic smirk.

"Don't give me the credit," he told his dad. "They picked it out by themselves." Beverly and LaRue were quick—and proud—to agree. The rest of the family took delight in that.

After the gifts were opened, Mom marshaled the troops into the kitchen. While everyone was gathered around the table eating, Dad and Alex began to talk about the war. All the talk in the newspapers was about the "phony war." Little fighting had actually taken place, except at sea. The *Graf Spee*, a German pocket battleship, had sunk a number of British freighters in the Atlantic and then, recently, taken a pounding itself and had to be scuttled off the coast of Uruguay, near Montevideo. So far, that was the only major victory of the war for the Allies, and it had come at a heavy cost.

"Hitler's the one talking peace now, I notice," Dad told Alex.

"Sure, he always gets what he wants and then tries to lie his way into a treaty—which he breaks as soon as he sees an opportunity to grab something else. Everyone wants peace so badly they let him pull the wool over their eyes."

"This world is a scary place right now," Dad said. "Russia has always talked so high and mighty about the glories of communism, and now that gangster Stalin is trying to take over Finland, as if he can't stand to see Hitler have all the fun."

"Look what Japan has done, too," Alex said. "They think they have a right to *lead* all of Asia, whether Asia wants to be led or not."

Wally had heard these kinds of conversations too many times before. He ate quickly, and then he said, "Dad, I have a present I want to take to Lorraine. I'll be back in fifteen minutes."

"No, Wally. Don't run off. I want to hold our Christmas meeting as soon as possible."

Dad was at the head of the table. Wally leaned forward and looked around Gene. "Come on. You'll all still be sitting here at the table for at least that long."

"Dad," Bobbi said, "Phil is coming over to get me. I'm going to run up to his house for a while."

"When?"

She hesitated, chewed, and then took a quick drink of milk. "Soon, I think. Maybe Wally could take off while I'm gone. I won't stay very long."

"No. Let's hold our meeting right now—or you'll all be running this way and that and we'll never get around to it. If Phil comes along, he can join us."

"Al," Mom said, "I've got a turkey in the oven, and I've got to get the rolls mixed so they'll have time to rise."

"That's fine," Dad said. "But let's meet first. It won't take long."

"I'll tell you what, Dad," Wally said. "I can give your Christmas talk—quick. I know it by heart. We all do."

Wally laughed, but no one else did, and Wally saw Bobbi duck her head. Dad was staring at Wally, but he didn't look angry; he looked hurt. That was not at all what Wally had wanted. "Hey, I'm just kidding," he said. "It wouldn't be Christmas if you didn't give your talk."

Everyone was silent—and tense. And Wally didn't want that. He had really only meant to tease.

But then Alex stepped in. "Wally, when I was in Germany, I would have given anything to be here for that little meeting we always have. There's nothing better in the world than to hear Dad read the Christmas story."

"I know. I like that, too. I was just joking." He looked at Dad. "I'm sorry. Really."

And that was that, but Alex had said the right thing, as always. And Dad, obviously still ruffled by Wally's comment, said very little at the meeting. He asked Alex to tell about Christmas in Germany. Alex picked up on Dad's usual theme and explained how simple a German Christmas was, with lots of family togetherness and only modest gifts. Wally thought of asking whether jolly ol' Hitler also played St. Nicholas for the children, but he decided he'd better keep his mouth shut.

After the meeting, Wally did drive to Lorraine's to drop off his present, but she was about to leave for her grandparents' home, and Wally only saw her for a couple of minutes. So Wally drove out to the Nakashimas' and gave the boys each a little rubber football. He liked being around Mat and Sharon, and they always made him welcome, but they were busy, so he didn't stay long there either.

When Wally got home, he found his dad in the living room.

"Dad, I'm sorry about this morning," he said. "You all took me too seriously."

Dad looked at Wally for a time, and then he said, "Wally, I do preach too much. I know that."

"That's what fathers do. There's nothing wrong with that."

"Well, anyway, let's not worry about it." Wally heard the change in his dad's voice—the congenial tone that seemed to say, "Why don't we just tolerate each other?"

"Dad, I really am sorry. I'm going to try to . . ." What he had thought to say was that he was planning to do his best at college. But the instant the idea came to his mind, he knew he couldn't make any such promise. The truth was, he hadn't done at all well fall term. "Anyway, I'm sorry I caused some bad feelings—you know, on Christmas and everything."

"Let's just make the rest of the day as nice as we can."

"Okay." Wally turned and walked upstairs, but he felt as distant from his dad as ever. The strange thing was, both Wally and Dad actually were trying to smooth things out between them. Wally had felt that for months. But there seemed to be no going back. They had both said too much the day Wally had quit the track team, and neither one could forget it.

That afternoon, when dinner was over and the house was still full of family, Bobbi pulled Alex into the kitchen and said, "Grab your coat. Let's get out of here for a while."

"Where are we going?"

"Just for a walk. I can't stand the chaos any longer." She hurried upstairs and got her coat and hat, and she met Alex at the front door. They slipped out before anyone could ask them where they were going.

Outside, Alex took a long breath. He liked the briskness in

the air. As usual, smoke was hanging over the valley, but the eastern sky, above the mountains, was bright and blue. He pulled his gloves from his coat pockets and put them on. "So how's everything going?" he asked. "How's college?"

"All right." A puff of steam escaped with her words. "Dad thinks I ought to change my major, but I love my lit classes."

"What does Dad think you ought to study?"

"He wants me to go to nursing school at the hospital."

Alex laughed. "Once you get married, I guess it doesn't matter much what you studied in college."

"You sound like Phil."

"Why? What does he say?"

"He doesn't think I need to graduate. He gave me a cedar chest for my Christmas present. He just wants me to fill that up with pretty little things, and then I'm all set. But I want to finish school. I've even thought about getting my master's degree—or a doctorate—and teaching literature at a college."

Alex laughed again. "Oh, Bobbi, you never do think like anyone else."

"What's that supposed to mean? I'm thinking like you. You want to be a history professor."

"Sure. But I'm a man. You're going to be changing diapers and wiping runny noses before long. And let's hope, for Phil's sake, you can learn how to cook."

"Alex, what is it with Mormon men? You all think alike."

"Don't other men think that way?"

"Not all of them."

"Like who?"

"Never mind." Either Bobbi's cheeks were turning red from the cold, or she was blushing. Alex wasn't sure what that was all about.

Bobbi waved to Sister MacFarland, who was sprinkling rock salt from a little paper bag on her front walk. She had on a huge gray sweater that hung to her knees. She was a widow, but the sweater looked like something she had knitted for her husband. "Hello, you two," she shouted in her high-pitched voice. "I've got family coming over. I don't want them to fall on the ice."

Bobbi yelled to her, "You be careful. Don't fall down yourself."

Bobbi knew all the neighbors, and she kept track of them. She was like Mom. Alex could picture Bobbi as a good mother and housewife, even if she pretended otherwise.

"I can't believe all the hours you're putting in at work," Bobbi told Alex. "I guess you are your father's son after all."

"Hey, I work hard just to carry my share of the load, but the thought of being in that place all my life makes me shudder."

"So what are you going to do?" She pulled her stocking cap down over her ears.

"I don't know. Dad's working me into a real trap." The two had come to a corner, and Bobbi was about to cross the street, but Alex said, "We'd better just walk around the block. Mom and Dad are going to wonder where we've gone."

"What do you mean by a trap?"

"Well . . . this is all very hush-hush for right now, so don't say anything, but Dad knows this guy named Henry Rosen. He owns a machine shop that went broke during the depression. But now millions of dollars are pumping into companies that manufacture armaments. Rosen wants to re-tool the shop and start bidding on jobs to build parts—you know, go after subcontracts for big companies. There are supposed to be all kinds of opportunities."

"But what does Dad have to do with it?"

"Henry doesn't have enough money—or good enough credit—to get the operation going."

"I see where this is heading. Dad will keep the dealership going, and you'll see to his interests with the new company."

"Exactly. Except it's worse than that. He wants me to be a

full partner. He doesn't think this Rosen guy is much of a manager, so he wants me to be in charge."

"He's got a lot of trust in you, Alex."

"I guess so. And frankly, I'm surprised by that."

Alex saw some kids at the corner. They had new sleds but little snow to work with. They were taking short rides on a strip of ice along the side of the street. He thought of winter days when he had been a kid in this neighborhood. He and his friends had belly-flopped onto their Flexible Flyers and glided forever off these hills. Now the neighborhood was packed with houses, and most of the good runs were gone.

"Did you ever ride sleds up in Parley's Ravine?" he asked Bobbi. "Up by the prison, above Thirteenth East?"

"Of course. That's where everyone went."

"In the summers, I spent all my time up in that ravine. We'd hike all day. Catch snakes and horned toads. And then we'd skinny-dip in Canyon Creek to cool off."

"I even did that," Bobbi said, and she laughed. "Except the girls wore their underwear."

"We played war a lot," Alex said. "We'd have battles all day sometimes. Plan out our attacks—kill each other off a hundred times. "Bam! I got you. You're dead."

"Except guys would always say, 'No. You missed.'"

Alex laughed. "That's right. You played a lot with the boys, didn't you?"

"Yup. Maybe that's my problem. I should have been home baking cookies."

Alex was thinking about those war games. The bad guys had always been Germans—a holdover from the World War. And Germans had been nasty-looking guys who deserved whatever they got. "Bobbi, if I get in on this deal that Dad is talking about, I'll spend my days building weapons. That's not something I want to devote my life to."

"No. I wouldn't like that either."

The two turned the corner and were heading east, up a

little hill. Alex looked at Mount Olympus, the mountain he had longed to see the whole time he had been in Germany. Now, with the snow on the rocky peak and with the blue sky for a background, it was magnificent. Sometimes he wished there were a way to keep the world out—so he could hide behind these mountains and let other nations fight their battles.

"The thing is, these weapons will be used against Germany, and I promised the members I would never be their enemy. This thing makes me feel like I am."

Bobbi slowed and turned toward Alex. "You're also thinking about Anna, aren't you?"

Alex had been careful when he had spoken of Anna, but he had told Bobbi more than he had told anyone else. "Of course I think of her—and her family."

"You're in love with Anna, aren't you, Alex?"

Alex kept walking. He finally found the voice to say, "Bobbi, I was a missionary. I didn't say anything to her—not directly."

"I saw that picture of her. She's beautiful."

"Actually, that's not a great picture. She's much prettier than that. Bobbi, she's so beautiful it *hurts* to look at her."

"Wow."

"But it's not just that. She had that experience—the one I told you about—and it softened her. She's been close to God and back, and it's touched everything about her."

"Oh, Alex," Bobbi said, "I hope you two will end up together someday." She reached up and patted his shoulder.

"Bobbi, I'm going to tell you something I haven't told anyone else."

"Oh, good." Bobbi laughed.

Her face was flushed, and Alex was reminded of how she had looked as a kid, bundled up, out in the cold all winter. She had never liked to be inside. "On the ship, coming home, I was out under the stars one night, and I prayed that I would be allowed to see Anna again. I got this powerful sensation that God had heard me and answered—that it would happen."

"Then it will happen."

"I keep hoping the war won't last long, and I can get over there before too long."

"I guess there's no way to go there now."

"Not that I know of." Alex exhaled, and the steam blew around his face.

"Do you know if she's getting your letters?"

"No, I don't. And I've gotten no mail from her. But that doesn't mean she's not trying. We promised to write each other."

"Alex, you've got to reach her somehow."

"I know. I think about it all the time."

For a time no one said anything, and they came to the final turn and walked back down the hill. "I know this is hard, but I still envy you," Bobbi said as they reached the house.

"Why?" Alex asked. He stopped and tucked his hands into his coat pockets.

"You know why. Because you have your answer."

A few days later, Alex was returning to the dealership after lunch. When he entered through the side door of the showroom, he noticed two of the salesmen in the back corner. One was sitting at his desk, and the other had pulled up a chair nearby. Both were smoking cigarettes. President Thomas hated that, but he had a hard time finding salesmen who didn't smoke.

Alex had a tendency to stay in his office and shuffle paper, but he knew he had to get better acquainted with the employees, so he walked back to the men. "Hello, Sherm. Owen," he said. "Not much going on?"

"Deader than a doornail," Sherm said. He was a slick-looking man with a thin mustache and smoothed-back hair. "But it's always slow during the holidays."

"Yeah. I guess that would be the case." Alex couldn't think

of anything else to say, but he glanced at the desk and noticed the *Tribune* open to the sports page. He saw a big picture of Joe DiMaggio. "What's Joltin' Joe up to this time of year?" he asked.

Owen was wearing a white shirt but no coat. He hooked his suspenders with his thumbs and stretched them out a little, and he smiled, showing a broken front tooth. "He made twenty-five thousand bucks last year. But he says that won't be good enough next season; he wants thirty."

Alex let out a little whistle. "*Thirty* thousand dollars?"

"Yeah. Can you believe that? And he's just a kid. Gehrig gets thirty-five—Hank Greenberg more than that. Plus they get a few grand more for saying they drive this car or that, or they smoke a certain cigarette. Somethin' ain't right about it. Too many guys are knocking their brains out to make two or three thousand a year."

"What about Joe Louis?" Alex asked. "What does he get for a fight?"

"Even more. He must be the richest nigger who ever lived."

Sherm laughed. "I doubt it," he said. "His manager probably keeps him in fried chicken and watermelon and takes the money for himself."

Alex was uncomfortable with that kind of talk. He thought of the things Brother Stoltz had said about the attitude toward Negroes in America. But he didn't comment, and just then Sherm said, "Hey, kid, you'd better get to work. Here comes your dad *and* your grandpa."

Alex turned and looked. "Grandma too," he said. They were all walking into the showroom through the front doors. Alex was glad for an excuse to get away from the salesmen. He waved to his grandparents and then walked toward them.

"Alex, my love," Grandma Thomas shouted from some distance away, her voice resounding in the spacious room. She held both arms wide as Alex walked to her, and then she gave him a big hug.

"Good to see you, Alex," Grandpa Thomas said. He shook

Alex's hand. Grandpa was clearly the prototype for President Thomas. He was a big man with the same shadow of a beard, the same dark eyes. But President Thomas's hair remained black, and Grandpa's hair was now mostly white. He was also rather thin after having had surgery in the fall.

"Entertain your grandmother for a minute, will you, Alex?" Dad said. "Dad and I need to take care of a couple of things."

"I don't like the sound of that," Grandpa said. "I don't usually let a car salesman get me into his office."

"I'll choose a new car for us," Grandma said. "You go set up an easy payment schedule."

Dad and Grandpa both laughed and walked away, and Alex looked toward Grandma Thomas. "Have you seen the new Hudsons, ma'am?" he asked.

"No. Let's look." Grandma walked to one of the cars and then gave the back tire a little kick. "Isn't that how you test these things?" she asked.

"Not with those pointy shoes," Alex told her, and she laughed. Grandma always chose rather sensational clothes— exotic hats and brightly colored dresses. Today she had on her full-length chinchilla coat that she had worn every winter for as long as Alex could remember.

"So do you know what your dad and your grandfather are up to?" she asked. She opened the door to the Hudson and sat down in the front seat.

"No, I don't."

"They're cooking up a deal that could make *you* a rich man. I guess you know something about that by now."

"Yes, but I didn't know Grandpa was in on it."

"Your dad was afraid to lose all his own money, so he decided to speculate with some of ours." She laughed, but then she said, "Actually, Grandpa's pretty excited about the idea."

"I wish I were."

Grandma Thomas looked up. "Are you serious?"

"Well . . . yes."

"Alex, I think you can make a lot of money on this deal."

"I've never been that interested in money," Alex said. He shrugged apologetically.

Grandma got out of the car slowly, and she stood in front of Alex, closer than was comfortable. "Alex, let me tell you something. I've tried poor, and I've tried rich. And rich is better. Trust me on that."

Alex smiled.

"I was raised on a farm with five sisters and three brothers. I grew up with no more than two worn-out dresses at any time. Your grandpa took me out of all that, and I don't want anyone in our family ever to know that kind of poverty again. It's time now that you think about building something for the future of your own family."

Alex didn't know what to say to that. He had never thought of building an estate—or of raising his family to a higher status.

"Grandma, I don't see anything in the scriptures that says I ought to give my life to making money."

Alex saw his grandma's eyes widen, her jaw stiffen. "Now wait just a minute," she said. "Your grandfather was bishop for twenty-six years. And look what your father has done. These are noble, hard-working men. And don't forget, you're the one who's benefited. How would you like to live without a refrigerator in your house, or a washing machine and electric range? Or what about that car I see you driving now?"

"Grandma, I grew up with an icebox and a coal stove, and Mom washed by hand until just a few years ago."

"Yes, and my question still stands. Would you want your own family to live without all the modern conveniences you have?"

Alex smiled. "All right, Grandma. I won't pay any attention to the scriptures. I'll just listen to you."

She gave him a tender little sock in the jaw with a doubled-up fist. "You little devil. You watch your tongue," she said. "You're just lucky I love you so much."

When Dad and Grandpa returned, Alex could see that the deal had been struck. As soon as Grandma and Grandpa walked away, Dad said, "He wrote a check. We're ready to get this thing going."

"Okay. But Dad, don't forget what we talked about. I want to get back to college as soon as I can."

"Son, this is an opportunity of a lifetime. You won't need college."

"I told you before—I'll get the operation going, but I'm not in for the long haul."

"We can talk about that later, Son, but for right now, I need your commitment. More and more, the automotive companies are building tanks and airplanes, not cars. Before long, I may not be able to get any cars. This parts business might be the only thing that puts food on the table for our family."

"That's fine. I told you I'd help you through the transition. But I haven't changed my mind about what I want to do."

"I understand that," Dad said, but he was smiling as though he were quite confident Alex would change his mind.

Alex smiled too. But he could see that he was on a collision course with his father.

2 1

Spring came slowly in 1940. The weather warmed for a few days at a time, but storms, even snow, continued to return. The mountains were still white, down to the foothills, in early April.

Many of the talks at General Conference were about the unstable conditions in the world. President Heber J. Grant had traveled to California earlier in the year and while there had had a stroke and was partly paralyzed. He was convalescing and hadn't been able to return in time for conference, but he sent a message to be read. Millions of people didn't know what the Saints believed, he said, and the gospel had to be taken to all the world. The task was great, but it had to be carried out, even though conditions in the world made it difficult.

The Thomases listened to conference, and after each session, President Thomas waited for the news on KSL. Hitler was massing troops on the Western front, and a major invasion of France or Belgium seemed near. But that week, on April 9, German forces attacked Denmark and Norway, countries that had remained neutral. Denmark fell without a fight. Norway offered what resistance it could, with some British help, but Germany had its victory before the month was over. Hitler claimed he had had to take possession of Danish and

Norwegian ports to protect himself from British ships that could lie in wait for his navy in the North Sea.

"Hitler turns everything around," Dad told his family at the dinner table. "It's the British freighters that have to watch out for Hitler's U-boats in the North Sea. They're getting sunk all the time."

Alex hated all these reports. He wanted the war to end quickly. He was also anxious to get the new business rolling so he could step away from it by fall. But so far, the wheels had turned slowly. Henry Rosen hadn't picked up a single contract, even though he had already spent a lot of money re-tooling the machine shop.

Alex had continued to send letters to Anna and to other members in Frankfurt, hoping to hear something from someone. But he still got no answers. Somehow he had to make sure Anna knew he was waiting for her. At one point he even hatched a plan to get into Germany as a war correspondent. He made some overtures to an editor at the *Tribune*, but the local papers didn't have the finances to sponsor a correspondent, nor could Alex pay his own way, and besides, the red tape turned out to be monumental. So that idea was hopeless, but somehow he was going to find a way to reach her.

Early in May, on a Friday night, Bobbi and Phil went dancing with a group of friends. The "gang"—mostly Phil's friends—parked their cars downtown, and then they all rode together on the open-air trolley to Saltair, on the shores of the Great Salt Lake. Woody Herman's "Thundering Herd" band was making a guest appearance, and even though the dance floor was huge, by the time the group arrived, the place was packed. It was a cool evening, but lovely, and Phil was always at his best when he was dancing. He knew how to lead, to use a gentle sort of firmness to move Bobbi exactly as he chose.

Bobbi danced with some of the other boys in the group during the night. She especially liked to change partners when a fast number came along. At one point, rather late in the evening, the band began to play "Blowing Up a Storm." "Whew!" Phil said, "It's getting hot in here. Let's walk outside for a minute." Bobbi knew, as much as anything, that Phil didn't want to do the jitterbug.

So Phil walked her outside to the dock, and for a time they leaned on the rail and watched the reflection of the moon on the waves. After a time, Phil looked at Bobbi. "Turn this way," he said. "I want to see your face in the moonlight."

"No thanks," Bobbi told him. "That only makes my freckles stand out."

"Hey," Phil said, "don't talk that way. I love your freckles. Not to mention your silly little nose—and that dent you get in your forehead when you're mad at me."

"So what am I supposed to say? I love that big mole on your shoulder?"

Bobbi glanced to see Phil roll his eyes, and she knew she had pulled the rug out from under the little scene he had tried to create. But the whole thing was so annoying. He didn't love any little "dent" in her forehead. He hated more than anything to have her mad at him.

Phil tried again. "Honey, I think you're perfect. I hope you know that. I just hope I'm *passable* in your eyes."

Suddenly Bobbi was frightened. She felt in that instant she had finally made up her mind. On Christmas day, when Alex had talked about Anna, Bobbi had told herself she couldn't marry Phil. But time and again she had given way to the inertia of the situation. The break seemed impossible, and she had always talked herself into Mom and Dad's point of view: Phil was such a "good catch."

Bobbi still saw David fairly often, and she found herself flirting a little at times just because she longed to have his interest. But that seemed to bother him, and he was having nothing of it. He had become cordial at best, and even a little resentful. But David had nothing to do with Bobbi's decision now.

This was about Phil. It was one thing to work out differences with a partner; it was something else to be annoyed—really put off—so very often.

Bobbi bowed her head and pretended to be looking at the water, but she shut her eyes and said, "Lord, I can't marry him. Please help me tell him." What she felt was a flood of relief. This was the right thing to do.

"Should we catch the train back before the whole crowd is trying to get out of here?" she asked, and she managed to sound at ease. The moonlight was rippling in the gentle waves, and she tried to let the quiet, the calm, get inside her.

"No, let's not go yet."

"But I have something I want to talk to you about."

"Wedding arrangements, I hope. We need to settle on a few things. Invitations, for one thing. My mother is in a big fuss about that."

Bobbi was amazed. Surely Phil, if he knew her at all, should have sensed something other than wedding plans in her voice. "Would it be all right if we leave soon?" she said.

"Okay. I don't mind. Let's have one last dance, and I'll try to spot someone from our group—just to let them know we're bailing out early."

And so they danced one last time, and Phil held her close. The band was playing "All of Me," and Phil sang it in her ear. "All of me. Why not take all of me? Can't you see, I'm no good without you?"

The irony wasn't lost on Bobbi, and now she was getting nervous. She wondered whether Phil could feel her shakiness. But he spotted one of his friends, Gerald Rich, and told him, "We're heading back—after this dance."

"How come?" Gerald asked, and his date, a girl named Margaret, said, "Stick around. The night is young."

"I think Bobbi wants to get me alone," Phil joked, and he took Bobbi under his arm and gave her a little squeeze.

Bobbi knew that somehow she had to change the mood so

this wouldn't be like a bomb dropping out of nowhere. She said very little as she and Phil rode the train back into town, even though Phil kept trying to make small talk. By the time they had reached the car, Phil was asking, "Bobbi, is something wrong?"

"Well, yes," Bobbi said. "I told you I have something I need to talk to you about."

"Okay. Fine." But he didn't seem all that concerned. And that was maddening to Bobbi. It gave her strength.

Bobbi waited for Phil to start the car, but she hadn't planned what she would say, and she hardly knew where to start. Finally, she said, "Phil, I don't know how to do this. There's no good way. I'm just going to say it straight out."

"Honey, what's the matter?"

"Phil, I *can't* marry you. I don't love you. Not enough. And you don't love me enough either." She struggled with her ring, partly because it was tight, and partly because she was shaking, but she got it off. "So I'm going to give you back your ring. And the only thing I know to say is that I'm very, very sorry." She was crying by now, somewhat to her own surprise.

"Honey, wait," Phil was saying. "I must have done something to upset you. Let's talk this out."

He drove to the side of the street and parked under a lamp-post, where the light showed his face clearly. He carefully moved the gearshift into neutral and set the hand brake, and then he turned toward her. She could see this was a "situation" for him—one he had to manage and get past. But he didn't really believe what she had told him.

"Phil, there is nothing to talk about. I've wrestled and wrestled with this. I always thought you were a wonderful choice for a husband, and I thought I would feel more love in time. But I don't. I feel awful telling you that, but it's true, and I don't know what else to say." She found that her voice was steadying as she prepared herself to resist whatever approach he was about to take.

"Bobbi, we've always had our ups and downs, and I think that's only natural. But don't make a decision quickly and throw away everything we've been building."

"I haven't made it quickly. I've made it much, *much* too slowly. In fairness to you, I should *never* have taken this ring." She held it out to him again, but he didn't take it.

"Now wait. Let's take some time, and you can tell me the things that are troubling you. I'm sure we can solve any problems we might have."

"Phil, you aren't listening. I don't *feel* enough for you. I don't know why. I should; I know that. I even wish I did, but I can't get married to someone I don't love. That wouldn't be fair to either one of us."

"But isn't it possible you've let your emotions get carried away, and you're seeing the situation too negatively?"

"Phil, this is all *about* emotions. Love is an emotion. It's not logical. I think the world of you, but I don't love you. And you *act* at love, as though you've learned a script. But I don't really feel it from you."

Phil let the idea run through his mind. He was silent for a long time. "Could we give this a week and see whether this isn't just—"

"No, Phil. I can't go through any more of this."

"Have you prayed about your decision?"

Suddenly Bobbi was angry. "Phil, don't start that."

"Don't start what?"

"Yes, I've prayed. And I have *never* received the peace I've wanted—until now." She grabbed Phil's hand and pushed the ring against his palm. He finally took it. "Please take me home."

"Is there someone else?"

Suddenly Bobbi felt caught. All the confidence was gone from her voice when she said, "No. Not exactly."

"It's Stinson, isn't it?"

"What?"

"People have told me, Bobbi. I just didn't believe them."

"There's nothing serious between us, Phil. And that has nothing to do with the way I feel about you."

Phil turned forward, jammed the car into gear, snapped the clutch, and took off much faster than usual. For maybe two minutes he was silent, but after the initial acceleration, he evened out his speed. Finally he said, in very measured words, "Bobbi, I've given my all to this relationship. Every time you asked me to change, I tried to do it. And I compromised about the wedding date, over and over. I think love is something that takes some effort. And I don't think you've given much of that."

Phil had a point, and Bobbi knew it. He had tried hard. But something in his self-righteous tone was almost more than she could stand. "You've always been very good to me, Phil. There's no question about that. But I've tried harder than you might think. What I want is to *feel* love—not to labor at it."

"Bobbi, that sounds like something out of one of those novels you read. Majoring in English has filled your head with a lot of ideas that will ruin your life. I still think Stinson is the main one behind this."

"Please continue," Bobbi said. "Because if you continue, I'll get angry, and anger is so much easier to deal with than the pain I feel about this whole thing." She wiped the tears from her cheeks with the back of her hand.

"Well, fine. Get angry if you like. But I'll tell you, I'm angry too. You've strung me along for all these months, and now you've humiliated me. That's not easy to take."

Bobbi didn't answer. But she was relieved. Her decision was so clearly right.

"The whole time I've been going with you, you've been telling me what's wrong with me: what I should and shouldn't say, what attitudes you didn't like. But I haven't said a word about your faults. You're not affectionate, Bobbi, and you think you're smarter than I am. I'm tired of all that."

This was actually rather refreshing to Bobbi. It was nice to hear what he really thought. "Well," Bobbi said, "at least we both know I've done the right thing to break this off."

But Phil paid no attention. "Bobbi," he said, "there are lots of girls at the U who have envied you. Beautiful girls. I'm not going to sit around and feel sorry for myself. I'll probably have a date tomorrow night."

"I don't doubt it, Phil. I'm sure you'll do just fine for yourself." Plenty of sarcasm was clinging to her voice, but then she added sincerely, "I'm the one who will have a harder time finding someone. That's very clear to me. And Phil, I do hope you find someone who will make you happy."

Phil let some time go by, and he sounded honest when he said, "Look, I didn't mean that. I don't even know what I'm saying. I'm having a hard time with this."

And that helped. Bobbi did like Phil, and she did feel bad about the pain she had caused him. When he stopped the car in front of her house, Bobbi said, "I really am sorry, Phil. I know I'm the one who let this continue when I shouldn't have. I really do hope things work out for you and you get everything you want out of life." She touched his arm and said, "Good-bye." Then she got out of the car and hurried to the house.

When she reached the door and glanced back, he was sitting with his head against the steering wheel. She wondered whether he really was that distraught, or whether it was a little act to make her feel guilty. What she did know was that the public embarrassment would be the hardest part of all this for him.

In any case, she did feel guilty. And she also felt angry and sorry and happy and scared and lonely and right and wrong— and a host of other things. The only thing she was absolutely certain of was that she didn't want to talk to her parents tonight. And so she hurried upstairs without letting them know she had come in, and she went to bed.

But early in the morning she heard the phone ring: a long burst and a short one, the Thomas ring on the party line. She wasn't sure what time it was, but her room was still dark, and it was a Saturday morning. Sometimes Dad got calls at odd hours of the day, but Bobbi was pretty sure she knew what this call was about. She didn't have to wait long before she heard steps on the stairs, and then she heard a little rap on the door. "Yes?" she said, already relieved by the lightness of the knock. That could only be her mother.

The door came open. "Bobbi, may I talk to you?"

"Sure. Did Sister Clark call?"

"Yes." Mom came to the bed and sat down. "Well, I'm not entirely surprised, of course. But I must admit, I'm disappointed."

Bobbi was disheartened by the tone of tragedy in her mother's voice. "I should have done it a *long* time ago," she said. "That was my big mistake."

"Yes, I suppose." Mom sat for a time, and then she said, "Bobbi, are you absolutely certain this is what you want?"

"Yes, Mom. It's what I have to do. You're the one who told me not to marry him if I didn't love him."

"Yes, I know. I understand that. And I agree with you. But every time I see you two together, you seem so perfect for each other. And we all like him so much."

Bobbi tried to see her mother in the dim light, but she could see only her dark shape, her head down, her shoulders slumped. She looked like a statue of a defeated warrior—a plump little warrior with curly hair tight around her head. Bobbi did feel sorry for her. It would be so much easier just to please her.

"What about this Professor Stinson? Is there anything to that?"

"No. Is that what Sister Clark thinks?"

"Yes. That's what Phil told her."

"Mom, I've told you all there is to tell. I like David, and he likes me, but there's nothing *going on* between us."

"That night last winter—just before Christmas—when you

suddenly had to read papers for a professor. Were you with him that night?"

Bobbi was glad for the dark. "Yes."

"Oh, Bobbi." Sister Thomas's head had gradually risen, but now she dropped it forward again.

"Mom, I'm sorry I lied. But that was the beginning and the end of everything. We talk once in a while now, but he knows as well as I do that it would never work. At least I've learned what love feels like—and I know that I don't love Phil."

"Bobbi, every time you open your mouth this whole thing sounds like a bigger mess to me."

"No it isn't. It's a very simple matter. I was going to get married, and now I'm not."

"Well, I'll go down and tell your dad. And I'll do my best to make him understand. But you might as well expect the worst. He's not good at this sort of thing."

Bobbi couldn't help laughing. "Tell him I'm pregnant. Then, when you take it back, a broken engagement won't seem so bad."

"Bobbi!" But Mom giggled. "I almost think that would be easier on him. He understands how to deal with sin. It's independence that he can't handle." She got up.

"Mom, maybe I should tell him."

"No. I'd better talk to him first. Get dressed. If you hear an explosion, wait until it calms. Otherwise, give me fifteen minutes or so, and then meet us in the kitchen."

"Are you going to mention David?"

"No. Not even Dr. Stinson. Your father can only take so much." She laughed briefly, and then she left.

Bobbi got out of bed and put on a pair of slacks. She knew Dad hated her to dress that way, even on a Saturday morning, but it wouldn't make a lot of difference today. She brushed her hair a few strokes and decided that was enough to get her by for now. She sat on her bed and waited, but she heard nothing. After about twenty minutes, she walked downstairs and into the kitchen. Dad was seated at the table. Mom was standing at the stove, cooking eggs and bacon. Dad took a long, serious look at Bobbi. He already had his white shirt and tie on. "I want you to think some more about this," he said. "Phil deserves that much. I won't fool myself and pretend I can talk you into anything, but I want you to give this whole thing some serious thought and prayer before you cast everything aside."

Bobbi sat down at the table and in a soft voice said, "Dad, you've trained me all my life to pray about my decisions. And now you assume that I've made this one on my own. This is the hardest decision I've ever made, but I do believe it's the right one, and I've prayed about it every day for months."

He was watching her all this time, but his face didn't soften.

"I love you, Dad. I respect you. I try to do what you teach me. All I can tell you is that I don't love him, and I'm not going to marry him."

"Barbara, just tell me this. What is it you want? Tell me one quality Phil lacks. Tell me one fault he has—of any consequence. Tell me the name of one young man in this whole valley who would make a better husband."

"I only prayed to know what I should do, Dad. I didn't ask God for a list of better prospects."

Dad didn't like that, and Bobbi could see it, but he was trying hard not to lose his temper. Mom had probably given him plenty of advice about that. "Barbara," he said, "are you sure you haven't gotten some romantic idea in your head that fireworks have to go off when you meet the right man?"

Bobbi thought about that for a time. "Actually, Dad," she said, "I think it's just the opposite. Phil is so good looking and so romantic that I let some of that cloud over what I really felt about him."

"Which is what?"

"Dad, he's not genuine. He says the right things. He looks

right. He even *does* what is right. But it's all on the surface. I don't trust what he says to me."

Dad was staring now. "I don't see that at all," he said.

"I know. But that's what I feel when I'm with him."

"And you think you're going to find someone who *is* genuine?"

"I don't know. I hope so."

Dad leaned back in his chair. He was obviously running everything through his mind. "Barbara," he said, "I think this forces some other decisions in your life. I don't feel good about paying for you to study literature. I'm not sure it's having a good effect on you—and I don't see the value in it."

"Dad, we've talked about all this before."

"Yes, but I feel different about it now. I think there's a strong chance you're going to have to make a living for yourself. It would make a lot more sense to switch over to education—or nursing—like I've said all along."

"Is this my punishment?"

Dad didn't like that. He pushed back his chair and stood up. "I care what happens to you, and I'm looking way down the road. Nothing you're doing right now makes sense. Passing up a young man like Phil is a huge mistake. And getting a degree in English—without a teaching license—will do you no good at all. You can study whatever you want, but after this term, I'm only paying for something that will get you a job."

"Al, wait a minute," Sister Thomas said. "This is no time to make a decision about something like that."

President Thomas looked at Bobbi, but he spoke to his wife. "I don't know why not. I've been thinking about this for a long time—the same as Barbara has been thinking about Phil. And I've come to a conclusion—the same as she has. I see my daughter making a big mistake, and maybe I can't stop her, but I don't have to pay for it."

Bobbi stepped around the table to her father, who was standing with his arms folded. She put her hand on his forearm.

"Okay, Dad. I'll think about all that. I'll go into teaching or nursing—or I'll find a way to pay for my studies myself." Bobbi saw him react to those final words, and she wished she had never said them. "But Dad, remember how you felt the day you married Mom. That's how I want to feel when I get married. That's not such a bad thing, is it?"

She saw him soften. But he didn't say anything. Instead, he did something that Bobbi had never seen him do. He picked up his suitcoat and left the house—without eating his breakfast.

2 2

It was early evening on a rainy day in May. The Stoltzes had eaten their evening meal of potatoes and cabbage and bread—since meat was hard to come by these days—and now they were sitting by their radio, with the sound very low. German troops had driven westward on May 10, 1940. They had taken Holland without much difficulty, and they were slicing through Belgium with terrifying ease. Nazi broadcasts reported the victories in glorious rhetoric, leaving the impression that few, if any, German soldiers were meeting death in the campaign. The Stoltzes knew, however, that they could learn more by listening to the BBC reports, which were broadcast across the continent in German. By law, Germans couldn't listen, and doing so was dangerous, but Anna had the impression that many people did.

Then a knock, hard and persistent, came at the door. Anna was instantly frightened, and she saw the same fear in her father's face. She knew of no one coming to visit, and this was not the knock of a friend. Brother Stoltz turned off the radio. "Stay here. I'll go to the door," he said, and already the knocking had begun again.

Sister Stoltz let her husband go, but she and Anna held the kitchen door open and watched. Brother Stoltz opened the door only a crack, but a loud voice announced, "I must come in," and a man pushed his way into the room. Anna saw the long black leather coat. Gestapo. "I must speak with your daughter," the agent said. He glanced around, and then he spotted Anna and her mother in the kitchen doorway.

"My daughter? Why would you want to see her?" Brother Stoltz asked. This was not a good tone to take with the Gestapo, and so Anna stepped into the room. She felt the man's eyes on her body as he studied her up and down.

"My goodness," the officer said. "No wonder your American friends liked what they saw here."

"What do you want?" Brother Stoltz demanded to know. Anna stepped to her father's side and took his arm. She wanted him to be calm. And careful.

"We know about your many meetings with foreigners, Herr Stoltz. We are very concerned when we see these things happen. We are forced to watch people like you very closely."

"Who are you?"

"Oh, excuse me. Have I been rude? I am agent Kellerman. Gestapo." The man was wearing no uniform, but every German knew the coats. He flashed a badge in front of them.

"Our meetings were with missionaries from our Church," Brother Stoltz said. "Those young men have returned to the United States now."

"Yes. You are a member of a sect, as I understand it. An American sect."

"We're members of The Church of Jesus Christ of Latter-day Saints."

"I thought you were Mormons," Kellerman said, and he smiled, his thick lips pulling back, showing his blunt teeth.

"Some people use this name for our Church, but it's not the correct title."

"Oh, it isn't? I'm very pleased that you corrected me about this. I wouldn't want to be in error. Would you also correct me if I am wrong about another matter? Your daughter now writes letters to America. She keeps up contact with these foreigners. Is that also a falsehood?"

"She may have written, but—"

"I have written. I don't hide that. The young men were my friends. I have sent letters to them."

"And what do you tell them, young lady? Do you tell them about conditions here? Do you spread lies? Do you speak against the Führer? Do you perhaps talk about troop movements, or weapons . . . or any such matters?"

"No. I don't."

"And how can we be sure of that?" He reached inside his coat pocket and pulled out several letters, all in air-mail envelopes. They had been opened. "We can stop your letters, you see, open them and read them. But how can we know your intentions? And what if one slips by us? Perhaps you employ a code to communicate secrets. This is what concerns us."

"I didn't know there was a law against writing letters to America," Anna said. "I won't write any more." Her mother and Peter had come into the room now. Sister Stoltz stepped close to Anna and put her arm around her waist.

"A law against writing to America? Certainly not. But we must be careful. We are at war, you understand." His voice had risen, his heavy face filling with color. "Americans help our enemies make war against us. How can it be good for you to communicate with such people?"

"The young men are her—"

"Young *man*. One young man. A young man who defied the Führer, who refused to salute our flag, who may have been here for reasons other than the religious ones he claimed."

"That is not so," Brother Stoltz said. "I assure you, he taught his religion, and he is a fine young man—with great love for the German people."

"It was only that," Sister Stoltz said.

"And . . . I assume . . . this fine young man had great love for *this* German girl." He eyed Anna up and down again. "Did you give him . . . *favors* to make him love the German people so much?"

"Herr Kellerman," Brother Stoltz said calmly but with a hushed intensity in his voice. "I must ask you to leave now. My daughter will write no more letters to America."

Kellerman stepped closer to Brother Stoltz. "I will decide when to leave. You will not decide for me. If you make a whore of your daughter—let her sleep with foreign *pigs*—that is up to you, but don't think you can insult me without reprisal."

Anna grabbed her father's arm, tried to stop him as he stepped forward, but it was already too late. "You are the *pig*," he said. "You will *not* speak this way about my daughter."

"No, Heinrich. Don't do this," Sister Stoltz pleaded. She also stepped forward and took her husband's other arm.

"And what will you do to stop me?" Herr Kellerman pulled his nightstick from his belt.

Brother Stoltz was shaking with anger. Anna tightened her grip. "It's all right," she whispered. "Let this go."

But Brother Stoltz said, "You have no right to come into our home and speak to us this way. Even Hitler would not grant you that right."

"Now you have said too much. Now you have shown yourself to be the traitor I suspected you were. You will come with me."

Kellerman stepped toward Sister Stoltz and pushed her away. Then he grabbed Brother Stoltz by the arm.

"No. Please," Sister Stoltz said. "This is all a misunderstanding. We are good citizens. We want no trouble. She won't write again."

"You stay back, Frau Stoltz. And *you*, come with me now." He pulled at Brother Stoltz's arm.

"I have no intention to go with you." Brother Stoltz pulled his arm loose and stepped back. "I have only said—"

Suddenly the nightstick flashed, striking Brother Stoltz viciously across the right shoulder. He dropped to his knees and cried out in pain, and then he fell forward and rolled onto his side. He tucked his arms close to his body and let out a dreadful moan. Anna knelt and grasped him around the waist. "No. Please," she was crying. "He only meant to defend me."

Sister Stoltz also knelt next to her husband. "Oh, Heinrich," she cried.

Somewhere in the background, Peter was pleading, "Don't hurt him anymore. Please, don't hurt him."

"All of you move back—instantly," Kellerman demanded. And then he grabbed Brother Stoltz by the elbow and jerked. Brother Stoltz let out another cry of agony, and then he clambered to his feet. Anna saw how white his face was, the sweat collecting on his forehead. He hunched forward and gripped his elbow tight against his body. His breath was coming in long, labored gasps.

"Now, Herr Stoltz, you will walk quietly from this room. And the rest of you will stay back." He pushed Brother Stoltz, who stumbled forward and then managed to walk out the door. Kellerman followed, and then he stopped in the doorway. "You are not likely to see this man again. He is a traitor. The rest of you, of course, are no better. Don't think you have seen the last of me." He closed the door.

Anna had gotten to her feet, but her mother was still on the floor, bent over. Anna and Peter knelt next to her, and all three gripped each other. For maybe half a minute, they clung to each other and said nothing, but Sister Stoltz had begun to cry out loud, the sobs wrenching from deep within her. "He'll come back," Peter was saying. "He'll talk to them, tell them he's not a traitor. It will be all right."

But Anna said nothing. She didn't doubt for a second that Kellerman would carry out his threats. As the door had closed behind her father, it seemed to her that he had been swallowed, that there was no coming back, and life couldn't possibly go on.

But her mother stopped crying, seemed to gather her

strength for a moment, and got to her feet. "I know someone. I will talk to Herr Schlenker. He's with the Gestapo. A high officer. But I've known him all my life. He's not like this Kellerman."

She hurried into her bedroom and then came back with her raincoat. "I'll go now," she said. "I'll see what I can do. Pray for me. And pray for Papa. I must hurry." And she left.

Anna and Peter knelt together, and they did pray. Anna clutched Peter next to her, and she pleaded with the Lord that another miracle could come to their family, that somehow their father could be saved and brought back to them.

Brother Stoltz was sitting on a wooden chair in the center of a little room. He was so full of pain that he could hardly think, the horrible ache running down his arm and side and up his neck right into his brain. The slightest movement sent fierce, stinging pains shooting in all directions.

Kellerman was standing in front of him, and on each side were other men dressed in civilian clothes. "Herr Stoltz," Kellerman said calmly, almost tenderly, "you have already made it clear that you have no loyalty to the Führer. We know you are a traitor. And so we can only assume that you and your pig of a daughter are sending secrets to America. If you want to save your family, you must admit to this."

"It's not so," Brother Stoltz said. "We have done nothing wrong." He was leaning forward and trying to hold perfectly still. He shut his eyes and tried to let the pain quiet.

Suddenly he felt a blow on the side of his head. The impact sent flashes of light through his brain and sent him sprawling on the stone floor. Pain exploded everywhere. He tried to curl up and hang on, but two of the officers grabbed him by his elbows and hoisted him back onto the chair.

"Please. Please," Brother Stoltz was saying between breaths. He wanted to explain that his shoulder was broken, that he could feel the bones moving, but he couldn't get that many words out.

"Simply tell us the truth," Kellerman said, his face close to Brother Stoltz's. "I cannot save you now. You are a doomed man. But I can save your beautiful daughter. Your wife. Your son. Simply admit what you have done."

But even in the depths of all this pain, Brother Stoltz knew better. If he admitted anything, Kellerman would only use it against his family. He, himself, would soon die, and this pain could end, but he wouldn't say anything the man could use against his wife and children.

Suddenly Kellerman struck him across the face, maybe with the night stick, maybe with his fist. Brother Stoltz only felt the smashing pain, felt himself falling backwards, and then he saw flashes again and felt a terrific pain in the back of his head as he struck the floor.

His next awareness was of something cold in his face, and he was coughing, choking. Someone had dumped water on him, and the pain was flooding back, the confusion. He felt his arms jerk, both at the same time, and then he was slammed back into the chair. But he also felt a kind of calmness coming over him. The pain was turning to numbness, and he knew he had passed the point of caring about that. He could not live much longer, he was sure, and then peace would come. He just had to resist saying anything. "Lord, help me," he said inside his head. "Please save my family."

"Now. I must ask you again, Herr Stoltz. Did you try to send secrets to these Americans? Simply say yes, and this will end. If you continue on this way, we will go after your family. We will bring them here, and we will let you watch as we punish them for your traitorous acts. Now say yes, admit to what you have done, and we won't have to do that."

"Lord, help me," Brother Stoltz kept repeating, but he said nothing out loud. "Give me strength. Please protect my family."

Suddenly something struck him across his knee, sending a new pain shooting through his leg. This fresh agony was almost too much. Brother Stoltz didn't think of admitting anything, but he asked the Lord for mercy. "Please. Let me die, Lord," he prayed, maybe silently, maybe aloud. He only realized that he was on the floor again when the men grabbed his arms and pulled him up, wrenching his elbow and sending the wild pain shooting through his body. He felt himself hit the chair again, but he couldn't see, and the numbness was returning. He was sinking into unconsciousness when water struck his face again.

"It's sad to see that a man cares nothing about his family," Herr Kellerman was saying. "There are things we can do to them. There are things that my friends and I can do to your pretty daughter—things we might enjoy very much. Perhaps we should bring her here now. Is that what you want?"

Brother Stoltz didn't answer. What he wanted to do was to strike this man just once before he died. But he couldn't move.

"Simply say yes. Simply admit you are a traitor, and this is finished. Otherwise, we will go get her. And we'll have our pleasure with her right here before your eyes."

Brother Stoltz took a long breath, and then he said with the last of his strength, "You will answer to God for this." Another pain struck him, somewhere. It was all jumbled now, and he felt himself slipping away, but he was relieved that the end had come.

The next time he felt anything, something cold but soft was on his face. And someone was speaking. "Can you hear me?" It was a man's voice, but not Kellerman's. Brother Stoltz had no interest in answering. This only meant more agony, not death.

"I have called for an ambulance. I'm bringing help," the man said. "Hold on for now."

Brother Stoltz was not sure whether he was in the same place. He forced his eyes open and saw a blurry face.

"Your wife came to me," the face said. "She told me what was happening. Kellerman had no right to do this to you. I know the kind of man you are. If someone had insulted my daughter this way, I would have reacted the same way."

From somewhere in the room came the hollow voice of Kellerman, subdued now. "He denounced the Führer. I will not put up with that."

"I know what he said," the man said, the one close to Brother Stoltz, and somewhere in the confusion it had become the voice of Herr Schlenker, the Stoltz's neighbor. "His wife told me. He only said that Hitler would not allow such things to happen. That says he puts trust in the Führer."

"No. She is lying. He said, 'Even Hitler would not allow this.' You know what he meant."

"You are a shame to the Gestapo, Kellerman." The voice moved away, and Brother Stoltz opened his eyes enough to see that Herr Schlenker had stood up. "These are not Jews or Slavs. These are good German people. I have known them for many years. You pushed your way into their home. You made filthy remarks about their daughter. Don't tell me they are traitors. I know you. You seek opportunities to inflict pain. You are an insignificant man—powerless—and so you work your evil on anyone you can. You are disgusting."

Brother Stoltz was praying again. "I thank thee, Lord," he said, thinking mostly of his family. At the same time, he was frightened. More pain was now ahead of him.

When Brother Stoltz awoke, he knew that time had passed, not just hours but days. His wife was there, sitting by his bed, and she seemed like an angel, hovering next to him. "Frieda," he said.

And suddenly her face was next to his, their cheeks together. "Oh, Heinrich. You're back with us."

"How long has it been?"

"Four days. They have given you morphine constantly. The pain was so terrible."

Brother Stoltz felt the pain return to his consciousness but knew it had been there all along. The worst, now, was in his leg.

"Kellerman broke your shoulder and twisted the bones. The doctor has done the best he could to set them, but it's not good. Your kneecap is broken, too. It will take a long time for all this to heal. But you are alive. You'll be all right."

"Did they do anything to you? Or to Anna or Peter?"

"No. I ran to Herr Schlenker's house that night. I told him what was happening. He said it was wrong, and he stopped Kellerman before it was too late."

The memories were streaming back now. He remembered Schlenker telling Kellerman that the Stoltzes were good Germans, not traitors. "He was wrong," Brother Stoltz said. Even back then, at the time, Brother Stoltz had known that Schlenker was just as wrong as Kellerman.

"Yes, I know. He had no right to do those things to you."

"No. It was Schlenker who was wrong. I am not loyal to the Führer."

"Be quiet. Soften your voice."

"I don't want to soften my voice. We have to stop this."

"Heinrich, Hitler is driving west. Holland has already fallen, and he is forcing his way to the coast through Belgium, driving back the French and the English. He's having his way."

"He must not win. People have to stand up for what's right."

"Please, Heinrich, don't speak this way. We must say nothing at all. Herr Schlenker said it's the only way we can survive. Anna has promised to send no more letters. And I have promised that we will be good citizens. Herr Schlenker trusts us. We must not do anything to change that."

"Frieda, think what you are saying. What if I had been a Jew? Would Schlenker have saved my life then? He only did it because we are neighbors—Germans. But he is still with the Gestapo. He wouldn't have raised a finger to stop Kellerman had he known what I really think of Hitler."

"I know. I know. But . . ." She sat for a time, touching her husband's cheek with her hand. Finally she said, "Heinrich, once Anna almost died, and we prayed. God let her stay with us. Now you might have died, but we prayed. And we have you back. Now we must be thankful. We must stay alive and keep the Church going. That's the one thing we can do. That's how we can show that we are thankful."

"Frieda, don't worry. I won't do anything careless. But I can't let this happen without doing *something.*"

"Heinrich, rest now. Sleep. You are still upset from all that has happened."

Brother Stoltz decided he had said enough, frightened his wife enough, but he also knew that God would give him some chance, sooner or later, and that he would strike a blow against these Nazis who were spreading evil across the earth.

2 3

On the first of June, Alex moved into a little apartment on Seventh East in Salt Lake. It had been nice to have Mom fuss over him and wash his clothes, but he had felt the need to take his life into his own hands. And everything had changed now. Al Rosen had finally gotten a contract, and the plant had airplane parts to produce. Alex was busy getting the operation under way. He had always been one to carry out his job, whatever it was, and putting in sixteen or eighteen hours a day—and sometimes staying at the plant all night—didn't really bother him. At least the work took all his time and concentration.

Alex rarely saw the family except at Sunday dinner, which he always went home for. He and Wally finally had something to talk about. The government had announced by then that the first-ever peace-time draft would take place in the fall. A lottery would only select a few men in the first round, but the army, manned by fewer than 200,000 troops, would bulge to well over a million by the fall of 1941. Both Alex and Wally knew that the chances were strong that at least one of them would be taken.

Wally was thinking, after putting the decision off for a year, that he might go ahead and sign up with the navy after all. One spring night, on the dance floor, Lorraine had whispered, "Wally, I wish I didn't love you. I should have broken up with you before I felt this way." The words sent chills down Wally's sides, and he had been blissfully happy for a few days, but it didn't take long to realize that she had meant exactly what she had said. She did wish she didn't love him, and she began to do more to distance herself. Wally was devastated. He had never studied enough for his classes, but in his discouragement he virtually quit trying. He showed up for his finals and passed all but one, but barely, and in truth, he didn't ever want to go back to school. The military was looking like his only option.

Bobbi was spending her weekend nights alone, usually reading, and preferred to be in her bedroom rather than sitting with her parents, whose disappointment was so obvious. She did see Phil on campus fairly often. He seemed to feel a mixture of pity and animosity toward her, but outwardly he was friendly. He didn't say anything about Ilene, the girl he was dating, but everyone else reported the latest to Bobbi—all the time. Rumor had it that Phil was already "getting serious."

One morning, when Bobbi was in the LA, she saw David in the hall. He seemed solemn, maybe upset. "If you have a minute, I would like to talk to you," he said in a business-like tone.

"Sure," Bobbi said, and the two walked to his office. Bobbi was self-conscious about people seeing them together, but she was curious about what might be wrong. When they reached the office, he twisted his desk chair around and dropped into it. "I'm leaving," he said. He pushed a lock of hair off his forehead.

"Leaving? When?"

"After finals. As soon as I can get ready."

"Where are you going?" Bobbi sat on the chair by the door.

"I've been offered an assistant professorship at the University of Chicago."

"But I thought you were staying here a few years."

"That's what I planned. But this came up. It's a good opportunity for me, and it seemed for the best. I don't want to see you anymore. It just makes life difficult for both of us."

Bobbi understood that, of course, but David was the one person who understood why she had given Phil's ring back, and he knew how sad she was about giving up English as her major. She had tried to make amends with her father by agreeing to go to nursing school in the fall. David thought it was a stupid concession, and Bobbi understood his point of view, but she wanted her father to know she was willing to accept his counsel.

"Why didn't you tell me before?" she asked.

"I don't know. I applied a while back, but I didn't think anything would come of it."

"Do you like the idea of living in Chicago?"

"I think so. Why not? I'm sick of this place." He sounded lifeless; he was staring off across the room, looking at nothing.

Bobbi saw that it really was the end, and she began to cry. "I should have stopped all this before it happened."

"Oh, Bobbi," David said, "Sometimes things happen spontaneously. And when they do, people ought to enjoy the gift. But you won't leave any room for that."

"I'm sorry. I just—"

"I know! Let's not go over all this again. I don't want to see you before I go. I'm angry right now, and it's probably better if we both remember that. I want to stay angry until I catch a train heading east."

Bobbi stood up. "Okay," she said, but the tears were flowing hard now. She felt in her skirt pocket for a handkerchief and found nothing. "I do hope everything turns out well for you." She turned toward the door.

"Bobbi, wait." He stood up. "I'm sorry. I'm being ridiculous. Let's just say good-bye and"—he was walking toward her—"I don't know. Chalk it up to experience."

He was close to her, but he didn't touch her. She whispered

"good-bye" and turned to leave. But in that instant she seemed to be turning away from the last glimmer of light in her life. She stopped and turned back, touched his face. He pulled her to him and held her in his arms. "Bobbi, how can we hurt each other this much? Come to Chicago with me. Marry me. Let's not think of all the reasons it wouldn't work; let's just *make* it work."

She couldn't think what to say, but she knew it was what she wanted. The other way, him gone and her in nursing school, seemed an impossible alternative.

"Bobbi, you know what you're feeling. Don't throw it away. Will you marry me?"

"I don't know."

"But you'll consider it?"

"Yes."

He took hold of her shoulders and pushed her away enough so he could look at her. "Don't think too much. Don't be *wise.*"

"I want this too, David. But I do have to think."

"Bobbi, listen. There's plenty in Mormonism I admire. I could do all right with it. I could even join, if that would make things better with your family."

"How could you do that?"

"I would embrace all the things I do believe in—the way of life. I'd quit drinking. Go to church. Whatever."

Bobbi smiled. She wondered whether he had any idea what he would be getting himself into.

"Bobbi, neither one of us can be happy without each other. I don't know why, but that's how it is. And we can't turn our backs on that."

Bobbi felt that was true, that she would never find anyone else like him.

"You need to make your decision right away. I'm going to leave in a couple of weeks."

"I want you to go. I want some time alone. You get established in Chicago, and then—"

"Bobbi, don't do to me what you did to Phil." He cupped his hand under her chin and lifted it. "I can't be that patient."

"All right. But you have to give me some time—more than two weeks."

"Okay."

He tried to kiss her, but she said, "No, David. I can't. I want you too much." She walked out and shut the door between them.

Sister Thomas read the paper every day, and she clung to every quotation from public officials who claimed that the United States would only build armaments but never fight in Europe. The Germans had driven the English and French back to Dunkirk on the English Channel and had come close to obliterating the entire force. Only a monumental effort had saved the troops, as almost every ship and fishing boat in England had been put into service and, blessed by good weather, had crossed the channel to transport the soldiers home. A small force of British and French troops had held out against the pressing German army, and most of the soldiers had been evacuated. The "miracle of Dunkirk" had saved thousands of lives, but it hadn't changed the reality that the Allies had been defeated quickly and easily.

Winston Churchill vowed to the English people "We shall defend our island, whatever the cost may be. We shall fight on the beaches, we shall fight on the landing grounds, we shall fight in the fields and in the streets, we shall fight in the hills; we shall never surrender"—but Sister Thomas took note of the last words: "until, in God's good time, the New World, with all its power and might, steps forth to the rescue and the liberation of the Old." Sister Thomas cringed to think what he meant: that the United States would have to save England.

On June 17, huge headlines in the *Deseret News* announced,

"FRANCE QUITS." Hitler's forces had pressed straight for Paris. Germany's Blitzkrieg warfare, which used air cover, lightning-fast movement of troops in trucks, and powerful *Panzer* tanks, had overwhelmed the French, who were still using tactics from the World War.

When France capitulated, the question was, how long could England hold out? Hitler offered peace and seemed confident that England would give up without a fight. Churchill only stiffened his will, however. The "Battle of France" was over, he said, and the "Battle of Britain" was about to begin. The whole world was waiting to see what Hitler would do next. Would he cross the channel and fight England on its own shores? And if that happened, Sister Thomas asked herself, how long until America got involved? How long before her sons were involved?

For the immediate future, however, Sister Thomas was more worried about Bobbi. She and Bobbi had had some long talks lately, and Bobbi had been open about her attachment to David Stinson. Sister Thomas was feeling the need to make at least an initial attempt to help her husband understand Bobbi's situation.

On a warm evening in late June, she was sitting on the front porch. The sun was going down, and she finally stopped stitching and merely gazed off to the west, where a few lumpy clouds were losing the last of their reddish tint. The crickets were making a racket, but she hardly noticed. She was trying to think how she could start the conversation with her husband. He was at his office in the stake building but would be home any minute.

President Thomas finally pulled into the driveway and parked in the garage out back. When he walked around the house and approached the porch, Sister Thomas could see the weariness in his face. But he did take off his coat and sit down next to her on the love seat, and Sister Thomas knew she might not get another opportunity like this. "How did your appointments go?" she asked first, hoping to get a sense of his mood.

"All right, I suppose. I met with a broken-hearted young woman though. She's only been married a couple of years, and her husband walked out on her—just took off."

"What did you do?"

"Not much I could do. She's a nice girl; it's not her fault. Mostly, I let her get it all off her chest, and then I tried to make her feel like the end of the world hasn't come. She seemed to feel a lot better by the time she left."

Sister Thomas decided her husband was in a pretty good state of mind after all, and she had better not pass up her chance. "Al, I had a long talk with Bobbi this afternoon. I need to fill you in on what's happening."

"Happening?"

"Yes. I know, when I tell you about this, you'll tend to feel that it can't work. But after listening to her whole—"

"Bea, tell me what you're talking about."

"But you have to listen and not just react."

"I never just react," he said. And he laughed at himself.

Sister Thomas looked toward him. The light was almost gone now, and she was rather glad she wouldn't have to see his face. "You remember Dr. Stinson, the English professor Bobbi got to know this last year?"

"'Got to know' is one way to put it. It's his fault Bobbi didn't marry Phil." President Thomas had had a man-to-man talk with Phil, which had served mainly as a chance for President Thomas to apologize on behalf of his family, but it was then Phil had claimed that things had gone fine until Dr. Stinson had gotten close to Bobbi and had become a bad influence on her.

"Well, anyway," Sister Thomas said, not wanting to get into all that, "he's gone now, as you know. He's in Chicago. But before he left, he proposed to Bobbi."

"Oh, for crying out loud. I would hope Bobbi had enough sense to tell that guy to kick a rock down the road."

"He's actually a fine young man, Al. He's considered quite brilliant, and he took a job at one of the best universities in the country. His future is—"

"Bea, don't start this. The man is not a member of the Church, and he's probably as godless as most of those professors the U keeps shipping in here from the East."

"Not really. He was raised in a religious family, and he gained great respect for the Church while he was here."

President Thomas stood up. He reached over and flipped the porch light on. "Are you trying to tell me that Bobbi wants to marry this guy?"

"Just listen for a minute. He's willing to join the Church. He likes what the Church stands for, and he would be glad to be part of it."

"Listen to yourself, Bea. What kind of commitment is that? Like he's doing us a favor." President Thomas tossed his coat on the love seat, and he pushed his hands into his pants pockets. "We don't need some half-committed Jack Mormon in the family. Is that the sort of man we want to raise our grandkids?"

"I'm not saying he would be our choice, Al. In a way, he isn't what Bobbi has had in mind either. But things happen, and her feelings are very strong for him. She's never known such a kindred spirit, someone she can share so much with."

"Bea, are you talking Greek or Chinese? I don't seem to understand a word you're saying." He banged the side of his head with his hand. "Maybe my ears aren't working right."

"Al, please. Stop and think for a minute. Bishop Findlay's daughter married out of the Church, and everyone felt bad for her. But after a year or so, her husband joined, and he's strong in the Church now. At least David is willing to join, and his commitment may well deepen as time goes by."

"Or last about as long as the honeymoon." He had begun to pace back and forth in front of his wife.

"What I'm trying to tell you is that Bobbi has fallen in love. David isn't from one of the families around here; he isn't the young man we would have chosen. But we might have to accept him, because Bobbi is thinking very seriously of marrying him."

"And she's going to do what she wants to do, regardless of what we have to say about it. Is that the idea?"

"I just think that if we handle this right, maybe she'll stay close to us, and David will be active in the Church. If we force her to take a stand, she'll resent it, and so will her husband, and we'll lose contact with them."

"So it's a done deal, and all you're trying to do is get me to buy into it?"

"No. She's thinking. And I do think she wants our understanding and help. But if you throw a tantrum, you'll lose all chance to have a say in this."

Sister Thomas had spoken to her lap, carefully and slowly, choosing her words. Now she looked up. President Thomas was smiling just a little, ironically. "So you think I'm a bull searching for a china shop, do you?"

"Those are your words, not mine."

"Bea, I don't know how to soft-pedal things. I fight for the things I believe in. I don't bargain them away."

"But this isn't a fight."

President Thomas took a long look at his wife, his hands still on his hips, but finally he picked up his coat and sat down. "So what do you think? Do you want her to marry him?"

"No."

"Did you tell her that?"

"Well . . . no. I tried to help her think about the implications of her choice."

"Maybe you'd better handle this."

"No, Al. She wants to talk to you. She doesn't want to do this behind your back."

"But what can I say to her? You know how I feel."

"Al, she feels that David is her only chance for happiness. That may be wrong, but we can't say, 'Choose unhappiness.' We have to offer something more than that."

"Oh, Bea. I don't think I'm up to this."

Wally was working for Mat again this summer, but one June afternoon, he got off his tractor and got himself a cold drink from a pump at the top of the orchard. He was dead tired, and so he stretched out on the grass and shut his eyes for a moment. When he felt a kick on his boot and heard Mat's voice, he realized he had fallen asleep, but he also knew that time had passed.

Wally sat up, gave his head a quick shake, and then got to his feet. "I'm sorry, Mat."

"Wally, this happened before, and you know what I told you."

"Yeah, I do. But don't worry, it won't happen again."

Mat was a kind man, but Wally could see that look—almost like President Thomas's—that said he wasn't going to be easy to deal with this time. "You worked hard for me last summer, Wally. But this year you show up looking like you haven't slept, and you go about your day like you're only half here."

"I'm sorry. I've got to start getting to bed earlier." Wally ran his hand over his back and down his legs, brushing away the dead leaves and dried grass that clung to his overalls.

Mat was looking at Wally closely, as though he were trying to figure out what was going on inside him. "I'm sorry," he said, "but I told you when I caught you sleeping before that I wouldn't put up with it a second time. You're fired."

"Oh, come on, Mat. Don't do that. Can't you just dock my check for the time I missed? Or dock me the whole day?"

"Wally, this is not about the time. This is about honor."

"Oh, come on. I slipped up a couple of times, but I've worked hard for you."

Mat turned away. "Come down to the barn. I'll pay you what I owe you." He walked ahead, down between the rows of cherry trees.

Wally said to his back, "This is ridiculous." But that's not what he was thinking. He respected Mat, and he was humiliated to be dismissed this way. And more than anything, he was sick at the thought of going home to tell his father. So, along the way, he made his decision. He waited and watched Mat look through the time sheets and write out a check, and then he said. "Maybe this is good, Mat." He tucked the check into his pocket. "I've been saying for a long time that I was going to get out of here. Now I'm going to do it. I'm joining the navy."

The barn was fairly dark, but a narrow shaft of light was falling across Mat's shoulder. Wally could see in Mat's eyes how bad he felt to be doing this. "Why the military?" Mat asked.

"I want to go somewhere, see some new things."

"You might see war."

"Yeah, I know. That's why I don't want to join the army. I don't want to crawl around on the ground with a rifle."

"Wally, if we fight Japan, the navy will be right in the middle of it."

"Japan?" Wally knew how Japan had been expanding its empire, pushing onto the mainland and into some of the islands. But he had never thought much about going to war with Japan.

"I think it will happen, sooner or later."

"Why? I don't understand what's going on over there."

"Militants have control of Japan. They've convinced the people that it's Japan's divine destiny to expand its power."

"That sounds like something Hitler would say."

"Maybe. But it's sincere. The Shinto religion teaches that Japan has a divine place in history. People there don't like the way western nations take advantage of Asia—always coming in to colonize and take control."

"So the Japanese want to take control instead?"

"They say they want to create a 'co-prosperity sphere' for all Asians. They feel it's their fate—to show the way."

"So they attack China? Some way to lead. Where do they get off thinking they're better than other people?"

"Wally, almost all people think they're better than someone. Don't you think you're better than a Jap?"

"Come on, Mat. Don't say that."

"But don't you? Maybe you think of me differently. But what do you think of most Japanese?"

Wally was embarrassed. "I guess I haven't thought about it," he said, but he knew he didn't sound convincing.

"The point is, Japan feels justified in what it's doing, and it isn't likely to pull out of China—or agree to the other American demands. At some point, the U.S. will put its foot down, but I doubt Japan will back off—and that could mean war."

"How do you feel about that?"

"Japan isn't my country, but it breaks my heart to see this happening. Most Japanese believe in Buddhism as well as Shinto. Right now the militants are twisting Buddhism to their own purposes, but that's not the religion I learned from my father. He was a gentle man, and generous. Most of the Japanese I know are like that. I hate to think what will happen to so many good people—on both sides—if we go to war."

All this was rather unnerving to Wally. He had thought a lot about joining the navy but very little about fighting. "Well," he said, "if a war comes, I'll get drafted anyway. So I'm no worse off if I'm already in the service."

"My father taught me to ask about the essence of things. I always ask myself *exactly* what I want when I choose an action. Have you thought about the military that way?"

"Not really."

"Wally, you need to know what you're looking for before you begin your search."

"I want to start over—that's the main thing. And this is the only way I know how to do it."

"Life doesn't start over. One step follows another."

Wally wasn't sure what that meant. "I guess I need to think about that," he said.

"But you won't, Wally. You're moving ahead blindly. I hope you open your eyes soon—or something opens them for you."

Wally sensed that Mat was probably right about that, but he didn't say so. "Well, anyway, I'm sorry about what happened. I appreciate everything you've done for me."

Mat nodded. "I hope things go well for you, Wally. When you find out what life means to you, come back and tell me."

"Okay." Wally walked from the barn, but the closer he got to his car, the deeper he felt his shame. Mat had deserved more than Wally had given him, and he knew it.

Wally didn't go home. He drove to the Do Drop Inn and killed the afternoon, and then he went home at his normal time. He said nothing about getting fired, and as soon as dinner was over he drove to Lorraine's and asked her to go for a ride with him. She hesitated at first, but he told her he had to talk to her about something, briefly, and she agreed.

"What's this all about?" Lorraine asked as soon as Wally got into the car.

"I'm trying to make a decision. I need to know something."

"Okay." She sounded a little wary.

"Lorraine, if I buckle down and prove to you that I can do well in school, would you . . ." Wally knew he couldn't ask it that way. She was staring forward, stiff and uncomfortable. It was all too clear to him what she would say. "What I'm asking is, are you holding out any thought that you might marry me someday—if I finally get my life going the way it ought to?"

Lorraine continued to look forward, and for the moment, she didn't answer. She was working as a waitress this summer, and she had cut her hair shorter than ever before because of the heat in the little restaurant, but Wally looked at the luster, the oak color, and he longed to touch it, longed to have her turn to him and say, "That's what I want more than anything."

"Wally, I'm sorry to say this, but I don't think you'll ever change. You're always resolving to buckle down, but you never do. And I don't see any sign that I can hope for something better in the future."

"If I knew you were going to marry me someday, I'd have a goal. I could do it then. The only thing I want, Lorraine, is to be with you the rest of my life."

"Not for eternity?"

"Of course for eternity. That's what I meant."

"But that's not what you said, Wally. Religion is always an afterthought to you."

"Okay. Fine. I have my answer. Now I can move forward."

"And do what?"

"I'm going to join the navy—the way I should have done a year ago."

The whole thing was finally over. Wally made a U-turn and drove back to Lorraine's house. He dropped her off without saying another word. Then he had a good talk with himself. He didn't need Lorraine, and he didn't have to mope around and feel sorry for himself. He was going to go see the world, and the idea was exciting. Now he just needed to get Mel on board.

· C H A P T E R ·

2 4

The next day, Friday, Wally got up and put his overalls on, and he pretended to go to work. But he took some street clothes with him, and he changed at Mel's house, and the two drove downtown. They parked outside the Federal Building, and then they walked in and found the navy recruiting office.

The only problem was, a sign was hanging on the door: "Open at 1:00 P.M." Wally and Mel were about to leave when a man across the hallway stuck his head out the door. "Sorry, fellows, Jim had to go out for a while this morning. He told me to watch for anyone coming by. Have you got your minds made up on the navy?"

"Yes, I think so," Wally said.

"Why's that?"

"I don't want to crawl in the mud."

"How about flying? I'm with the Army Air Corps. That's where all the opportunities are these days."

What happened in the next half hour was magical to Wally. This man—Sergeant Martella—had all the facts and figures. He said the air corps was young and growing, and the opportunities for advancement were ten times better than in the army or navy. And yet there were air bases all over, so the chances to see the world were just as good.

"We have a terrible shortage of airplane mechanics in this country," he told the boys. "But you might want to *fly* a plane rather than maintain it. Once you're in, a couple of intelligent young fellows like you—college men—could apply for officer's school and then get pilot training."

The idea of flying an airplane almost took Wally's breath away. But Mel said, "Mostly, I just came along with Wally. I think I'm going to stay in college."

"Okay. But let me give you one thing to think about." The sergeant was a dark-complexioned man with thick hair on his hands and tufts of hair jutting from his nostrils. "You *are* going into the military. The only question is when you'll go. We're already in this war, right up to here." He held his hand just under his nose. "Every healthy guy your age is going to go. The ones who get in first will be the ones with the advantage."

Mel didn't argue. In fact, he nodded, as though that made sense to him.

"I'll tell you something else," Sergeant Martella said. "Roosevelt is putting most of his defense budget into airplanes. So the air corps is going to keep growing."

"I can see that," Wally said. He looked at Mel. "I think this is the way to go."

"Okay. Here's the thing," the sergeant said. "You boys are old enough to sign, but don't do anything until you've thought about it. Take these papers home, and use the weekend to talk things over with your families. Just don't wait too long. We have a quota, and it's almost filled for this month."

"Maybe we should sign now," Wally said.

"I can't do that," Mel said. "I've got to talk to my dad."

"That's exactly right," Sergeant Martella said. "But remember, I can't say for sure you can get in. There's a physical and some exams you have to pass. We don't just take everyone who comes along."

Wally wanted more than ever to sign, but he decided he would break the news to his dad and then come back on

Monday. He just hoped Mel wouldn't lose his nerve. So Wally talked hard as he drove Mel home—extracted something of a promise from him that the two would join together—and then he drove to his dad's dealership. He found President Thomas sitting at his desk, processing paperwork, as usual.

"Dad, can I talk to you for a minute?" he asked.

"Sure," his dad said. He looked concerned, as though he expected something to be wrong.

"I just got back from talking to a military recruiter. The way I see it, war is coming, whether we like it or not, and it might be better to go in now and get a jump on the guys who'll join up later on." He had wanted to sound logical and careful, but he had blurted the whole thing out as though the idea were nothing more than an impulse.

His dad's eyes widened, and for several seconds he stared at Wally. Then he shook his head. "No," he said. "You've got better things to do with your life than pack a rifle around."

"That's just it, Dad. I'm not going to. I'm going into the air corps. I'll be working on airplanes, maybe even flying them. I know I'm not really applying myself in college, but this will give me a chance to find out what I want to do."

"Wally, don't shovel that stuff at me. What you want is to get away from home. Nothing good would come of that."

"Dad, I don't need permission. I'm old enough to sign."

"Don't talk to me about being 'old enough to sign.' The last I checked, I'm still your father."

Wally was standing in front of his father's desk, feeling like a kid in front of the principal. "Dad," he said, "I'm going. I'm an adult. I can make my own decisions."

"And that's what this is all about, isn't it? You want to be free—and not have to answer to your family."

"No. I've looked into this. It's a good opportunity."

"Wally, I offered you a chance to become a partner in my business. So don't talk to me about opportunities. You already let your biggest one pass you by."

Wally was finding some strength. He took a breath. "Dad, I know what you think of me. And I'm going to prove you wrong. I've settled on something I want to do. Now let's see whether I can do it."

Dad looked at Wally for a long time. And then, to Wally's surprise, he said, "All right. Good. You join the air corps. It's time you start taking responsibility for your own actions."

"Dad, I promise you right here, right now, I'm going to do some big things with my life. This is just the first step."

"Wally, you told me once that your plan was to be the family quitter. Once you join the service, quitting is not one of the options. Let's see how you do when you *can't* quit."

"Fine. I'll come back here in my officer's uniform someday, and I'll show you what I've done."

Wally walked out. He felt strong and excited. And all weekend he talked with confidence, rehearsed the things Sergeant Martella had said, not only to others but to himself. He pushed aside all doubts, but the truth was, he felt a sort of breathless fear that he had jumped off a cliff and was falling headlong into the unknown.

Wally let no one else bother him, but he did feel bad about the way his mother was taking the news. As they walked to Church on Sunday evening, he tried to explain, once again, all the solid reasons for his decision, but she kept saying, "Wally, you don't know what the world is like. I hate to think of the kinds of temptations you'll have to deal with."

Sacrament meeting was held at seven in the evening during the summer months, but the heat was terrible tonight, no matter what time it was. As the Thomases sat down in their familiar spot on the left, toward the front, other ward members already had their fans going—the ones provided by a local funeral home—and the whole place seemed to be in motion. But even with the windows open, there was hardly a breath of air, and the speaker was old Brother Dixon from the high council. He not only lived in the past but always gave more or less the same talk.

Brother Dixon always started his talks by saying, "I want to speak to the youth tonight," and then he began his "when I was your age" stories. Sooner or later, he would get around to the Word of Wisdom. As a young man he had chewed tobacco, and he had fought the addiction for many years. His willpower had triumphed in the end, but he wished now that he had kept himself clean from the sins of the world.

Toward the end of the talk, Wally glanced to see his mother wiping her eyes with one of the little lace handkerchiefs she always carried in her purse. She had worn her white summer hat—straw, with a little yellow bow and some tiny dried flowers on the brim—but it was perched in her lap. She sat straight, with her feet together, grasping the brim of the hat with one hand and holding the hanky in the other. During the closing hymn, she dabbed, over and over, at the corners of her eyes. Wally put his arm around her shoulders, and for the first time all weekend, he allowed himself to question whether he was doing the right thing.

When the meeting was over, Wally escaped the building more quickly than the others, and so he walked home alone. He was feeling subdued, and he didn't want to talk anymore. He went to his room and changed, but he was still buttoning his shirt when the phone rang. Bobbi yelled up the stairs that the call was for Wally, so he walked downstairs and picked up the receiver. He wasn't surprised that it was Mel calling, and he was even less surprised that Mel had "talked things over" with his dad and had decided "not to join the service right now."

"Don't make up your mind yet," Wally said. "I'll come over, and we'll think it through before you make a final decision."

"No, Wally. You'll try to talk me into it."

"Come on, Mel. You promised me."

"Not exactly. I just said . . . well, anyway, I'm not signing up."

"Okay." Wally gave up. "That's fine. I just thought it would be nice to go together."

"I know. I'm sorry."

Bobbi and Mom had heard the conversation. As Wally hung up the phone, Mom said, "Wally, if Mel isn't going, don't you think you should think about . . ." But Wally didn't listen to the last of Mom's plea. He kept going and walked out the front door. The truth was, his resolve *was* weakening, but he had made his declaration of freedom, and to back off would mean swallowing his pride—not just with his dad but with Lorraine. He decided to drive to her house and tell her what had happened. Somewhere in his brain was lodged a tiny hope that she would ask him to stay, but Wally didn't want to admit that to himself.

Sister Gardner came to the door when Wally knocked, and she seemed surprised to see him, but she invited him inside. And then Lorraine showed up in the front hallway, looking skeptical, maybe even annoyed. "Could we talk for a minute?" Wally asked.

"No, Wally. We've talked enough."

"Just let me tell you something. And then I'll go."

"Okay. Tell me."

Wally felt sick. He saw the firmness in her face. "Just come out on the porch for a minute. It's hot in here."

She walked past him and pushed against the screen door, which stuck for a moment and then sprang open. She held the door until Wally was outside, and then she let it swing shut. She was wearing a pretty dress—light blue, with white polka dots. It fit loosely, but Wally could see her lines. Her face, her smile were pretty, but those perfect lines—and the way her skirt swung around her slender legs—had always been too much for him.

She was standing stiff now, her lips pressed into a straight, thin line. "Let's sit down for a minute," Wally said.

He walked to the swing seat on her front porch and sat

down. The house was fairly new, a square, squat place, in dark brick and white trim. The concrete front porch was covered but not screened like the older houses. Still, it faced the west, and it was a nice place to sit and watch the sun go down.

Lorraine continued to stand. "Go ahead. Say what you have to say."

"I just came to tell you that I'm signing up for the Army Air Corps tomorrow. I talked to the recruiter, and it's all set. My dad isn't standing in the way. I wasn't very nice the other day—and I just wanted to say good-bye and wish you the best."

"How soon do you leave?"

"I don't know for sure."

She nodded. "Well, I hope it works out well for you."

Wally had been dismissed. He stood up. "It's nice to know that you're all broken up about it," he said.

"Is that what you wanted?"

Wally hadn't planned to tell the truth, but he found himself saying, "I guess I did. That's how stupid I am. But I should have known better. Good-bye, Lorraine." He got up and walked to the steps and then down to the sidewalk.

"Good-bye, Wally," she said, and her voice was muted now, all the edge gone.

Wally turned and looked at her. She was standing on the porch in that pretty dress, her hair curled around her face. The setting sun was glowing, gold, and the color of her skin and hair were brightened, heightened. He could hardly bear the pain that hit him. He looked at her for only a few seconds, and then he said, "I love you, Lorraine. I always will."

He turned quickly, but she said, "Wally," and he stopped. "I'm sorry," she whispered. "I love you too, but it never would have worked." Tears were glistening in her eyes. She turned and grabbed the screen door, which caught again and then rattled as it finally pulled loose. She hurried inside. Wally watched as she disappeared, her blue dress hazy through the screen. As he turned away, the image was still there in his head:

her standing on the porch, illuminated by the sunset, whispering "I love you too." He had the feeling that picture would hurt him just as much in twenty or fifty years as it did right now.

Wally drove home, and all the way he steeled himself to deal with the last onslaught from his family. But it didn't come. No one tried to change his mind. He went to bed early and slept fitfully, and the next day he drove downtown, where he signed the papers.

Wally learned on Monday that he would have to wait until September before leaving for California for basic training. The rest of the summer looked endless. With no job, he had nothing to do. He thought he would use the time to fool around, but as it turned out, he found nothing that entertained him. He went to movies with Mel and took out a couple of girls he had known in high school, but he was antsy, eager to get going.

Mom had finally accepted that he really was going, and she had some nice "chats" with him about living the gospel. Wally tried to reassure her. But Dad said very little. He was actually more friendly than he had been for a long time, and Wally felt some sense that he regretted the conversation that had led to all this—but he never once said so. What Wally felt most was a painful awkwardness between the two of them.

On Wally's last night at home, Mom cooked a farewell dinner. The next morning he would report to Fort Douglas, near the U, where he would take his final physical examination and process his paperwork. Mom prepared a big meal—like a Sunday dinner—of roast beef and mashed potatoes, corn on the cob, and a cold watermelon for dessert.

Everyone laughed and joked, and Wally put on one of his shows, teasing LaRue and Beverly and making claims about visiting exotic islands—with pretty dancing girls.

"Yeah, you'll probably end up in Texas or Alabama, or somewhere like that," Gene said.

"That's all right," Wally told him. "You know those southern belles. They know how to treat a guy."

"You look for a *Mormon* southern belle, you little snip," Mom told him.

Dad was quiet all this time, but finally, after dessert, he said, "Wally, have you thought about receiving a father's blessing before you go?"

"I hadn't thought about it. But sure. That'd be good."

So everyone walked into the living room, and Wally sat on the piano bench, which Alex set in the middle of the room. Dad took a moment before he placed his hands on Wally's head. They were big, heavy hands, and Wally liked the feel of them. He shut his eyes and listened to Dad's voice fill the room.

"Walter Daniel Thomas," he pronounced, "with the power of the Holy Melchizedek Priesthood, and in the name of Jesus Christ, I lay my hands upon your head to give you a father's blessing."

The words came easily after that, the phrases familiar to Wally. But gradually he heard his father's voice begin to strain. "I bless you with the Lord's protection, to keep you safe in war or peace, to grant you strength and resistance to disease. I promise you that if you will turn to the Lord, he will deepen your faith. Take with you the love of this family, Walter; hold it in your heart."

Dad stopped, then, and took some time, maybe to get his emotions under control. "Walter, know this is your home and always will be. You are part of all of us, sealed up unto eternity. I bless you, Son, that you will come home to us safe and well, and full of the Spirit of the Lord."

When he was finished, he lifted his hands, slowly, and the room was silent. When Wally stood up and turned around, he saw tears on his dad's face. Wally nodded, unable to say anything. But then everyone came to him, and one after the other, they took him in their arms. Gene did it quickly and then hurried away. LaRue and Beverly clung to him, both crying and squeezing him around the middle. Bobbi sobbed, wetting his hair.

Alex gave Wally a quick hug and some hard pats on the back, and then Mom held on to Wally and whispered a kind of blessing of her own. When Wally finally stepped away, he saw that Dad was unsure what to do, so Wally stepped toward him, but in the same instant he lost his nerve and merely reached his hand out. "Thanks," he said. Their eyes met only briefly, but an understanding seemed to pass between them. Wally was too moved to say anything, and so he merely mumbled that he needed to pack, and he went upstairs.

Wally found Gene lying on his bed, his face in the pillow. He sat up when Wally came in. "It's no big deal," Wally said.

"It feels like the end of our family," Gene said, and he broke down.

"No. No, it isn't. I'll be back. Lots of times. Alex came back, didn't he?"

"He didn't leave—not exactly."

And Wally knew what that meant. "Gene, I'm not mad at anyone—not Dad, not Alex. I just need to do this."

"Will you get leave sometimes—so you can come home?"

"I'm not sure. I think it depends on where I go."

"I wish you could be home for Thanksgiving or Christmas—or something like that."

"Yeah. Me too. Maybe I can." But then Wally forced a little laugh. "Hey, tell the truth. You're happy to get the room to yourself," Wally said.

But Gene couldn't laugh. He got up and walked from the room. He almost bumped into Alex, who was now at the door. "Say, listen," Alex said. "I've got to head out. But there's something I wanted to talk to you about." He walked into the room. Wally sat down on his bed. "This business I'm running for Dad is taking off. We already have more work than we can handle. There will be plenty of room for you to be involved, if you're interested someday."

"Right now," Wally said, "I'm seeing a lot of opportunities

in the air corps. I might apply for officer's training and then stay in for a career."

"Well, see how you like it. But Wally, I'm going to make a lot of money, and it's crazy, because money doesn't mean that much to me. I feel like you ought to get in on it."

Wally had told himself that he wanted to make his own way, but tonight everything seemed different. "Maybe, Alex. We'll see."

"You're going to be learning about airplanes, and we're producing a lot of airplane parts. You'll have a good background. And it will give you . . . you know . . . a reason to feel good about coming back, after you've had some other experiences."

"Okay. We'll see," Wally said again.

He stood up and shook Alex's hand again. Then he went back to his packing. But Bobbi soon stuck her head in the door. "Got everything about ready to go?" she asked.

"No," Wally said. "I don't even know what I'm doing. I can't think straight."

Bobbi sat down on Gene's bed. Wally's leather suitcase, which Mom and Dad had given him as a going-away present, was open on his bed. He had stuffed in socks and underwear and some of his favorite sports shirts.

"Are you taking any white shirts? And ties?"

This, of course, had to do with going to church. "I could. Or I could wear my dress uniform to anything I have to dress up for. That's what that sergeant told me."

"It might be good to have one white shirt, just in case."

"Yeah. I guess." But he didn't move.

"Are you going over to say good-bye to Lorraine?"

"No."

"I know you broke up. But you've been friends for a long time. You could just say good-bye, couldn't you?"

"No. We did that." And yet the idea had been on his mind all day. "Mel talked to her," Wally said. "He told her I was going, and she just said, 'Tell him good-bye.' She didn't say anything about stopping by."

"I'll still bet she'd like to see you."

"I doubt that very much." The curtness in his voice seemed to stop Bobbi, but Wally was sorry to have sounded that way. "What are you going to do about your professor?" he asked.

"I haven't told Mom and Dad yet, but I wrote and told him I can't marry him. He called me long distance the other night, and he asked me to reconsider."

"How did you feel about that?"

"I don't know. When I heard his voice, I almost agreed to catch the next bus, but I knew I couldn't do that. He wants to stay in touch, but I think it's better if we don't."

"So that's it? It's all over?"

"That's what I keep telling myself." She laughed. "But I can't seem to get my heart in tune with my head. Every time I say it's over, it . . . isn't. I still feel really close to him."

"So what do you do about that?"

"I don't know. I envy you. I wish I could go away."

"You'll get married before long. Some other guy will be crazy about you one of these days."

"Not likely. I don't seem to be inspiring that kind of devotion in any other little hearts."

"You will. If I weren't your brother, I'd fall for you for sure."

This was not the sort of thing Wally normally said, and they both knew it. Bobbi laughed. "Thanks," she said. "I'm going to miss you around here, Wally. Sometimes you're the only one who can make me laugh."

"Dad can take over. That guy is *funny*."

Bobbi laughed, but then she said, "What did you think of the blessing he gave you?"

"It was . . . good. I liked it."

"He does love you, Wally. We all do. These years—when we're all growing up and making decisions—are hard. But let's stay a family. Okay?"

"Okay."

Bobbi got up and kissed Wally on the cheek. "I'll see you in the morning," she said. "I'll say good-bye then."

"Could you do this first?" he asked, and he pointed to the shirt, which he had had little success folding.

So Bobbi folded the shirt, tucked it in among the other things, then she left. Wally tried to think what else he needed, but his mind wouldn't focus, so he walked to LaRue and Beverly's room. LaRue was standing by her closet, in her underwear, apparently looking for play clothes. "Wally!" she said. "Get out. I'm not dressed."

Wally smiled and turned around. But after a minute or so, she announced, "All right. You can come in now."

Wally turned around and stepped into the room. Beverly was on her bed, with three dolls before her, all sitting up against a pillow. She was talking to them as though they were real, and as though LaRue and Wally were not in the room.

"Hey, Bev," Wally said. "Those kids are bad. They don't listen to a thing you say."

"Yes they do," she said seriously.

"Well . . . you two aren't going to have me around to tease you all the time. Gene will have to do it for me."

"Gene doesn't tease. He doesn't even talk," LaRue said.

"He thinks. I talk."

"You ought to think before you talk." It was the sort of thing she always said to Wally, but she seemed to regret it instantly. She walked to him. "I don't want you to go," she said. "I want everything to be just like always."

Wally nodded. He was about to say, "Things have to change," but the words wouldn't come. He knelt and hugged LaRue, and then Beverly, who also came to him. "I'll miss you two," he said, and then he got away, went back to his room. He sat on his bed and stared at his shelves, the pictures, all the balls. His years in this room came over him in a procession of images, and he couldn't, for the life of him, remember why he had wanted so badly to leave. He had the feeling that when he walked from the room in the morning, he would be leaving himself behind. He wanted to cry, but all his emotions seemed locked inside, and he couldn't get himself to feel much of anything—except an overwhelming sense of loss. He thought of trying one more time to talk to his father, but he knew he couldn't do it.

Brother Stoltz knew about German air raids on England.
Speculation had it, both in Germany and in England, that
Hitler was trying to weaken the power of the Royal Air Force
before invading the island in the fall of 1940. Late in the summer, however, the RAF began to bomb Germany, and then on
August 25, for the first time, bombs fell on Berlin. Germans
were stunned. Hermann Göring had promised that Berlin's anti-
aircraft protection was so sophisticated that bombers would
never penetrate to the city. Everything Germans read or
heard—and all of Hitler's speeches—had made victory over
England seem not only certain but imminent. And yet, now the
British were attacking, and the idea of another war on German
soil was disheartening to the people.

Gradually, German bomber attacks began to concentrate
more on London. Raids came almost every night, and clearly
the purpose of the "Blitz," as the attacks came to be known, was
to terrorize and weaken the spirit of the people. Brother Stoltz,
because he listened to the BBC, knew the extent of the bombing on both sides, but he said nothing to President Meis or others in the branch. He doubted that anyone was working for the
Gestapo, but a repeated statement, an accidental remark picked

up by an informant, could lead to big trouble. Kellerman would surely be tracking Brother Stoltz's every move.

As Christmas approached, Brother Stoltz was certain England was nowhere near submission. In spite of the Blitz, not only on London but also on Liverpool, Manchester, Birmingham and other cities, RAF pilots in Spitfire fighters were taking heavy casualties on the *Luftwaffe*. And British attacks on Germany were widening to seaports and to large industrial cities. Japan and Italy, in the Tripartite Pact, had agreed to fight with Germany against any declared enemy, and that convinced most Germans that the United States would stay out. But Roosevelt had announced a plan to lend or lease aircraft and other armaments to England and its allies, bolstering his commitment to resist Hitler. From all appearances, now, the war would not soon be over.

Brother Stoltz was walking again. His knee still gave him pain, and it probably always would, but it had healed better than his shoulder. His arm was still held with a sling. He could move his elbow and manage to use his hand, but even that caused him pain. He had returned to his teaching and went about the work patiently, but every day was exhausting, and every night was made tedious by his inability to sleep.

Sister Stoltz often reminded him that he was lucky to be alive. And he usually agreed. But sometimes the frustration was hard to deal with. One morning while trying to tie his shoelace by himself, he suddenly yelped from the stab of pain in his shoulder. Anna knelt by him and said, "Here. Let me do it."

Brother Stoltz said, "A man wants to tie his own shoes. This merciful God we speak of might at least grant me that."

Anna patted his back. "I'm sorry you have to suffer this way," she said.

Brother Stoltz was clearly embarrassed. "I didn't mean to say that," he said. "It's my old self speaking. I prayed that my life might be spared. Now I complain about a little pain."

But Anna knew it was a great deal of pain, and she knew

how much her father's spirit was suffering. There were certainly others who hated the Nazi methods as much as he did, but no one dared to say so, and so the disillusioned remained unknown to each other. "At least I can't do that damnable Nazi salute with this broken shoulder," Brother Stoltz told his family, but he could never say such a thing outside his household.

Anna was working now. She had a *Gymnasium* education, and she had always planned to attend a university, but everything had changed in Germany. She worked, by assignment, as a secretary for a company that made military uniforms. She typed letters and kept books, and she did the bidding of a sour old manager who leered at her when she walked across the room. Sometimes his overtures were anything but subtle, but he never touched her, and she prayed every night that would never happen.

She had not written any more letters, nor had she received any. She told herself that by now Elder Thomas had probably married. She couldn't spend the rest of her life brooding about that. She had to follow her father's example and live with the reality that lay before her. That's what she told herself. But she looked at Elder Thomas's picture every day—called him "Alex" in her mind—and she prayed that he was happy and well. If America entered the war, she wondered whether he would have to fight. She hoped he could be kept safe.

Christmas was happy, however, no matter how difficult everything was, and one simple act made it so. Two days before Christmas, Brother Stoltz had sent Peter on his bicycle into the country, and Peter had been able to buy some fresh produce. Food had to be shipped to the western front, and raw materials were being used to build weapons, uniforms, trucks, and tanks. It had become difficult to buy personal items: soap, tools, paper, school supplies. But worst were the shortages of sugar, butter, fruit, and vegetables. Germans had grown used to living on bread, potatoes, and cabbage, and on little else.

Peter, however, had managed to buy some carrots and a

sack of apples. The boy must have looked forlorn when he explained how much his family hoped to have a nice dinner on Christmas. A farmer finally said, "I'll sell you these. But tell no one else where you got them."

The Stoltzes sent Peter with a few of the carrots and apples to the other families in the branch. And then, on Christmas eve, Brother Stoltz said, "Come with me, Peter." With the help of a cane, and with Peter on one side of him, he had left the house. Anna had assumed he was going to buy some little gift for the family, and she hadn't made a fuss even though she knew how hard it was for him to walk very far. But when he had returned two hours later, both Anna and her mother were greatly concerned. Father looked exhausted as he dropped onto a kitchen chair, but he was smiling. "I did something the Führer would not like, and I feel better than I have in a long time."

"What? I hope it wasn't foolish," Sister Stoltz said.

"Only a little foolish," he said. "And very satisfying."

"Oh, Heinrich, what have you done?"

"Peter and I went to visit Bruder Goldfarb. I had never met him, and it was time someone from the branch paid him a visit. We gave him four carrots and two nice apples. He cried and kissed both of us. It was wonderful. He's a man I would like to know better."

Anna and Sister Stoltz were staring at Brother Stoltz. "You can't do this," Sister Stoltz whispered.

"I did it. I pretended I was an old Jewish man, hobbled and bent, and Peter was my helper."

Peter grinned. "No one even looked at us," Peter said. "It was easy. I wasn't frightened."

Anna was proud of her father. She could see, however, that Sister Stoltz was afraid. "Please, never again," she said.

But Brother Stoltz didn't promise. And his spirits were clearly raised. There was no Christmas tree this year, no candles, and Christmas dinner was simple, but the Stoltzes sang together, and they read the story of Christ's birth.

Anna kept thinking of the Christmas two years before when Elder Thomas and Elder Mecham had been with them, and Anna had been so young and yet so flirtatious with poor Alex. She understood how wrong she had been, but she also remembered the way he had looked at her. It was one of her favorite memories.

"I wonder what Elder Thomas is doing today?" Peter said. "I wish he could visit us."

Brother Stoltz nodded, and Sister Stoltz said, "Yes. That would be nice." She glanced at her daughter, gave her a tiny nod. "Let's sing now," she said. "What shall we sing?"

"*O, Du Fröbliche,*" Anna said. It was a song of joy: "Oh, you joyous; oh, you blessed; oh, you mercy-bringing Christmas time." It was also Alex's favorite Christmas hymn.

Alex promised to come over to the house early on Christmas morning, but Beverly and LaRue were put out when he didn't get there until 6:30. The minute he opened the front door, the girls bounded down the stairs and ran to the tree. Bobbi came down soon after in a terrycloth bathrobe, her hair wrapped in a scarf. Mom had to go upstairs and roust Gene out of bed. But once he found his way onto the stairs, he picked up speed and hurried to see what gifts he had.

Alex stood and watched all this until Mom said, "Aren't you going to see what Santa brought you?"

"Did he leave my stuff over here?" he asked. "I thought he'd missed me."

"Don't put on an act," LaRue said. "Me and Bev know about Santa."

Dad had been up for a while, but he was still wearing pajamas and slippers and the wool robe Mom had given him for Christmas the year before. "Now listen, girls," he said with only a slight smile, "Santa brought those things, and if you don't think so, turn them back in."

"Never mind. We believe," LaRue shouted, and she giggled. She was cradling a doll in her arms. "This is the one I wanted," she said. "It wets its diapers."

"Well, now, only Santa would bring something like that. If I were buying, I'd get you both pretty red Sunday coats."

Both girls jumped to their feet immediately. "What?" Beverly said. "Where are they?"

"Never mind."

But it was too late for that. Mom had to tell them to open the two large boxes under the tree, and then the girls had to try on the coats—and kiss their dad.

Alex looked through the shirts and ties and stockings that Mom and Dad had gotten for him, and then he sat on the couch and watched everything happen. During the fall Alex had almost lived at the plant. He had spent his time solving problems and worrying about deadlines. But the quality of their products had been first rate. Manufacturers were now offering the little company contracts without requiring bids. Everyone was talking about the boom that was coming in 1941, with all the dollars being pumped into defense, and Alex was right in the middle of it all. There was a certain excitement in that, and most of his days were so intense that he hardly had time to think whether he liked what he was doing. But today was Christmas, and Alex had awakened with Anna on his mind— and a sense that his life was sadly lacking in the things that mattered to him.

He wondered whether she was all right. He watched the papers to see whether bombs had dropped on Frankfurt, and so far he hadn't read of any. But it had to come in time.

"Alex?"

"Yes."

It was Bobbi. She was holding out a package. "This is for you," she said. "From me. But it's not what you need."

"What do I need?"

"A woman. You need to get married."

Mom said, "You should talk, Bobbi."

"I don't a need a woman," Bobbi said. The girls giggled.

Mom sighed. "Last Christmas I thought a lot of things would be settled by now. You and Phil were engaged, and Alex was back with us, safe. Wally was in college. It felt so good. I just had no idea so many things would change this year."

"Have you heard anything from Wally lately?" Alex asked—to change the subject a little.

"We finally got a letter a couple of days ago—after about a month of not hearing anything. He said he'd sent a package, and he was sorry he'd sent it so late. You know Wally."

"How is he doing?"

"All right, I think. His letter was awfully short and full of jokes. But I got the feeling he was homesick. He said he wished he could be home for Christmas."

Bobbi laughed. "He wouldn't even mind our Christmas meeting, I'd bet." She patted her father's knee.

"I just wonder how he's doing," Dad said. "He hasn't said one word about church. Brother Spendlove had a son in the Philippines, and he said there's not much chance of attending Mormon meetings."

"I'm just glad he's a long way from Europe," Alex said. "Even if we get into the war, I doubt he'd get shipped all the way over there."

"If you're so concerned about staying out of the war, you shouldn't have voted for Roosevelt," Dad said.

Alex decided not to argue the point—not on Christmas. He and his dad had gotten in some rather tense disagreements about politics this fall. Roosevelt had won a third term in office, which was irritating enough to President Thomas, but worse, he had carried Utah easily. And Herbert Maw, a Democrat, had taken the governor's house, defeating Henry D. Moyle in the Primaries. Brother Moyle was a Latter-day Saint—and another Democrat.

"I wonder what Wally is doing today?" Mom wondered aloud. "Do you think he'll get a special dinner?"

"I'm sure he will," Alex said. "But I hope he's homesick. On my first Christmas away, I think I finally realized how much my home meant to me."

"Sing that German Christmas song for us," LaRue said. "*Stille Nacht?*"

"No. The other one. The happy one."

"*O, Du Fröhliche?*"

"Yeah. I think so."

"Not right now. Maybe during our meeting." But Alex didn't want to sing. He looked over at Bobbi, who smiled and gave him a little nod, as if to say, "I think I know what you're feeling."

The family had been together the night before, and Alex and Bobbi had found a few minutes alone in the kitchen to talk. Alex had asked her whether she was still in touch with David. "We still write," she had said. "He's been my friend these past two years. I can't seem to give that up."

"If nothing is going to come of this, maybe it would be better to stop writing and end the pain."

"I know. That's what I keep telling myself."

"But you can't bring yourself to do it. Right?"

She nodded.

"I'm going to end my pain this year—or at least ease it."

"How?"

"If I have to commandeer a British bomber and land in Frankfurt, somehow I'm going to talk to Anna."

"And what will you say to her?"

"I'm going to ask her to marry me—and promise to wait for her, no matter how long this stupid war lasts."

Wally was sitting in a bar in Manila. He didn't drink beer very often—and he actually didn't like it—but he drank one or maybe two, now and then. The excuse he used was that some-times it was the only cold drink he could get.

Earlier, the Twentieth Pursuit Squadron, the fighter unit Wally was with, had eaten a huge Christmas feast, and now, in the late afternoon, as the heat was subsiding a little, Wally and a few friends had taken a taxi into the city and were relaxing a little. It was an odd Christmas, entirely different from his expe-riences at home, and he was feeling rather strange.

Wally could never have imagined a better life than the one he had had since leaving Salt Lake. He had been homesick as the train had pulled away from the valley, and he hadn't loved basic training at Hamilton Field in Southern California. But air corps training was light compared to what the grunts in the infantry had to put up with, and when Wally had volunteered for a unit heading to the Philippines, his training had been cut short.

From that time on, he had been living a dream. The trans-port ship was a commercial ocean liner. It was crowded in the beginning, but most of the troops got off in Honolulu, and only Wally's squadron continued. Every lowly private bunked in a state room. The food was great, the service embarrassing, and the soldiers spent their days swimming or lounging like vacationers. Wally learned to play blackjack the hard way, los-ing most of his cash. But he needed no money, and he was glad to learn his lesson early. He made up his mind not to play cards again.

When Wally let himself think very much, he sometimes still felt pangs of homesickness. But he had met a fellow from outside Pocatello, Idaho, who was a Mormon, and another guy from Kalispell, Montana. The three young men, all westerners, seemed to understand something about each other. Warren Hicks, the boy from Idaho, had Mormon parents, but the fam-ily hadn't made it to meetings very often. Jack Norland, the Montana boy, was actually more of a "hick" than either of the Mormons. He had never been out of western Montana before signing with the air corps, and it was remarkable how little he seemed to know about anything except cutting hay and raising cattle. He was good-natured, however, and ready to try anything, and in that sense, he sometimes brought out the worst in Wally.

The ship first anchored in the Yangtze River, off Shanghai, and Wally saw things he had never known before. The Japanese were in control of Shanghai, which had been devastated by artillery and bombs. Homeless people roamed the streets, and some came out to the ship on boats, where they begged for food or waited by the garbage chute for anything they could grab.

Some American families came on board in Shanghai, and the ship sailed back into its paradise of an existence, now with young American women on board for the soldiers to pursue. Wally tried to show Warren and Jack what a lady's man he was, but he learned that his thought of kissing one of the girls, out under the stars, was hardly what the more experienced men had in mind. He couldn't believe the stories that were soon circulating, and he passed them off as bragging, but still, he knew he was a long way from Sugar House.

Wally had expected grass shacks and tropical jungles in the Philippines, but what he discovered there was the modern city of Manila on Luzon Island, and palm-lined Dewey Boulevard with the beach on one side and elegant Spanish homes on the other. Nichols Field, not far from Manila, looked more like a plantation than a military base. Wally's quarters were not fancy—a barracks upstairs in a large, screened building—but the ground floor was filled with pool tables, card tables, and easy chairs.

The heat and humidity were oppressive, but even the weather had its compensations. Roll call was at 6:30 each morning. Breakfast was at seven, and at noon the workday ended. The afternoon heat made work next to impossible, so most of the soldiers lounged about or slept. The evenings were free for swimming or basketball or for trips into town.

Pay for new recruits was only twenty-one dollars a month, but each soldier gave five dollars of that to locals, who took all the KP duty, made beds and cleaned the barracks, and even washed laundry. The airmen lived an easy life: half a day of work and no end of free time. They didn't have much money, but nothing cost very much. They ordered special shoes and tailored uniforms, and they looked classier than troops almost anywhere else.

Wally had almost no complaints. He hadn't wanted to be a mechanic, so he was glad for the chance to serve as a supply clerk. He got an immediate jump in rank and income—thirty-six dollars a month—which made life even more pleasant. Eventually, those who took mechanics' training got more money, but that didn't bother Wally. He felt as though he had been granted a long vacation. He could have used a little more privacy than the barracks offered, but his days were full of fun, and he was seeing things old Mel would probably never see in his life.

Wally knew—based on what Mat Nakashima had told him—that war could come to the Philippines. But something in the peacefulness, the rustling of palm fronds, the constant wash of the blue-green ocean, and especially the persistent heat, made hostility seem unlikely, even too much effort. Besides, General Douglas MacArthur had trained the Philippine Scouts to protect themselves, and he had developed a defensive plan. Experienced soldiers claimed that if the Japanese tried to take more of the Asian islands, the Philippines would be the last they would think of attacking.

Wally trusted that, and he was glad he had joined the air corps. Chances were that he could make corporal before long, and his supply sergeant was training him to take over that job. Wally could be a sergeant in almost record time. Something like that never would have happened in the army or navy.

"Another beer?" Jack was asking. Jack had never been a drinker at home, but he was catching on fast here.

Wally shook his head. He had already had two, and that was normally his limit.

"Forget the beer," a man named Barney—one of the older guys in the unit—bellowed. "I say we take these boys to the Golden Gate Bar. It's time they became men." There were five airmen at the big table—besides Wally, Warren, and Jack—and they all agreed immediately that this was exactly the right plan.

Wally knew for sure he wasn't going to get involved with a prostitute, but he was curious to see what went on at a place like that. He looked at Warren, who was shaking his head. "I don't want to go over there," he told Wally. But not five minutes later, the eight men had piled into two taxis, and they were motoring down the street toward the Golden Gate Bar.

The place turned out to be dumpy and cheap—much like the bar they had just left—but when another round of drinks was ordered, a "waitress" arrived with each drink, one for each of the soldiers. A little woman—really just a girl—chose Wally. She was vaguely pretty, in spite of the heaviness of her makeup and a certain exaggeration in her attempt to be seductive. She placed a beer in front of Wally, put her arm around his shoulders, and held her face so close that she was almost touching his cheek. Then she whispered, "What can I do for you?"

"Nothing," Wally was quick to say, and a bit too loudly. Most of the men laughed. Wally glanced at Warren.

"Let's get out of here. I don't like this," Warren said.

"Okay," Wally told him. "Let's just see what happens for a minute."

He watched Barney put his arm around a woman and pull her against him. Like the others, she didn't have much on—a low-cut blouse and a short skirt that was split along the side. Barney was a heavy man who wore his shirt unbuttoned halfway down whenever he was "out of uniform." He never said a sentence without some vulgarity in it. Wally was not really surprised that this woman, who was no youngster, would let him maul her, but then she began rubbing up against him.

"Let's get out of here," Warren said again.

Wally nodded. The other men were beginning to paw their own waitresses, and the young woman who was still behind Wally reached around him and began to rub his chest. Suddenly a sense of shame struck Wally. He pushed his chair back, stood up, and looked at Warren. "It's Christmas," he said.

"I know. This makes me sick." He got up too.

"We'll see you guys later," Wally said. "Are you coming, Jack?"

Jack seemed to waver. But Barney shouted, "Stick around. I think that girl has a Christmas present for you."

Jack shrugged and said, "I guess I'll stay."

Wally and Warren got out. They found a taxi, and they headed back to the base. They said very little along the way, but when Warren said, "I wish I could be home today," a surge of homesickness hit Wally that was more powerful than anything he had felt since the day he had left Salt Lake.

Wally calculated the hours and tried to think what time it was at home. But Christmas had not come yet. The Philippines were across the international time line, a day ahead of Utah. Wally felt the loss of Christmas Eve, and of Christmas morning still to come, and suddenly he wanted to be home.

When he got back to the barracks, very few of the men were there. He was glad for the quiet and the relative privacy. He got inside the mosquito netting, and he lay on his bed. He tried to picture it all—LaRue and Beverly running downstairs, Gene ambling down behind them trying not to act too excited. Everyone there, together. And then he thought of his dad reading the Christmas story. Wally considered looking for his Bible, of reading the passages in Luke himself. But he couldn't do it—for all kinds of reasons. And so he lay there in the heat and tried not to think of home anymore. The trouble was, his thoughts wandered where they wanted to go—along

Thirteenth East, and there, on the porch, he saw that lovely figure in the sunset, wearing a light-blue polka-dot dress. He suddenly threw back the mosquito netting and stood up. He had to think of something to do. But nothing appealed to him, not even swimming in the ocean.

2 6

It was a cold February day, and snow had been falling all night. Alex had been in his office since very early that morning. He was trying to keep up with all the government paperwork. Recently, he had hired a second shift to keep up with the contracts that were coming in, but that had only meant more supervision—and more paperwork.

Alex was ordering new machinery all the time, and his operators were sometimes novices who had to be supervised. Some of the parts had minute tolerances, and a small mistake could cause an entire order to be rejected. Alex was actually quite mechanical, and he learned quickly. His foremen were, for the most part, much older than he was, but they respected his ability to troubleshoot and to work patiently with new hires. The problem was, they sometimes depended on him too much, and he spent more time than he had to spare out on the floor.

Henry Rosen liked to travel, to pitch the company to weapons builders, and to take big shots to lunch. What he didn't like was to deal with day-to-day operations. But that was all right. Alex preferred running things by himself to having Henry there acting important and getting everyone confused.

Alex sometimes escaped the plant to eat lunch at a nearby

diner, where he could be left alone for a few minutes. More often, he told himself he would get away soon and then ended up skipping meals. Every time Mom saw him these days, she shook her head and told him he had to start eating better. And so it was probably her idea that Dad showed up on this cold day with a basket of fried chicken.

President Thomas stepped up to Alex's little office and stood in the open doorway. "Dinnertime," he said.

Alex looked up, surprised. Dad came by often, but he had never brought food before. "Oh, thanks," Alex said. "Come in."

"Push a few of those papers aside and I'll join you. Your mom cooked enough for the whole plant, I think."

"I'd like to push all these forms right into the wastepaper basket. It's unbelievable how much red tape I have to deal with." He picked up a stack of papers and slipped them into a folder, and then he pushed some forms off to one side.

Dad sat down across from him. The office was a shabby little room with a worn-out carpet and windows on all sides, shaded by venetian blinds. Alex kept the blinds open enough to see out on the floor of the plant.

"With all the money that's coming in these days, you ought to spend five dollars and get yourself a decent lamp," Dad said. "I can't believe you work in this light."

"I've been meaning to buy something for a long time. I just never get the time to do it."

"Alex, you need more secretarial help—or an assistant manager. You can't keep pushing yourself like this."

"I know. I plan to hire some more people."

"When?"

Alex laughed. "As soon as I get time," he said.

"Well, you've got to do it soon. I'm worried about you." Dad pulled a plate from the basket and handed it to Alex. "Your mom really fixed us up here." He pulled out utensils and cloth napkins and a bowl of potato salad with waxed paper over it. "Grab some chicken. There's a nice breast piece right there."

Alex did take the breast, and he could hardly believe how good it tasted. It reminded him of how much he missed his mother's cooking—or any sort of home cooking.

"Alex," Dad said, "I had no idea what I was getting you into with this business. I thought Henry would carry more of the load, and I didn't know it would get this busy."

"Well, I do have to get more help."

"I'll tell you, Alex, I couldn't be prouder of you. I knew you had the talent to manage a business, but I didn't expect you, at your age, to step forward and make such a go of this thing. I've talked to the men in the shop, and they tell me they've never worked for a man they like better."

Dad bit into a thigh piece and stayed after it until he had finished it. He wiped his hands and mouth then, and he forked in a big bite of potato salad. He ate the way he did everything else: as if it was a job that had to be done and he had better go at it hard until it was finished.

"Alex, things are falling into shape for you. Now it's time to step back and think about some other priorities. You're twenty-four. You need to find yourself a wife, get a family started." He pointed to the basket. "Oh, say, Mom put hot rolls in there too—baked this morning."

Alex reached in and got a roll, but he didn't say anything. Dad went after another piece of chicken, consumed it, and dropped the bone on his plate. Then he wiped his fingers again before he said, "Your mom was telling me about some of the young women she would like to see you court—girls from the best families. There's not a girl in Sugar House who wouldn't jump at the chance to go out with you."

Alex laughed. "Sounds dangerous," he said.

Dad seemed unsure how to react to that, but he tried to smile. "Tell me this," he said. "How do you feel about being a business manager now? Doesn't it turn out to be a lot more interesting than you expected?"

"To tell you the truth, no," Alex said. "I'm doing the best I can. But I can't really say I enjoy it."

Dad took his time to react, as though trying not to come on too strong. "I don't understand that, Alex. Just think of the doors that are opening up for you."

Alex was still bothered by the idea that he was making weapons, but he didn't want to get into all that again. And so he merely said, "It just doesn't engage my mind. I like ideas. I like to think."

"Are you telling me you still want to be a history professor?"

"Yes, I do."

"Alex, you're helping your country here. And you're getting set up financially so you'll never have to worry again."

"Look, Dad, there's no use our debating about this. I told you from the beginning, I'll manage the plant long enough to get it going, and then I'm going back to school."

"Alex, if I were you, I wouldn't be so quick to turn away from the great *blessing* you're receiving. You could have your fortune made in a few years, and then you can devote your life to anything you want. You know what Elder Smith told you— that you could serve in the highest councils in the Church."

Alex didn't answer. He saw all too clearly what Dad had in mind: get married, make some good money early in life, and then become a Church leader. It was Dad's notion of the fulfilled life, and there was nothing wrong with it, but Alex simply couldn't see himself traveling that road.

For a time, Alex and President Thomas merely sat and ate, but Alex felt the tension. Dad was obviously frustrated. Eventually, after putting away one more piece of chicken and a second helping of potato salad, President Thomas leaned back in his chair and said, "Alex, is this still about building weapons? Is that what's bothering you?"

"That's one of the things. Yes."

"Your mom tells me you're still attached to this German girl—the one you baptized."

This sounded like an accusation, and for the first time, Alex was a little irritated by what was happening. He glanced at his dad, but he didn't say anything.

"Son, you can't let this German girl color everything you're accomplishing here. Hitler needs to be stopped, whether she lives in Germany or not. And you absolutely *can't* think about waiting to marry her."

Alex wiped his mouth and then dropped his napkin on his desk. He took a long breath and then tried to smile. "Dad, come on. That's my decision, not yours."

"I'm just being realistic. You need to get married, and you may not see this girl—"

"Her name is Anna."

"All right. Anna. But you may not see her for years, if ever. And there's more to it than that. Bringing a foreign girl here is difficult. I've seen other missionaries do it, and sometimes it works out, but it's never easy."

"But it's still my decision."

"So what are you telling me? Are you going to wait out this war? I know she's a pretty girl, but—"

"Wait, Dad. Give me some credit."

"Well, I don't know what's on your mind. I don't understand this at all."

Alex leaned forward and put his elbows in his desk. "I haven't told you how I feel because I knew how you would react. But I'll tell you now."

Dad leaned back and nodded, but he looked as though he were waiting to be slugged.

"Before I left on my mission, I told you my testimony wasn't strong enough, and you said, 'That's what a mission is all about. You'll learn to get answers.' And that's exactly what happened. I learned to get answers—and I got my answer on this. Anna is the right girl for me."

Dad didn't argue, but he didn't look convinced.

"I asked the Lord whether I would ever see Anna again, and I got the clearest answer I've ever had in my life. She's going to get through this war, and I'm going to have my chance to ask her to marry me."

"Alex, the only way this war is going to be short is if Hitler defeats England this summer. Otherwise, it's going to last for years."

"I know."

"And you're *absolutely* sure you want to wait?"

"Yes."

Dad sat for a long time, his eyes distant and full of concern, but finally he said, "Son, I would never tell you not to follow the Spirit, but I hope you haven't deceived yourself into believing what you want to believe."

"If that's what I've done, then I don't know the Spirit, and I don't really have a testimony. It's that simple to me."

Dad was stopped. He thought for a time again, and then he leaned forward. "I'm sorry," he said. "I have no right to question your knowledge of the Spirit. I didn't mean to do that."

"Thanks." Alex sat for a few seconds and then reached across the table and touched his dad's hand. "Dad, you will love Anna someday. You'll thank the Lord for her."

"I hope so, Alex." Dad got up. He stuck his plate into the basket. "Does she know how you feel?" he asked. "Will she wait for you?"

"I've written her, but I don't know whether my letters have gotten through. Can you think of any way I could contact her—like through the Church?"

Dad left the chicken and potato salad on Alex's desk, but he put the plates and utensils and napkins in the basket. He seemed to be thinking. "I could talk to J. Reuben Clark," he finally said. "He was with the State Department for a long time, and he served as an ambassador. He has contacts all over."

"He made some kind of official visit to Berlin during that first year I was on my mission."

Dad nodded. "Yes, I'm sure he's been there many times, and I know he keeps in touch with the American ambassador to Germany. Maybe there's a way to get a letter to the ambassador, and from there to Church leaders."

"Dad, that would be great."

"All right. I'll call him. I'll see what he says. Or maybe I can make an appointment for you. I'm sure you can make a better case than I could."

"Do you still think I'm making a mistake?"

Dad had taken a step toward the door, but he turned back now, and he looked at Alex. "Son, this breaks my heart. I hate to see you put off marriage that long, and I worry whether it will all work out. If you had told me she was a swell girl and you couldn't live without her, I would tell you to stop kidding yourself. But you're telling me God is guiding you in this, and I'm not going to take that lightly."

"Thanks, Dad." Alex smiled. "I'll tell you something else. She's the prettiest girl who ever *lived*."

"Sorry, son. I married the prettiest girl who ever lived—a long time ago." Dad smiled, but only with some effort. As he turned to leave, Alex saw in his eyes, in his posture, how deeply disappointed he was.

When Alex stepped into the office, President J. Reuben Clark, first counselor to President Grant, glanced up and said, "Yes. Sit down." He was making a note on a sheet of paper, and he finished before he finally set his pen down and looked at Alex. "You're Al Thomas's boy, I understand."

"Yes." Alex sat in the chair President Clark had pointed to, directly in front of the big, dark-walnut desk.

President Clark was a heavy man with a round face and a thick double chin. His hair was full, mostly gray, shading to white at the temples. His desk was covered with papers, and he had seemed deep in his work, but now that he had set it aside, his smile was welcoming.

"So how is your father? Is he like me, still feeling bad that the Saints have no more sense than to vote for FDR?"

"I don't think he ever held out much hope for anything else." Alex wasn't about to mention his own vote.

"That's smart. I always think that if I make a good speech, I might change some minds. But I never do." He laughed at himself, the flesh under his chin shaking. President Clark was the most prominent Republican in the state and was nationally known for his opinions on international relations. Alex knew that plenty of people did listen to what he said.

"I remember President Thomas telling me that you served a mission. Where was it you went?"

"The West German mission. I was there when the war broke out."

"That was a busy time around this office, I'll tell you." President Clark pointed to his phone. "I ran up a mammoth telephone bill trying to keep in touch with what was going on. It's good we didn't wait another day before we got you out."

Alex smiled. "We were a little busy ourselves," he said.

"Tell me something." President Clark leaned back and rested his arms on his heavy chest. "How did the members of the Church feel about Hitler?"

"Most didn't say much. But the ones who spoke up usually said they thought well of him."

"Now, see, that's what I've been saying." He waved a finger in Alex's direction. "I'm not going to sit here and tell anyone that Hitler is a fine fellow. But people here don't understand what he's done for Germany. The Treaty of Versailles was wrong. It was punitive beyond reason. The Germans had no hope of recovery until they defied that treaty. What I say is that England and France created Hitler, and now they can live with him."

Alex would have liked to talk more about that, but he was

nervous. He wasn't sure how President Clark would react to his request. He ran his hands along his trousers and then leaned forward a little, his hands on his knees. "President, I don't want to take a lot of your time. I merely wanted—"

"Tell me a little about yourself, Alex."

"Well . . . I went to the U before my mission. I have a year to go to get my degree in history, but right now my dad and I have started a business. We're making parts for the big munitions companies."

"So have you decided not to finish school?"

"No. Not at all. I want to go back as soon as I can. Actually, I'd like to do what you did—go east to graduate school. I want to be a professor."

President Clark seemed to consider that, but he looked rather solemn for the first time. "Well, I'll tell you, I don't regret for a minute what I did. I got my law degree at Columbia, and then I stayed in the East. I made my way in Babylon and did all right, and then the Church called me home to do this job. So that worked out fine for me. But I used my law training to get some work done—work I believed in. Sometimes I'm not sure whether these fellows with Ph.D.s believe in anything at all. I'd be careful about going that direction."

"You *do* sound like my dad."

"Well, now, that's a compliment. Thank you very much." He laughed out loud. "Tell me now, what can I do for you?"

Alex had thought out his little speech, but suddenly his reason for coming was embarrassing. This was a man who had worked out treaties between nations, negotiated with world leaders. "While I was in Germany I baptized a family," Alex began—carefully. "I need to get in touch with them. I've written, but I get no answer. I was thinking that a letter could be sent through the American ambassador, or maybe through Church channels. I need to know *for sure* that the letter gets through."

President Clark looked mystified, his eyebrows, much darker than his hair, gathering over his eyes. "I could possibly get something through, but we use those channels only for very important matters. I can't be a conduit for ordinary mail."

"I understand." Alex took a breath. "I . . . well . . . I want to marry the daughter in this family. The Lord has answered my prayers about that. But she doesn't know my intentions."

President Clark smiled. He looked down at his desk for a time. "Alex, I could tell you that's too minor a matter to require diplomatic intervention—but I'm sure you would disagree. So let me answer another way." He waited until Alex looked up at him. "Find a local girl. Marry her. Let the German girl find a husband in Germany. This war could last a long time, but even if it doesn't, I still think that's good advice."

Alex didn't feel he could argue with a member of the First Presidency, but he also couldn't accept the answer. "Can you think of some other way, then, that I could possibly contact her?"

President Clark chuckled. "Then I take it you're not going to accept my advice?"

"Well . . . no. President, I haven't had a lot of experiences in my life where I was *sure* the Lord had spoken to me. But it happened once when I blessed Anna, and her life was restored. And it happened again when I asked him whether I should marry her."

"Well . . . if it's right, the Lord will preserve her for you."

"All right. And maybe I'll just have to live with that. But I want her to know how I feel, and that I'm waiting. I think it might help her get through the war."

"What if she's not as interested in you as you are in her?"

"We didn't say anything to each other about that—but I knew how she felt."

President Clark smiled again. "Oh, my," he said. He drummed his fingers on his desk.

"President," Alex said, "I'm sorry I've taken your time." Alex got up.

"Now wait a minute." President Clark motioned for Alex to

sit down. "I was born in 1871, Alex. That's the dark ages to you. We didn't think the way you young folks do. But I'll tell you one thing. When a man falls in love, I guess it always feels about the same way. And if some old fellow had told me to forget about Luacine and find another girl to marry, I wouldn't have listened to him any more than you're listening to me."

"President, I meet the girls around here, and they're fine. But Anna almost died. When she came back, her spirit was changed. I've never met a young woman who's so close to God."

"And I suppose she's rather a plain young woman? You only love her for her spirit."

Alex felt his face get hot. "No," he said, without looking at President Clark. "She's beautiful."

"I had a feeling she would be." Alex was still unsure what President Clark was going to say, but he sensed something positive, so he looked into his eyes. "All right, since you won't take my advice, go out to my secretary's office and write your letter. I'll see if I can get it through. I can't make any promises, but I think I know how to do it."

"Thank you, sir." Alex stood again. He tried not to show his elation. "Let me say one more thing," President Clark said. Alex nodded and waited. "Some people call me a pacifist, and I'm not sure that's exactly the right word to describe me, but what I do know is that war is evil and Christians should avoid it if they possibly can."

Alex was surprised. He knew that President Clark was known for his opposition to American involvement in the war, but he seemed to be saying more than that.

"Alex, I hate to see you building parts for weapons, but I also hate to see you sell your soul in graduate school. I want to see our bright young people step forward and lead this world. I did a little of that. Future generations could do a lot more."

"I guess I don't see myself as a leader."

"Do you think I did when I was growing up in Grantsville?

I was just a dirt-poor, barefoot kid. You're way ahead of what I was. That's easy to see."

"I do want to do something worthwhile with my life."

"Alex, Roosevelt is already in this war. He can't build airplanes for England and then claim to be neutral. So we'll be sending troops to Europe, maybe before the year is out, and that means you'll probably be fighting Germans, not marrying them. And once the shooting starts, you'll be ducking bullets, clinging to life, and if you're not careful, you'll be hating the German people. War only sounds good in the newspapers back on the home front. In reality, it's the most evil force that Satan has invented. The horror of war is not just that people get killed—it's that it creates killers. And it throws young people into vile, corrupt environments. You remember that. If you end up having to go, find a way to keep the Spirit alive in you."

Alex nodded.

"We can't forget our purpose, Brother Thomas. This war is splitting our church up—separating us from our own brothers and sisters, stopping our missionary work, diverting our attention from the real work we have to do. It breaks my heart. I look at a young man like you, and I see Satan trying to enlist you in his service—wreaking havoc, spilling blood—when you need to be building the kingdom, raising up a family unto the Lord."

President Clark's volume—and power—had gradually risen, and Alex was moved. "I don't like spending my time building weapons," Alex said. "No one seems to understand that."

President Clark nodded, but then he smiled. "Well, sometimes I get up on my high horse, and I have to be careful. But tell me this. If you end up killing Germans—hating them—are you going to be able to love your Anna?"

"I'll never hate the German people."

"I hope you're right. But you think about what I've just said. Go write your letter, but be very careful about the promises you make."

27

Bobbi hadn't gone into nursing with any enthusiasm, but as it turned out, she liked it. She had always loved to learn, and she found the science—biology, anatomy, chemistry—more interesting than she had expected. But what she liked best was being in the hospital, even with the long hours and the miles she ended up walking every day. Knowing people who were suffering made her own problems seem less significant, and she liked the contact, the little chats, the life stories she heard, and even the physical touch.

She had never wanted to deal with bedpans and vomit and all the rest that she associated with nursing, but that was actually the most comforting to her—to find that she could accept smells and secretions as part of life. She no longer had to see people in some best-dressed state to accept them. Some people were nasty in their suffering, others serene. But people seemed to become what they really were in that state, and for the most part, Bobbi liked them that way.

Still, Bobbi missed the university and the literature that she now had no time to read. And the simple fact was, she still missed David. She missed her talks with him, the sharing, and the wonderful way he had of probing her mind and liking what he found there. She missed the beauty she felt in herself when he looked at her. Sometimes at night, she lay awake and imagined him holding her, kissing her the way he had those few times, and she was almost certain she would never feel that much pleasure again.

She was not dating. She wanted to believe that she was out of touch, being away from the university, and that she wasn't meeting many boys. And yet, she suspected that she was not very attractive, that Phil's devotion to her had been a sort of aberration, and that David's was a meeting of minds of a kind that wasn't likely to come around again.

Bobbi had always been happy. It wasn't in her to feel sorry for herself, and she didn't do that now. She took life as it came, and she was cheerful most of the time, but when she stopped to look inside herself, she felt a relentless emptiness, and she was worried that it would never go away. Her answer for that was not to look inside very often, not to let herself dwell on her own problems, but a little sense of loss never seemed to leave her.

One night early in April, she was finishing a long day at the hospital and was feeling particularly dragged out. She got her coat from her locker, and even though it was already late, grabbed a couple of books she needed to study when she got home. Then she headed out the front doors to her bus stop. But there was Phil standing at the bottom of the steps in a wool topcoat and a classy felt hat. It was a cool evening, and he had his hands tucked into his pockets as though he had been waiting around long enough to get cold.

When he finally spotted her, she saw his face light up. "Hi," he said, quite naturally. "Could I give you a ride home?"

"Is that legal—for an engaged guy?" She laughed.

But he took the question more seriously than she had meant it. "Not really, I guess. But I want to talk to you."

"Okay."

"You look good." He was standing rather close, with his shoulders hunched, looking down at her.

"White is a good color for me," she said, and she laughed. But she glanced down and realized that little white was showing. She had her gray tweed coat on. She knew she had worked too hard to think of something to say, and she was embarrassed.

But then, with that strong hand of his, he was taking her arm, turning her. His touch still seemed to say, "I'll take care of you." He opened the door for her, held her arm as she got in, and then he tucked her coat against her so it wouldn't catch in the door. It all seemed so normal, so right.

When he got into the car, he started it and then pulled out from the curb, but he didn't head south, as she had expected. He turned east and drove through the avenues.

"I just wanted to talk to you for a few minutes, Bobbi."

"I'm glad you did. It's nice to see you. When are you getting married?"

"The date is set for June. But Bobbi, I'm still in love with you. I just wanted to ask you whether there was any chance that we could get back together."

Bobbi's first reaction was a lovely kind of satisfaction, but she knew she had to be careful. "You mean you would break up with Ilene, and we would start dating again?"

"Yes."

"What if everything went the way it did last time?"

"I don't know. It would be a mess, and my family would be upset with me, but I'd like to take the chance. I can't tell you how awful it is to be in love with you and planning to marry someone else."

Bobbi was touched. Phil sounded more vulnerable than she ever remembered him. Maybe he had grown—and deepened. Maybe Bobbi could thrill her parents and end this loneliness she had felt the whole past year. If David wasn't an option for her, maybe Phil could be again.

"Bobbi, things are better now. I'm almost through my second year of law school, and you're moving ahead in nursing school. Maybe this delay is what we needed. Now we could go forward, and we wouldn't have the stress we had last time."

But the analysis was wrong. Phil never had understood the problems between them.

"I've learned a lot in the past year. I've dated some beautiful girls, but they all seemed shallow. There's something special about you, Bobbi. You weren't trying to *catch* me. You were always yourself with me."

"But Phil, we're so different."

"We both love the Lord. That's the center of everything. And we have things to offer each other. Maybe our differences will become our combined strength."

The words were right. And Bobbi felt herself wanting to believe them. Maybe this was meant to be. She had always known Phil would be a stalwart, a good father, a steady influence in her life. Maybe she could learn from that steadiness, and maybe she could help him take more interest in the things she loved. "Phil, I don't know. It would be so complicated to do this now. We'd be the talk of the whole town. You've already had pictures of two fiancées in the *Deseret News.* Do you want to have the paper re-run the first picture?" She laughed.

"I don't care about anything like that. I would simply go to Ilene—tonight—and tell her I'm sorry but that it isn't going to work. And then, to look right, we could wait a month or so before we actually dated in public. It would simply seem that Ilene and I had broken our engagement, and then, that you and I, at a later time, had begun to date again."

But this was not spontaneous. This was something he had thought out very carefully. And something else became clear for the first time. She had wondered why he hadn't come inside the hospital to wait in the lobby, but now she knew. He hadn't wanted to be seen.

"Phil, what if I say no? What are you going to do?"

"I don't know."

"Maybe you should decide what you want to do about

Ilene first. If you decide you don't want to marry her, break up. After that, we could go out a few times and see what happens."

"I'm not comfortable with that, Bobbi."

"Why not?"

But Phil had no answer. He had turned south and was driving past the university campus. It all reminded Bobbi of days they had spent together, when the two of them would sit on the lawn and talk. That was a nice thought, but it also reminded her of a frustrating argument that had started one day when he had complained about being required to take a music appreciation class.

"I just need to know whether I have any chance with you, Bobbi."

"So if I say that you don't have a chance, you'll marry Ilene?"

"Maybe. I haven't decided. But it's hard for me to—" He stopped as though he saw too late the trap Bobbi had set.

"Phil, you're trying to negotiate a new deal. But you want to hang on to the old one until you see whether you can get a better one." She turned and looked at him more directly than she had before. She was beginning to feel some confidence.

"Maybe that's true, Bobbi. But it's not so bad as you make it sound. I care about Ilene."

"You're ready to cut and run, if you get the chance."

"You did that to me, Bobbi." He looked her way and smiled, as though to be charming, and to cover the frustration that was obviously building in him.

"Not because I got a better deal, Phil. I looked into my own heart, and then I did what I felt I had to do."

"What about Dr. Stinson? Are you telling me he had nothing to do with it?"

Bobbi was ready to protest for a moment, but then she admitted, "Okay, he did play a role. It wasn't that I thought I would marry him when I broke up with you. But I did see what I was missing."

"Thanks."

"All I mean is, he and I understood each other. And I want that."

"If he had been a Mormon, you would have married him then?"

"Yes."

Bobbi knew what Phil was doing: sizing up the contest, accepting the truth he hated—that he had lost to another man.

"Well, Bobbi, you *are* a Mormon. And I love you. Ilene is a wonderful girl, but I still feel more for you."

"Maybe. Or maybe I'm the one girl who turned you down, and you just can't get that out of your head. Maybe the instant I said yes, you would regret everything—and run back to Ilene."

Phil leaned back and gave the steering wheel a little slap. "Bobbi, I don't know. Maybe that's right. I don't think so, but maybe it is. The long and short of it is, you're sending me packing again. Right?"

There was a certain hardness in his voice now, and Bobbi felt relieved to hear it. But she told him, "Phil, you have no idea how close I just came to saying okay, let's try it."

"Then do it. Just give me one more chance."

"And then what? If you dropped Ilene and we dated again, I would be trapped. I couldn't possibly change my mind at that point. My family wouldn't let me."

"I don't see that, Bobbi."

"Of course you do. You thought this all through—every aspect of it. You don't do things by impulse, Phil."

"I just don't want to lose you." But his voice had lost all its certainty. And now he was driving toward her home.

"I'm sorry, Phil. I'm touched that you would think of me this way, but it's obvious that we would drive each other crazy if we got married."

Phil shrugged. "You're probably right," he said, and Bobbi

had the feeling he had just then decided to marry Ilene after all.

When Bobbi walked into her house, she could see a glow slipping under the kitchen door and lighting the dining room a little. She wondered who was up and around, so she walked through the living room, into the dining room and then pushed the kitchen door open. "Oh, Mom. Hi. I thought you'd be in bed."

"That's where I'm going. The kids messed up some dishes after dinner, and I was just washing them up."

"You ought to let LaRue and Beverly do that. They're the ones who always eat after supper."

"I know. I ought to do a lot of things. You sound like your dad."

Bobbi saw a kind of weariness in her mother's face that was unusual. She stepped into the kitchen. "What's wrong?" she asked.

"Nothing. I'm just tired. Are you going to bed now?"

"Soon. I have to read for a little while. Is there anything edible in the refrigerator?"

Mom laughed. "I'll let you decide that. But if you eat something, clean up your own mess."

"I'll just make some toast."

Mom was heading for the door. But suddenly Bobbi didn't want to be alone. "You won't believe what happened tonight," she said. Mom turned around. She was wearing a faded brown house dress she'd had for many years, and her face seemed a little faded too. Bobbi thought again that she wasn't just tired, that something was wrong. "When I got off work tonight, Phil was waiting. He wanted to talk to me."

Bobbi saw a little spark appear in her mother's face, but it faded just as quickly. "You didn't give him a chance, did you?"

Bobbi hadn't expected that reaction, and the words stung. "Actually, I tried," she said. "He drove me home, and we talked. But it was the same old thing. I don't feel any different."

Bobbi walked to the cabinet and opened the bread box. Mom didn't bake bread very often anymore. Bobbi found a loaf of Wonder Bread inside, which she didn't like much, but she got out a couple of slices anyway.

Mom was still standing by the door. "Bobbi, sometimes I think you're looking for something in a man that you never will find."

Bobbi placed the slices of bread in the toaster and then closed the little doors on both sides. She turned around. "Mom," she said, "Phil didn't want to marry me. He wanted to own me. He was shopping for a wife, and then he wanted a house, some kids, and maybe a dog to go with me. Once he had paid off my mortgage he would have put my title in a safe-deposit box, and that would have been that."

"That's how men think."

"All of them?"

"I don't know. All I've known."

"Even Dad?"

Sister Thomas walked over and sat down at the table. Bobbi came to the table too and sat across from her. She saw the sadness in her mother's eyes. "What's wrong tonight?"

"Oh, nothing much. Your dad and I just had a little spat."

"What about?"

"Money. As usual. I told him I need more for my household budget—with all the prices going up. And he started in on one of his little speeches about all of us being too extravagant."

"I thought he was doing really well in this new business."

"That's the mistake I made—bringing that up. He went off on a harangue about my spending money that we don't have yet. If the war ends this spring, he could be stuck with a worthless plant and . . . blah, blah, blah."

Bobbi laughed, and then so did Mom. "You'd better get that toast," she said.

Bobbi got up quickly, having forgotten all about it. But the toast still wasn't as dark as Bobbi liked it. She shut it back in the toaster. "I thought you told me that you fell head over heels in love when you met Dad."

"Oh, Bobbi, don't make so much out of this. I'm just put out with him tonight. That doesn't mean I don't love him."

"I know. But you just said all men think like Phil. Didn't it bother you when you saw that in Dad?"

"I don't know how to answer that. I wanted a husband. I met a handsome man who loved me. And I fell in love with him. I don't remember ever considering all these things you worry about."

"Okay. But think about it now. You said men expect to own their wives. Is that all right?" Bobbi opened the toaster again, and this time she pulled the toast out and set the slices on the cabinet. She walked to the refrigerator to find some butter.

"Bobbi, try not to get toast crumbs in the butter. You know how—" But she stopped.

"How Dad hates it. I know."

Sister Thomas laughed, but then she looked at the clock. Bobbi had the feeling that she was measuring the cost of staying up any later. All the same, she said, "Bobbi, when I was growing up, girls were taught certain attitudes that we never questioned. My parents told me what to do, and I accepted that. I stayed a little girl, really, until I got married. Then my husband began deciding everything. At first, I didn't ask myself whether that was right. It was what I was used to in my own home."

"That seems sad, Mom."

"I don't know whether it is or not. But there's a streak in me that doesn't like it. I pop off. I say things to people that I know darn well your dad wishes I wouldn't say. Sometimes I exaggerate my opinions—just to show that I can think for myself. The funny thing is, Al never has tried to stop me. He likes to be in control, but there's a fairness about him, and he's not one to tromp on anyone. So he let's me get away with it."

Bobbi was pouring a glass of milk by now. And then she

brought her little meal to the table. "Mom," she said, "you seem pretty strong to me. Dad always jokes about having a wife he can't buffalo."

"But that's just the problem, Bobbi. I always feel as though I'm swimming upstream, and what I long for is a little more respect. Your dad is entirely confident that he knows more than I do, that he's smarter. He tries to be considerate of me, and he lets me have my way at times, but deep down, he'd prefer to run the whole show."

"Mom, that sounds awful."

Sister Thomas reached across the table and tore off a corner of one slice of toast. "Oh, Bobbi, you're young. You idealize everything too much." She took a little bite out of the toast. "I love your dad. I admire him. I trust in the guidance he gets from the Lord. And I like him. You kids see the worst of him sometimes because you're all pushing him so hard right now. But he's a gentle man, a loving man, and he's trying to do what he thinks is right. He's playing the role he was taught to play—and all I do is confuse him."

"Are you two friends?"

Sister Thomas took a long time to think about that. "Yes," she said eventually. "But not as much as I'd like. And I suppose that's the thing that is hardest for me. I became Bea Thomas before I ever knew who Bea Snow was, and I wish your dad had been more willing to let me become myself. But he was so strong, so sure, that he simply pulled me along with him. When I finally started taking a stand on a few things, he hardly knew how to react."

"David Stinson listens to me, Mom. He's interested in my thoughts—gets excited about them. If we got married, we'd be *partners*."

"Maybe. You don't know that for sure."

"But if I've got a chance for that kind of marriage, should I throw it aside—and marry someone like Phil?"

"I thought you had your mind made up not to marry David."

"I thought I did too. But it was really Dad who made up my mind for me. We had some good talks, and he tried not to make any demands. But I knew what it would cost me if I went against him, so I just gave in."

"So what are you saying?"

"I don't know. Tell me what I should do."

"I can't do that."

"Tell me what you think then."

Mom sat for a long time again. And as she thought, tears filled her eyes. "Bobbi, I don't want you to marry David. I want you to do life the way I've done it. That's my *feeling*. But at the same time, I know I've missed something. I work behind the scenes. I manipulate. I suggest, cajole, apologize, flatter—do anything I can just to have a say in what happens. But if I told your dad that, he wouldn't even understand me; he'd be hurt and baffled and maybe even angry. So I just go on managing that way, and it's hard work. I wouldn't want you to go through the same thing. You're too independent. It would destroy you."

"Thanks, Mom."

Sister Thomas got up from the table. "But I already wish I hadn't said anything like that. You're too quick to jump on things and magnify them. The most important thing in this life is a temple marriage. I have all eternity to work out my relationship with your dad. You may not end up getting that from David, and he may not be nearly so understanding and open once you're married. You have to consider all of that—think about it *very* carefully."

"I know."

"And pray about it."

"I do. All the time."

"Well, don't just pray. Listen. That's not your greatest talent." She smiled.

"I know that too."

Mom left, and Bobbi stayed up for a long time. In fact, even though she eventually went to bed, she never did go to sleep. She saw how complex her question really was, but she also felt more clearly than ever what she wanted out of life.

In the morning, she waited until she knew her dad was eating breakfast, and then she went downstairs. "I need to tell you something," she told him. She was standing just inside the kitchen door, in her robe. "David and I have stayed in touch all year—as I'm sure you know. He still wants to marry me. This summer I'll have some time off at the hospital, and I have some savings, so I've decided to take a trip to Chicago. I'll stay in a hotel there, and everything will be proper. But I need to go. I need to see him again and decide for sure what I want to do."

President Thomas looked shocked, but he didn't say a word.

"I know I told you the whole thing was over, but the problem is, I can't get him out of my heart. I think about him all the time. I'm not going to Chicago to marry him; if I decide to do that, it would happen later. But I have to reach a decision for myself—one I can feel good about."

President Thomas leaned his head back and shut his eyes. "Well, I won't say a word. The new rule—and I'm not sure where it came from—seems to be that a father can't guide his children. He's some sort of dictator if he does."

"Dad, don't do that to me. It's not fair. I've listened to everything you've said. And I've talked to Mom. I'll take all of that into consideration."

"Thanks. That's very kind of you." Bobbi had to get out before she lost her temper. She turned and pushed against the door, but her dad said, "Bobbi, this isn't about *opinions*. This is about your life. I have a right to tell you what I think is best for you."

"And I have a right to think you're wrong."

Bobbi left.

2 8

Anna was home alone. She had come home from work before her mother, who was now working too. Sister Stoltz had not sought work, but a government official had visited her and explained that her records indicated she was unemployed with no young children in her home. She would therefore be expected to work in a new factory in Frankfurt that was producing boots for soldiers.

Brother Stoltz and Peter were usually home by this time, but Anna knew that today they had planned one of their trips into the country to purchase fresh food. Inflation had made their money of less worth than before, but they had gained some contacts with farmers who sometimes sold them the things they wanted. Brother Stoltz could no longer ride a bicycle, but he had bought a second-hand motorbike, which he could handle if he didn't over-tax himself. The problem was to obtain a gallon of gasoline once in a while. Late in June, Hitler attacked Russia. His troops, in three parallel thrusts, had been racing ahead, stampeding the Russians. Germans, for the most part, were excited by this move. Russia had always seemed more an enemy than France or especially England, and the early success seemed to assure a quick victory. But shortages were now a larger problem than ever, and gasoline was especially hard to obtain.

Anna was tired today. It was July of 1941, and a hot day. The factory where she worked had been sweltering, and tempers were on edge. The manager of the plant was getting pressure to turn out more uniforms, and he was passing that pressure along to his workers. Anna tried to keep up, but no amount of work was enough to satisfy her boss.

So this was the hour she longed for every day—when she could relax for a time. Evenings passed too quickly, and mornings came early. Then it all started again, six days a week, sometimes seven. Recently, the first bombs had dropped in Frankfurt. So far, the British had targeted the industrial part of the city, far across town, but when the sirens sounded at night, everyone had to hurry down to the basement, and those lost nights of sleep only added to the stress.

Anna made rose-hip tea, although she longed for some cool apple juice. She sat at the kitchen table and tried to take joy in having a few minutes to herself. When a knock came at the door, she assumed it was a neighbor, or perhaps President Meis, who sometimes stopped by. She opened the door carefully, however, having learned to be wary. She had opened it only a few inches when she saw that it was Kellerman. She froze.

"Good afternoon," he said. "It's nice to see you again."

Anna said nothing. What could he want after all this time?

"May I step in for a moment?"

Anna couldn't think what to do. She didn't want to let him in, and yet she feared saying no. In her confusion, she hesitated, and suddenly he stepped forward and pushed against the door. Anna stepped back and Kellerman walked in, and then he shut the door behind him.

"Is your father here?" he asked. He spoke politely, but Anna felt the undercurrent, the implied threat in his voice.

"Yes," she said. "He walked down to the courtyard for something. He will be back in just a moment."

Kellerman smiled, his thick lips stretching wider than usual. "Oh, my dear, you lie so well. If I didn't know better, I would believe you. How does one so pretty, so innocent, learn to lie this way? Did your American friends teach you this?"

Anna didn't answer, but now she was more frightened. How did he know she was lying? Why would he come when he knew her father wasn't there?

"I need to know something. Tell me the truth or I will search your apartment. Is your mother here?"

"No. She's still at work. I expect her any minute now."

"Yes. This is a closer answer. But not for half an hour at the very least."

Anna thought she knew now what was happening. She began to think what she could do. He was standing between her and the door. She would have no chance to get out that way.

"I am aware that your father and your brother have gone to the country again. They enjoy their little trips, I notice. I'm surprised your father gets around so well, but I'm pleased for him." Kellerman enjoyed his irony with another facetious smile.

"And they like to purchase vegetables and fruit, maybe some cheese. Is this not so?"

"Yes."

"Isn't that nice for you? It makes you look so pretty to have these healthy, fresh foods."

Anna was thinking of the kitchen: the drawer where the knives were.

"And being such good Christians, your father and brother take these foods to members of your sect. Is this not so?"

"Certainly."

"That *is* wonderful. It's exactly the way religious people should behave. All this kindness is inspiring, don't you think?"

He took a step forward, and Anna moved back. She almost bolted, but he stopped, and she waited.

"But then, I'm not certain that it's Christian to feed Jews. And there is also the question of law. For your father and brother to enter the ghetto, a place forbidden to them, and to take food to a Jew—something also forbidden—perhaps that makes this difficult question more complex? Do you think so?"

"My father is a good man. If he takes food to people, it's only out of kindness."

"Yes, yes. This question *is* difficult. But then, if a man has insulted me, has made me look bad before my leaders—perhaps I cannot be truly dispassionate. And not being as Christian as your father, perhaps a desire for revenge clouds my thinking."

"He wants no trouble. Honestly, he doesn't."

"That may be so, and perhaps there is no Christian answer." Kellerman took another step forward. Anna stepped back again, toward the open kitchen door. "Perhaps the only answer is a Jewish one. I understand that Jews like to strike a bargain— and I can do that. Would you like to strike a bargain that would save your father's and your brother's lives?"

Anna's breath seemed to stop entirely. Her vision had become hazy. She wanted to run.

"Perhaps if you were *very* kind to me, I would be willing to let your family live. You are such a pretty young woman, and I think you could please me very much. Surely, it would be worth it to you—to save both your father and your brother from certain death, as traitors to the Führer. Wouldn't you say so, Anna?"

She had made up her mind to surprise him—to dash into the kitchen without warning, but she kept hanging on, fearing what might happen once she got hold of the knife.

"You understand, my dear Anna, I am going to have you. This can happen gently and sweetly, or it can be rough. I don't mind either way. But it will be easier for you if you cooperate. And better for your father and brother."

"You're the liar," she said. "You will do the same to them either way. You won't let them live."

He smiled again. "Anna, I like you. You are bright and straightforward. And I am glad we understand each other. This is not about saving your father, is it? It's about saving yourself. So let's bargain over that."

"There's no bargaining with Satan."

Kellerman laughed, and for a moment he glanced away. At the same instant, Anna spun and ran. She got to the cabinets and pulled at a drawer, which caught for a moment and then gave way too quickly. Several of the knives and utensils flew across the room and scattered on the floor. But Anna saw the big knife she wanted, a butcher knife. It had flipped up, with the handle over the edge of the drawer. She grabbed it and spun toward Kellerman as he stepped into the kitchen.

He was not hurrying. He was smiling. "Oh, little Anna, this is much more fun than I expected. You can't imagine how much you please me."

"Lord," she whispered, "please help me." She was crying, but she hardly realized it. Kellerman was moving slowly toward her, smiling.

"We take training, you know, we agents, in dealing with circumstances of this kind. We learn to take knives from big, fierce men. And so I see no great challenge in this. Still, it excites me. That's what I like about it."

"I'll kill you. I will."

"That's good. I'm glad you think so." He stopped three or four steps away. "And I'll also make you a promise. I'll only injure you as much as I have to. Any time you submit your will to me, I'll stop hurting you. In fact, if you would like to put the knife down and be nice to me, I'll not hurt you at all."

She didn't move. She held the knife out, waist high, pointing toward him. He took a short step forward, and she crouched a little more, ready.

"Let me warn you of one thing. Never use a swinging motion when you try to stab a man. That gives him too much time to see the blow coming. You must stab quickly, and straight, and it's best to catch him by surprise. Would you like to try?"

Another little step forward.

She straightened up, and she let her hand fall to her side. "Please don't hurt me," she pleaded. "Please, don't."

He laughed and took another step forward. At the same moment, she drove the knife straight at his chest. And she did catch him by surprise. His left arm came up quickly, but the knife got through, tore through his uniform and sliced the top of his left shoulder. At the same time, his right arm crashed against the side of her head and dropped her. She hit the floor hard, and everything spun for a moment, but she knew he was coming after her. She rolled and slashed with the knife and felt it cut into him.

But now he was on top of her, driving her into the floor, his left forearm across her throat, choking her. She twisted hard, trying to get air, and as she did, she saw a flash of red, of flowing blood.

He grabbed her shoulders to keep her from twisting, and he drove her back against the floor, pinning her. But now she saw a terrible gash across his left cheek, through part of his nose and down through those fat lips. The flesh was laid open, deep, and his mouth was contorted.

"You *whore*," he screamed at her. "I'll have you anyway." But blood was gushing down his cheek and off his chin and nose, running in a stream onto Anna's face and throat.

Suddenly he released her shoulder and slammed his fist at her face. She was able to see the blow coming and turn, but he struck her cheek and ear, sending an explosion of pain through her head. At the same time, she heard him grunt, and he pulled back, releasing his hold on her. She took the chance to slam her fist into his shoulder—into the wound she had made there.

Kellerman grimaced and then rolled off her and clambered to his feet. He touched his face, felt the gash, and then pressed his hand against it, but the blood oozed through his fingers. Anna could see the panic in his eyes, as though he had realized for the first time just how bad the wound was.

"You will die for this," he bellowed, and he kicked at her. His foot was aimed at her stomach, but she caught it with her hands and kept it from striking very hard. She tried to grasp his boot and knock him off his feet, but he pulled back and only stumbled. All the same, it gave Anna time to spot another knife on the floor, against the wall. She scrambled after it, grabbed it, and jumped to her feet. She crouched again and waited for his next move.

But Kellerman wasn't ready for that. He pulled his hand away from his face and looked at the blood. The collar of his white shirt was soaked red now, and he was holding his left elbow against his body, probably to reduce the pain of the shoulder wound. "I'll have you yet, and then I'll kill you, slowly. You will *suffer* for this, and so will every member of your family."

He looked about himself and saw a tablecloth on the kitchen table. He jerked at it, sending an empty fruit bowl flying, and then he forced the cloth against his face. He took a last look at Anna, who was still waiting. He seemed to waver for a moment, and then he hurried from the room.

Anna listened to him tramp out to the landing and onto the stairs, and she ran and slammed the door and locked it. Then she dropped to her knees. For a couple of minutes she cried, letting herself vent her emotions. But she began to realize that she couldn't do this. She had to find her family. She had to warn them. Kellerman might not be back quickly, but he would send others, and it wouldn't take long.

She unlocked the door and started out, but she thought of

the blood all over her. She ran back to the kitchen, grabbed a dishtowel, wet it, and wiped away the blood from her neck and face. But a big circle of blood was also on her blouse. She tore the blouse off and ran to her bedroom. She grabbed another one, the first one she could see, and began to put it on as she ran back to the front door. She flew down the stairs, and then she stopped at the downstairs doors to tuck the blouse into her skirt and smooth her hair a little. She walked more carefully into the street and then began to walk toward her mother's place of work, controlling her impulse to run.

She had only crossed a couple of streets before she thought she saw her mother in the distance. She couldn't hold herself back any longer, and she let herself run. But the woman was not her mother, and Anna had to fight herself not to look too strange, too wild, as she reached the woman. She slowed, looked away, and then, once she had walked on past, couldn't help but run again. She had covered most of the distance to the factory when she finally did see her mother, walking toward her.

"Mother," she said, trying hard not to fall apart, "we're in trouble. We must find Papa and Peter. Kellerman came to the house. He tried to . . . hurt me. I cut him with a knife. I slashed his face. He left, but he'll be back."

"Where's your father?"

Anna saw the terror in her mother's face and found it unnerving, but it helped her control herself. She knew she had to think straight. "He and Peter went to the country. We have to find them."

"There's no saving us, Anna. What can we do? You can't stab a Gestapo agent."

"Mama, he was trying to rape me." The color was already gone from Sister Stoltz's face. But for a moment, Anna saw her eyes roll back, and she thought her mother was going to faint. Anna grabbed her. "We must get away from Frankfurt," Anna said. "We must hide somewhere. Come. Hurry."

The two of them walked fast, ignoring those who looked at them on the street. They said very little, except that Sister Stoltz said, "We have to go home. Even if they find us there. If your papa and Peter have come home, we must warn them."

Anna knew that was so, but what then? How long could they wait? Was there some way to find them? Anna and her mother had never gone on these excursions. They had no idea where to look.

At the apartment house, they saw no one outside, and so they hurried upstairs. When they reached the apartment, Sister Stoltz fumbled to get the key in the door, but it suddenly swung open. Anna and her mother lunged backward, but at the same time, they saw Brother Stoltz, looking at them wide-eyed. "Are you all right? What happened?"

And then Anna realized what he had seen in the kitchen: blood on the floor, blood on the dishtowel, knives and utensils scattered about. "Kellerman was here," she blurted out. "He came after me."

"He tried to rape her," her mother said, crying for the first time.

"I cut his face. He said he would come back and kill us all. What can we do?"

Brother Stoltz reached out and grabbed them, each by a wrist, and pulled them inside. Anna saw that Peter was there, behind her father. He looked terrified.

Brother Stoltz thought for another few seconds. "All right. Move quickly, but we must not panic. We must do this correctly. Each of you get a change of clothes. Put everything in one suitcase. No." He stopped and thought. "What do we have? A laundry bag. Put the clothes in that."

"I want the family pictures, and the old Bible."

"No. Nothing. Just a change of clothes and any money we have. Don't take identification papers either. Somehow we'll have to get false papers. I don't know how to do any of that, but first we must get out of this neighborhood and leave no trace to follow."

And so everyone hurried off to grab a change of clothes. Anna took a quick look around and thought of one other thing. She grabbed the little picture on her desk, the one of Elder Thomas and Elder Sawyer standing with her on the day she was baptized. She folded her clothes around it and took them to her mother, who stuffed them into the laundry bag.

Mother hurried to the kitchen then and grabbed bread and wurst and cheese. She put them in a net and was about to return to the living room when Brother Stoltz came into the kitchen and said, "Leave the food. People will notice it."

"I'll put it in the bag with the clothes."

"No. They'll smell it. We can't do anything that looks suspicious. We must go—now."

Not three minutes had passed since Anna and her mother had come home, and they were all leaving. Anna saw her mother lift a little Delft plate from a shelf and tuck it in with the clothing before she closed the door.

Anna was anxious to get away quickly, but at the same time, she knew the immensity of what had just happened. The family had just shut its doors on *everything*: all their possessions, their home, their way of life. Everything was gone. Even if they managed to stay alive somehow, nothing would ever be the same.

And she felt, in some terrible way, responsible.

Brother Stoltz peeked out through the front doors, then looked back and whispered, "All right. We are going for a walk. Step out with me and walk normally down the street. We'll get a few streets away, and then we'll take a streetcar—get to another part of town as quickly as possible."

"What then?" Mother asked.

"Let's just get that far, for now. I'm thinking."

"We need to pray."

"Yes. But quickly." He bowed his head, and so did the

others. "Father, we are in great trouble," he said. "We need a miracle. Please help me get my family away, and help me, somehow, to keep them alive." He closed the prayer.

"Pray for you, too," Peter said.

"It's all right. Now, let's step outside. Look natural."

And so they stepped out into the bright afternoon sun, and they walked slowly down the street. The corner seemed miles away, and Anna wanted to run to get around it, but she took normal steps, even greeted a neighbor who passed by, as did everyone in the family.

After they turned the corner, they picked up their pace a little. All the while, Anna watched for any sign of anyone coming—perhaps Gestapo agents in a car. But everything seemed normal—just the end of a hot day, and people heading home from work or going out to stand in line with their ration cards at neighborhood shops.

The family followed a zigzag pattern until they reached a streetcar stop several blocks from home. They boarded the first streetcar that came by, a crowded one heading west across town. Anna was feeling better as they moved farther away from home, but the other sense, of everything lost, was coming on stronger. She saw that tears were running down her mother's face, and she grasped her around the waist. "You must not cry," she said. "People will notice," but tears came to her own eyes.

Brother Stoltz saw both of them struggling and said, "Get off at this next stop." And once they were all off, he talked to them. "You must look normal. You cannot looked frightened. And you must not cry."

"Where are we going?" his wife asked.

"Let's go north."

"Can't we stay with someone? What about members of the branch? Maybe someone could hide us for now."

"No. Kellerman will check with all the Mormons first. We cannot put them in danger. They must not be forced to lie for us either. It's best that we leave without contacting anyone.

President Meis will understand that something like this must have happened. He knows about Kellerman."

"Could we speak to Herr Schlenker again? Maybe he will stop Kellerman the way he did before."

But Anna had thought of that. "Kellerman knows that you took food to Bruder Goldfarb," she said. "He must have had you followed."

"Did he say this?"

"Yes. He said you had gone to the ghetto and taken food to a Jew. He even knew you had given food to others. He must have been watching everything you and Peter have been doing."

"Not him. But he has his spies." Brother Stoltz rubbed his hands over his eyes. "Schlenker won't help us now."

"We watched so carefully," Peter said. "We thought no one had seen us."

"There's no beating these people," Brother Stoltz said.

"Then what can we do?" Sister Stoltz asked, and she began to cry again.

"Get out of Frankfurt."

"But where can we live?" Anna asked. "We have to register, anywhere we go. We can't use our names. We can't get work. Can we get out of Germany somehow?"

Brother Stoltz was shaking his head. "No. I doubt that. But if we stay here, we face certain death. For now, let's get farther away. I'll have to think of something. I'll do everything I can to keep you alive."

But it was he who was showing his emotions now. He took his wife under one arm and reached for Anna with the other. Peter moved in close and put his arms around his mother and sister. The four of them clung to each other for several seconds, but then Brother Stoltz said, "Come now. We must not do this. People will notice."

They stepped away from each other.

"We'll get on the next streetcar. But everyone must keep

control this time. I'm thinking that somehow we can get to Berlin. There has been more bombing there. Maybe displaced people won't seem so out of the ordinary, and we can find a way to hide."

It did sound reasonable—the first idea that offered some hope. But how would they get to Berlin? By now, the Gestapo were certainly looking for them, and one of their agents had been wounded. This was not something the Gestapo could allow. All the police in Germany would soon be on the alert.

2 9

Brother Stoltz stepped out of the shadows and waved for his family to come ahead. Sister Stoltz, Anna, and Peter had been waiting behind the cover of some shrubs just inside the fence of the railroad yard. Now they slipped out and hurried across two sets of tracks. When they reached Brother Stoltz, he motioned for them to move in close to the train, out of the gleam of an overhead floodlight.

"This train is heading north," he whispered. "I found a car that's marked for Berlin. Follow me. Be very quiet."

And so the four sneaked along the side of the train, and they stayed in the shadows and watched for any of the railroad employees who might be in the yard. The Stoltzes didn't dare buy tickets for a passenger train. A freight train seemed the only answer. But they were not exactly experienced at hopping freight trains. Anna was terrified.

Brother Stoltz stopped by a boxcar. He pointed to a sheet of paper posted on the side. It was shredded and faded, but it did read: "Destination: Berlin." "I pounded my fist on the side," he whispered. "It sounds empty. Help me get the door open. I couldn't do it by myself."

Anna knew that was perhaps because of his damaged shoulder, but she also wondered whether the door wasn't locked. It seemed a mistake to try something like this when they didn't know what they were doing. But Father kept telling them that they had no choice, that they couldn't walk all the way to Berlin.

It had been a strange night. The Stoltzes had taken the streetcar to the last stop, and then they had had no idea what to do. But Brother Stoltz had talked to a beer delivery man outside a *Gasthaus*. Brother Stoltz had asked him what direction he was heading in his truck, and the man had said, "North, to Butzbach." Brother Stoltz had told the man his car had broken down and he needed to get his family home. If the man could drop them off in Friedberg, it would be a huge help to them.

"My company won't let me do that," the man had said at first, but he had taken a good look at the Stoltzes, seemingly abandoned with evening coming on. "But I guess it would be all right. You would have to ride in the back."

And so the Stoltz family had sat among kegs and cases of bottled beer. But they hadn't minded that; they were happy to be traveling inside where no one could see them. The only problem was that Friedberg was not all that distant from Frankfurt, and so the trip was only a small step in the right direction. But when they had arrived in Friedberg, Brother Stoltz had told the others about his idea to catch a ride on a freight train. Even if it didn't take them toward Berlin, if it would take them farther away from Frankfurt they would be better off.

Now he had found a train that seemed to be on its way to Berlin, and that offered some hope. Peter grabbed the handle on the door and pulled, but it didn't budge. He pulled again, putting all his weight behind it—and still, nothing.

Brother Stoltz reached up and tried to add the strength of his left arm to Peter's attempt, but any strain of that kind pulled too hard on his right shoulder. Anna saw him tug hard, once, but then grimace with the pain.

"Let me try," Anna said, and she stepped in front of Peter.

But just as she was about to pull, she heard footsteps. The train tracks were lined with coal cinders, and as the Stoltzes suddenly froze in place, they knew that the crunching sound was coming toward them. And then a light flashed in their direction. "Who's there?" a man shouted.

Peter took a couple of quick steps away, but all the others sensed that it was already too late to run. The crunching sound, the light, were coming closer, and the voice sounded again. "Stop right there. What are you doing?"

No one answered. Anna now wished that they had all run. Anything would be better than standing there with that light on them and a faceless voice making demands.

"What are you doing?" the man asked again.

Anna was surprised by her father's answer. "Trying to get on this boxcar," he said very simply.

"You cannot do that."

Father laughed. "I know. We found that out. It seems to be locked."

The man behind the light seemed confused by Brother Stoltz's friendliness. He said nothing for a time. But then the light clicked off. As Anna's eyes adjusted, she could see a small man, older, wearing overalls. "You are the family on the run, aren't you? We got a report," the man said.

"From the Gestapo?" Brother Stoltz asked.

"I don't know. I suppose. We are to watch for you."

"Do you want me to tell you why we're trying to escape?" Brother Stoltz asked.

"No. It is not my concern." But the man was soft spoken.

"A Gestapo agent tried to rape my daughter—this young lady." Brother Stoltz put his hand on Anna's shoulder. "She fought him off. Bravely. She cut him with a kitchen knife—the only means she had to defend herself. Now the Gestapo is looking for us—and you can imagine what will happen if they take us in."

"The report we have said nothing of this. It said only to watch for you—to hold you."

"Do you have any daughters?"

"That's not important."

"But do you?"

"Yes. Two."

"What would you do if one of these brutes came after your daughters?"

The man didn't answer. He stood, quiet, for a time, and then he said, "This is what you say. But I have no way to know what's true. Come with me."

"And what if we turn and walk away? Would you stop us?"

"I can call for help. There are others not far off. Please, come with me."

"I'm telling the truth. A Gestapo agent tried to force himself upon my daughter. He knocked her down, struck her. Look at her face. If you turn us in, we will die."

The man was looking at Anna now, perhaps trying to decide whether the story was true. Anna ran her fingers along her cheek, showing him the bruise.

"We're going to walk away," Brother Stoltz said. "Please don't stop us."

"Wait. Where will you go?" Anna heard a new quality in the man's voice—like a grandfather's concern.

"We're trying to get to Berlin," Brother Stoltz said. "Maybe we can disappear there more easily than most places."

"That's the wrong train for Berlin."

"This paper here—"

"No. That's old. This train goes north to Kassel and Hannover."

"That would be all right," Brother Stoltz said, as though he were accepting an offer. Anna didn't know what was happening.

But the man said, "No. Come with me." And then, when no one moved, he added, "I'll get you on a train to Berlin."

It was almost too good to believe, but the Stoltzes followed, and the man took them between two cars, over the coupling, and then across some other tracks. He didn't hurry, but he stayed in the shadows, and he didn't speak.

When he came alongside another train, he waited for everyone to move in close to a tanker car. "I think you will do best in an empty coal car," he whispered. "It won't be comfortable, but you won't be seen if you stay down. The box cars are mostly loaded, and when they're empty we keep them locked."

He began to walk again, staying close to the train. When he stopped at a coal car, he whispered, "Climb in here."

"Thank you so much," Anna said.

"Hurry," he said, and he began to walk away. But then he came back. "Listen," he said, "don't take the train all the way into the main yards in Berlin. You won't get out of there without being spotted."

"Where can we get out?" Brother Stoltz asked.

"I'm not sure. Try a small town somewhere, close to Berlin. But I don't know the stops. I can't help you with that."

"What about—"

"I must go. That's all I know to tell you. Good luck."

"Thank you," all the Stoltzes whispered. And then they climbed into the car, sat down, and stayed low. They hadn't thought to ask when the train would be leaving, and as it turned out, they had a long wait. It was almost one o'clock in the morning before the car jerked and then began to roll.

By then, Peter, lying with his head on the laundry bag, had fallen asleep. The others were leaning against the inside walls of the coal car. Anna knew she wouldn't be safe any time in the near future—maybe ever—but once the train made it out of the yard, she began to breathe more easily. It was a nice night, with the stars clear, and somehow, in that setting, it did seem a little harder to believe that their lives were in danger. But now she had more time to think, and the images all came back. She thought of the gash she had put in Kellerman's face, the horrible open cut across his cheek and mouth. She had never thought of hurting anyone so terribly, but she also remembered his threats, his power, the leering way he had studied her. She shuddered to think of the evil, the ugliness, of the man. She felt soiled by it all, and she wished that she could take a hot bath. The night was warm, but she felt cold. She wrapped her arms around her middle and tried to stop shaking, but she said nothing to her parents, who had enough to worry about.

During the night the train made a couple of stops. At one of those it did some switching, either taking on or dropping some cars. It was hard to know what was happening in the dark, and Brother Stoltz kept telling all of them to keep their heads down. They had no idea where they were or how far they had come.

The sun rose early, however, and as the first light illuminated the horizon, Brother Stoltz raised his head a few times to look around. As the train passed by a town, he was able to spot a name on a train station. "We have a long way to go," he said. "At this rate, we'll be all day getting to Berlin."

"Maybe it's better if it's dark when we get there," Anna said.

"Yes. Maybe." But then he began to laugh.

It was the last thing anyone expected. Anna looked over at him and knew immediately, however, why he was laughing. She smiled too.

"What is it?" Sister Stoltz asked.

"Look at Peter," Brother Stoltz said. "Look at all of us. We're covered with coal dust."

And it was true. Especially Peter, who had been lying on the floor, was covered with the black dust. He had rolled over at some point, and he was caked on all sides with black.

"Yes," Brother Stoltz said, "We'll arrive at night—all covered with coal. No one will ever spot us."

Anna tried to laugh a little, for Papa, but she saw that this was a little too much for Sister Stoltz. The woman looked exhausted, battered, and somehow the laughter was more than she could handle. She shook her head. "Please don't," she said, and she sounded angry. Anna reached over and put her arm around her, pulled her next to herself. And she understood. It didn't seem likely that they would ever be able to relax again, to know a little comfort, and this laughter was only a reminder of that.

"It's all right," Brother Stoltz said. "We're going to be fine. I've felt better since we met that man in Friedberg. I have the feeling God sent him to us."

It was a surprising thing for Father to say, and Anna felt it like a flood of relief. She knew her mother felt the same thing. Sister Stoltz let her body relax against Anna. "Yes. Yes," she whispered. "I think that's right."

But their problems were far from over. The day seemed to last a week, with the sun burning down on them and nothing to eat or drink. And every stop brought on terror. The Stoltzes crouched low then and hoped that no one would look in the car. One of the stops involved considerable switching, and Anna kept worrying that their car would be dropped from the train, or that coal would be dumped on top of them. But even worse was the wait that followed. For some reason, the train sat in the yard almost two hours.

The Stoltzes moved to the opposite side of the car, where the shade had now shifted, but the heat was still suffocating, and all of them were very tired. Sitting on the hard, metal floor was uncomfortable—and they couldn't talk or even move very much. Anna did fall asleep for half an hour or so, but she awakened more tired and hungry and uncomfortable than when she had drifted off.

The train finally did move, and then all afternoon it chugged forward, the smoke billowing overhead, dropping ashes into the car, the tracks rattling noisily, and the steel under them getting harder by the mile. Everyone was terribly thirsty, and yet there was nothing they could do about that. "We'll get water tonight, and food," Brother Stoltz told them. "We just have to get by for this one day."

The sun was beginning to go down when the train stopped in a good-sized railroad yard. The Stoltzes didn't look up, but they could hear the trains around them and hear voices and footsteps from time to time.

Anna watched Peter, who had been lethargic and quiet all day. She could see that he was nervous. With no cover over the car, Anna constantly felt that a head was suddenly going to appear, and a Gestapo agent would have them trapped where they would have no chance to escape. She watched continually, and yet she longed just to stand up, stretch, and have a look around. She had realized by then that her ankles and shins were getting sunburned, as were her face and arms, but she had no way to protect herself.

As darkness gradually came on, Brother Stoltz did finally take a look outside. "This is a big place," he whispered.

"Maybe Leipzig," Peter said.

"No. Not that big. I'm thinking Halle. But maybe we're closer to Berlin than that. I simply don't know."

"How will we know when to get off?" Sister Stoltz asked, and Anna could hear the strain in her voice.

"I'm not sure," Brother Stoltz said. "Once the train is going again, I'll try to spot some town names."

But the train waited quite some time again, and by the time it finally began to move, Anna felt as though she couldn't stand much more of this. Getting away from Frankfurt had been relieving, but before long, the other reality had to be faced. They would have to get out of some railroad yard without being stopped. And then what? Where would they go? How could they survive? Anna wanted more than anything to go home. She wanted to sleep in her own bed. She wanted the things she had left behind—her books, her school pictures, the new beige dress she had bought with her own money, her diary. She hadn't brought so much as a hairbrush. Running away had meant saving their lives, but now, what were they running to?

When the train departed, Brother Stoltz made a stronger attempt to determine where they were. Eventually, he realized they were much closer to Berlin than he had guessed, and now the train wasn't stopping. He kept peeking up and then saying, "We're coming into the city. We need to get off somehow, before we reach the main stop."

But on and on the train continued, and Anna felt the panic growing inside. She saw it in Peter, who was squirming constantly now, and in her mother, who was deathly still.

"Listen," Brother Stoltz finally said, "I can feel the train slowing. We can't be far away. We need to get off now."

"While the train is moving?"

"Yes. It won't be so bad. We can climb over the side, drop to the ground, and roll."

"Heinrich, how can I do this? How can *you?*"

"We must. That's all. You heard what the man in Friedberg said. Come on now. Peter can go first, and then he can hurry and catch up with us. Anna will go second. And I will go last."

"I can do it," Peter said, obviously pleased to be chosen.

He got up and pulled himself over the top edge of the car and onto the ladder. "Can you see anything?" Brother Stoltz called to him.

"Not too much. But it's not going fast. I can do it. Jump quickly after I do. Don't leave me here alone."

"Don't worry. We must hurry after you. Go ahead."

And suddenly Peter disappeared. Anna climbed up quickly after him. She saw buildings not far from the tracks, but close by she saw nothing but darkness. She had no idea what she would be jumping into. She only knew there was no time to wait. She jumped, feet first, and instantly she knew the train was going faster than it seemed. Her feet hit, and she was sent flying. She tried to roll, but she landed on her front, scraping into a bed of cinders.

Anna rolled over and popped up to her feet, but she felt her arms and chin burning, and she knew she had cut herself. She spun as she heard Peter running toward her. "Anna, are you all right?" she heard him call.

"Yes. Are you?"

"I hurt my knee," he said. "It's not too bad. Hurry." And he ran on by. Anna saw that he was limping. At the same moment, Anna thought of her mother. What would happen to her?

Anna began to run, and in the distance, she caught a glimpse of a dark figure letting loose from the train—disappearing. "Mother, mother," she called, and she ran hard, passing her little brother.

When Anna got to her mother, she found her struggling to get to her feet. "I'm all right," she said, but she didn't sound all right. "Run for Heinrich. I'm scared for him."

Peter had caught up by then. Anna could hear that he was crying, and she knew he was hurt more than he wanted to say. "Stay with Mama," Anna said, and she took off running again.

Anna saw nothing, heard nothing, and now she realized, they had made a mistake. Her father should not have gone last. He must be struggling to get out of the coal car. But then she caught a glimpse of his silhouette. He was on the ladder, getting ready. But darkness enveloped him, and she didn't see him jump. She kept running as hard as she could, even though her lungs were burning with pain.

And then, ahead of her, she heard him moan. "Papa, papa," she shouted, and she dropped down next to him. He was taking long, agonizing breaths, but when he realized she was next to him, he said, "Don't worry. I'll be all right."

But he wasn't all right. Anna could hear that in his voice. "Did you land on your shoulder?"

"No. I turned the other way. But it . . . I don't know. I'll be all right in a moment. How did your mother do?"

"I think she's all right. Peter hurt his knee. It's you I'm

worried about." Anna knew that her father's shoulder had twisted in some way. This could only make things worse.

"Help me up. I can get up now."

When she tried to lift him, however, the twisting was too much. He cried out, and then he said, "Wait." He took a few more gasping breaths, and then he sat up, pulling himself forward without using his arms. "Now get behind me. Help me stand."

The last car of the train passed by, and suddenly the night was surprisingly quiet. Anna got behind her father and wrapped her arms around his chest, but she had the feeling that she helped very little, that he forced himself up through sheer will, on his own. And when he reached his feet, he had to stand and breathe again, every breath a groan.

Still, he began to walk, back along the track, and they hadn't gone far before they heard Sister Stoltz and Peter crunching through the cinders.

"Heinrich, how are you doing?" Sister Stoltz asked, even before Anna could see her.

"I'm fine," Brother Stoltz said.

"He's not fine," Anna told her. "He hurt his shoulder again."

"No, no. It's nothing new." Anna and her father stopped as they reached Peter and his mother.

"Peter has cut his knee. I can't see it very well, but it's bleeding badly."

"It's nothing," Peter said, no longer crying, and trying hard, Anna could tell, to sound as brave as the others.

As it turned out, Sister Stoltz had come out better than anyone. Her elbow was sore, but Anna was scratched up worse, and Peter, besides the cut on his knee, had torn up his forearms. The cinders had apparently been more solid, hadn't given way as much, where Peter and Anna had jumped. It was good, they all concluded, that the parents hadn't jumped first.

"We can't stay here," Brother Stoltz finally said. "I don't

know where we are exactly, but we need to clean up and get our other clothes on, so we won't draw attention to ourselves."

"I want some water," Peter said.

"Yes, I know. We all do. We'll find some. But it may be morning before we can get any food."

They left the tracks and walked toward the buildings in the distance, and they found that they were in a neighborhood of apartment houses and shops. They soon found a school, however, with a little playground outside. They hid behind a pair of large spruce trees and changed their clothes. Before Peter put his fresh trousers on, his mother tore up his old shirt and tied a bandage around his knee.

Brother Stoltz suffered terribly in getting his shirt off and another one on, but he got it done, with some help. And then, once he got his breath again, he told the others, "Let's throw away our old clothes, but tear up a rag or two that we can use to wipe our faces and hands. We'll find some water now."

So with fresh clothes on, they walked down the empty street until they found a park—and in the park, a fountain. Brother Stoltz warned everyone not to drink too much, too fast, but Anna found the advice hard to take. She drank a great deal, and she did feel a little sick after, but the hunger pangs were not so bad with something in her stomach. And it did feel good to wash her hands and arms, and her face. She couldn't get it out of her head that Kellerman's blood was still all over her.

"We need to stay out of sight until morning," Father said. "If the police catch us out here now, they'll want to know who we are. Maybe we can get a little sleep on the grass."

And so the Stoltzes tried to rest. But Brother Stoltz, even though he managed, with help, to lie on his back, was in far too much pain to sleep. His strained breathing continued to worry the others, and only Peter fell asleep quickly. Anna did drift off after a time, but she never really slept deeply.

When the sun finally began to rise, and the birds began to

sing, Anna was struck by the strangeness of the world going on quite normally. She realized then that her father, at some point, had gotten up. He was sitting on a bench some distance away. When he saw Anna stirring, he came back to the others. He looked at Anna and for the first time realized how badly she had scraped herself. "Oh, my dear," he said, and tears came to his eyes. "I'm sorry for what you've been through." He pulled Anna to her feet and folded his arms around her. She was tempted to cry, but she held on.

"I wish I could promise all of you a better place to sleep tonight," Brother Stoltz said. "I can't do that, I suppose, but I do promise you that I will try."

"It's not your fault, Papa," Anna said. "It's mine."

"No! Don't ever say that, Anna. You did nothing wrong—absolutely nothing. I'm just thankful that you did what you did, and that he wasn't able to defile you."

Anna wanted to believe that. But still, without understanding why, she felt a dreadful filthiness that she didn't know how to clean away. Her mother came closer and put her arm around her, and the closeness did help.

"I've been thinking everything over," Brother Stoltz said. "We need names we can use, and we need a story. Then we need to get into the city near a bombed-out area so we can claim to be dispossessed of our papers and our belongings."

They walked back to the bench where Brother and Sister Stoltz sat down, with Peter and Anna on the grass in front of them, and they invented names: Hofmann for a family name, because it was common. Norbert and Maria, Karl and Ursula. Then they walked in pairs until they found a streetcar. They boarded it without seeming to be together, and they rode toward the city center until Brother Stoltz spotted some damaged buildings and got off. The others followed.

They walked until they found an outdoor market where people were doing their early morning shopping. Brother Stoltz bought bread and cheese and milk, and then they split off in pairs again and shared the food. Anna had never tasted anything better in her life, and she watched Peter come back to life as he got some nourishment in him.

After they had eaten, Brother and Sister Stoltz walked back to the children. "Stay here," Brother Stoltz told the others. "Stroll around. Sit on a bench over there. Split up at times, perhaps, but keep each other in sight. I'm going to try to find the Church—or a member."

"What if the Gestapo tracked us to Berlin somehow?" Anna asked. "Wouldn't they check all the members' homes?"

"I've thought a great deal about that," Brother Stoltz said. "The only way to track us would be through the man in Friedberg, but he would be inviting his own death if he told anyone. He's not going to say anything, I trust, so the Gestapo have no reason to look for us here any more than anywhere else."

"What can Church members do for us?" Sister Stoltz asked.

"I don't know, but we know they're people we can trust. Maybe a member can hide us until we figure out a place to go."

And so Brother Stoltz left. Anna felt herself a little more relaxed now that she could move about more freely. And she felt stronger now that she had eaten, but her hands continued to tremble, and she constantly studied anyone who approached her. No matter what she tried to think about, the image kept coming back. The wound. The blood running off Kellerman's chin and onto her face. The fanatic anger in his eyes. What she knew was that the man would never stop looking for her. Her father wanted her to believe that the Gestapo had lost the trail, but Anna was not sure of that.

Brother Stoltz came back much sooner than she had expected—less than two hours later—and when she saw him, she knew that he had good news. His face had not looked this confident, this relaxed, since they had left their home. He gathered the family together, and then he said, "I found the address of the church, and I went there. A caretaker was cleaning up, and he gave me the branch president's name and address. I found him home before he left for work. He lives on the edge of the city—in a house. President Hoch is his name." And now tears came into Brother Stoltz's eyes. "He was careful. He was dubious about my story at first. But then he said, 'Bring your family. Have them come to the back. We have a cellar in the house. You can all stay there for now—until we think of something else."

"It's another miracle," Sister Stoltz said. "It's what you prayed for."

"Yes. Exactly. We're going to live. The Lord wants us to live, or he wouldn't be opening these doors for us."

Anna put her arm around Peter's shoulders. She was fighting not to cry. But Brother Stoltz said, "Don't shed tears. Don't do anything out of the ordinary. Let's go now. Two at a time."

Anna got herself under control, and then she and Peter followed, staying back. Still, Anna kept watching, checking behind her and studying every person she passed on the street. Her face was bruised and scratched—maybe someone would notice that. She wanted the cover of the cellar, the darkness. She wanted to hide where no one would ever look.

30

Bobbi had always been careful with her money, but she withdrew most of her savings for her trip to Chicago. The train ticket alone was $59.35. Still, this would be her chance to have some new experiences. And as it turned out, she loved the streamliner: the novelty of sleeping in a berth in an air-conditioned Pullman car; the luxury and comfort of the dining cars; the indulgent treatment from the porters and waiters. It was all like living in a movie. She also enjoyed the mountains of Colorado, the plains of Kansas, the rolling hills of Missouri and Illinois, and she was impressed by the grand, showy train stations in Kansas City and St. Louis.

By the time the train pulled into the station in Chicago, however, she was nervous, and she almost wished she hadn't come. But when she stepped off the train and found David there, she found herself slipping naturally into his arms, feeling deeply happy for the first time in a long time. He kissed her longer than she liked in the middle of all these people, but when he stepped away and looked at her with his tender eyes, she had no doubt that she had done the right thing in coming. Her decision seemed already made.

"It's awfully hot," he told her, and he reached for her suitcase. "It must seem humid to you."

She could barely hear over the noise of the trains and the people. She was amazed at the size of this place, with all the big coal locomotives lined up alongside the modern streamliners. "It's been humid since Kansas City," she said, "but my hotel will have air conditioning." She smiled at the thought of it. She was staying at the Stevens Hotel, downtown, the largest hotel in the world, with three thousand rooms. The price was terrible, $4.50 a night, but she didn't care. She had never stayed in a hotel in her life, and she wanted to experience the best.

Just getting to the hotel, however, was almost more excitement than Bobbi was prepared for. She had tried to picture what it would be like, but the vibrancy of the huge city was beyond anything she had imagined. The noise, the intensity, the movement—the grand picture of it all—was splendid and frightening at the same time. The skyscrapers were overwhelming: hundreds of buildings clustered together, every one of them taller than the highest building in Salt Lake. David kept pointing out the window: "That's the Field Building—over fifty floors. But look this way and you can see the Chicago Board of Trade—the tallest building in Chicago." Bobbi would lean one way and then the other, always oohing and aahing, even though she wondered what the taxi driver must think of her.

When the taxi crossed Wabash street, under the L—the elevated train—Bobbi heard the thunderous rattle of the trains and, below, saw the jam of trucks and cars, the mass of people on the sidewalks. It was chaotic and wonderful, so glittering above, with buildings reaching into the sky, but dirty and seedy at the street level. She had no idea why she liked it.

The next few days were perfect. Bobbi's room at the hotel was on a corner of the nineteenth floor. Northward, she could see the downtown "loop" area, and to the east, Lake Michigan. Beneath her, on the shores of the lake, was Grant Park, where she could see the giant Buckingham Fountain, illuminated by colored lights at night. Everything in the room was exquisite:

the tiled bathroom with the big bathtub, the fancy draperies, the elegant cherrywood bed. She had trouble calming down enough to sleep at night, and so she sat up late, gazed out the window, or took a long bath and, like a princess, lounged in all the luxury.

David came for her in the mornings, and he took her everywhere. They spent most of one day at the Art Institute in Grant Park. They saw works by all the great American painters whom Bobbi had studied, and when David guided her into the collection of French impressionists, tears actually came to her eyes. She was looking at paintings by Monet, Renoir, Manet. She had seen Renoir's "Two Little Circus Girls" in her art-appreciation text, but now she was seeing the real thing. It seemed impossible.

One afternoon David took Bobbi to a White Sox baseball game at Comiskey Park, then to dinner in Little Italy, and that night to an opera in the lavish Chicago Civic Opera Building—with a stage that was thirteen stories high. David loved so many different kinds of things, and he made everything fun. He took her walking in the loop one morning, down State Street, where they wandered through the opulent departments of the Marshall Field store. But then they stopped for lunch at a shabby little chili parlor on Wabash. And after lunch, they walked north along Michigan Avenue, the "Fifth Avenue" of Chicago, where they window shopped, waited to watch a drawbridge rise over the Chicago River, and then continued on to the famous old gothic Water Tower. David had told her to wear her swimming suit under her clothes, and as the afternoon heat came on, they swam in the lake and then rested on the beach.

David had to leave Bobbi on her own one day, and she spent the time in Grant Park at the museum of natural history and then at the aquarium. But that evening David took her to China Town for dinner, and then he strolled with her around the campus of the University of Chicago. Bobbi had read

Sandburg's Chicago poems and Theodore Dreiser's *Sister Carrie*, and she finally complained that she was seeing mostly the glamour of the city, so the next day David took her on the L to the south side, and there she saw rows and rows of broken-down tenements, vast areas where virtually all the people were Negroes. Bobbi had the feeling she would never be exactly the same after seeing poverty of a kind she had only read about before.

That night David took her to a little jazz joint, in a better part of town, and David talked about the origins of jazz, all the way from Africa, something Bobbi had known very little about. But he seemed to be making a point: all these ethnic groups—this diversity—gave Chicago something that Salt Lake would never have.

It was all dazzling and fascinating, and every day was something new. They ate wonderful food of all kinds, and they met people who spoke all sorts of languages. David constantly made her laugh, but he also held her hand, touched her hair, stole kisses. They spent way too much money—twenty cents, at least, every time they climbed into a taxi—and dinners that cost five or six dollars for the two of them. It was almost like a honeymoon, except that each night David said goodnight at the door to Bobbi's hotel room.

Bobbi was in love. She didn't have to ask herself about that. And he adored her; she felt that in everything he did and said. As her time began to run out, she felt certain he would ask her, once again, to marry him. She told herself to be careful, not to answer on the basis of this golden experience, but she was already quite certain she would never feel anything this powerful for another man.

On Thursday night, when she knew she would be leaving on Saturday morning, she finally invited David into her hotel room. They sat across from each other and talked, but then, as he prepared to leave, they stood by the door and kissed. It was all very soft and sweet in the beginning, but they didn't stop after a kiss or two. They continued to hold each other, continued to kiss, and Bobbi felt a hunger that she had never experienced before. She could feel his hands on her back and sides, moving, caressing, felt the firmness of his body against her, and she told herself to stop, not to let him get the wrong idea, but she didn't want to stop, and their kisses were taking her to a numb, light-headed state that pushed aside her usual wisdom.

David was beginning to breathe hard. He suddenly grasped her tighter and whispered, "Bobbi, do you want me to stay?"

For a moment she couldn't think what he meant. And then she was startled at the idea—and even more startled how much she wanted to say yes. But already she was pushing him away. "David, I love you," she was whispering. "I love you—but no. We can't do that."

And somehow she expected him, then, to propose marriage, and she expected to say yes. She wanted the wedding to happen as soon as possible.

"It's all right. I'm sorry. I shouldn't have asked." He took hold of the doorknob. "I'm really sorry."

She didn't mind that he had asked, actually loved the idea that he wanted her that much, and she stepped back to kiss him one more time. "It's all right," she said.

"No. I'd better go. I'll see you in the morning." And he slipped out the door.

After, she took a warm bath, and as she lay in the water, she was alarmed at her own vulnerability, the force of her desire. They had gone too far, and she couldn't let that happen again, but she loved him and she had to marry him. She couldn't feel this need for someone and then walk away. Everything would have to work out.

The next morning David came over a little before ten. The two of them took the elevator down to the coffee shop in the hotel, and Bobbi ordered an omelette, with toast and milk.

"I just want a cup of coffee. Black," David told the waitress. It was all he ever had. He didn't like breakfast.

"It's almost lunchtime," Bobbi said, laughing. "You ought to be hungry. I'm famished." She flirted with her eyes. She wanted him to know that she wasn't worried by what had happened the night before, that she was still basking in the closeness.

But he seemed subdued, even a little distant.

"Do you know," she said, "that in my entire life, until this week, I have never had breakfast with someone who was drinking coffee. I'm afraid I'm spending my days with a sinner."

He leaned back and smiled, his eyes quiet. "Only a Mormon could find sin in something as nice as a morning cup of coffee."

She had only meant to tease, but she was embarrassed, partly because his coffee actually did make her uncomfortable. She hoped he was still willing to commit to the Church; he hadn't brought that up all week.

The coffee shop was quiet, with only a few tables occupied. A waitress with a white paper cap was standing behind the counter. She was chatting with a cook who was having his own cup of coffee. The cook was a Negro, and the woman white, and yet they seemed at ease, talking and laughing. Bobbi was not shocked but curious. She had never known a colored person, personally, and had rarely even been around people of other races. She mentioned to David, again, how affected she had been by her experience on the south side, but David had little to say about that. She wondered what he was thinking this morning.

Bobbi tried a couple more times to get a conversation started, but then David said, rather abruptly, "Bobbi, we need to talk. There's a lot we need to think about."

She reached across the table and touched his hand. "So now *you* want to think. You told me not to do that."

He didn't smile. In fact, he looked troubled. "Bobbi, I want to marry you. You know that. But I've seen some things this week that worry me."

Bobbi was taken by surprise. She had felt cosmopolitan and

open-minded all week. She thought she had handled things well.

"I think, if we got married, I'd have to return to the University of Utah. I don't think you could be happy here."

The waitress arrived with Bobbi's omelet and David's coffee, and she asked, absently, "Anything else?"

"No," David said. Bobbi was already telling David, "I don't understand." She studied his eyes, but he seemed unwilling to look her straight on. "I can't believe this is you talking, David. I thought all we had to do is love each other."

"That would be enough for me. But you need your family. You don't seem yourself here. I tend to push you too hard to be someone new, and you try too hard to prove you can make the adjustment."

"I don't feel that at all, David."

"Bobbi, I know who you are. You need Thanksgiving and Christmas at home. You need the life you know: the dance festival, the road show, the Twenty-Fourth of July. Your church is who you are. It becomes obvious when you're taken out of your element."

Bobbi looked at her food, but she wasn't hungry now. She felt the lovely joy of the past few days slipping away. "What are you doing, David? You're the one who always said it could work."

"I know. I want it to work. But I don't want to ruin you."

"You're a good person. That's what matters to me."

Bobbi saw the confusion come into David's eyes. "I don't know whether I'm good by your definition, Bobbi. If I joined your church, I would stick out like a sore thumb."

"David, you said you could join. Why are you doing this now? I'm finally ready to commit—and you're trying to run away and hide."

"Bobbi, you aren't hearing what I'm telling you. I love you. I want to marry you. I just don't want you to get into this and then find out that I'm making you miserable."

"Or that we're making each other miserable?"

"That's possible too, I guess." He picked up the cup of coffee. "Bobbi, to most people in the world, coffee doesn't have a lot of meaning, but you know you wouldn't want me to drink it in front of our children. And frankly, that seems ludicrous to me. I would give it up. That's not the problem. But I'm not sure I wouldn't resent it."

"But coffee *isn't* good for you, David. Why can't you look at it that way and not worry about whether it's a sin or not?"

"I guess I could. But you can't. I watched you at that jazz club. All the smoke and alcohol and loud music was part of the atmosphere for me, but you were hanging on for dear life, telling yourself you could live with it for one night."

"So you're giving up on me because of coffee and . . . whatever?" She slid the plate away, put her elbows on the table, and ducked her head.

"Bobbi, I want you. But that's selfish. I'm trying to do the right thing."

"I'm going to see whether I can change my train tickets—and leave today."

"Bobbi, don't. I want to find a way. I just think we need to see things as they are and then work from there. I don't know whether I could get a job at the U again, but I could try. "

"No. I won't do that to you. You love this job. You love Chicago."

"I know. But . . ." He dropped backward in his seat, clamped his eyes tight for a moment. "Bobbi, last night I could have ruined your life. If I hadn't asked—and given you a moment to think—I might have ended up staying all night. And that, to me, would have been beautiful. But it would have destroyed you. On the train, going home, it finally hit me: if we were together, I would pull you away from everything you stand for."

"I'll go upstairs and pack—before check-out time. Will you see about the train schedule?"

"Bobbi, please don't leave yet. Let's—"

"David, stop. Let's just part as friends. I don't want to get angry."

"Angry? Why?"

"You're the one who filled me with all the nonsense: 'Don't be practical. When two people are in love, they have to be together.' I told you and told you that life didn't work that way—but I was so miserable without you that I . . .'" She had to stop or she was going to cry, and she didn't want to do that.

"Bobbi, I still feel the same way. I just don't know whether you will."

"Don't put this on me, David. You're all *talk*, it turns out."

David folded his arms across his chest. Bobbi could see the pain in his eyes. "You've got a point," he finally said. "When I couldn't have you, I longed for you. But now I'm scared—for both of us."

"Better now than later," Bobbi said, but she couldn't work up the anger she wanted; she felt a dreadful sadness setting in. She got up, leaving her breakfast uneaten.

That afternoon she and David stood by the train again, in the noise and the humid heat—but everything was different. Again they kissed, but this time lightly and quickly. David shed some tears and told Bobbi how sorry he was, but Bobbi didn't cry. She felt as though she had been turned to stone.

When Bobbi got back from Chicago, a day early, she took a taxi home. She could have called her parents, but she didn't feel like doing that. It was fairly late in the evening when she walked in carrying her suitcase, and Dad and Mom were in the living room listening to the radio.

"What are you doing home already?" Mom asked.

"I caught an earlier train than I planned at first."

And then they waited. Bobbi was tired and depressed, and the emotion came through in her voice—but no one asked the question. So Bobbi decided she would get it over with. "I'm not going to marry David. You don't have to worry about that."

That might have been the end of it, because she picked up her suitcase and headed for the stairs, but Dad couldn't resist. He got up and walked to the parlor. He looked up the stairs and said, "Bobbi, what happened?"

Bobbi kept going. "We just made a decision."

"Well, it was a wise one. I'm very proud of you."

Bobbi had reached the top of the stairs. She set her bag down and turned around. "You don't understand, Dad. *I* was ready to marry him. But *he* decided that it wouldn't work."

"Bobbi, I'm sorry. All I meant was—"

"I know what you meant."

Bobbi turned, picked up her suitcase, and walked on to her bedroom. But she didn't unpack. She sat on her bed, and finally she let go and cried. What had grown in her during the time on the train was not only the gloom about her future but also shame. She had been ready to compromise so much of what she had always believed, and it was David who had had to tell her that she couldn't do it.

Mom came upstairs in a few minutes. Bobbi didn't tell her much more, but she had decided one thing, and she did say that much. "I need to move out, Mom. I just want to be alone, like Alex. I'm too old to live with my parents."

"How will you pay your rent?"

"I don't know. I spent my money."

"Maybe I could find work—and I could help you."

"Work?" Bobbi couldn't have been any more surprised had her mother suddenly spoken in a foreign language.

"It's something I want to do anyway. I have my reasons."

"Dad will throw a fit if you even bring it up."

"Well, maybe. But it's not fair for you kids to have *all* the fun. It's my turn to get him upset."

Bobbi laughed softly, but she was also still crying.

The weather in the Philippines didn't change much. More rain fell in the spring and summer, and that pushed the humidity higher, but the temperature was about the same. By the summer of 1941, Wally had taken over the supply room and had made sergeant. He doubted anything like that could have happened in the other branches of the military, so he was glad he had chosen the air corps, and he was also happy he had seen a part of the world that he might never have seen.

But there was another side to all of this. One day was very much like another, and a three-year hitch was a long time. Wally was beginning to realize he was going nowhere. True, with a high school diploma he had some advantages, and officers' training was a possibility. But that would mean staying in the military, and Wally had lost interest in that. He didn't like being told what to do. Besides, officers did all right, but no one was going to get rich in the service.

Wally still had dreams of making a lot of money, and he wasn't sure, now, how he was going to do that. He had been anxious to get away from his dad, but he had traded his dad for his C.O., and now he needed to get on with his life. He wanted to open some sort of business, and he wasn't sure how he was ever going to get the money together to do that. He might have to take Alex up on his offer, but he still didn't want to do that.

Wally's entire unit had recently been transferred to Clark Field, an air base with a dirt runway and a few hangars, near Fort Stotsenberg, an army base. The place was close to the mountains and a little cooler, but it was eighty miles north of Manila, which made trips to the city more difficult. Angeles, the closest town, didn't have much to offer except a decent place to eat called Chicken Charlie's. For now, the men all bunked in a hangar, but a new supply shack was under construction, and Wally's C.O. had promised him he could bunk there. It wasn't fancy, of course, but at least he would have a place to himself. The squadron had received new Curtis P-40 fighters, the latest in pursuit airplanes, plus a few B-17 bombers.

This brought the unit much more up to date, but it also created more work, and duty now lasted all day.

Wally continued to drink a little beer and occasionally some gin. The men all said it was safer to drink alcohol than the local water, and gin only cost thirty-five cents a bottle. Every now and then, for no real reason, Wally would also smoke a cigarette or a cigar. He didn't really like smoking that much, but when everyone stopped to take a break, it was just something to do, and the military handed out cigarettes, free.

Wally knew that his parents would be upset if they knew he drank, or that he smoked a little, but he didn't plan to do it all his life. Once he moved back to Salt Lake, where people were so strict about that kind of thing, he would quit, and that would be that. Here in the islands, everything was different, and having a drink or a smoke didn't seem that significant.

Warren Hicks had gone through some changes in the past year. He had started studying his Book of Mormon every day. And he liked to raise questions about points of doctrine. He had even begun to write home for certain books he wanted to read. That was baffling to Wally. He was religious, he told himself, and he wasn't one of those guys who got drunk and got in fights or who ran off to prostitutes. In fact, the men teased him about being a "Goody Two-Shoes." But Warren was getting into all this straight-laced stuff, chastising Wally, and always wanting to talk about the Second Coming or the meaning of the Atonement. Wally believed in those things, but he didn't see that there was a lot to say about them. In fact, that was the problem with Church; everyone talked about the same things over and over.

Wally did go to church services almost every Sunday. There was no Mormon group, but a chaplain gave a sermon, and quite a few of the men went. Wally felt compelled to go, partly because he could write home and reassure his parents—when he got around to writing—and partly so that Warren wouldn't ride him. But there was more to it than that.

He had always gone to church, and he told himself he always would. It was his way of saying to himself, "See, all these people don't have to worry about me."

Wally knew also that he did, someday, want to go home to Salt Lake. Every now and then he would get so homesick that he could hardly stand the thought that he had signed up for such a long tour of duty. He was sure Lorraine would be married by the time he got back, but he knew he wanted someone like her, and he was pretty sure he would only find a girl like that at home.

Warren asked Wally one day whether he ever prayed. "Not in the regular sense," Wally said. "I don't get down on my knees and—"

"I don't either, Wally," Warren said. "I don't want everyone staring at me in the barracks. But I lay in bed and pray, or sometimes I go out into the jungle, and then I kneel down. I always feel better after I do that."

"Well, that's probably good. I ought to do that," Wally said. But he didn't do it.

Most of the men liked Wally more than Warren. Wally joked around with everyone and swore just enough that he didn't seem prissy, and he was the champion of "wanglers." When someone needed something, everyone always said, "Talk to Wally Thomas, the supply sergeant. If he can't get it, it can't be got."

Warren didn't get preachy with the men, but he lived more strictly. He had stopped going to Chicken Charlie's because of all the drinking. But Wally liked the food: whole deep-fried chickens with French fries and homemade bread, all for one peso. And he didn't mind the guys' drinking so long as they didn't get out of hand.

But one night that summer Wally's friend Barney was loaded up on gin, and he started grabbing at one of the waitresses, who made it clear she was not a prostitute. Barney wouldn't take no for an answer, however, and kept bothering her. When he reached behind her and began to slide his hand under her skirt, she stepped back and slapped him across the side of his head.

Barney grabbed his ear and then burst out of his seat and reached for her. The waitress made a quick retreat, and in a moment, the manager—Charlie—came through the swinging doors of the kitchen. He was wearing the customary fancy white shirt that most Filipino men wore. "Boys, boys," he said, smiling, "enough is enough. You don't want me to call in the MPs, do you?"

Barney was not so drunk that he wanted to get in trouble with the police. He made a gesture of truce, holding his hands up and grinning, and then he sat down. "Send her back with my chicken," he said. "That's all I want from her." But as soon as Charlie had disappeared, Barney said to the men at the tables, "Who does that little slut think she is? All I'd have to do is flash five pesos in front of her and she'd be begging me to take her to the back room."

"I don't think so," Wally said. "She didn't like you grabbing her like that. She's probably a good Catholic."

Barney laughed. "She's a good little *gook*, that's what she is. I've been all over these countries—China, Japan, Burma. Gooks are all alike—Japs, Chinks, Filipinos, it doesn't matter. You show them enough money, they'll sell *anything*."

"That's what some people say about Americans."

"What?"

The table was suddenly silent, and Wally wished he had kept his mouth shut. He had broken the rule—no one ever spoke well of Asians. But Wally had chafed at that from the beginning. He remembered too much of what he and Mat had talked about.

"Look, Barney," Wally said. "People are just people. There are good and bad ones everywhere in the world."

Barney laughed, showing his broken front tooth and the deep tobacco stains on the rest of his teeth. "No," he pronounced. "These gooks aren't people. They don't care nothing about life. If you don't watch your step, they'll pull you off in an alley and slit your throat—just for your ring or your watch. You can't trust any of 'em. I know—I've been around 'em."

"That's right," one of the other men said, a guy named Clyde. He was another old mechanic from the flight line. "I wish the Japs would quit messing around and attack us. In about two weeks, the American navy could wipe out that whole stinking island, and then we wouldn't have to put up with them anymore."

Barney swore. "They don't have the guts to take *us* on," he said. "They can go shoot up the little chinks all they want, but they know better than to take on America."

"Back home, I worked for a Japanese man," Wally said. "He was about as nice a guy as you'd ever know. And he used to talk about his family—who had moved to the States from Japan. They were Buddhists, and they were very kind, very good people. They weren't anything at all like what you're talking about."

"You don't know that. That's just what this guy told you."

"I know what kind of man he was. He was fair with me. He's one of the best men I've ever known."

Again the silence, and then Barney said, "Wally, what do you know? You've never been anywhere. Me and Clyde here know a lot more than one Nip guy back in the States."

Wally decided to let it go. When the waitress came back, however, he felt bad for her. She seemed a reserved young woman, not comfortable with the atmosphere she was working in. She had agreed to return to the table where she had been insulted, but she obviously didn't like it. And Barney certainly didn't apologize. Wally did try to be kind to the woman, but he wasn't sure that she noticed.

Bobbi stayed to herself most of the time during the rest of the summer. She was putting in long days at the hospital, so when she did come home she had an excuse to disappear into her room. But she wasn't pouting. She was merely trying to make the best of things and to move on with her life. Sister Thomas told her one day, "Oh, Bobbi, in some ways I envy you. You've already had two great adventures in your life. Two boys in love with you. Two heartbreaks. I never did have so much excitement." And that was a turning point for Bobbi. She began to tell herself that she was lucky to have had both these experiences. She couldn't find much to regret, except for the pain she had caused Phil, and she was glad to know she could love.

President Thomas was trying his best to do things right. He was friendly, not pushy, but he seemed nervous around Bobbi. And he could never go more than a couple of weeks without probing a little. The thesis behind his questioning was always the same: What are you doing to find a husband? And not very deep beneath the surface was a little reprimand: Don't you wish now that you had married Phil? Or maybe Bobbi only imagined that part.

Bobbi and her mother continued to talk about Bobbi getting an apartment, and Mom kept saying she had to talk to

President Thomas, but she didn't do it. Then one Sunday evening, after disappearing with her husband into the back office for more than an hour, she came upstairs to Bobbi's room.

"Bobbi," she said, and she let a hint of a smile appear. "I'm going to take a job. It's all arranged. I'll be starting this week, maybe even tomorrow."

"And Dad said it was okay?"

"Yes."

Bobbi had been sitting at her desk, reading. She got up and came over to her bed and sat down. Her mother sat down next to her, and now Sister Thomas was grinning. "Are you sure?" Bobbi asked. "Did he understand what you were asking him?"

"I didn't ask. I told him."

Bobbi laughed out loud. "What in the world is going on around here?"

"Well, it's not so shocking as you might think. Your dad has been fussing for months and months that Alex needs help at his office. Alex always agrees, but he never bothers to hire anyone. So I told him I wanted the job, and he offered it to me. I've just been waiting for the right time to break the news to your dad."

"What did he say?" Bobbi couldn't help laughing again.

"There wasn't much he could say. I told him I'll send the girls off to school in the mornings and be here when they get home. And I told him it would help Alex get out of the plant a little more often. How could he disagree with that?"

"I thought he was opposed to women working—no matter what."

"He is. But he's probably counting his blessings that I haven't come up with something worse." She nodded emphatically, and Bobbi saw how flushed she was with her own pleasure.

"Well, I'm proud of you, Mom. You'll do a good job."

"But I don't think you understand what this is all about. Bobbi, in my whole life, I've never had a penny of my own. Your dad gives me a budget, but if he decides *he* wants something, he just buys it. I've never been able to do that. Besides that, I've always asked for permission when I've wanted to do something. This time I talked to him as an equal, and he seemed to accept that."

"That's great, Mom. What are you going to do with all your money?"

"The first thing I'm going to do is rent an apartment for you. I already told your dad that, too."

"No." Bobbi stood up and looked down at her mother. "You said you wanted the money for yourself."

"No, I didn't. I said I wanted to have some money that I could spend the way I choose. And right now, I see you needing a change—needing some independence—and I want you to have it. It's something I never experienced."

So in September Bobbi moved to an apartment not far from the LDS Hospital. It was a cute little one-bedroom place, and Bobbi and her mother spent several evenings cleaning it. Then Gene and Dad helped move everything in.

Once everyone was gone, Bobbi sat among the boxes she still needed to empty, and she liked the idea of being on her own this way. But her mind soon turned to David, who was alone in Chicago. She wondered what he was thinking now, and she longed to talk to him. She also thought of Phil, who had gone ahead and married Ilene. The fact was, she wished she had also found someone, that her own life were more settled, but she decided not to spend this first evening in her new home thinking that way. She got up and began to put away her things.

Bobbi also had another plan. During the fall she talked to recruiters, and she decided she would join the navy right after she graduated. Her brothers had left the valley for a time and gone to distant parts of the world. Bobbi wanted her chance to do that too. She hadn't signed up yet, and she hadn't mentioned the idea to her dad, but she knew it was what she would do.

* * *

On Monday morning, December 8, which was December 7 back home, Wally was sitting outside the squadron mess shack eating breakfast. He wasn't feeling well. The squadron had thrown a party the day before for a departing Master Sergeant. Wally had had more than usual to drink, and he was feeling the effects of that now. He was surprised when he looked up and saw his first sergeant running toward the mess shack. As the man got closer, Wally was struck with the strange look on his face. He seemed startled, maybe even scared. "The Japs are bombing Hawaii," he shouted, and for a moment Wally thought he had heard wrong.

All the men at the mess shack stood up, automatically. "It's bad," the Sergeant said. He stopped in front of the men. "Everything is on fire. Lots of ships have gone down."

"What are you talking about?" someone asked, and that was Wally's response too. This was impossible.

"I don't know what's going on. I guess we're at war. The C.O. wants us all to fall in on the parade ground."

But no one moved. All the G.I.s stood where they were, obviously letting the idea sink in. Wally was trying to think what would come next.

"Just let the Japs try it here," one of the men said. "We'll show 'em." But Wally heard more astonishment than conviction in the man's voice.

The Thomases were sitting at the dinner table, eating and gabbing about this and that. Alex and Bobbi were both home, but Dad had called and said he was held up at the stake office; the family should go ahead and eat. Alex said the blessing, and everyone began to pass the food around—pot roast, potatoes, and a dozen other things. Mom always filled up the table with relishes and pickles, rolls and preserves. Everyone was talking and laughing when the telephone sounded the Thomas ring.

Gene got up and answered it. The family was still talking, and in a moment, Gene said, "Be quiet." Then into the telephone, "Are you sure?" Alex could tell something serious had happened, but he couldn't think what it would be.

"All right," Gene was saying, and then he hung the receiver back on the telephone and turned around. The color had left his face. "The Japs are attacking us," he said.

"What?" Alex said.

"They're dropping bombs on the Hawaiian Islands."

"Who was that?" Bobbi asked, sounding doubtful.

"Dad. He said to turn on the radio." Gene was already walking to the radio, but when he turned on the power, the tubes took time to warm up, and everyone waited. The first sound was an announcer's voice: "Wave after wave of Japanese bombers continue to strike. Most of the ships in Pearl Harbor are burning. Some have apparently sunk."

No one ate. Everyone listened, occasionally making a comment but mostly trying to accept the idea that this could happen. For two years every American had lived with the idea that war could break out. And sometimes speculation had brought Japan into the picture, but most of the talk had been about Germany. It had never seemed that it would happen this way.

Alex knew immediately that his life would never be the same. This meant war, and now he was sure to be drafted. He tried to think whether Germany would join Japan against America, and what would all this mean to Anna? His thoughts were racing, but behind it all, he felt a kind of nervous panic. Everything he had worried about, feared, would come down upon him now.

"What about the Philippines?" Sister Thomas asked. "What will happen to Wally?"

"I don't know," Alex said, but that concern had also struck him.

"The Philippines are so close to Japan."

Alex saw the fear in his mother's eyes. She was thinking of

her son who was already in harm's way, but Alex looked across the room at Gene, who was standing with his hands in his pockets, still listening to the radio. All three sons could end up in this. Gene was only sixteen, but who could say how long this might last?

"We'll kick those Japs' pants for them," Gene said. "They don't scare me. I wish I could join up right now."

"Hush," Mom said. "You have no idea what we might be in for."

"What about the Germans?" Bobbi asked. "Will we go to war with them, too?"

Alex nodded. "I think so," he said. "Germany and Japan have signed an agreement. Hitler must have known this was going to happen. I don't see how we can fight Japan and let Hitler take Europe."

"But how can we fight them both?" Sister Thomas asked. "And what's to keep the Japanese from bombing San Francisco—or even Salt Lake? If they'll bomb Hawaii, how do we know they won't keep right on coming?"

"I don't know, Mom," Alex said. "I don't know what they're thinking. But I can't picture them doing that."

"They're going to draft you, aren't they?" Mom said, and tears spilled onto her cheeks.

"I think so."

On and on the voice on the radio continued. The announcer kept giving the same information, repeating it for all those tuning in. But now and then something new would come in, and the picture was becoming more frightening. Most of the Pacific fleet had been docked at Pearl Harbor, and most of it was damaged or destroyed. The Japanese had pulled off a complete surprise, one the United States could not easily recover from. It really did seem that the country was defenseless along the West Coast.

Alex had glanced at LaRue and Beverly a couple of times, and he had seen the concern in their faces. But when Beverly began to cry, he finally realized how scared they both must be. He pulled Beverly onto his lap and held her. "Why do they want to drop bombs on us?" she asked between her sobs.

"Don't worry, honey. I'm sure they won't," Alex told her, and he patted her back.

But Alex's mind was still busy. The number he had drawn for the lottery was high, which would have kept him out of the service at the rate the draft had been going. But what would happen now? All healthy young men would probably be called up. He saw it as a picture in his mind: him slogging through mud, being shot at, watching people die around him, perhaps dying himself. And he thought of shooting at people, killing them. It was something he had tried to imagine many times before, and in his mind, those he would kill were always Germans. The soldiers would be the same young men he had known while he was there—teenagers playing soccer in the streets, students walking home from school, even young Mormon priesthood holders blessing the sacrament and passing it in their branches. He would rather fight the Japanese, if he had to fight. He didn't know them. And now they had struck first, asking for the war that they were going to get. But Japanese young men couldn't be so different from Germans— or from himself.

Dad came home before long. He listened to the radio for a time, and then he sat down and ate his dinner. He said next to nothing, but Alex knew he was considering all the implications.

"What's going to happen to Wally?" Mom asked him.

"I don't know," he said. "We'll just have to wait and see." But he sounded worried.

Alex continued to hold Beverly and to pat her on the back. She had stopped crying, but she was clinging to him. LaRue, who looked as frightened as Beverly, was leaning against her mother, and Mom was holding her close. Alex wondered what must be going through the girls' heads. He thought of the little children in Primary in Frankfurt. Did they have the same thoughts about the British? Would they feel that way about America before long? So many children, all over the world, were going to suffer. He gripped Beverly's skinny little frame and tried to make her feel safe.

"We've been hearing about a possible second World War," Mom said softly. "That's what this is now."

Alex never finished his meal. Neither did Mom or Bobbi or the younger girls, but Gene finally came back and gulped down his food, and Dad ate everything on his plate. When he was finished, he wiped his mouth with his napkin, placed it on the table, and said, "Alex, come with me for a few minutes. I want to talk to you."

He walked to his office. Once inside, he took a seat at his desk, and Alex sat in one of the two old overstuffed chairs. Sometimes Dad held interviews at home, extended callings, or counseled young couples planning to get married. Now he sat hunched over his desk with his hands gripped together. "Alex," he said, "this could be very bad for Wally."

"Will the Japanese start attacking all the islands—or what do you think they're up to?"

"I have no idea. But those bases are too close to Japan for the Japanese not to knock them out if they can. I don't see any way he's going to sit there and not get pulled into this thing."

"General MacArthur has been over there for years, training the locals to fight. Maybe Japan won't dare try an invasion."

"I'm hoping the same thing. But even if the Japs don't try to take the islands, they're sure to attack Clark Field and the other airfields and ports."

"It's nuts, Dad. What makes the Japanese think they can take on the United States?"

"We're not ready, Alex. They've knocked out most of our fleet. Japan may be a small country, but they've been building a huge navy, and now they've grabbed us by the throat. I think we could be in big trouble."

"Just the islands, or here, too?"

"I don't know, Alex. But if Hitler should finish off England in the next little while, and if we can't mobilize fast enough to handle Japan in the Pacific, we might have to sign treaties and let Japan and Germany and Italy divide up the world among themselves. Isn't that a pretty picture?"

"A month ago I thought Moscow was about to fall, but the Russians are holding on. Maybe Hitler's taken on too much, fighting in Africa and Russia and England all at the same time."

"We'd better hope so. I'm afraid the winter is slowing the Germans more than the Russians are. Moscow might fall quickly in the spring."

"If England and Russia fall, Hitler won't stop. He'll join with the Japanese and come after us. Those countries would never be satisfied until they had all the resources of a big, rich country like ours."

Dad nodded. "Evil is trying to take over the world, Alex. That's what it comes down to. And the responsibility to stop it is going to be on our shoulders. I've been as stupid about this as anyone. I just kept thinking we could stay out of it."

Alex thought he saw where all this was leading. But Dad took him by surprise. "Alex, maybe it was meant to be that you're operating our plant. Everyone is going to be called on to serve. But you're already in the middle of the effort."

"I don't know, Dad. You can run the operation—or Henry Rosen. Young men like me are going to be drafted."

"No. The military can't start taking more people than it's ready to train. And not everyone will go. I don't see why any one family has to send all its sons."

"It might take all of every family's sons if we're going to fight Japan *and* Germany."

"Maybe. But Alex, you have a purpose in this life. I've known it since the day you were born. You know what Joseph Fielding Smith said about you." Dad hesitated, placed his hands flat on his desk, and looked into Alex's eyes. "Today, when I got the word, I said to myself, 'I have three sons. What will happen to them?' I thought of Wally, and I knew he was in great danger. And I thought of having to send you now and maybe Gene later. But then I had a feeling come over me when I thought about the position you hold at the plant. I just don't see you as a warrior. I see you as someone who will do his part by serving here, as someone who will be preserved for higher purposes."

Alex wanted to believe that. But it sounded self-serving, too convenient. "I don't know whether the draft board will look at it that way, Dad."

"I know some of those men. I can talk to them and make sure they understand your position. The plant is just starting to roll. If someone tried to take over—especially Henry—I hate to think of all the problems that would follow. Soldiers are worthless without weapons, and you're the one putting those weapons into their hands."

Alex saw some logic in that, but he was still bothered by the money. Both he and his father, along with Henry, could get rich out of this. The war only assured them that more contracts would be coming their way. "Dad, I feel like we're trying to talk ourselves into excuses. I can't stay here and profit off the war while other boys go out and fight. I'd feel like a coward."

"No. Don't say that. You keep the parts going out and you'll be a hero. In any war there are more support troops than gun-toting infantrymen. Plenty of patriots are going to run down and sign up and then end up pleased as punch to be whacking away at a typewriter instead of pulling a trigger. You're going to play a bigger role in this war than anyone like that."

Alex tried to accept that. The idea that he could stay home without guilt and not have to do any shooting was certainly comforting, but he was still uneasy with the idea.

"Alex, there's something else you need to think about."

"What?"

"The girl you met over there. Anna."

Alex had thought of her from the beginning. He was trying

to think what it would all mean, but he told his father, "It doesn't change anything for me, Dad. I've known for a long time that we would probably end up in this war."

"Alex, it could last for *years.*"

"I know."

"Have you heard anything more from President Clark?"

"No. He got my letter through to a German Church leader, but by the time the letter got to President Meis, the Stoltzes had left Frankfurt, and no one knows where they are."

"Why would they pick up and leave?"

"I'm not sure. But I'm worried that they might have had trouble with the Gestapo."

"Maybe they got hauled off, if that's the case."

"I know." Alex had hardly thought of anything else for weeks, and he hardly needed his dad to put it in such bald terms. "Alex, are you sure you want to hang on to this idea? Wouldn't you be better off to start thinking in terms of finding someone else?"

"No. I wouldn't."

Dad obviously knew better than to say any more. He simply nodded. Alex accepted that as a sizable act of compromise on his part. But saying nothing was almost a more powerful argument. Alex only saw the reality more clearly: his chances of ever seeing Anna again had to be remote.

"Well," Dad said, "let's go listen to the radio. I hope our whole Pacific fleet isn't lost."

The two got up then and walked back into the dining room, where Alex found his mother, her face white with concern. She looked up at Alex and President Thomas. "My heart breaks to think of all the pain that is coming. I wonder what it will mean for Wally."

Bobbi, who was sitting next to Mom, reached her arm around her shoulders. "I feel like he'll come back," she said. "Remember how Dad blessed him when he left?"

"Yes, I do," Mom said. "But maybe it's not fair to ask for

special blessings. So many boys are going to die. Why should our family expect to be spared?"

The question cut to the heart of things. The room fell silent except for the continued voice on the radio. And now the announcer was beginning to name the ships that had been sunk and the numbers of sailors who were on board each of them.

It was President Thomas who finally said, "I guess now we'll find out what our family is made of. We've always had it too easy."

3 2

No one at Clark Field knew what to expect, but Wally had never seen the men so solemn. They stood about in little groups and talked—trying to make sense of all this. They cursed "Japs" in the foulest language, but at the same time, they wanted to know how America could have let this happen. How could a huge armada of ships make it all the way from Japan to Hawaii without being detected? How could all the U.S. ships have been sitting there, just waiting to be destroyed? A begrudging tone of respect had also come into the men's voices. The "little Nips" had turned into cursed "yellow bellies," but the Japanese had also taken upon themselves the proportions of a serious enemy.

Everyone was supposed to be at his post. But Wally's post was the supply shack. He walked over and surveyed his supplies, and now he looked at everything from a new point of view. His 45-caliber pistols had been issued to the senior noncoms. What he had for defense were four racks of 12-gauge, sawed-off shotguns. Those were to protect against the possibility of an attack by parachute troops or to put down any local disorder. A lot of good they would do if the Japanese were to land on the island. The only serious weapons were a few Lewis

30-caliber machine guns, one per squad, but in training, the old relics had always managed to jam after a few bursts of fire.

The unit did have some anti-aircraft guns, and the men had dug several trenches around the hangars and the operations and mess shacks. Wally remembered how much the men had complained when they had had to dig those trenches, but the protection was welcome now. The airmen themselves weren't entirely untrained for an attack, but they were unprepared mentally. An easy indolence had become a way of life. How could men like that suddenly turn into warriors? Wally told himself that he wasn't afraid, and he certainly didn't feel any sense of panic, but a numb disbelief kept telling him that war just couldn't come here.

One thing Wally did believe was that the pilots in their unit would hold their own in the air. Shortly after the C.O. had spoken to the squadron that morning, all the fighters had taken off. The P-40s were to stay in the air most of the time—to intercept any attack, but also to protect themselves from being bombed or strafed on the ground. Ground crews would have to work hard to keep them in the air.

At about eleven the airplanes returned, and crews refueled them and gave them quick maintenance checks so they would be ready to take off again soon. A little more ease spread through the base as word came back that the pilots had spotted no enemy airplanes or ships. All the same, the pilots were unusually serious, and they were eager to get back into the air.

The maintenance crews were busy, but Wally had no part in any of that, so he decided to walk over to the mess shack and get something to eat. He donned an old World War steel helmet—the only kind available—and he got his mess kit. He locked up the supply shack and began to walk across the field to the mess shack, a distance of a couple hundred yards. He hadn't gone far, however, before he heard the sound of airplanes. He stopped and looked at the sky. He knew that fighters from the other bases on the island were also supposed to stay in the air, and so he assumed these must be from one of the other two squadrons.

At first he saw nothing, but then, coming in quite low, he saw a flight of aircraft dotting the sky. It was comforting to see such a large force protecting the island. But something didn't make sense. He could gradually see that the airplanes were too large and slow to be fighters. Somehow, the air corps had managed to get a whole fleet of bombers to the Philippines. This would add some real power to their defenses.

He watched for a few more seconds, enjoying the sight. The bombers banked to the left over Fort Stotsenberg, next to the airfield. They were almost overhead before Wally saw the insignia: the "Rising Sun" painted under each wing.

"Jap bombers!" Wally screamed, and already he could see the bombs begin to fall. He dropped to the ground, in the open field, and grabbed his helmet with both hands. The horrible whistle of the bombs blocked out other sounds until the first of them hit the earth with a deafening explosion.

The target, of course, was the flight of P-40 fighters on the ground—and the B-17 bombers. Wally watched from a safe distance, but the scene was horrifying. Pilots ran for their airplanes and tried to get them rolling onto the runway. Crews were trying to help. But bombs were falling at a furious pace, the whole earth jumping and airplanes exploding. Some of the pilots got their planes moving, but Wally watched them blow apart before they ever got into the air. He knew the men in those planes, knew the crewmen who were running for their lives.

"Run, run," Wally screamed into the roar and confusion as he watched four men dash toward a trench. But all of them dropped at the same time, cut down by shrapnel from a huge explosion just behind them. Another man, a sergeant Wally knew, was sprinting hard for the trench when he slowed, kept trying to run, and then dropped to the ground with a huge, red hole in his back. At least some of the men were making it out of the inferno and were diving wildly into the trenches.

In just a few minutes the whole flight of aircraft was torn apart. Explosions kept going off in the middle of them, and then secondary explosions followed as the fuel tanks blew. Everything seemed to be on fire. Only three P-40s managed to get through the chaos and off the ground.

Bombs were striking the hangars now, too, tearing them apart, and heavy black smoke was rising everywhere, obscuring most of the sky. Wally saw a bomb hit the mess shack and blow it apart. He hoped no one had been inside.

Once the bombers had passed over, Wally jumped to his feet and ran back to the supply shack. He fumbled for his keys and opened the door, and he grabbed himself a shotgun and some shells. He had no idea whether a parachute landing might be coming with the bomb attack, but he knew he wanted some kind of weapon in his hands.

As he headed back out the door, he almost crashed into Len Granfield, a staff sergeant. "Wally, give me a shotgun," he shouted. Wally turned back and grabbed a gun and a box of shells. Neither said another word. They both ran outside, but Wally had no idea where to go. He wanted to get to one of the trenches, but now that the bombers were gone, Japanese Zeros were swarming over the field. They were strafing with machine guns and firing their big 20-millimeter cannons at the same time. Amid the staccato of the machine gun fire was the constant "whomp, whomp, whomp" of those cannons.

Wally looked about, tried to think where to go, and then he spotted a pile of sand that construction workers had dumped near the supply shack. Len was already running for it, and Wally followed. He could hear a Zero diving toward them, the machine-gun fire already sounding, and the whistle of bullets in the air. He dove behind the pile and then watched the sand fly around him as bullets pounded into it.

For a moment he felt safe until he saw another Zero

coming in from the opposite direction. He and Len jumped up and shuffled around the sand, and then they got down on their knees. Again the bullets pounded into the sand and didn't touch them.

Hunched down that way, a strange memory came back to Wally. He saw it for only an instant, but with amazing clarity. He was a boy, back in Sugar House, down the street in a vacant lot. He and his friends were playing war. He was hiding behind a tool shed, waiting, ready to jump out and fire at "the enemy."

Some jumbled thoughts followed: a picture in his head of the little red wagon he had gotten for Christmas one year. He had left it outside and someone had stolen it. Wally had never really gotten over that. And then he saw fireworks going off one night at the Twenty-Fourth of July rodeo. His dad was holding him and telling him the noise was nothing to be scared of.

Maybe he was about to die. He had heard that a person's life passed before his eyes before he died. And yet, the memories were merely impulses firing through his mind. His conscious focus was on the next Japanese fighter coming in.

"Why aren't we shooting back?" Wally screamed, although he never knew whether Len heard him in all the noise and confusion. But Wally couldn't hear anything that sounded like anti-aircraft artillery.

Another Zero was diving at them. Len and Wally scrambled around to the safe side of the pile of sand again. And they did this dozens of times before everything ended.

There was only one good moment, when one of the P-40s that had gotten off the ground disappeared with two Zeros on its tail but then swung back into view, out of the smoke, and hit one, then the other Japanese fighter with gunfire. One of the Zeros dove directly into the ground and exploded. The other began to smoke badly and disappeared. But Wally had no time to take much joy in that, nor did it give him the slightest degree of hope. He knew that the Japanese were receiving almost no resistance.

Eventually, there was little more for the Japanese to accomplish. The fighters had strafed all the damaged American airplanes and fired into the burning hangars and operations shack. They had even zoomed over the living quarters and fired into them. Finally, they began to peel away and disappear beyond the smoke. Wally waited and watched for some time, but finally Len said, "They're all gone," and Wally allowed himself to drop onto the sand. He rolled onto his back and lay there panting. He realized that he was still clinging to his shotgun even though the barrel was jammed with sand. He tossed the thing away, and for a couple of minutes he lay where he was, taking long breaths.

When Wally and Len finally got up and took a look, they saw that almost everything was burning. The planes were virtually all destroyed, which meant the Japanese could return any time. There was no way to stop them. Wally had no idea how many of his squadron were dead, but he had seen a number of them die before his eyes.

Yet, it was strange how little fear Wally felt. The whole thing was like a scene out of a war movie. It had all happened, and Wally had reacted, but he couldn't comprehend what it was going to mean. He had a strange sense that he was utterly vulnerable to another attack, and yet, it was more a sense of recognition—just a fact—than it was a concern.

Later that day, word would come that the gunnery base on the opposite side of the island had been wiped out completely. The fighters there had also been destroyed, and one of the first bombs had hit a mess shed full of airmen, killing all of them. Clark had not lost as many. Seven pilots were dead, and fifteen enlisted men, along with dozens more who were wounded or burned.

For some reason, the Japanese had not attacked Nichols Field. Maybe it would be next, but at least the men at Clark were glad to know that some American airplanes were still operating. The three planes that had survived the attack on their own field were hardly enough to mean anything.

As it turned out, it was the C.O., Major Teuscher, who had piloted the American P-40 that had knocked down the two Zeros. And after the battle, he managed to land on the broken field. So Clark Field was not without its leader—the young "old man" the men respected so much and who now had been raised to a higher level by his heroics in the air.

By late afternoon, the Major had organized the surviving troops and instructed them to abandon the field. They were to bivouac near a river a couple of miles inland. Wally, as supply sergeant, earned the dubious right to carry the C.O.'s bed roll to the site along with his own equipment: one blanket. He didn't begrudge the major. The man had earned plenty of respect that day. All the same, the hike through the jungle was difficult, especially with the added weight, and Wally was com- pletely spent by the time he made it to the bivouac site. It was dark by then, and no one was doing much to set up any sort of camp. Men were dropping their blankets in the first good spot they could find and then crashing onto the ground. No one seemed interested in talking. Wally's mind was full of all kinds of images, thoughts of the dead, confusion about the future, but he had neither the energy nor the desire to discuss any of that with the others.

Wally was hungry, but he soon learned there was no food. What he wanted more than food was sleep anyway. So he wrapped himself in his blanket and in only a few minutes was sound asleep. He hadn't slept long, however, when someone began to shake him. Wally couldn't see much in the dark, but he heard a familiar voice say, "Sergeant. It's Lieutenant Cluff. I need your help."

It took Wally a moment to get everything straight, and then it all thundered back into his head: where he was, what had happened. Lieutenant Cluff had been his supply officer at one time. Wally liked the man and had worked well with him, but that didn't mean he was pleased to be awakened this way.

"The C.O. wants me to go back to Clark. We're getting some replacement planes in from Nichols. I came up in a Jeep, on the road, but I'm going to have to walk back, and I don't know the trail. Do you think you can help me get there?"

"Sure," Wally said. He rolled onto his side and then got up, slowly. His body ached, and he still wasn't thinking very clearly, but something told him he had to do what was asked of him right now. He had to come through; everyone had to do that. "I can get there," he mumbled.

"Okay. We need to get going."

"Do you have any food?"

"No. But we can get something back at the field."

It wasn't worth it. However hungry he was, right now he just wanted to sleep. "Have you got any kind of light?"

"No. We'll just have to find our way."

"All right." Wally stumbled off in the direction he thought he would have to go. There was some moonlight, and Wally soon found the trail. For some time the two walked in silence. If airplanes were coming, the field was going to be kept open. That could only mean more attacks. He wondered whether the squadron had a chance of defending itself any better the next time.

"How are you feeling, Wally?" Lieutenant Cluff finally asked.

"Tired. But I'm okay."

"Scared?"

"Not too."

Maybe another minute went by before the Lieutenant said, "It's hard to believe. I didn't think any of us would die over here. Davis and Samuelsen were both good friends of mine."

"I know. I was friends with Holbrook." The reality of these deaths seemed to strike with more force now. Wally had lived amid these jungles for a long time, but everything seemed more eerie, the sounds strange again, the way they had been when he first arrived. He wished that somehow he could escape the island and go home.

Lieutenant Cluff let some time pass again before he said, "I just can't die out here. I've got to get back to my family."

Wally didn't know what to say to that, and so he didn't respond. The trail was not hard to follow, but the jungle growth cut out most of the light. Wally had to move slowly and feel his way along. His uniform was already soaked through by his own sweat and the humid air.

"I've got two daughters at home," Lieutenant Cluff said.

Wally had known that Cluff was from Indiana, or maybe it was Illinois, but he had never heard him mention his children.

"I don't fear my own death all that much," the Lieutenant said. "But I don't know how my wife would handle it—and my little girls."

"I guess it's good I don't have to think much about things like that," Wally said. "My parents would feel bad, I'm sure, but I have a big brother who's their pride and joy. It'd be a lot harder for them to lose him."

"Come on, Wally. Parents don't think that way."

Wally tried to think about that. He knew that everyone would miss him. Still, if his parents had to lose one of their children, they could let go of him more easily than the others. But until this moment, he had never thought about it that way, and the truth of it hurt him. "Well, Lieutenant, I'm not—"

"You can call me Don."

"Okay." But Wally didn't do it. "I'm not saying that my parents wouldn't feel bad. But they would get over it. They have five other kids who never trouble them as much as I do." Wally had reached a clearing. He could see the sky, the stars. A memory of summer camp in the mountains, back when he was a boy, struck him. In those days it had never occurred to him that he might be any less valued than the other kids.

"It doesn't work that way, Wally. Your child is your child."

Wally wasn't sure. He knew what a disappointment he had been to his father. Before, however, that thought had always come to mind as a reproach against Dad; now everything seemed changed. Men had died that morning, suddenly and easily, and he could have died the same way. It occurred to him how little he had to show for his life, how little effort he had given.

"One of my girls is four, and one is two," Lieutenant Cluff said. "I haven't seen the baby since she was six months old."

He didn't add to that. But the point was there. Wally felt the man's agony, and he found himself wishing he had something to care that much about. He wondered what Lorraine was doing now. He had never written to her, but his parents mentioned her in their letters now and then. She had asked about him, they said—and she wasn't married. But that's all he knew.

Suddenly Wally wanted to stay alive, and for the first time, fear struck him. He wanted—needed—more time so he could do things right. All that talk about making money, starting a business, being out on his own—what was that? He had spent a year and a half away from home, and he hadn't kept a single commitment to his mother and father, or to himself. He wasn't one step closer to knowing what he believed or what he wanted to do with his life. And now the Japanese would be coming back, attacking the base again. What if he never made it home?

And then Wally was struck with a thought so surprising and yet so obvious that it was stunning. All this time his dad had been right—annoying and sometimes overpowering, but still right. Why hadn't he had the sense to stay home, learn his dad's business, grab the opportunity to go to college? What had he been thinking? Suddenly he wanted to sit down with his dad and talk everything out, to say to him, "Dad, let's start over. I was just a kid and I did and said a lot of stupid things."

Behind him, in the dark, he heard Lieutenant Cluff, still

thinking out loud. "My older daughter—Patty—could only talk a little when I left. Now she's saying everything. My wife writes two or three times a week, and she tells me all the things she says. She's a smart little girl."

"How long have you been married?" Wally asked, mostly just to show he was listening.

"Five years. A little more. My wife got pregnant the first month. But that was fine with us. We wanted kids."

And then he kept talking. He told about meeting his wife in high school, getting married when he was nineteen, and then deciding to join the army when times were still pretty tough. He had applied for officer's training and gotten it, and then had received the chance to shift from the regular army to the air corps. Everything had worked out well, and he liked the service. But he had only seen it as a good job during the depression. He had never really expected to end up in a war.

Wally listened without fully concentrating on the story. He was thinking more about his family. They would hear, soon now, that the Philippines had been attacked. They would worry. Bobbi and Mom would show it the most, but everyone would worry. He wondered how Beverly and LaRue would react. And Gene. He wished he could see them at least one more time.

"You're a Mormon, aren't you?" Cluff asked.

"Yeah."

"You don't seem all that religious to me. Are you?"

"I guess not—not the way you mean it. But I was raised to be a good Mormon. My dad's a leader in our church and everything. What about you? Are you religious?"

"I guess so. In a way. I'm about like you. My parents took me to church every Sunday my whole life, and the first time I got away from home, I stopped going. It wasn't anything I even thought very much about. I just didn't find much interest in listening to sermons."

"What about your wife?"

"She's the same way about church. But she thinks about things like that a lot more than I do."

"She'll be praying for you," Wally said.

"I know. She will. I've said a few prayers myself today. I guess you have too."

"Not yet," Wally said, actually embarrassed, but not willing to lie about something like that.

"Do you want to stop here, maybe, and . . . you know . . . say a prayer with me?"

Wally kept walking. "I don't know, Lieutenant. I haven't prayed for a while, so it seems a little wrong to start asking the Lord to bother with me now."

"I'm no authority, but I do believe in God. And I don't think for a minute that he thinks that way. Let's stop here, before we get back to Clark."

It wasn't exactly an order, not in the military sense, but Wally didn't have the nerve to say no. And so he stopped.

"Do you know a prayer?"

"We just . . . say what we think needs to be said."

"Why don't you say it then. I've never really done that."

Wally hesitated. He wasn't ready. But he couldn't think what to tell Lieutenant Cluff. "Okay," he finally said. He ducked his head and folded his arms, the way he had done in Primary, long ago. "Our Father in Heaven," he said, but the words almost stuck in his throat he was so ashamed. "We ask thee to bless Lieutenant Cluff. If I were to die here, it wouldn't matter so much, but Lieutenant Cluff has a family, and he needs to get back. Protect him, Lord. Put a shield around him to stop the bullets. Give him strength to withstand whatever comes. And bless his wife and children with comfort."

Wally closed the prayer, unable to ask anything on his own behalf.

"You didn't need to do that," Cluff said. "I meant to pray for both of us—or all of us."

"I know. But you're the one who needs to get back."

"You sounded like a priest or a minister or something. I've never heard a prayer like that."

"I do have the priesthood. Young guys in our church start out with the priesthood at twelve." Wally wasn't quite sure how to explain all that.

"I feel better," Lieutenant Cluff said. "I really do."

"When I said it, I felt like you would get through. I think you will."

Wally wasn't sure what he was doing—imitating his father, he supposed. But he really had gotten a feeling that his friend would live through this. That was strange, but it was also comforting. Dad—and Alex—would have handled it better, expressed themselves more eloquently. But something in helping this man—or at least asking for help—felt good.

Wally thought of adding his own prayer—for himself—as he began to walk again. But he couldn't do it. He just didn't feel that he had a right to ask.

3 3

By the time Wally walked all the way back to the campsite on the river, it was three in the morning, and he was so tired he could hardly keep moving. He found his blanket, lay down on the ground, and fell instantly asleep. He didn't wake up until the sun was high in the sky.

By then, some of the men had gone back to the airfield. Bulldozers were repairing the runway. With all the hangars destroyed, the new airplanes had to be hidden under the cover of brush and trees. It was going to be a tough job, and it had to be done fast. Around noon, trucks finally showed up to haul the rest of the men back to Clark Field from their bivouac site.

Most of the men had still not eaten, and they were tired and bedraggled, so they had little to say as the truck lurched and bounced over the rough road. Wally could see that the men were experiencing the same thing he was: disbelief. How could this have happened? From one day to the next *everything* had changed. And beyond all of them lay a future that was as troublesome for its unclarity as it was for its threat.

Wally had a picture in his mind that kept coming back. It had happened so quickly at the time that he hadn't thought much about it, but in the night on the trail, and again now, he saw it all over again. When he had been hiding behind the pile of sand, and the Zeros had kept diving and strafing, he had looked up once to see one of those planes, very low, coming in just above the trees. The airplane had angled toward the hangars, not toward Wally and Len, and Wally had watched as it passed on by. For just one instant, Wally had been able to see the pilot himself, and Wally was sure the man had been smiling.

It had all been a blur, and yet the thought that the pilot had enjoyed what he was doing was infuriating. Wally couldn't imagine himself feeling that way. He knew all the men who were dead. He knew that their families would soon be getting word about these deaths that had occurred on the first day, in the first hours, of the war. He could imagine how much pain would come just from this one attack.

Wally thought he could kill that pilot and feel good about it. He had never known such hatred in his life. He thought of Mat Nakashima and all the things they had talked about, but this seemed to have nothing to do with any of that. All he knew was that men in airplanes, men with machine guns, were trying to kill him. He didn't care what country they were fighting for—or even *who* they were. They wanted to kill him, and he wished he could kill them first.

Wally was still lost in his own thoughts as the truck bounced over the road. And then he heard the noise. Airplanes. "Japs!" someone yelled, and the men began to bail out. Wally jumped to his feet and then swung over the side of the truck. As he landed on the ground, he glanced at the sky and saw two Zeros slicing diagonally across the road, guns firing. He dove into the underbrush and rolled.

The pilots had apparently not seen the trucks until they were almost past. They had fired quick bursts of gunfire that had slashed harmlessly through the trees beyond the road. But someone shouted, "They'll be back. Get good cover."

Wally jumped up and struggled through the bracken to get deeper into the jungle, and he tucked himself under some ferns and thick bushes. Then he waited. The pilots had to know that the men were close to the road. If they happened to strafe along his side, the greenery over him was certainly not going to stop any bullets. He thought of jumping up to scramble deeper into the woods, but the movement might bring attention to himself should the fighters return at that moment. And so he lay on the ground, rolled up like a potato bug, and he waited.

He could hear nothing, only his own hard breathing and the sounds in the jungle—birds singing as though it were a lovely day. It was all so strange and infuriating. What did those pilots think they were doing up there? Were they just flying around trying to find someone to shoot at—just for the pleasure? He wished with all his heart that he were a pilot, that he could get up in the air and take those guys on.

The fighters didn't return. All the same, the airmen waited for a long time before they finally came out of the brush. And when they did, Wally noticed a change in them. They had been frightened as they had jumped off the truck, and maybe they still were, but they were also angry. They climbed back onto the trucks, and they cursed and swore, called the pilots every disgusting name they could think of. Wally felt the same rage, but he didn't curse. He didn't want to do that now.

Anger was a much better emotion than fear, and the men seized it with relish. They bragged about all that the Americans were going to do once reinforcements and more airplanes reached the islands. "We're going to wipe out every one of those little slant-eyes," one of the men vowed. He was a mechanic who had been drunk almost every night for as long as Wally had known him. He was sober now, though, and he was dirty and unshaven. He looked fierce enough to fight, but Wally knew he wasn't really ready. None of these men were.

The tough talk continued all the way back to Clark, but the airfield was a frightening reminder of the reality the men were facing. The place was like a ghost town, and the skeletons

of the former hangars, the wreckage of the airplanes, now bull-
dozed into a heap, only made it clear how completely the
Japanese were in control. The squadron did have a few P-40s
again now, but the word was that they would be used mainly
to watch the movements of the enemy. There were not enough
of them to take on the Japanese in any sort of air battle.

The other talk was even more grim. Those who knew said
the American planes were a joke compared to the Japanese
fighters. The American pilots were probably equal in their flying skills, but the P-40s were too slow and awkward to hold
their own with the Zeros they would have to fight.

"How could Uncle Sam let something like this happen?"
the men kept asking each other. What were they doing out
here without better equipment, better preparation? Why hadn't
anyone known what the Japanese were up to? And men speculated quietly that maybe reinforcements would not be quick to
come. If the Japanese had attacked Hawaii and the Philippines,
where else had they attacked? Who else needed to be
defended? Did the army even have enough troops and airplanes to deal with so many fronts? And what was left of the
navy after Pearl Harbor?

That evening the men were instructed to set up camp in a
nearby canyon, just beyond Fort Stotsenberg, and to dig in.
Most of them did little that night but get a decent night's sleep.
But the next morning they went to work. The hard labor was
actually welcome after two days of inaction and too much time
to think. Most men were especially committed to digging
themselves deep foxholes, but they also worked at trenches
near the field and near the cooking area at their camp. And
they worked hard to get the airplanes protected. These planes
were their last offensive firepower, even if they weren't taking
on the Zeros that were still flying about, unmolested.

Wally's C.O. told him that each man would have to look
after his own supplies—a blanket and a few personal items—
so the position of supply sergeant, for the present, had little

meaning. Wally spent his time digging with all the rest. Each day, Japanese bombers returned. They bombed the airstrip and the already ruined hangars. Men had to stay on watch at all times, and workers had to scramble for the trenches each time another raid began. Fighters would also show up at odd times, coming in low and fast, sending sudden terror through the camp.

After three days the work was mostly finished. Men spent their time digging their own holes deeper or just sitting around talking. And Wally felt the fear deepening. The truth was, these men were trapped on the island with few resources, and no one knew when help would come. Most seemed to feel they would hold out all right against any land invasion, so long as help would come eventually. But the talk about blasting the Japanese away had stopped, and a clear reality had taken shape: Things were likely to get a lot worse before they got better.

Some of the men turned inside themselves and seemed consumed by fear. One sergeant spent almost all his time in his own foxhole and would come out only when hunger drove him to it. Another man, a big cook who had always been a sour cuss and a bully, now became almost paralyzed with fear. The men, recognizing this, loved to shout, "Here they come!" just to see him dive into his foxhole and lie there trembling.

Wally wasn't going to act like a coward, and yet, he did understand the impulse. The bombers continued to blow up the airstrip, and everyone had to wonder: How long before the pilots realized where the airplanes were? The area under the trees, near the field, had to be a rather obvious site for the planes to be sheltered. So when would the bombers and the fighters start working over the nearby jungle instead of the airfield and the bombed out hangars?

Daylight hours were constantly frightening. Only at night, when the Japanese didn't attack, could Wally relax. Sleep was a welcome escape, and even in a dirty foxhole, in the humid night air and among the bugs and mosquitoes, he slept well.

A few days after the first raid, Wally was working in the area near the hidden airplanes. Some pilots were about to taxi from the revetments and take off, so the fighters' engines were already roaring. Over the noise of the P-40s, Wally heard a vehicle approach. He turned around to see a guy he knew, Sandy Hodges, driving up in a cut-down pickup truck. He had a big grin on his face, and Wally wondered what he was up to.

He braked and then bounced out of the truck. He had a box in his hand, which he slapped onto the hood of the truck. Then he reached in and pulled out a double handful of cigars. "Cigars! Cigars!" he yelled above the drone of the engines.

Wally wondered where Sandy had managed to scrounge a box of cigars, and he looked around to see who wanted one—but saw no one at all. Instantly, Wally guessed what was happening. He spun to look at the lookout tower the men had built. A red flag was waving in the breeze—the sign for an air attack. At the same moment, Wally heard the whistle of dropping bombs. The noise from the engines had apparently drowned out the sound of the approaching bombers, and he hadn't noticed the flag go up.

Wally spun and ran for the nearby brush, where the men had dug a trench. At any second, he expected shrapnel from the exploding bombs to strike his back. But he ducked under a hanging vine and dove into the ditch. Just as he landed, he heard a grunt behind him and then heard Sandy go down. He hoped the guy had only failed to duck for the vine and had fallen, but he feared the worst.

The bombs kept falling for several minutes, and shrapnel was flying overhead, cutting through the brush and palm trees. Wally didn't raise his head to look, but it was all he could do to stay down. He just hoped Sandy was staying flat and the shrapnel was passing over him, but chances were, he was cut up and bleeding.

The attack was soon over, and even though Wally knew that Zeros often strafed the area after the bombs stopped falling, he climbed out of his ditch and crawled quickly back to the point where the vine hung over the trail. But no one was there. Other men were climbing out of the trench now, and Wally shouted, "Where's Sandy? Did anyone see him?"

Just then Wally heard a yell from the ditch, off to the left. "Hey! Hey! Hey! Hey, you guys!"

Wally ran to the ditch, dropped onto his knees, and looked down. Sandy was lying on his back, dirty but smiling. He held up both hands, each still full of cigars. "Don't any of you guys want a cigar?" he asked.

Wally took a long breath, and then he sat down and began to laugh. Everyone else was laughing too, and it felt good. It struck Wally that he hadn't laughed for a long time, and he found himself continuing to enjoy himself even after the joke was long over. All the other men were doing the same thing—laughing much harder than was probably called for.

The days that followed didn't bring much more laughter. The men tried to stay in good spirits, and they settled into their new routine of waiting and hoping to survive. Gradually, however, word began to filter in that the Japanese had landed on the island, both north and south, and that the troops were pushing from both directions toward Manila. MacArthur had been training a civilian army—the Philippine Scouts—for a long time, and the men placed great hopes in them, if not in MacArthur. Those who had dealt with the general knew how pompous he was. Most took the view that he cared about very little other than furthering his own purposes. Still, the Scouts were fighting to save their own country, and though the Americans were limited in numbers and equipment, like the Filipinos, they had their backs to the wall. The talk was that the Japanese were not likely to have landed enough troops to overpower both the Filipino and American forces.

In the following week, however, the news was not good. The Scouts fought bravely at Lingayen Gulf, north of Clark Field, but their horse-mounted troops were no match for the firepower of the Japanese ships and airplanes along with heavy artillery and well-equipped ground troops. News on the radio of the valiant defense by Filipino and American soldiers was always impressive, but it invariably came with the information that those same troops had fallen farther back.

Clark Field was in the path of the attacking Japanese ground troops. Somehow, the United States had to get help to the island or the airfield would be overrun before long. The tension kept mounting—and Wally was beginning to accept fear as part of all his thoughts—but no one actually knew what was going to happen. And then, a few days before Christmas, word came that Clark Field was to be abandoned.

Wally knew his skills as supply sergeant were going to be important again. As his men fell back, he wanted to transport everything he could, even though he had few vehicles. One thing that occurred to him was that a big load of laundry had been taken to Manila before the first air attack, and those uniforms had never been returned. The men were wearing clothes that were filthy in spite of their attempts to hand wash them. He talked to his supply officer, who was able to persuade the C.O. to let Wally take a ton-and-a-half truck and drive into Manila.

Wally took Warren with him, and the two were able to make the eighty-mile trip into Manila without any difficulty. They obtained the uniforms from the laundry, even stopped at a YMCA for a wonderful, sudsy bath, followed by an ice-cream sundae, and then they headed back toward Clark.

In Manila, the people were nervous. Word had it that President Quezon and General MacArthur were getting off Luzon and heading for the little fortress island of Corregidor. The people took that as a sign that Manila was going to be left wide open for the Japanese to take. No one knew what that would mean, but panic was setting in. Some people were fleeing, but most knew nowhere to go.

The road heading back to Clark Field was already much

busier, and the going was slow. Most of the traffic was heading south, and troops, both American and Filipino, were moving heavy artillery, sometimes taking up both lanes of traffic.

At one point, Wally was forced to stop. A couple of men were looking under the hood of an army truck that was stopped in the lane of traffic. Wally leaned out his truck window and yelled, "Hey, what's going on?"

"I don't know. We're broke down," a G.I. shouted back.

"Yeah, but what's happening up ahead? Why is the artillery moving?"

"The Orange Plan," the man yelled back. "It's MacArthur's emergency plan. Everyone's supposed to head into the Bataan peninsula, west of Manila."

"What for?"

"Combine all forces. Then hold out for reinforcements."

Wally heard a honk behind him. He knew he had to move on, but he was confused. He looked at Warren. "He's giving up almost the whole island. Bataan is just a little peninsula. The Japanese can hit us with everything they have."

"The mouth of Manila Bay is south of the peninsula," Warren said. "We've got ships there, and forces on Corregidor. That at least keeps Japanese ships from surrounding the peninsula."

"What difference does that make?" Wally asked. He ran his sleeve across his sweating forehead. "They can hit the whole area from the west."

"I guess it's the only thing we can do." Wally heard the fear in Warren's voice.

"Maybe the navy is coming to get us off the island. Like Dunkirk. Maybe we're all withdrawing, and then they'll bring ships into Manila Bay and pick us up."

"What ships?" Warren asked. "Where would they come from? The few ships we've got in the Bay couldn't start to do anything like that."

"Well, then, what's going to happen, Warren? Can we hold

them off?" Wally glanced outside at the palm trees, the bougainvillea vines. This island had seemed such a paradise when he had first seen it. And now it was turning into a trap.

"I don't know, Wally," Warren said. "I think we're in trouble."

Neither said anything for a time, and Wally knew that Warren was as scared as he was. "We've just got to take this one day at a time," Wally finally said, but he knew he was trying to calm himself, and that no really good answer lay ahead.

"I've been praying a lot," Warren said.

Wally didn't comment. He had felt good that night, praying with Lieutenant Cluff, but he hadn't prayed since. He still didn't feel right about it.

When Wally and Warren finally arrived back at Clark Field, Wally had new worries. He knew he had to do what he could for his squadron. He pushed and negotiated, got some leverage through Major Teuscher, and managed to get a five-ton truck from Fort Stotsenberg. And then he went to work on the supply officer. Why leave supplies and uniforms behind for the Japanese to confiscate? The supply men saw the argument and told Wally to take anything he could get on his truck.

So Wally filled the truck to the brim and beyond. He not only got all the uniforms, socks, and underwear he could, but he also stacked in blankets and tents. He found the post exchange abandoned and unlocked, so he grabbed up boxes of toothpaste, soap, towels, shaving equipment, and anything else that looked useful. By the time he had finished loading everything on and then draping the supplies with canvas, the old truck was dangerously top heavy. But he liked the way he felt. If his squadron was going to have to hold out under a long siege, all this stuff was going to make the men's lives a little easier.

The P-40s were the first to clear out. They took off, bound for Bataan Field, another little dirt airstrip. Meanwhile, mechanics were stripping every spare part from the airplanes that had been damaged in the air strikes.

Finally, late in the day on Christmas Eve, the convoy got ready to roll. Wally was driving the big, over-balanced truck, which only got more top-heavy as a dozen men or so climbed on for a ride. The squadron simply didn't have enough vehicles to transport everyone, and so men began to scrounge cars where they could. One group of men showed up looking very pleased with themselves. They were driving a big old LaSalle convertible they had confiscated somewhere.

Along with Warren, Jack Norland managed to crowd into the cab of the big truck. Soon after the convoy began to roll, the sun set, but the word passed along not to turn on any headlights. Wally was now happy to have men on top of the truck, who could serve as extra eyes to spot hazards ahead.

As the convoy passed through the little town of Angeles, Wally said good-bye to Chicken Charlie's. "Carefree" was a word he had used but never thought much about, but now he already missed those days when he could wander into town, eat a chicken, and act rowdy with his friends. He wondered whether he would ever be able to do something like that again.

When the convoy reached another town, San Fernando, a little place Wally had passed through many times on his way into Manila, the trucks pulled to a stop by the city square. Word passed down the line that this would be a rest stop.

Wally didn't get out of the truck. He leaned forward and rested his head on the steering wheel. But about then bells began to ring in a church tower somewhere.

"Midnight," Warren said. "It's Christmas."

Wally pretended not to hear—pretended he was asleep. He couldn't have said a word. He pictured his home, his living room, and a memory—just an image—came to mind. Dad had been holding one of his Christmas meetings, and Bobbi had gotten up and walked to the piano. Wally saw it all—entirely—and was able to scan the walls, see everything as though he were sitting in the room again. He saw the old piano, and Bobbi in her blue dress with the gold buttons. He saw the front window, a panel of stained glass along the top, and the yellowish light in the room. He remembered the wallpaper, the shelf in the corner. And he saw the girls and Gene sitting on the floor, Mother in her chair—and Dad.

Wally remembered how much he had hated those meetings, how tough he had been on his father. It all seemed so strange now to think he could have felt that way.

What time was it there? What did his family know about what was happening to him? When would he see them again? When would he be home for another Christmas?

Wally tried to drift away. He just wanted to sleep and not think, but the image was in his head, and he couldn't get rid of it. There was his dad, sitting in his big chair, holding his Bible in front of him, his reading glasses perched on his nose. Wally knew better than to think of the words—or his father's voice—but phrases came back to him anyway: "Glory to God in the highest, and on earth peace, good will toward men." Wally heard it like a hymn, with that full, strong voice, and he ached to be home.

· C H A P T E R ·

3 4

The Thomases tried to make the best of Christmas morning. A heavy snow had fallen the night before, which would have been wonderful most years, but it didn't help much today. Everyone wanted to be cheery for the sake of the girls, but LaRue was twelve now, and Beverly ten, and even though they expressed some excitement about their presents, they felt the gloom as much as the others. Every day in the newspapers there were new reports of Japanese submarines spotted off the coast of California, and each of the major West Coast cities had taken a turn at public panic when real or imagined Japanese airplanes had been sighted. The whole nation was still waiting and wondering whether the Japanese would attack the continent. Roosevelt was talking about higher taxes and great sacrifices, with shortages of almost all goods, and young men all across the country were signing up "for the duration plus six months." Worst of all, wherever the Japanese had attacked, they were winning deadly, decisive victories, and reports from the Philippines were not good.

After the presents were opened, whatever fun the family had been able to generate died quickly, and the room fell silent. The year before, President Thomas had been worried about

Wally's behavior. This year, obviously, he was worried about his life.

He waited until the girls were carrying their things upstairs, and then he said to Bobbi and Alex, "I don't like what I'm reading about Wally's situation. Our troops just keep falling back."

"I know," Alex said. "I've been following the news every day." Actually, he knew even more than he wanted to say. That week he had talked to a high official in the Boeing company in Seattle—a company Alex had some contracts with. The man had predicted that the United States could not throw its full power against Germany and Japan at the same time. The weapons weren't ready, but even more, there simply weren't enough troops. This next year would see huge growth in the numbers, but all those people would have to be trained.

"I'm in touch with people in Washington," the man had said, "and I'm hearing a lot of 'Europe first' talk. One man—and I've got to say that he's very highly placed—told me the Philippines would have to be sacrificed."

"Sacrificed? What does that mean?" Alex had asked.

"You tell me. Those boys over there don't have a chance."

Alex didn't want to tell his family any of that. He wanted to believe that the man was mistaken. But Alex saw nothing, heard nothing, that gave him much hope.

"I keep telling myself that maybe Wally needs an experience like this," President Thomas said. "Maybe it's the one thing that will humble him." He hesitated for a few seconds and then added, "But I wish I had done things a little differently with Wally. It got to the point where he and I couldn't talk to each other—and that was my fault as much as it was his."

Bobbi said, "Dad, he was just trying to grow up. It was a hard time. You two will get along fine when he gets back."

That only introduced the other question. Dad looked toward Bobbi, but his eyes seemed distant, and he didn't say anything.

"We need to have our Christmas meeting, Dad," Bobbi said.

Alex saw his dad's eyes move away from Bobbi's. "Maybe we shouldn't have a meeting," he said quietly. "Wally never liked my preaching."

"I'll bet he'd love to hear you right now."

"Well, let's just read the Christmas story from the Bible. I think he did like that part."

Once Mom could get away from the kitchen, and Gene could be hunted down, the family gathered as they had done for so many years. Dad asked Alex if he would read the verses in Luke, but everyone protested. They wanted Dad to do it, and he did. But when he was finished, everyone was struggling.

Gene ducked his head. When Mom put her arm around his shoulders, he said, "What's going to happen to Wally? Why won't anybody around here tell me the truth?"

Gene had come into his own in the past year. He was sixteen and pimply and a little awkward looking, but he was beginning to show what a fine athlete he was going to be, and it was almost as though he felt some need to take over for Wally as the family comedian. Everyone knew he had a stronger sense of connection to Wally than Alex did. He was always the one to bring up childhood memories, or to tell stories about things he and Wally had done together.

No one answered Gene for a time, but Alex thought it only right that all of them, even the girls, were prepared for the possibilities. "It doesn't look good," he said. "Our soldiers don't have the weapons or the numbers of troops they need to hold off the Japanese. And there's no way to send in reinforcements."

"Why can't they all just come home?" LaRue asked.

"We don't have the ships to get the soldiers off the island," Alex answered.

"Will the Japs shoot Wally?" Beverly asked.

No one said anything for a time. No one even looked at Beverly. Then, finally, Mom said, "We hope not, Bev." But tears had begun to run down Mom's cheeks.

Alex looked around the room. The full truth of the situation was finally out in the open, and Alex saw nothing but fear in everyone's eyes.

Wally drove the truck all night. The convoy moved slowly in the dark, and once the trucks left the Manila road and headed onto a dirt road into the Bataan peninsula, the going got rough. Wally strained to see, without headlights, and there were times when he was afraid he would turn the truck on its side. It was still dark when the C.O. halted the convoy and passed the word down the line for everyone to find a spot in a bamboo thicket and get a little rest.

Wally and Warren and Jack each grabbed a blanket and dropped in the first spot they could find. Wally had a little more trouble falling asleep than the other two, but he drifted off after a time. It was nine o'clock before someone came by and said, "The cooks have breakfast ready."

Wally was still very tired, but he got up and carried his blanket back to the truck. Then he and his friends walked along the road to a place where the cooks had managed to pull a few things out of the back of the mess truck. Breakfast was coffee and bread and jam, except that the bread tasted more of gasoline than of jam.

Wally had fallen into the habit of drinking coffee with his breakfast, but he turned it down this morning, even though he was left with nothing else to drink. He had always felt a certain nagging guilt when he broke the Word of Wisdom, and right now he didn't want to be carrying any extra burdens.

"Merry Christmas," Warren said.

He didn't seem to mean it ironically, but Wally felt it that way. "I don't think Santa found us last night," he said.

"The Japs probably shot him down," Jack said, but no one laughed.

"The word is, we're not moving again until night," Warren said. "We'd be too easy to attack in the day."

That made sense, and Wally was glad they were in a spot

where there was plenty of cover for the trucks. But the day would be long, sitting and waiting, and Wally couldn't get it out of his head that it was Christmas, not a day to be stuck in a flea-invested bamboo thicket. After "breakfast" Wally and his friends caught a little more sleep, and then they passed the time doing nothing, talking at times, thinking more. Just after noon a supply truck came down the road, and to everyone's surprise the cooks received the makings of a pretty good Christmas dinner. The canned turkey wasn't quite like Mom's, and the mashed potatoes looked more like potato soup, but all in all, it wasn't bad. The food seemed to lift everyone's spirits a little—just not enough.

Wally sat on the ground and leaned against the wheel of his truck. He and his buddies speculated about where they might be going and how the Japanese would respond to their retreat into Bataan. But that kind of talk was depressing, not to mention frightening, and talk about home was even worse. Before long they had all three become quiet. They tried to sleep again, and Wally managed to drift off a couple of times, but he was uncomfortable and nervous, and he didn't sleep much.

Late in the afternoon, a mechanic from the squadron, a fellow named Arnold Karn, walked over to them. "Hey, fellas," he said, "some girls have opened up for business in a little shack down the road. There's already a long line, so if you want your chance, you'd better get down there."

Wally, of course, wasn't interested, and neither was Warren. Wally glanced at Jack to see what he would say, but he shook his head. After Arnold walked away, Wally felt much more depressed. Something about men acting that way only reminded him of how far he was away from home and of the things he associated with Christmas in the Salt Lake Valley. He thought of the time he had taken LaRue and Beverly shopping downtown—the decorations, the girls in their new coats and hats, the funny tie they had bought for Dad. And then he thought of Lorraine and the pretty red dress she had worn one Christmas day. He knew he would never marry her, but he wished he could see her one more time. It would be nice to sit on her porch and talk for a while, tell her what he was thinking. Maybe she would even see some changes in him.

He thought of the last time he had talked to her. He could see her standing there on the porch, the golden light making her hair and skin so beautiful. He heard her whisper, "I love you too, but it never would have worked." There were things in this world too lovely not to hold onto, and he had let Lorraine get away. But then, she had been right. It wouldn't have worked— not then.

And then a tune came into his mind: "I get along without you very well. Of course I do." But he couldn't let that get into his head. He sat up. "So what do you think?" he said, laughing. "Who's going to win the Rose Bowl?"

Jack had been asleep. He rolled over on his blanket and looked at Wally. "What?"

"Who's going to win the Rose Bowl?"

Jack dropped his head back onto his blanket. "Who cares?"

"Who's playing?" Warren asked. He had been lying on his back with his arm over his eyes, but clearly he had not been asleep. Wally sensed that he wanted to talk—that, like Wally, he was ready to stop thinking.

"I don't even know," Wally said. "I thought maybe you guys knew."

"It's Duke and . . . somebody. Oregon State College, I think," Jack said, but he still sounded disgusted about being awakened.

"What are you talking about?" Wally said. "Last year you were laying down bets with all takers."

Jack nodded. "I know," he said. He sat up slowly and then leaned against a spindly little palm tree that was struggling to survive under the canopy of bigger trees. "I got cured on betting. Last summer, when Ted Williams was batting over .400

halfway through the year, I gave some big odds that he'd never keep his average that high all year."

Wally knew about that. He laughed. But Warren, who was sitting cross-legged close to Wally, said, "We missed a great baseball season at home." His voice had taken on a surprising sadness. "DiMaggio had that huge streak—hits in over fifty straight games."

"Fifty-six," Wally said, and he felt Warren's mood grabbing him, so he tried to think of something else. "Jack, what was your greatest moment on the football field?" he asked.

Jack obviously knew what Wally was doing, but he finally responded. "One time in high school I broke loose on a long run," he said. "Seventy yards or something like that. It was pretty late in the game, and that touchdown put us ahead. We won, and after"—he finally smiled—"everyone treated me like a big hero."

"What about you, Wally?" Warren said. "You played football too, didn't you?"

"I sat on the bench. My big plays were all with the cheerleaders, after the game." Wally grinned, and then he pretended to hold a girl and give her a big kiss.

"Didn't you really get in the games?" Jack asked seriously.

"Not much," Wally said. "My best sport was track. But I quit that in the middle of my senior season."

"Why?"

But now the conversation had taken the wrong turn. Wally pulled a long stem of grass from the ground and rolled it in his fingers. "I just . . . didn't like it. The coach made me run the four-forty, and it about killed me. Maybe my dad's explanation was right—he said I was a quitter."

"If you were good, why did you quit?" Jack asked.

"I don't know. I had it in my head that I had to beat my brother's record. When I found out I didn't have it in me to do it, I just decided . . . to heck with it."

"Sometimes you still talk like you're in competition with your brother," Warren said.

"I know. But now, it seems stupid." Wally stuck the grass in his mouth for a moment, but then he took it back out and said, "I wish I could have a chance to do certain things over in my life."

"Hey, we're young," Jack said. "We'll have plenty of chances."

"Sure. If . . . you know . . . we get back."

"We're not going to die, Wally," Jack said. "So don't start talking that way."

Wally nodded, but he glanced at Warren. And he saw the same solemn awareness in Warren's eyes that he felt in himself. "Right now," Warren said, "I wish I'd never come over here."

"Yeah, me too," Wally said. "Next Christmas I'd like to be home."

"Yeah, well," Jack said, "me too. As far as that goes."

The Stoltzes spent their lives in the Hochs' cellar. Bombs fell quite often, always during the night, and officials devoted their days to keeping the city operating. That meant it was possible to hide out in a basement with little thought that authorities would bother to come around checking—and the Stoltzes were thankful for that measure of safety. For the first few days, the cellar had been a second chance at life, after death had seemed so close. Gradually, however, life in cramped, dark quarters had become a tedious imprisonment. A better answer always seemed necessary, but one day followed another, and the Stoltzes remained in the little room, hardly big enough for all of them to sit in comfortably.

The cellar was for storage—for fruit and canned goods, for produce in summer—not for people to live in. The rock floors and walls were cold and hard. Only a tiny window, high on one wall, emitted a little light. An electric light made reading possible, but reading material was limited. During the day, the

Stoltzes sat on two small mattresses; at night, they slept on those same mattresses, with feather ticks for covering. Peter slept next to his father and tried not to take up much room. Brother Stoltz struggled all night, every night, to find any rest. The pain in his shoulder and knee made every position unbearable after a time.

When Christmas came, tedium was beginning to turn into despair, but the Hochs tried to do what they could to make things pleasant. President Hoch was too old to be called into the military himself, but he had a son in France, and another, a married son, was part of the Czech occupation. Both sons were safe for the moment, but the Hochs feared the future and were not really in merry spirits. All the same, Brother Hoch came home with a Christmas tree. It was actually only a branch from a fir tree. He had found it in a park, where a bomb had ripped the tree apart and burned most of the branches. But this branch was healthy, if not exactly shaped right, and Brother Hoch built a stand for it. On Christmas Eve, the Stoltzes came upstairs, and the two families decorated the tree with ornaments—but no candles—and then sang Christmas carols.

The next morning, on Christmas, the Hochs had a little gift for each of the Stoltzes. Both President and Sister Hoch worked now, Sister Hoch because it was required of her. Brother Hoch had worked for the city before the war, keeping up parks and gardens, but all that was gone now, and he spent his days doing salvage work—primarily removing rubble and digging out those left alive after bombing raids. It was a discouraging, never-ending task. Every week he faced new heaps of debris, often a new one created overnight, with fires still burning and the smell of burnt or rotting flesh.

At every bombed-out building there were relatives waiting for news, or there were those who had just heard what they dreaded to hear. Sometimes, President Hoch got someone out—someone trapped but still alive. But more often he found people who might have lived had the rescue effort moved more quickly. These were people who had slowly died of hunger or exposure. Sometimes they had clawed until their fingers were bloody. Others were found sitting in air pockets, trapped, serene, as though they had accepted their deaths and merely waited.

President Hoch told Brother Stoltz more about this than he wanted to hear. It seemed, however, that President Hoch needed to tell someone, as though to carry it in his head night and day were too much for him.

The Hochs had to deal daily with one major problem: They had four extra mouths to feed, and rationing cards limited the amount of meat, butter, produce, and other commodities they could buy. Brother Stoltz had turned over all his cash to the Hochs, and that helped to buy potatoes and flour, but they had to be careful about how much food they were seen carrying into the house. They used some of their stored food, and they kept a small garden out back, but they also relied on others. They said little of this, but the Stoltzes knew that members of the branch were bringing food. President Hoch assured Brother Stoltz that he hadn't told other branch members that he had refugees in his home. Letting that word out would be too dangerous for the Stoltzes *and* the Hochs. But he must have appealed for help in some way, because the food kept coming.

Today, however, was Christmas. President Hoch told the Stoltzes, "I know your existence in our cellar is very difficult, but let's find some joy in the idea that you were able to find us—and that we are all alive."

"We'll never be able to thank you enough," Sister Stoltz said. "We can only pray that somehow better days lie ahead."

Anna had a hard time seeing how that could happen. She sat near the tree—the branch—on the floor, and she tried to find pleasure in the decorations, the little gifts, but she could see no way out. Even if the war ended, the Stoltzes' problem with the Gestapo would not go away unless Germany lost the war, and that was not going to happen quickly.

As the bombs dropped on Berlin, other possibilities seemed just as likely. Sooner or later, the Hochs' house could take a direct hit, and all of them would die. Or the Gestapo could somehow find out that the Stoltzes were there, and the family would be dragged off to prison—or worse. Or perhaps, most unthinkable, the war could drag on, and Anna would spend her young adulthood in this prison. The Hochs were kind to put their own lives in danger this way, but the fact was, life was going on somewhere, and Anna was seeing nothing. She spent her days waiting, with almost no hope of any change, any fun, any satisfaction. Her father had taken it upon himself to continue her education, and Peter's, but he had few books to work with. Brother Hoch tried to bring home something from time to time, books he salvaged from destroyed homes, but it was hit and miss as to what he could find.

"It doesn't matter. The important thing is that you keep learning," Brother Stoltz told his children. "We have to keep our minds going if we want to survive."

Anna did believe that, and sometimes she was able to lose herself in her books for hours at a time. But the terrible reality was still there. She never saw the sky. When she went upstairs to use the toilet, she saw sunlight filtering through curtained windows, but she couldn't part those curtains and look out. She lived in a world where exercise was nothing more than running in place, and where the only joy was the occasional laughter the family could make for itself.

But Anna did dream. She imagined a life someday, after all this. She pictured herself strolling through the woods, hearing songbirds. She liked to remember what it felt like to be outside, to go where she wanted, to walk to a grocery store, or to ride a bicycle. Sometimes, still, she imagined herself seeing Alex. She had his picture, although she sneaked a look at it only now and then, and she sometimes allowed herself a little fantasy, always the same. He would fight his way through the danger, hunt until he found her, and then lift her and her family out of this place. When the bombs fell at night, and the rumble came closer and closer, she would shut her eyes and picture it. But after, when the bombs stopped, she would find it all very childish. She never mentioned Elder Thomas to her parents, but she kept him as "Alex" for herself, and when her family mentioned him, she acted as though she took little interest in the subject.

After dinner, Peter told the Hochs about a wonderful Christmas when the elders had been with them in their home in Frankfurt. Sister Stoltz cried at the memory, and Father reminisced about the branch and then told the story of his conversion. Sister Hoch was a quiet, warm person with a round face and round, dark eyes. "Ernst brought me to the Church," she said, and she laughed. "I wasn't going to join a *sect*, no matter what he told me. But he was so kind, and I wondered what made him this way. That was the beginning of my interest."

Brother Hoch told more of the story, how he had joined the Church in Leipzig after the missionaries had taught his family for more than a year. But when he had met Sister Hoch, he had fallen in love *instantly*, he said, and he had made up his mind he would never give up until she believed as he did. Five years actually passed before she joined, but he refused to give up, and after she joined, they finally married.

All this time Anna said nothing, but she loved this story, and, of course, she thought of Alex. She wondered what he was doing on Christmas day. She tried to imagine Salt Lake City—the white, two-story home he had told her about, the brothers and sisters. In her image of things, Alex was there, and he wasn't married. He still had her picture. He kept it close, where he could look at it often.

Anna had heard the news that America had been attacked by Japan and that Hitler had declared war on the United States. Anna wondered whether Alex would become a soldier. What if he died fighting the Japanese, or worse, fighting Germans? He was such a gentle man, not someone to kill, and certainly not someone who ought to be killed.

The Stoltzes stayed upstairs much longer than ever before. The Hochs kept the curtains drawn, but for Anna, being out of the cellar seemed almost like being free, and so the day was good. But that evening she had to go back, and the temporary freedom only made the confinement seem worse. But Sister Stoltz suggested that the family sing Christmas songs, and that helped some, even if it brought back difficult memories.

35

President Thomas was sitting in his office at the dealership one day late in March when he looked up to see Mat Nakashima standing in his open doorway. "Hello, Mat," he said, but already he saw the concern in his friend's face. "What's wrong?"

"I'm wondering whether you can help me."

"Sure. What is it?"

Mat stepped into the room, his hat in his hand. He was wearing a suit, something he avoided most of the time. President Thomas motioned for him to sit down. "You know my brother—the one we call Ike?"

"Yes. Sure."

"He's been arrested."

"Arrested? What for?" President Thomas couldn't have been more surprised. Ike was like Mat, a hard-working man, very highly thought of in the south end of the valley.

"He went to California for the winter—to work. He was living with my uncle and aunt in Fresno. Now the government is rounding up the Japanese—all up and down the coast."

Suddenly President Thomas understood. He had heard that this was happening. "Yes, I know, Mat. But I didn't think they were arresting people like Ike."

"They're taking anyone of Japanese heritage. It doesn't

matter how many generations back a family has been in the country."

"They're looking for spies, Mat—fifth columnists. You can understand how people feel."

Mat looked at the floor for a few seconds, and then he said softly, "President, they aren't rounding up German Americans."

"Germany hasn't attacked us. Japan has. Japanese submarines have been spotted right off the coast."

"German U-boats are sinking ships on the other coast."

President Thomas hardly knew what to say. "It's nothing against any of you. It's just a way of being careful."

Mat took a long look at President Thomas, but he didn't try to argue.

"Listen, Mat, they don't know who to pick up and who not to. Maybe I can get in touch with some people. I know a local FBI agent. If I let the right people know that Ike grew up here, maybe they'll let him come home."

"What about my uncle and aunt?"

"That's going to be harder, I suspect."

"President, they've lived in California for thirty years. They farm. They pay their taxes. They have *citizenship*. They're just as American as you are. This isn't right."

President Thomas believed that, but he also knew the panic that was spreading across the country. America had never been attacked before. "Mat, people do things differently during a war," he said. "I'm not saying it's a good thing. But when people are this scared, they need reassurance. Right now, I'm not sure it's safe for your relatives. People feel so much resentment against all Japanese."

Mat stood up. "President Thomas, never mind," he said. He stepped toward the door. "I'm sorry I bothered you."

"No, wait. I'm just trying to explain."

Mat set his hat on his head. For the first time he looked angry. "Explain what? That no matter how long Japanese live in this country, they're still *Japs?*"

President Thomas couldn't think what to say. For the past two months he had never had an hour go by without wondering what was happening to his son. He had lain in bed at night and wished that American ships could somehow get to the Philippines, that they could blow those treacherous Japs off the face of the earth. But now, here was his friend Mat, who had grown up in his ward, who had turned to him in times of hardship. "Mat," he said carefully, "no one has anything against you, personally."

"President Thomas, when people talk about Germans, they talk about Hitler and the Nazis—the bad people who have misled the Germans. But every day I hear that "the Japs" did this or did that. Couldn't the leaders be at fault in Japan, too?"

President Thomas felt the power of the argument, felt confused by all his conflicting emotions. He stood up and walked around his desk. "Look, Mat, you're misunderstanding me. I don't feel good about any of this. I'll make some calls. I'll see what I can do for Ike."

"All right, President. Thank you." Mat stepped to the door. "And I'm sorry. I'm very upset right now."

"Maybe this is all just temporary—until the government can sort things out."

"I hope so."

"Well, let me get on the phone, and I'll get back to you before the day is over." He reached out, and Mat stepped back and shook his hand.

But when the day was over and President Thomas had spent the afternoon on the phone with local officials, and then with men in offices in California, he had little hope to offer Mat. In fact, although President Thomas didn't say it, he wondered what might happen to Mat himself—even though he was not on the coast. President Thomas was almost sick from all the times he had heard "slant-eyes" or "sneaky little nips" roll so easily off men's tongues. But when his thoughts returned to Wally, he found it hard to deal with his own attitude. He knew he was supposed to be a man of God. He had been taught—had taught—all his life that he shouldn't hate anyone. But Japanese soldiers were advancing into the Bataan Peninsula, could overrun American forces any day. He had read it in the paper just that morning. How was he supposed to feel about men who wanted to kill his son?

President Meis was sitting at the kitchen table in Sister Goldfarb's apartment. "I'm afraid I have some bad news," he had begun. She was waiting now, gripping her hands together, her face white.

"Your husband has been taken away. I don't know exactly when it happened, but his shop is boarded up, and he is gone."

Sister Goldfarb sat for a long time, nodding, tears in her eyes, but President Meis could tell she wasn't surprised. "How do you know this?" she finally asked.

"I heard rumors, so I went there."

"Weren't you afraid to be seen in the ghetto?"

"Yes. I was."

She didn't say anything, but her eyes were clearly asking the question.

"I'm ashamed of myself, Sister Goldfarb. I wish I had never told him to stop coming to church."

"You were not wrong to be afraid. I don't blame you for that." Sister Goldfarb folded her arms around her slender body, as if she needed to cling to something—and had only herself.

President Meis was always careful what he said, but there were things he needed to express. "At first, I kept telling myself that Hitler was good for Germany. But I see what's happening. Bruder Stoltz stood up to the Gestapo, and now he's gone. His entire family. A Gestapo agent came to my house, his face bandaged, and he demanded that I tell him where the Stoltzes were hiding. I had no idea, but he knocked me down and kicked me anyway. I don't know whether he found the Stoltzes."

Sister Goldfarb nodded. "Where are they taking people?" she asked. "Where are they putting the Jews? Do you know?"

"In concentration camps. That's all I hear. Some, I know, are in Poland."

"Will the Nazis kill my husband?"

"I wish I could tell you that they won't, but I'm not sure. Terrible rumors are starting to spread. It doesn't sound good." He ran his fingers along the edge of the table, over the oilcloth cover. He couldn't stand to look at her. "Maybe it would be better if we lost the war—quickly. Your husband might have a better chance of being set free."

"You are a traitor to say such a thing," Sister Goldfarb said.

"I know."

"Are others beginning to feel this way?"

President Meis found himself whispering. "I don't know. I'm sure that some do."

"You were good to come here, President."

"I want you to come to church. I plan to visit you and your daughter. There are things that are right. I want to do them."

Sister Goldfarb pulled a little handkerchief from her apron, and she wiped her eyes, but she was under control. "Yes, there are things that are right. But you must live, and so must I. And I must protect my daughter. So please don't come again. I'm afraid the Nazis will want her next—because she's Jewish in their minds."

"I plan to check on you. I won't come often, but I will from time to time. And others in the branch will contact you. We do want to help. I'm sorry we didn't do so sooner."

"It's all right." She patted his hand.

When Sister Thomas opened the door, she found Lorraine Gardner standing on her porch. "Oh, sweetheart, it's so good to see you," Sister Thomas said, and she swung the screen door open. The day was unseasonably warm, spring really coming on now.

"I was just wondering what you had heard about Wally," Lorraine said, and she sounded subdued.

"Come in, dear." The two walked into the living room and sat next to each other on the couch. "You're so beautiful," Sister Thomas said. "Prettier than ever. Poor Wally would give anything to see you right now. I'm sure of that."

"Has he written?"

"No. But I don't think he can get mail out. We only know what we read in the papers—the same as everyone else."

Lorraine sat with her feet together, leaning forward a little, her hands in her lap. "How's your family holding up?" she asked, a little absently, as though her mind were on other things.

"We're doing the best we can."

"Wally and Bobbi have always been so close. I'll bet this is hard for her."

"It is. She told me the other night that she wants to join the navy. I hope she gets that out of her head."

"I've been thinking the same thing."

"Oh, why, Lorraine?"

"I don't know. The world seems changed all of a sudden. College seems pointless when the whole planet is at war."

"Maybe so. But we have to keep normal things going, too. We can't just let everything fall apart."

Lorraine didn't answer. She was still leaning forward, looking down. Her silky hair covered most of her face. "What's going to happen to Wally?" she asked. "Can't America get any help to the men over there?"

Sister Thomas took a breath. "I'm not going to cry," she said, but tears were filling her eyes. "I've cried until there shouldn't be a drop of water left in me." She took another breath. "There's no sign, so far, that we can get any troops there—or any transports to get them out."

"I wish—" But Lorraine's voice broke. Sister Thomas reached out and pulled her close, and the two cried together.

"The last time I saw him," Lorraine finally said, "I wasn't nice. I told him all his faults."

"Well, he certainly has plenty of those." She leaned back, still holding Lorraine close. She looked across the room at the picture of Wally that she had put up recently. He was in his blue air corps uniform, grinning, looking cocky. She liked to think he hadn't lost all of that spunk.

Lorraine saw the picture and got up and walked to it. She stood and looked at it for quite some time before she turned around. "He was so good to me, Sister Thomas," she said. "I don't know whether anyone else will ever love me so much."

"Oh, Lorraine." Sister Thomas stood up, walked to Lorraine, and took her in her arms again. She felt the shaking in Lorraine's thin little body. "I just have to tell myself that some things are meant to be, and if he's supposed to live, he will."

"I want to see him again."

"Yes. I ask the Lord for that every day."

"Why do people think up reasons to kill each other?" But Lorraine was sobbing hard now, and so was Sister Thomas. Neither said anything for some time. They clung to each other and cried until they couldn't cry any longer. And it did help a little. But it didn't change anything. Sister Thomas didn't know what was happening to Wally, and the worst was that she wasn't going to know anything for a long time—maybe forever.

Bombs were dropping very close. The whole earth seemed to be in upheaval, the explosions rocking the house, shaking even the stones of the cellar floor. Anna huddled next to her mother, but she didn't scream. She shut her eyes and tried to see the scene she had rehearsed so many times in her mind. She imagined Alex opening the cellar door and climbing down the steps. "I've come for you, Anna," he always said.

And then a blast hit so close that the room filled with flaming light. The crash jolted the house, and upstairs, things fell.

Anna thought she heard a window break. But everyone was still alive; the bomb hadn't made a direct hit. Anna cringed and waited for the next one to drop. But the next one was not quite so close, and then the sound began to move away, until it was like the rumble of far-off thunder. It was then that the cellar door opened, and Anna saw light from above.

"Are you all right?" President Hoch called out. And now Anna could see that the light was a candle. The electricity was probably knocked out.

"Yes," Brother Stoltz said. "How much damage was done?"

"Some windows. A few things knocked off the walls. It's not serious." He took a couple of steps into the cellar and then sat on a step. He was wearing his heavy coat. Because of severe coal shortages, the house was never heated at night now. "In the morning," he said, "there will be people about—repairing, checking on things. We must be very careful."

"Yes, of course," Brother Stoltz said.

"I don't understand it," President Hoch said, and for the first time ever, Anna heard anger in his voice. "Why do the British bomb *civilian* neighborhoods? What's wrong with them?"

"President Hoch, what do you mean? Look what we've done to London."

President Hoch was sitting with the candle in front of him, its light gleaming in his wide-open eyes. "What are you talking about?" he said.

"Don't you know? Haven't you listened to British radio?"

"Of course not."

"You should, President Hoch. We're destroying cities all over England—just the same as they are doing to us. It's madness. It's like no other war, ever."

President Hoch was still staring, obviously in disbelief. "This is not true," he finally said. "We only bomb military sites. The Führer has said it is so."

Brother Stoltz gasped with pain as he rolled onto his side, and then he slowly got to his feet, grimacing as he straightened up. "President Hoch, I'm sorry. I don't want to say things that upset you. You have been so kind to us. But you need to know the truth. We are bombing all the large cities of England—and the British say we did it first."

President Hoch sat for a long time, silent, before he said, "I see the results of this war every day. I see what the British bombers do. I can't believe Germans would do such a thing to anyone. You're hearing only lies from England. That's why the Führer tells us not to listen."

Anna saw her father's head drop. "Ernst," he said, "why do you think I'm so twisted and broken? Germans did this to me—not some enemy."

"I know this. But I don't know why, and I don't want to know. I'm helping you because you're my brother."

"That's good. You're a wonderful man. But you're letting Hitler have his way—the same as I am—and he's destroying everything in his path. If I could get to the man somehow, I would take his life—and feel completely justified. I could save millions of lives by doing it."

Anna saw the shock in President Hoch's face, something close to panic. "I can't let you speak this way. Not in my house."

"I won't. Not again." His voice softened then, and he added, "Ernst, I'm sorry. I know we have to leave here soon. We've accepted too much of your generosity already."

"No. You are welcome to stay. But don't talk to me about the Führer. I must be loyal to my country. It's the only thing I understand."

"I know how you feel. I am also loyal to my country. But not to Hitler."

President Hoch sat for some time, seeming to consider. Finally, he said, "I can't think two ways at once. But let's not speak of this again. Sleep if you can, and then come up to the toilet very early, before the sun comes up."

"Yes. Thank you. I'm sorry to alarm you. I won't cause you any trouble."

"It's all right." He climbed up the steps and shut the door.

Anna lay in the darkness when he was gone. She could see a hint of red from the little window. Buildings were burning outside somewhere. People had died. Anna hated to think that the same thing could happen to her and her family. She was scared to think what still lay ahead for them. But she wasn't so unhappy as she had once been. She had something now that changed everything. Somehow, Alex had gotten a letter into Germany. It had apparently come through a Mormon diplomat before the attack on Pearl Harbor had brought the United States into the war. The letter had reached President Meis, in Frankfurt, and it had stayed with him for many months, but at a meeting of Church leaders—rarely held these days— President Meis had asked whether anyone knew the where- abouts of the Stoltz family. President Hoch had waited until the meeting was over, and then he had approached President Meis. "The Stoltzes are alive and well. I think it not wise to say any more than that."

"I understand," Brother Meis had told him. And then he had given President Hoch the letter and asked him to wish the Stoltzes his best.

When Anna read the letter, she was beside herself with joy. Alex expressed his love so sweetly, and he assumed nothing. He told her that he longed to think she felt the same about him, but by now, with the passing of all this time, she may have put him out of her mind. He was willing to wait for her, how- ever long the war lasted, but if she had found someone else— or was simply not interested—he understood. He hoped she could get a letter back to him.

So Anna was happy to know she was still loved, but she was fearful about the future. The letter had been written the year before, and much might have changed by now. For one thing, Alex might think she had not even tried to answer. So Anna begged President Hoch to find a way to get a letter out. President Hoch told her that he had lost his main connection—the Mormon diplomat who had now gone home—but he would try to work through a Church connection he had in Denmark. He couldn't promise anything, however. Anna had written the letter, and President Hoch had passed it on, but there was no telling whether it had gotten out. And worse, there was no way of knowing whether Alex had received the letter, or ever would, since there was now no way for him to write back. Anna had not even said where she was, or explained what had happened. She was too fearful that the letter would be intercepted and that her family would be found out.

Still, for the first time since moving into the cellar, Anna had something to hope for. If she never saw Alex again, at least she would have the satisfaction of knowing that he loved her, and that she had made a commitment to him—whether he knew it or not.

It was nine-thirty in the evening, so Bobbi was surprised when someone knocked, but she was happy when she opened the door and saw Alex. "Do you want to take a walk?" he said. "It's warm out tonight."

"Oh, yes. I have far too much to do, but I'd like to get out." She gave him a little hug. "Alex, it's so good to see you. Are you doing all right?"

"Yes."

She was surprised at how happy he looked. "You have something on your mind, don't you?" she said.

"Come on. Grab a sweater. I'll tell you."

Bobbi was intrigued, but she didn't bother with the sweater. She thought she would be warm enough. She was wearing jeans and a big flannel shirt that had once been Wally's. Once outside, Bobbi said, "I talked to Mom today. Is she really doing all right at the plant? She talks like she runs the place."

"She soon will," Alex said, and he laughed. "She already knows the operation better than anyone else down there."

"Except you."

"I'm not so sure about that. You can't believe how much of the paperwork she's doing for me now."

The two turned east, along Fourth Avenue. They had to duck to get under a low-hanging limb, but as soon as they were past the tree, Bobbi said, "So what's going on?"

"Well . . . I'm engaged."

"*What?*"

"I guess you could call it that. I got a letter from Anna today."

Bobbi stopped. "Are you serious? How did she get it out?"

Alex had taken a step ahead of Bobbi, but he turned and looked back. "I don't know how she did it. The letter was posted in Salt Lake. So someone brought it here for her. I think it must have come through Church channels somehow."

"But she didn't receive your letter, did she?"

"Yes. She finally did."

"Did she explain why her family moved away from Frankfurt?"

Alex began to walk again, but slowly, and Bobbi caught up. "Well . . . not really. She was careful in her wording. She said, 'We moved very quickly one day,' and I think that could mean they were in trouble—maybe with the Gestapo. I have the feeling she and her family are in hiding, because she didn't say where they were. But at least I know she's alive."

"She said something more than that, or you wouldn't look like the cat who ate the canary."

"Well, yes." He looked toward Bobbi and grinned. Alex was wearing a white shirt, but he had taken off his coat and tie. "She said she loved me, and she wants to marry me. We're committed now. We've both promised to wait for each other—no matter how long this stupid war lasts."

"Oh, Alex, that's wonderful. It's what you've hoped for, isn't it?"

"Sure. But it's pretty awful, too. I'm really worried that she's in danger. And a lot of things could happen between now and the time I get to see her again. It's one thing to feel that way now, and another to keep feeling that way for years."

"I think it's beautiful, Alex. Somehow, this whole thing is going to work out." Bobbi's eyes were filling with tears, and she knew she was feeling joy for Alex but also some envy.

"Well, we're caught in a strange situation, but at least there's a harmony between us. We're thinking alike. We still love each other."

"The Lord is helping you, Alex."

"Yeah. I think that's right."

Bobbi heard the huskiness in her brother's voice. "I wish we could hear from Wally now," she said. "That would be the other thing that would make me happy."

Bobbi wished immediately that she hadn't said it. It was just too painful to bring up when Alex had finally had something good happen. The two walked in silence for a time. The trees in the avenues were budding out now, and Bobbi could detect the sweet smell of blossoms.

"Bobbi, I've got something else on my mind." Alex shoved his hands into his pockets. "I don't feel good about staying out of the war."

"I thought that was all settled—you're helping the effort here at home."

"I know. But I feel like a draft dodger. Most of the guys I know from high school have already signed up—and I read every day about some movie star or athlete going in to volunteer. Bob Feller said he couldn't stay home and play baseball when there was a war to be won."

"What about the things President Clark told you?"

"Mostly, he was saying that nothing good comes from war, and I agree with him there. But we didn't choose to get involved. The Japanese made that choice for us."

"The way things are looking, though, you're more likely to end up fighting Germans than Japanese."

"I know. And President Clark warned me what could happen—that I'd end up full of hate for them—but I don't know what else to do."

"Can you shoot people and love them at the same time?"

"I don't know. But I keep thinking about Wally. How would I be able to look him in the eye when this is all over?"

"It might sound strange to you, Alex, but I'm thinking somewhat the same."

"What do you mean?"

Bobbi heard the electric trolley rattling along down on Third Avenue. The sound had become so much a part of her life since she had moved to the avenues, where trolley lines ran along Third, Sixth and Ninth avenues. "I've made up my mind to join the navy," she said. "My life may not ever be in danger, but at least I'll be part of the effort." Bobbi was feeling chilly now. She folded her arms around her middle. "It's like our family is in the war now, and we have to come to Wally's aid. It's the only way I know how to do it."

"When would you go?"

"Right after I graduate. I've applied, and I've been accepted. The only thing I haven't done is sign my name. Once I do, I'll have to deal with Dad."

In the subtle moonlight, Bobbi could see the big Victorian homes looming above her, and something in the civility of those homes seemed to suggest that the world had no right to change. The war was such an ugly intrusion into everything that was orderly and right. "Are you scared?" Bobbi asked.

"I'm terrified. I don't want to spend *years* of my life doing things I hate. And I don't want to die before I see Anna— before I'm sealed to her. That's the worst thought of all."

"At least you know she feels the same as you do."

"But that only adds to the worry." He walked for a time, but then he seemed to recognize what Bobbi must be feeling. He put his arm around her shoulders. "Are you okay?" he asked.

"Sure."

"No, come on. Tell me what's going on. Are you feeling all right about the way things have worked out for you?"

"I think so. Sometimes I wish I were the sort of person who could have fallen for Phil—and accepted life on his terms—or taken the leap and married David. But either way I would have given up some part of who I am. I'm pleased with myself that I didn't do that."

"I'll say this. I'm glad you didn't marry Phil. I never did like the guy. He was too slick for me."

"Oh, Alex, thank you. I've needed someone from the family to tell me that." She leaned in closer to him.

"Good things are going to happen to you, Bobbi. I'm sure of that. You deserve better than you've gotten so far."

"Thanks, Alex. I needed you to come by tonight." She turned and kissed him on the cheek. "Let's be happy. It's the only way to fight back against this stupid war."

"Not the only way. I've got to get some things straightened out at the plant; then I'm going to break the news to Mom and Dad; and then I'm going to sign up."

Bobbi hated to think of it: another brother in danger, one more terrible fear to live with, the family split further apart. "Alex," she said, "how are we going to get through this?"

"I've thought a lot about that lately. Dad always makes the early Saints sound so brave, but I doubt they were any braver than we are. They just did what they had to do. And that's what we're going to do now."

That sounded right. But Great Grandmother Thomas, during her trek to Utah, had buried two of her children out on the plains. Bobbi felt sure she could deal with hardship, but what if she had to deal with death? How could she give up one of her brothers?

36

Wally's squadron set up camp on the southern tip of the Bataan Peninsula. Wally and Warren had driven ahead and located a site near a stream, under the heavy tropical canopy. The men all dug foxholes, and that's where they slept, with a single blanket for bedding. Each day they hiked three miles to Mariveles Field, an airstrip close to the beach and across Manila Bay from the fortress island of Corregidor, where MacArthur had set up his headquarters. The men worked in the tropical heat to clear revetments for airplanes they expected from America. Rumor had it that a squadron of fighters would soon be on its way, and the men had to work hard to be ready for them.

Nights were frightening now that the Japanese had begun nighttime bomber raids, and the days were hot and exhausting. That would have been difficult enough had the troops had adequate food. Somehow, there had been a disastrous lack of preparation in putting "Plan Orange" into operation. No food, medicine, or weaponry had been moved with the troops. The G.I.s were aware of huge reserves of food near Manila, but almost none of it had gotten to the peninsula, and now that food was probably feeding the enemy.

The men ate only twice a day, and Wally, as supply sergeant, drove his truck about ten miles every evening to a supply station farther up the peninsula. At first he received ten round loaves of bread each day, along with rice and canned goods. But before long the men were forced to live on rice and whatever they could scrounge for themselves. Teams hunted monkeys or searched for carabao—a native water buffalo—which were rumored to live in the jungles. Others fished or searched for edible plants: banana stalks, bamboo shoots, roots. But the carabao were not to be found, and the fishing was difficult. Monkey hunting did supply some meat, and Wally soon found that he didn't mind it, although he tried not to think about what he was eating.

Through January the work on revetments had continued, but no airplanes arrived, and from radio reports the men knew that Japan was moving through the islands of the Pacific without difficulty. As the Japanese pushed to Northern Australia and then west into Indochina, Borneo, Malaysia, Burma, and on toward Singapore, the soldiers listened to Singapore radio broadcasts. The promise was that the British would never let Singapore fall, but then word came that two of England's great battleships had been sunk, and Singapore had been taken.

It was unnerving. By then, Wally's squadron had moved into abandoned Marine barracks near Mariveles Field. That made the men sitting ducks, and air raids often sent them flying for cover. What was worse, the truth was becoming obvious: airplanes were not coming, and neither were ships. These mechanics, cooks, and support personnel were now infantrymen, and their assignment was to defend the southern end of the peninsula. The heavy fighting was coming from the north, as Japanese troops drove the Filipino Scouts and American troops deeper into the peninsula. For now, because of the power of Corregidor, the southern beaches were not so threatened, but the Japanese constantly landed teams of guerrillas, who moved into the caves in the bluffs along the bay. From there they sneaked out to snipe and harass.

The G.I.s, in squads, combed the forests and tried to flush

out the guerrillas. Wally sometimes led a squad on night patrols. His men had been provided with nothing better than ancient Enfield rifles for weapons, and their aged hand grenades didn't always explode. Snipers fired at Wally on a couple of occasions, and he found himself about as brave as the next guy. But he was scared. He never slept well, and because of the watch schedule—six hours on, six off—he was always tired. He hardly remembered what it was like to sleep a night through.

Constantly, the news to the north was disturbing. The troops fought valiantly and, at times, pushed the Japanese back temporarily, but by late February, a great deal of ground had been lost. Wally's squadron eventually moved out of the barracks and back to the bivouac area, so they were under better cover, but food was getting more scarce and foraging more difficult. A horse or a domestic carabao sometimes died in an air attack, and the squadron would get some of the meat. For a day the men would feast, which helped get some strength back, but everyone talked constantly about the time when all food lines might be cut, even the daily ration of rice. Then what would they do?

So far, supplies of powdered quinine were holding out, and that kept the men from getting malaria, but the lack of nutrition was causing many of them to come down with beriberi, which caused their feet and legs to swell and ache. Others suffered from almost constant diarrhea, which led to dehydration. So far, Wally had avoided any serious illnesses, but he felt weak and tired almost all the time.

Wally's squadron had once dressed like dandies. The same men had now turned into a rough-looking bunch. They tried to stay clean and to shave, but they were losing weight, and the lack of sleep, the illness, the heat, the fear, were causing a numbness that Wally could see in everyone's eyes. Still, the men told each other they could hold out, and reinforcements would eventually come. They cursed MacArthur. "Dugout

Doug," they called him. And they cursed the politicians who had allowed the country to become so weak and unprepared, but they continued to believe that America would not let them down.

On April 8, Wally made his daily trip to the supply station. It seemed stupid to make the trip so often and to bring back such a little bit of food, but that's the only way he could obtain the squadron's ration of rice. Harvey Opdike, one of the cooks, said he would ride along. Harvey had the ability to laugh no matter what happened, so Wally liked to have him around.

This night, when Wally pulled the truck off the dirt road into the rendezvous site, no supply truck had arrived. That wasn't all that unusual, but Wally and Harvey waited for more than an hour and the truck still didn't show. By then, American and Filipino troops, not far away, had begun a barrage of artillery fire. When return fire started coming in, Wally knew he was in a bad spot. The truck was parked under dense foliage, but heavy stuff was crashing into the forest around them. The trees stopped the shrapnel, so only a direct hit would get them, but the noise was thunderous—really shattering to the nerves.

By about ten o'clock, the firing slowed and then died out. For a time the jungle was strangely still, not even any birds singing. But the quiet gradually became almost as nerve-racking as the noise had been. "I don't think the truck is coming," Wally finally told Harvey. He hated to return without food, but he was anxious to get away from the front line.

Harvey laughed. "We spend most of our time talking about hating rice," he said. "Now, a little rice sounds mighty good."

"If we go back without any, the guys might boil *us* for dinner."

"I doubt that. We ain't nothing more than stew bones about now." He pinched at his ribs. Actually, Harvey still had a layer of fat over his ribs, but he had been a heavy man at one time. He was a country boy from Alabama, but he was knowledgeable on an amazing variety of topics.

"So what do we do?"

"There ain't no use sitting here. That truck is probably blown sky high. Either that or those boys heard all that artillery and just decided to forget it for tonight."

And so Wally backed out, got the truck turned around in a tight spot, and headed toward the main road. But he was shocked by what he saw when he got there. Earlier, on the way up the peninsula, he had seen a few Filipino troops heading south, but now the road was clogged with men and trucks.

Wally swung down from his truck and approached a Filipino officer who was marching south with the others. "What's going on?" Wally shouted.

"The lines have broken. We have surrendered." The officer was an older man in a tattered, filthy uniform, and he looked broken, his eyes like empty caverns.

"What are you talking about?"

"The Japs have overrun us. It's all over." The man pushed on past Wally and continued down the road.

Wally climbed back in the truck. "That guy—that officer—said we've surrendered."

"What? Maybe the Filipinos, but Americans wouldn't surrender—not to a bunch of Japs. That's just bull. Let's get back to our squadron."

Wally edged the truck forward, into the crowd of troops, but the movement was extremely slow. The trucks ahead were hardly moving, and men were streaming around them, moving faster on foot than in the vehicles. An hour passed and Wally hadn't moved ahead much more than a mile. Then an enormous explosion rocked the truck. For a moment Wally thought a bomb had dropped. He was about to jump from the truck when Harvey grabbed his arm. A concussion from another explosion whistled through the trees and rattled the truck, and the whole sky lit up again.

"We're destroying our ammo," Harvey said. "Those big

ammo dumps are going up." He slammed his fist against the dashboard. "I don't believe this. We're giving up."

It was really happening. And here were Wally and Harvey stuck in a traffic jam, hardly moving. "This is a mess," Wally said. "What do we do?"

Harvey could make a joke out of almost anything, but he found nothing funny in this. "I don't know. We'll be all night at this rate—and then some. We've gotta get back to the squadron."

For the next couple of hours, Wally kept hoping that things would start moving better. But it didn't happen, so he and Harvey decided the truck had lost its value. Wally found a place to pull it off the road, and he and Harvey left on foot, cutting off through the jungle and over a mountain.

Wally was still trying to get used to the idea of a surrender. "What'll the Japs do to us?" he asked Harvey. "Aren't there rules they have to follow?"

"Japan didn't sign the Geneva convention agreement," Harvey said. "I don't know what to expect from them."

Wally wondered. Maybe if the Japanese set up some sort of prison camp and fed the prisoners, it wouldn't be all that bad. "They won't just march in and kill us off, will they?"

"I don't know. I don't trust 'em—I know that."

Wally didn't ask again. But all during the night he wondered what was coming. It was almost morning when he and Harvey finally walked into the bivouac site. They spread the word about the surrender, but most of the men didn't want to believe it. Major Teuscher had flown out in one of the few remaining P-40s a few days before. He was part of a plan to escort some supply ships into Manila Bay. But that meant Wally's squadron was directed by an acting commander, a lieutenant named Russell Dark.

Wally found Warren and Jack and pulled them aside. "It's a mess up there," he told them. "Everyone is on the run. We don't have that much time until the Japs get here."

Wally saw the confusion, the panic, in Warren's face, but Jack was trying to act tough. He raised his rifle to his side, as if to fire from the hip. "I say we keep fighting," he said. "Everyone knows what Japs do to prisoners. Let's die fighting."

"What do you mean? What do they do?" Warren asked.

"In China, they lined people up and shot them. When they did take prisoners, they starved them to death."

"That's just talk," Wally said. "You heard that from Barney and all those guys. They don't know."

"I don't want to be no prisoner of war—I know that."

Jack sounded brave, but Wally could see how scared he was. Warren was absolutely white with fear. For the first time, the full reality of the situation was settling in on Wally, and he felt his chest locking up, but he said, "Look, we'll get each other through. At least we'll be alive. We can last them out until Uncle Sam gets some troops in here to clear the Japs back out. Maybe that won't take too long."

Jack didn't argue. He set his rifle butt on the ground. "Let's go into the jungle and have a prayer," Warren said. Wally glanced at Jack, and then he looked down at the ground. "Right now, I need to scrounge some food for the squadron," he said. "The navy should be willing to break loose with some supplies. I'm taking the ton-and-a-half truck down to the bay. Do you want to come with me?"

"Sure," Jack was quick to say, and Warren didn't press the issue about praying. He and Jack piled into the truck with Wally. When the three of them reached the navy base, the supply clerks told them to take anything they wanted, so they began looking through all the gallon cans in the storage tunnel. "Prunes," Wally said. "That doesn't sound so bad right now."

Jack suddenly broke into a big laugh. " 'White navy beans' this can says. Beans and prunes—that ought to be a fine combination. Maybe we'll be able to defend ourselves after all."

Wally laughed, but he felt the nervousness, not just in his

friends but in the navy clerks. Still, a belly full of food would help his men, so Wally and the others started hauling cans to the truck, and when they returned to the bivouac area, they found that beans and prunes sounded just fine to the men. They ate as though it were their last meal. Wally found that his stomach filled very quickly, but he kept stuffing more beans into himself. It seemed wonderful to eat all he wanted.

He and the other men were polishing off the last of the beans when a series of pops sounded nearby. It took a moment to realize that machine gun fire was whizzing overhead and crashing through the trees. Everyone hit the dirt, and for a couple of minutes no one moved.

"It came from the road," someone finally grunted.

Wally had no idea what to expect. Maybe the Japanese weren't taking prisoners. But he heard Lieutenant Dark say, "Sergeant Thomas, come with me. Let's see what's going on."

The other men stirred, but most stayed down. Wally and the lieutenant got up, but they crouched as they walked carefully along a path through the jungle. As they neared the road, they came to a sudden stop. A Japanese tank was parked on the road, and an officer was standing with his head and shoulders sticking out from the turret.

The officer said, "Come forward." Wally fought back an impulse to turn and run, but the officer said, in excellent English, "You must give up your weapons." He hesitated, and when Lieutenant Dark didn't respond, he added, "Bring all your rifles and handguns to the road. Stack them here. Weapons in one pile, ammunition in another. You must do this by noon tomorrow. Your commanding officers have surrendered unconditionally. You have no choice but to do as I say."

Wally and the Lieutenant stood silent, unmoving.

"We might have killed you. We have chosen kindness. But you must not try to escape. If you don't cooperate here, we will kill *everyone* on Corregidor."

The officer's head disappeared, and then the tank rolled

ahead, the sound of the tracks resounding in the trees. Wally
and Lieutenant Dark said nothing to each other. It all seemed
unreal. But they walked back to the troops, and Lieutenant
Dark repeated the message. Wally watched the men. They
could hardly believe what was happening. "What will they do
to us?" Lieutenant Cluff asked.

Lieutenant Dark shook his head. "I don't know."

"We can't do this," one of the pilots said, a fellow named
Carter who was one of the old-timers with the unit. "Americans
don't surrender. This many Americans have *never* put their arms
down—not in all our history."

"Maybe we ought to head off into the jungle," Harvey said.
"We could hold out."

"I don't know how we'd eat out there," Lieutenant Dark
said, and he sounded unsure of himself. Wally wished Major
Teuscher were there. "Besides, we didn't make this decision.
Someone made it for us. I think we have to go along with this."

A big sergeant spat on the ground and swore. "Where's
Uncle Sam?" he said. "This ain't supposed to happen."

"Uncle found a way to get MacArthur off Corregidor,"
Harvey said. "Our lives must not be as important."

And that set things off. All evening the talk continued. The
men ate another meal, but not with the relish they had shown
before. Wally tried to take things hour by hour. He opened up
the supply truck and invited the men to take whatever they
wanted. He got himself a pair of coveralls and some new shoes.
He also grabbed some extra underwear, socks, soap, and a
safety razor. He stuck it all in a mosquito net.

So he was ready. There was nothing else to do but wait,
and what lay ahead was a very long night. Wally hardly slept
at all. He thought of home, thought of his decision to join the
air corps, thought of a thousand things. But mostly he wondered what his life would now be like. He tried to reassure
himself. Prison camp couldn't be much to look forward to, but
life would be endurable; he would make it.

Next morning the men in Wally's squadron stacked up
their weapons and ammunition, as instructed, and again they
waited. By now, no one had a lot to say. The time crawled by.
Not long after noon the first full units of enemy soldiers began
to arrive. The Japanese troops were scruffy looking, unshaven
and dirty. They carried heavy field packs on their backs, and
some of them were actually pulling artillery, like teams of oxen.

The G.I.s lined up, as instructed, and were expecting to be
marched off. But instead a squad of Japanese soldiers grabbed
the first men they approached, knocked them to the ground,
and ripped away anything that seemed of value: watches, rings,
pens.

Wally cringed and waited as more Japanese soldiers moved
into the squadron, spreading chaos. He told himself he must
not react when his own turn came. When two soldiers turned
to him, grabbed him by the shoulders, and shoved him to his
knees, he went down without a struggle. When one of the men
grabbed at his watch, Wally unbuckled the strap and handed it
over. Then one pointed to his East High class ring, and Wally
pulled that off too. Then the soldiers jerked him back to his
feet and grabbed the mosquito net he was still carrying. They
took almost everything, but they left his mess kit and a spoon.

That seemed to be the end of it. One soldier began to turn
away. But without warning, the other man suddenly struck
Wally in the mouth. Wally stumbled backward and caught
another blow in his chest. As he dropped to the ground, the
soldier's boot caught him in the right side. Wally rolled up and
hung on against the pain as he waited for the next shot. But it
didn't come, so he stayed down for the present and tried to get
his breath. Lying there with his eyes closed, he could still see
the rage in the soldier's face—the one who had kicked him—
and he couldn't understand it. What he knew for sure, however,
was that a nightmare had begun.

Wally took long breaths, let the pain in his side subside,
and then struggled to his feet. Something told him that he

couldn't let these men believe they had subdued him. He couldn't fight openly, but a mental battle had been engaged, and he was not going to be defeated. They could be as brutal as they wanted to be, but he wasn't going to cower.

Another airman next to Wally was taking a beating. He was a young guy named Anderson, one of the two squadron medics. Once the Japanese soldiers left him, Wally got down on his knees next to Anderson, even though he was still in a lot of pain himself. "Are you all right?" he asked.

Anderson moaned and then rolled onto his side. "They took my glasses," he said.

Wally knew how bad the boy's vision was, and he couldn't think why anyone would want his glasses. "It's okay. Get up. I'll help you." Wally knew instinctively that far worse was coming. All of them would have to keep getting up, no matter what, if they were going to get through this.

Once the looting and the battering was finished, the Japanese soldiers marched the men down to Mariveles Field, which was not far away. Along the way, other American and Filipino units were herded together—maybe five hundred men in all. Wally spotted Warren, and he worked his way over to him, and then Jack joined them. But they didn't say much; they didn't dare. Once at the field, the guards had all the troops lie down on the ground. For the moment, that seemed a relief. "What are they going to do?" Warren whispered.

"Don't worry about it," Jack told him. "We'll just take what comes."

And, of course, that was the only answer, but the time moved slowly as everyone waited, and one thing was becoming clear: Even in the intense afternoon heat, the guards were making no attempt to get water or food to the prisoners.

The day stretched on and on, and the uncertainty was as bad as anything. Men were allowed to walk to the edge of the group and relieve themselves on the ground, but otherwise, no one did anything. When the sun finally went down, still no food or water was offered. The guards stood at a distance, encircling the men on the ground, but they said nothing, made no attempt to explain what was happening.

Wally was still feeling pain in his mouth and along his side. But hunger, and especially thirst, were pressing aside every other concern. It was hard to think beyond those needs. If he could eat a little, and get some water in him, then he could handle everything else, but how long until that happened?

The prisoners sat, or they lay on the ground. Wally and Warren and Jack made occasional comments—mostly speculations about provisions—but they said little more than that. The night passed away fitfully, with little sleep, and when morning came, nothing changed. The prisoners received nothing to eat, and as the sun rose in the sky, it only seemed hotter and more sapping than the day before. But no one received water. Sometimes the Japanese guards wandered through the men, checking for valuables they might have missed, but they told the men nothing.

All day, again, the men stayed on the ground. Wally gradually felt a blessed sort of numbness. The lack of food and water was taking its toll, seeming to extract not just his strength but also his powers of concentration. He would shift his position, lie on one side for a time, then on the other, then sit up, but the deprivation was robbing some of his will. He already knew that this fight was going to be more difficult than he had imagined when the soldiers had knocked him down, and it would take place inside his own head.

The time passed slowly, but he continued to glance toward the sun. The only thing he could think to look forward to was the sunset, the reduction of that baking heat on his back and neck. He kept telling himself that the guards surely would provide food by evening and not put them through another night like the last. No one could let prisoners of war sit in a field and starve to death.

But there was no food or water again that night. And by

then, the numbness and exhaustion had stolen all life from the men's eyes. They sat, heads down, eyes shut much of the time, or they lay lifeless, sometimes curled up because of the pain in their stomachs. Wally would glance around from time to time and see his friends, already dehumanized and disheartened, and he wondered how much longer this could last. Men would start to die if water didn't come soon. Why didn't the guards just start shooting? Didn't they want to waste the ammunition?

The smell of the men—hundreds of them packed so close together—and the smell of all the human waste on the ground became increasingly sickening. And all during the ordeal, artillery fire boomed from above the beaches as the Japanese hammered away at Corregidor and return fire crashed into the hillsides. The noise, in time, became a loud but dull part of the numbness that was creeping into Wally's brain. The men were out of the line of fire for the present, but he wondered whether troops on Corregidor even knew where the prisoners were.

On the third day, guards began to ask who could drive a truck. Wally had no energy to drive, but he wondered whether he would receive food if he volunteered. "Do you think we should do it?" he whispered to Warren.

Warren didn't answer, but Jack looked over and said, "Why help them?"

Wally didn't know whether the trucks were to transport the men or if they were for some other purpose, but he had no desire to call attention to himself. He decided to keep his mouth shut. The guards pulled some men out anyway, but no trucks appeared. Wally had no idea what to make of that. Finally, in the afternoon, one of the guards called out, "Trucks come. You go north."

Wally twisted around to look. He thought the man meant that the trucks were in sight. Maybe they were loaded with food, and the men would be fed before they were transported. But he saw nothing, heard nothing, and the wait continued.

As evening came on, a guard stepped in front of the group

and spoke in English. "You are cowards," he shouted. "Japanese warriors fight to death. But you do not fight. And so we take you to prison. Do not expect kindness from us. You are lower than dogs. We must treat you this way."

He waited. Wally wanted to feel some of the anger he had felt at the first, but he had no energy to care about the insult. What he wanted was to see the trucks.

"Stand up now. Trucks will come. We march."

And so the men got to their feet. Wally felt his head swim. Not far away, he could hear the sound of the ocean, and he wished he could dive in. But trucks were coming. Maybe food and water. Wally told himself he had to hold out a little longer, and then everything would be all right.

The men were forced together, very close, and then told to move ahead. They marched down the airstrip to Mariveles Bay. There they saw a number of trucks, but they were American trucks that had been damaged in battle. There were no drivers, no sign that the trucks were to be used. The prisoners marched on by to the shores of the bay, and there they found more Japanese soldiers, with fixed bayonets. They glared at the Americans and shouted in angry voices, "Trucks come. You go." They forced the men onto the road that led away from the beach.

The prisoners marched as best they could in their weakened state. But as the sun disappeared, the darkness made the hike up the steep hill more difficult. The road was ankle deep in dust, and the men were so close together that they stumbled over each other. They sucked for breath, but they kept pushing ahead because they were being driven by the guards from behind.

Wally didn't know how long he could do this—how long any of them could—but the soldiers kept yelling about the trucks that were coming, and he told himself they surely must be telling the truth. Even these men must know that no one could walk very long after having nothing to eat or drink for three days.

Eventually, the Japanese directed the men off to the side of the road. In the darkness the prisoners stumbled to spots where they could sit down. Everyone was breathing hard, struggling against the exhaustion. Somewhere in the darkness Wally had lost contact with Warren and Jack. He had no idea where they were, and the loss was devastating. He had nothing to say to them; he merely wanted them there, near him. He had told himself all evening that the trucks were coming, but he was sure now that there were no trucks. There weren't going to be any trucks. That was just a lie to keep them going. Sooner or later, the Japanese had to feed them—just had to—but if they would make the prisoners go this long without anything, how much longer might they continue the punishment?

Wally felt something giving way inside himself. He was too tired already. How much more did these guards expect from him? He lay on his side and tried not to cry, to moan, not to let the ache, the numbness break him. He heard no whimpers around him, no cursing, rarely so much as a word. He knew that all these men were trying to decide the same thing: Could they do this? How long? Why not just quit—and die sooner rather than later?

But Wally couldn't quit—not this time. He needed to find some way to survive, needed strength. The decision to call on God was hardly a decision at all. The words were suddenly there in his head. "Oh, Lord," he found himself saying, "give me strength. Please. I know you don't owe me a thing, but I need help."

He lay there for a minute or so, and then he added, "Let me see my family before I die. Let me see my home again." He hesitated, and then he remembered to close his prayer in the name of Jesus Christ.

He hoped for some change, but he wasn't sure that he felt any. What he did know was that he had only just begun to pray. He started again, "Oh, Father in Heaven." And he continued all night. Sometimes he was fully awake, and sometimes he was somewhere close to sleep, but even then, he kept pleading.

37

Alex had gone to work very early on April 10, long before sunup. He had a million things to do. He was working on a new bid when one of his foremen, Max Sheldon, came in. "Mr. Thomas," he said, even though he was twenty years older than Alex, "I thought you'd want to see this." He handed Alex a copy of that morning's *Tribune.* Alex looked at the headline: "BATAAN ARMY OF 36,853 FACES DEATH OR CAPTURE."

Alex's breath caught. He scanned through the article and saw that the American and Filipino troops had been "enveloped." "The heroic epic of Bataan Peninsula ended Thursday," the article said. Most of the American soldiers were "slain or facing captivity." Alex dropped the paper on his desk and looked up at Max, but his mind was running in all directions.

"At least they seem to be taking some prisoners," Max said.

That was true, and for the past two weeks Alex had been fearing a complete massacre. This could mean that Wally had survived.

"I never thought America would have to surrender to *anyone,*" Max said.

"We got caught off guard," Alex said. "We weren't ready."

"Well, we'd better get ready—fast. Or this is only the beginning. We've got a long ol' road ahead of us."

Alex was looking at the newspaper, hardly listening, but he said, as much to himself as to Max, "I hate to think how many men are going to die."

"A lot of *young* men."

Alex looked up, and he watched Max's eyes. He was a wiry little man, already quite gray, with shaggy eyebrows. Alex tried to see under those eyebrows, to interpret what the man might be implying. Was he accusing Alex?

"Well, anyway, I thought you'd want that. Just keep it."

Alex thanked him, and then he read the rest of the article. The account, however, was incomplete. The Japanese had broken the lines and pushed the Filipinos and Americans back into full retreat, and General King had agreed to a surrender. But there was no word about how that was happening.

Alex leaned back in his chair and tried to think. He knew he had to go home and see his parents. They hadn't called, so they probably didn't know yet. He breathed deeply, and then he looked at his watch. It was five-forty. His parents were up by now. Dad might not go out for the paper immediately, but Alex knew he needed to get over there as quickly as he could. So he hurried out to his car and drove across town. Gasoline was being rationed now, and Alex didn't have a lot to spare, but he pushed the speed limits a little. He got to the house shortly after six. There were lights on upstairs, but he found the paper still on the porch, and he picked it up. The front door was unlocked, as usual, so he slipped in, stepped to the bottom of the stairs, and called, "Mom, Dad, it's Alex. I need to talk to you about something. Can you come down?"

"Just a minute," Mom called back to him. "What's wrong?"

Alex didn't answer. But his mother soon hurried down the stairs. As she got close to Alex, she must have seen the concern in his eyes. "Is it Wally?" she said.

"I think he's all right. Don't worry," Alex said, even though he didn't really know that. He took hold of her hand. Dad was now coming down the stairs. He had shaved, and he had his white shirt on, but no tie. Alex backed into the living room, still holding his mother's hand. He could see that she was frantic. As Dad stepped into the room, Alex said, "The *Trib* says our forces in the Philippines have been defeated. It sounds like a lot of the troops have been captured."

Mom grasped Alex's arm and clung to it. Dad was standing well away from Alex, but Alex saw him take a quick breath.

"This might save his life," Alex said. "I think there's a good chance he was taken prisoner and not killed."

But Mom looked terrified. Alex took her into his arms and then looked over her shoulder at his dad. Dad was stiff as a mannequin, his face revealing nothing. But he walked closer, and when he touched his wife's shoulder, she turned and embraced him. Dad looked at Alex, and his steady gaze seemed to say, "I'm not going to fall apart. *We* are not going to fall apart." "Were there any details?" he asked.

"No. Just that the troops were overrun, and there was nothing else to do but surrender. Here's the paper. You can read the article."

"How can we find out if he's alive?" Mom asked, still crying.

"We may not for a while," Dad said. "But the army wouldn't have a bunch of airplane mechanics on the front lines. I'd say it's pretty sure that he was taken captive."

"How will they treat him?"

"I just don't know, Bea," Dad said, and Alex heard the stress in his voice.

But it was Mom who suddenly said, "Come with me. Let me make breakfast." Alex and Dad followed her to the kitchen, where President Thomas picked up the newspaper and began to read. Mom was already tying on an apron, as though she had made a decision not to go to pieces, to keep moving ahead.

Dad sat down at the table with the paper in front of him. Mom began to rattle pans and pull things from the refrigerator. Neither spoke, but Alex was pretty sure he knew what they were wondering: If Wally had been taken captive, could he hold up?

President Thomas finished the article and set the paper down. He looked up at Alex. "I think Wally's alive," he said. "And he's a Thomas." He looked at his wife. "And a Snow. Our families are made of good stuff. He'll have to rise to this."

Alex heard someone walking in the house, and he thought maybe it was Gene. But the kitchen door opened and Bobbi stepped in. She was dressed in her jeans and the old flannel shirt Alex had seen her in before. She had the newspaper in her hand. "You've already seen it," she said. Alex could see she had been crying. "I think maybe it's good news, don't you? I think it means he's alive."

Mom walked over to her. "Maybe," she said. "That's what I'm trying to think. I just hope they'll treat him all right."

"How did you find out so early?" Alex asked.

"I got up to study. And I looked at the paper." She held up her own newspaper. "I borrowed my neighbor's car to get over here."

"I'm glad you're here," President Thomas said. "I want to have a family prayer. We need to combine our faith."

"That's a good idea," Alex said.

But Dad didn't move to call the kids. He looked at Alex and then at Bobbi. "I feel good about where we are right now," he said. "Alex and Bea are serving the cause down at the plant, and I think I'll be helping over there more all the time. My business is grinding to a halt, with no cars coming in. I also think about the shortage of nurses we're going to have, and I see some inspiration in Bobbi's choice to switch to nursing school."

But all that bothered Alex. Dad had pressured Bobbi to go to nursing school. It was *his* inspiration he was referring to. And he had not wanted Mom to work with Alex. All the same, Dad had opened a door. Alex wasn't sure his timing was right, but he decided he had to step through. "Dad," he said, "you're right about Mom. She's doing a great job at the plant. She could run the place."

"Well, I don't think—"

"Especially if you can get there more often from now on."

"I couldn't give it my full attention, Alex, and your mother could never be a boss to all those men." Dad had obviously seen, too late, the direction of Alex's thought.

"I don't know why she couldn't," Alex said. He took a step toward the table and looked down at his dad. "All the men think very highly of her."

Dad leaned back and stared up at Alex. "Is this about going back to college?" he finally asked. He seemed alarmed, maybe even angry.

"No, Dad. It's about doing what I have to do. I'm going to sign up with the military. I can't put it off any longer."

"No. I've talked to the men on the draft board. They agree with me—you're needed here."

"Dad, you just said that your business is winding down. You and Mom can handle the plant. You don't need me now."

"That's not true, Alex. Even with your mother helping out, you're still putting in long hours down there. It's going to take all of us to meet the demand."

"Dad, that's not really the point. I can't have my little brother in some prison camp while I sit at home and get rich. I won't do it. I'm going to the recruiting center today."

It was Mom who said, "Alex, please. Don't do that to me right now."

"Mom, I'm sorry. I can't live with myself anymore. I'm out of excuses."

Dad stood up. "Now listen to me, Alex," he said. "I'm telling you not to do this."

"Dad, we've been through all this before. I have to make my own decision."

The two of them stood facing each other, the table in between. Alex could see the desperation in his father's eyes. He seemed at a loss for an argument—but not for conviction.

"Dad," Bobbi said, and she stepped up next to Alex, "you might as well know now. I've signed up with the navy. I'm going in as soon as I graduate."

"What?" President Thomas's eyes widened. Alex looked down at the table. He knew the fight was on now, and he hadn't wanted that.

"Dad, you always talk about the great battle between good and evil, but now you want Alex and me to stay out of it. How can we do that?"

"Are you telling me you already joined?"

"Yes."

"Without talking to me?"

"Yes."

"Well, you're going to *unjoin*. You're not going into the service, Barbara. I'm not going to have one of my daughters involved with . . . that element."

"Dad, I'll be at a navy hospital somewhere. I'll be helping with the war effort and doing what you want me to do anyway—working as a nurse."

"No, Bobbi," Mom said, "you need to stay home and find a husband. You can't go running off in the middle of all this mess." She walked to Bobbi and put her arm around her waist.

"You're not going, Barbara," Dad said. "You've always gotten these wild ideas in your head, but this time I'm putting my foot down. You are *not* going."

"Dad, I already signed up. And I'm over twenty-one."

"Maybe so. But when I get through with those recruiters, they'll just be happy to give the paperwork back. I won't put up with them going behind my back."

"Dad, that's not what happened. I went in and applied. And I'm going."

"I've got to go too, Dad," Alex said. "It's not that I want to go. I have to."

Dad's face was like stone, but Alex saw the truth in his eyes: he knew he had lost, and he had no idea where to go from there. "I didn't talk to my father this way," he finally said. "I listened and learned." He walked around the table and headed for the door.

"Wait, Al," Mom said. "Your breakfast is ready. Don't leave. Let's all sit down and talk about this."

"Talk? What is there to talk about?" Dad said. "They aren't going to listen."

"Al! What are you saying? Is that what talk is? *Listening* to you?"

He looked at his wife. There was doubt in his face now, but still the fury. "I don't know how to do this," he finally said. "Our family is being pulled apart, and every time I try to stop it, you all accuse me of being a tyrant."

Mom walked to her husband, stood in front of him, and looked into his eyes. "Come on, Al. Every time you lay down edicts, you only shove them away."

President Thomas seemed to hear that, seemed to stop and consider, but then he turned and pushed the door open.

"Don't go, Al," Mom said.

"There's something I need to do," he said, without anger, and he walked out the door. In a few seconds, Alex heard him tromp up the stairs, his steps resounding in the kitchen.

Mom turned around and looked at Alex and Bobbi, who were still standing next to each other near the kitchen table. "This is all too much for him—all at once," Mom said. "Can you understand that?"

"Sure, Mom," Alex said. "But sooner or later, he has to let go of us."

"Oh, Alex, that's so easy to say at your age." Tears began to drop onto her cheeks. She was grasping a spatula in front of her as though she needed to keep hold of something real. "This is hard for us. I don't want you running off around the world—people shooting at you. I want you to come here on Sundays for dinner. I want you to get married and give me grandchildren. I want life to go on."

"That's what we want too, Mom," Alex said. "But we don't have that choice."

Mom walked to the table and sat down. She was still holding the spatula against her chest. Across the room, the eggs and bacon were sizzling. "You need to talk this out with your dad—not argue with him," she said. "We have to come to some kind of agreement that everyone can live with."

"We'll talk," Bobbi said. "There's just nothing to negotiate. We're both going."

"I know that," Mom said. She got up and walked back to the stove. "But let's do it right. Let's not have hard feelings." She took the pan off the stove and looked at the eggs. Alex could smell that they had begun to burn.

Alex heard footsteps on the stairs again, and he thought his dad was leaving for work. But the footsteps came to the door and hesitated for a time. Then the door came open and Dad stepped in. Dad looked ahead, not at anyone, and he spoke quietly. "I've been praying," he said.

Everyone waited. Alex heard the change of tone, and he did want to listen now.

"Let's sit down," Dad said.

Mom set the eggs aside, wiped her hands on her apron, and came to the table. Dad sat in his usual spot, at the end, with Mom on the corner, next to him.

Dad gripped his hands together and took his time. Alex could tell he wanted to start over and say things differently this time. "I don't want to lose both of you now—not with Wally where he is. But I tried to tell the Lord that, and I was overwhelmed by my own selfishness. I remembered what the prophet told us in General Conference. We only had the small group, with just leaders there, and he opened up to us. He told us we had to be ready to sacrifice more than we ever have before." Dad continued to stare at the table. "I've been telling you all your lives that you had to stand up for what's right—and as hard as it is for me to accept, I know that's what you're doing."

Dad didn't cry, although his voice had become shaky. He held himself together and said quietly, "I guess it might work for Bea and me to take over the plant. The only thing I ask, Alex, is that you hold off a little while so you can train us. And maybe by then we'll have some word about Wally."

"All right. But Mom can train you in most things. She really does know what's going on."

Dad nodded, but it was obviously not an easy idea for him to accept.

"Don't worry," Mom said, smiling, "I'll have you up to speed in no time."

But Dad couldn't smile. He twisted around to look at Bobbi. "I do worry about you leaving these mountains and going out among people who don't believe the same things we do."

Bobbi walked back to the chair, where she had been before. "Dad, don't worry about that."

"Will you move back home for a while now, before you go?" Dad asked.

"Sure. I'd like to do that."

So everything was settled, but reality began to set in for Alex. He felt that he was breaking a vow. He had promised his German brothers and sisters that he would never be their enemy. He hoped they would understand.

"It's time for the kids to get up, isn't it?" Dad asked.

Sister Thomas looked at the wall clock. "It will be before long," she said.

"Let's get them up and have them come down to the living room. We need to have a prayer while we're all together."

Mom got up from the table and walked upstairs. Dad and Alex and Bobbi went out to the living room. But when Gene and LaRue and Beverly came down, still in their pajamas and looking sleepy, Dad had to tell them that Wally had probably been taken captive—and then he had to address all the questions that couldn't be answered. After that, he explained what Alex and Bobbi were planning. The girls cried, and Gene looked at the floor. By the time everyone knelt down, the pain was so raw that Alex wondered how the family would survive it.

Dad's voice, softer than usual, was full of the anxiety everyone was feeling. "Lord," he said, "thou knowest our hearts and our troubles. Thou knowest the ache we feel this morning."

He cleared his throat and then said with more intensity, "Father, we know that we must join this battle against the forces of darkness, however much we would prefer not to. We plead with thee for protection, but we hold nothing back. We accept thy will. If death should visit our family, we pray for the strength to deal with the loss. And if we must suffer, we pray for the will to hold to truth and honor, and to survive whatever comes."

He hesitated for a long time, as though he were mulling everything over. "Lord," he finally said, "now is our great trial—our refiner's fire. We pray that we can keep the faith and grow stronger. We pray for the Church, for the Saints all over the world, who may have to fight each other, and who will perhaps die in great numbers. Let the Church survive, and let the membership come away from this war more deeply committed to the building of the kingdom. Bless the dear friends Alex made in Germany, and the good people of Japan. And help us to forgive those who have taken our son."

Dad's voice finally broke. "Father," he said after a moment, "give our son Walter the strength to endure. And if it be thy will, please bring him back to us alive, that he might establish his own family and pass the gospel on to our posterity. I need so much to speak to him one more time. It would be my own greatest blessing if I could have that privilege."

Dad was crying now, and everyone in the room was sobbing. Alex had plunged his face into the couch, and he felt his tears soaking into the fabric. Beverly, who was next to him, was shaking and clinging to his side.

"Finally, please bless Barbara and Alex as they prepare to part from us. Let them carry with them, from this blessed valley, the strength of these hills. Let them remember their heritage, that they are children of the promise, with a great destiny to fulfill. We ask that they return to us in good time, well and whole . . . but we accept thy will in all things."

He closed in the name of Jesus Christ.

No one got up at first. They stayed on their knees, all crying. When they did finally begin to rise, they took turns embracing each other. Gene clung to Alex for a long time, sobbing as though he would never stop, and the girls seemed almost beyond consolation as Bobbi and Mom tried to comfort them.

Dad stayed to himself. He stood straight, his eyes focused on the east window. Alex had the feeling that he was still trying to accept all this, still trying to convince himself that he could let go. Or maybe he was just looking at the mountains, trying to draw some strength.

When the sun came up, Wally was forced to stand, and to march again—across the southern end of the Bataan peninsula. He no longer hoped for trucks, and he had no idea whether he would eat this day, but he kept praying, repeating the words that had been in his head all night. He didn't expect quick results, didn't ask for any miracles; he concentrated on the task at hand. He needed the power to make it through this day, this hour.

The road, the crowded march, the heat, the hunger—all continued the same. And now the prisoners were in the target area of the artillery that was slamming into the mountainside from Corregidor. The explosions frightened the guards, who shouted for the prisoners to move faster. Wally was part of a massive group of men, thousands of them, herded forward on a narrow road that wound its way over a string of hills. The men simply couldn't go any faster, frightened as they were by the artillery themselves.

Wally knew that some of the shells must be hitting the road ahead of him, killing American and Filipino soldiers, and before long he saw the proof. He came upon mangled, bloody bodies left on the side of the road. But no one was allowed to stop and help, even though some of the wounded were still alive.

He was so numb now that it was hard to think much about what he was seeing. But ahead, he heard a man screaming. He watched as he came nearer, and then, just when he was almost there, one of the Japanese guards stepped to the wounded man and drove his bayonet through his chest.

The screaming stopped abruptly, but as Wally passed by, he heard the gurgling in the man's throat, and he heard the guard curse the man, then spin around and shout warnings to the prisoners. Wally's sense of his own peril deepened. He didn't panic, but a realistic awareness struck him that these guards were capable of anything. When he saw a severed head stuck on a pole—the head of a Filipino soldier—he assumed that this was a warning from the guards, a method of instilling fear. But Wally's fear couldn't get any deeper.

Wally wondered how long he could go on, whether he could hold up if this nightmare continued very long. What he knew for certain now was that he could keep going only if he got help from outside himself. And so he continued to pray as he concentrated on putting one foot in front of the other. His only other attempt was to keep track of Warren and Jack, just to know they were with him.

Wally sensed that this was his trek. He was like those pioneers his dad talked about every year on Christmas day. Wally saw no irony in that memory. In fact, he felt reassured that others had been through similar tests and that he could get through this one. But he hardly thought in words; he only felt a powerful impression that he had to keep going, that he had to stay alive so he could get back to his family.

The words in his head continued, almost without a break, always the same: "Father, please help me." He meant his father in heaven, of course, but he also thought of his father back home. And his mother. And all those who would be praying for him. It was strange that he finally felt so close to them, finally felt strength coming from them. His single focus now was the hope that he could get back to all the things he had run away from.

Bobbi drove back to her apartment, but then she sat on the front step, outside. She needed to go in and study, but she couldn't bring herself to do it. What struck her was that she had worried entirely too much about herself for the past couple of years. She needed now to see things on a much larger scale. On the day Pearl Harbor had been attacked, she had thought she understood the implications of it all—that everything was changed—and that a great sacrifice was going to be necessary if America was to turn the tide of the war. But now that war had come home. It had hold of her little brother, and it was ripping away at her family. For so long, she had been trying to establish her independence, but that seemed unimportant now. What she longed for more than anything was the safety her family had always given her. She soon found herself praying. She prayed for Wally, of course, and for a timely end to all this chaos, but she closed her prayer by asking for the one thing that she wanted most: "Lord, as we go our separate ways, please keep us together."

Alex went back to the plant. There was so much work to do. He sat at his desk and stared at all the paperwork before him, but his thoughts were full of Anna. He pictured the little arch in her upper lip that was so unexplainably beautiful, the soft curve of her cheekbones, and he dreamed that he could bring her home to Utah somehow, and that he could forget everything going on in the world. But he was at war with Anna—at war with all the German members he had loved so much. He was at war with part of himself. There had to be a way to love a people and war against a movement, a philosophy, but he had no idea how to fit such conflicting feelings inside himself. All the same, he prayed that somehow he could do battle and still love, and that when the war was over, he could be one person, still part of all the things he cared about: his family, his church, his German brothers and sisters. But what he felt, even after praying, was that he was asking too much. He had ended one battle with himself—and his father—by committing himself to go off to war. But he had entered a darker, more difficult realm, and he was not sure he would ever be himself again.

President and Sister Thomas sat across the kitchen table from each other and held hands. Sister Thomas prayed that she would have the strength to manage, to hold out through everything she would have to face. But President Thomas felt an odd sense of relief. He had seen a great deal of strength in his children that morning. From all appearances, they were made of the stuff he had been preaching about for such a long time. He was concerned about Alex and Bobbi, but they had stood up to him, and in doing so, they had actually chosen better than he would have chosen for them. Maybe Wally could do as well, and maybe the younger children were equally strong. He was struck with the strangeness of it all: that he would feel so confident on this of all mornings. And yet, an inner voice kept telling him that it was time to trust his children. The fire was coming, but he believed they would be refined, not destroyed.